fair game

fair game

New York Times Bestselling Author
Monica Murphy

Fair Game
Copyright © 2015 by Monica Murphy

Interior Design and formatting by

www.emtippettsbookdesigns.com

chapter
One

Jade

"I hate Shepard Prescott."

"Of course you do. Heaven forbid you're normal and think he's hot like the rest of the female population on campus." Kelli rolls her eyes, flicking her long, perfectly wavy brown hair over her shoulder. I dodge out of the way before all that glossy perfect hair smacks me in the face.

"Do you really think he's hot?"

The pointed look Kelli sends my way is answer enough.

It doesn't matter if I think or Kelli thinks he's good looking because he just is. There's no denying that fact. But his arrogant attitude and smug personality cancels out the sexiness.

"Seriously. He's an asshole." I stare at the back of the asshole's head. His hair is this streaked golden brown that almost looks like he paid for those highlights, which I really hope he didn't because, oh my God, that would make him even more pretentious. Though I'm sure he received those naturally glorious blond streaks by sailing on his family's yacht or whatever. Or perhaps sunning himself on the beach during one of the many tropical vacations he no doubt takes.

To say we run in different crowds is putting it mildly. He's older than me by two years. He's in a frat and I'm not in a sorority. He's rich as hell and I am most assuredly not. There is absolutely no reason whatsoever for him to know I exist and I'm fine with that.

Really.

"Even his name makes him sounds like an asshole. And his nickname is stupid too. *Shep.*" I grimace. All rich dudes have stupid nicknames I swear. "Sounds like a dog's name. 'Here boy. Here Shep. Mommy's got a treat for you'," I sing song then roll my eyes. "Ridiculous."

"I just bet Mommy's got a treat for him," Kelli says, her droll voice dripping with sarcasm.

"Pfft. Please. He wishes." I wave my hand, sending a cautious glance in Shep's direction. I may be mocking his ass but the last thing I want is for him to actually hear me.

"You're on a roll tonight aren't you?" Kelli sounds

bored. That's because we are bored. Holed up in a crappy little underground poker palace run by the supposedly legendary gambler Shepard Prescott and all of his rich, asshole friends. Our boyfriends brought us here so they could play against Shep and his gambling posse because they have a reputation. As in, they bet big so they tend to win big. But more often than not, they lose. Really big…

Our boyfriends are counting on the losing really big part.

"I can tolerate maybe two more rounds of this and then I'm walking," I mutter before I finish off the rest of the warm beer in my requisite red Solo cup. Grimacing, I set the cup on the table behind me and heave a big sigh, earning a quick glance from my boyfriend. Pretty sad he recognizes my irritated sighs but we really haven't been getting along lately so it's no surprise. He flashes me a tense smile before returning his gaze to the cards in his hand.

"He looks stressed." Kelli nudges my side with her pointy elbow, making me yelp. Does she sharpen those things or what? "Joel. Look at him."

I'm looking at him. And she's right. Joel does look stressed. What else is new? "He's been wearing that look a lot lately." Lack of funds will do that to a person. Instead of saving the money his parents gave him at the beginning of the semester to bail him out since he lost his part time job, he went and blew it on stupid stuff. Like that pair of designer sunglasses he promptly lost when he was at one of those lake parties, got drunk and went swimming with them on. In February.

My boyfriend doesn't always make the best choices.

"He doesn't have very many chips left either," Kelli mentions, leaning in close to me so she can see past Shep. But who can really see past that guy? He has shoulders as broad as a mountain. And all that wild does-he-pay-for-highlights-or-not hair that sort of springs up as if it has a mind of its own.

"Good. Maybe that means we can leave soon." I grab my cup from the table and bring it to my lips only to realize it's empty and I frown. Not that I want more warm beer but...

"Get her another." Shep raises his hand above his head and snaps his fingers, his finger pointed backward.

Right at me.

"How the hell did he do that?" I ask no one under my breath, glancing up at the barely dressed girl who's suddenly standing in front of me, fresh Solo cup in hand outstretched toward me. I take the drink from her with a mumbled thank you and she flashes me a toothy smile before she bounces away.

"Look." Another nudge from Kelli's pointy elbow — that should be an illegal weapon — before she's pointing at the wall across from us. There's a mirror mounted there.

And Shepard Prescott is looking right at us, a smug grin stretching his lips wide, revealing perfect white teeth.

"He's watching us?" I ask incredulously.

His gaze snags on mine in the mirror, those dark brown eyes never leaving me. I'm the one who has to look away first.

Asshole.

"What a creeper." A shiver moves down my spine but I ignore it. I sip my beer, thankful it's colder. They must've cracked open a new keg.

"Ha. If he's a creeper then I hope he abducts me in his tricked out van." Kelli bursts out laughing at her own crude joke.

"Ew." That we're joking about being abducted is one thousand times wrong. That we're joking about Shep Prescott abducting us is a million times wrong. "And what do you mean, his tricked out van?"

"So many creepers have those equally creepy vans. You know which ones I'm talking about." Kelli mock shudders. "So gross."

Our conversation has taken a weird turn and I blame boredom. We need to get out of here. But Joel's not paying attention to me. He's too busy gnawing on his lower lip and sweating bullets. Kelli's boyfriend Dane is hunched over his cards, as if he's afraid someone might catch a peek at his hand. And Shep Prescott is sprawled in his chair, legs spread wide, one arm slung over the back of an empty chair, his other arm resting on the table, cards fanned wide so anyone can see them. He looks just as bored as we are.

It's a good look for him.

Damn it.

"I'm done." Dane throws his cards down in disgust and gets up from his chair, moving so he's sitting on the bench behind Joel. He claps a hand on Joel's shoulder in a good luck gesture and plucks the beer out of some random chick's hand, downing it before he grins at her.

I feel Kelli tense up and I can't blame her.

Sitting up straight, I peek over Shep's broad-as-a-mountain shoulder to see exactly what he's holding. And oh my God, he's holding something amazing. When I was little, my grandpa taught me everything I know about poker and blackjack. My gambling knowledge always impressed Joel even when I tricked him with that irritating game of fifty-two pickup one time. He fell for it completely.

Thanks Grandpa.

Shep Prescott's hand is about as good as it gets. As in, he's holding a full house with tens and jacks. Talk about luck. I can only guess by the way Joel is still sweating and muttering unintelligible words under his breath that he's got nothing. Or he's the best bluffer ever.

I'm guessing the first option.

"You in?" Shep asks, his deep voice rumbling from his chest, low and intimidating. Joel looks up, his teeth still sunk in his lower lip and I notice all at once how incredibly young and foolish he appears. He's wearing a faux vintage Mountain Dew T-shirt he got at Target a few days ago with the gift card his mom sent him and his dark hair is buzzed short. Like he's ready to join the armed services or something. His face is clean-shaven and a little pale though there's a faint ruddiness to his cheeks. He looks like a baby compared to Mr. Suave Calm and Cool with the broad shoulders and sexy hair. I'm afraid he's about to get his ass kicked.

"Uhhh…" Joel draws out the sound, his gaze flickering to mine. I'm shaking my head no, slicing my finger across my neck, anything to get him to fold so he doesn't get suckered and lose everything. He's already close enough to losing it all as it is.

"What the hell are you doing?"

Everyone in the room goes silent. Kelli nudges my side with her damn pointy elbow again and I stop gesturing when I realize that Shep Prescott is talking…

To me.

I lift my head to find him glaring at me in that stupid mirror, his dark eyes almost black, his mouth thin. Oh, he looks pissed.

"Are you *cheating?* Is that why your boyfriend

brought you here?" he asks when I don't say anything.

"Um." I have lost all coherent thought. I've also lost the ability to speak.

This isn't good.

"Forget this fucking hand." He throws his cards face down into the middle of the table, right on top of the pile of chips, various dollar bills and even a small mountain of quarters that were part of that round's pot. Everyone playing had already dropped out, one by one, even Dane, until it was just Joel and Shep left. Some had even abandoned their chairs, moving on to grab more beer or play at another table. Or to leave the party with their tails tucked between their legs and their wallets empty.

Not Joel. He's holding out to the very bitter end. And now I'm getting him into some major trouble.

"Come here." Shep turns to look at me, his hard stare pinning me in place. I can practically feel his anger coming at me in big, hot waves. All my snarky comments, all my earlier bravado evaporates. "Sit by me," he commands, pointing at the empty chair beside him.

I stand on shaky legs and approach the table, ignoring Joel, ignoring the snickers from other people watching the spectacle unfold. Without even looking at Shep I fall heavily into the chair beside him, keeping my spine stiff, desperate to put as much distance between us as possible.

But it's no use. I can smell him. And he smells... fucking incredible. There are no other words for it. A combination of pine and lemon and dirt...okay I know that doesn't sound very appealing but oh my God, I'm tempted to lean in close and sniff his neck.

I don't, of course. Instead I grip the edge of the table and allow myself to look in Joel's direction. The expression on his boyish face is nothing short of misery. I'm starting to wonder if he had a good hand after all. Possibly better than Shep's? Did I ruin everything? Oh God, if I did, would Joel ever forgive me?

"Don't look at him," Shep murmurs, his voice so close to my ear I gasp and turn my head to find his face directly in mine. I can see everything. Every pore in his skin, every little hair in his thick brows, every inky lash that rims his too dark, all seeing eyes. "I want your eyes on me and me only."

Swallowing hard, I try my best to ignore the anger slowly building inside of me at his threat. But it's no use. "Are you kidding me?" Who does this guy think he is? So he's worth a fortune. So he's ridiculously good looking. So what?

He offers a lopsided smile as he gathers all the cards and starts shuffling like he's some sort of pro straight out of Vegas. "Nope. I catch you looking in his direction during this next hand and I'll kick his ass."

My jaw hangs open as I absorb his words. "You really are an asshole, aren't you?" I whisper.

The lopsided smile grows. "You're looking at a top of the line asshole, baby," he says.

I roll my eyes at the *baby* mention. I hate it when guys call me baby. Though…huh. No guy has ever called me that before. Not even Joel. Considering Joel is only my second semi-serious boyfriend and we've been going out for about six months, I guess that's not saying much but still.

The baby bit should offend me. But it doesn't. Neither does that smile.

What the hell is wrong with me?

"We'll play another round of five card draw, just you and me." Shep jabs his index finger in Joel's direction. "The pot stays as is. But we'll still raise. Consider this game," he pauses and I hear the smug amusement enter his voice, "high stakes."

Someone groans. I think it might've been Joel. Not that I'm allowed to look at him or anything.

"Your girlfriend here." He touches me. Freaking Shep Prescott risks losing a limb by actually sliding his arm around my shoulders, his hand gripping my upper arm firmly. I can hardly move, what with the way he's holding me. "You two make eye contact for even a second and you automatically lose."

"Not a problem," Joel says, his voice shaking the

slightest bit. I wish I could look at him. If I could I'd be telling him to grow some balls and man up.

"So we're ready?" Shep releases his hold on me, his fingers streaking across my back as he moves away and settles back in his seat. I send him my most evil glare but it doesn't even faze him. He simply resumes shuffling his cards, slouching in his chair as he does so, his legs going wide so his knee bumps against my thigh.

Ignoring the sizzle that shoots up my leg, I scoot away from him as best I can but he stops me in my tracks.

"You leave, he loses," Shep murmurs, so low I'm sure no one can hear him but me. "Don't forget that."

"Considering you won't let me, I don't think you need to worry," I say with a little snort that I immediately regret. Way to impress him.

But you don't want to impress him. You think he's an asshole.

Yeah. I need to remember that.

Shep

The girl with the sarcastic mouth just made the night infinitely more interesting. I'd been bored out of my skull knowing I was going to win. The pot was small, maybe five hundred bucks. Big fucking deal. The last dude sitting at the table was a nervous little freshman who hadn't backed down which surprised me. I figured he either had a better hand than me—almost impossible—or he was an excellent bluffer.

Also fairly impossible.

Then the girlfriend had to go and gesture behind me. She saw my hand. The little fucker brought his hot girlfriend to cheat and I hadn't even noticed. And I always notice that crap. Instead of making sure she was on the up and up while I stared at her in the mirror I put up for the sole purpose of catching cheaters, I caught myself checking her out.

Nice tits. Good skin, if a little on the pale side. Long red hair pulled up into a ponytail and freckles scattered across her cheeks and nose. Freckles pretty much scattered everywhere. Not my normal type but what did me in—besides her tits because they look damn good in that black tank top she's wearing—was her mouth. Bee stung lips. I can only imagine those lips wrapped tight around my...

"Are you going to deal or spend the entire night staring at me?"

I blink her into focus. She's a feisty little thing too. What's she doing with this freshman loser sitting across from me, looking ready to pass out at any given moment? I like her voice, despite all the shitty things she's been saying about me.

And I've heard every single comment since she

settled in behind me.

Ignoring her, I deal our hands and check my cards, careful to keep my expression neutral. A pair of queens and three junk cards. I won't discard until he does first. I'm the dealer so that's protocol and I don't want him to know that I only have a pair.

"What's your name?" I ask the girl.

She crosses her arms in front of her, plumping up her chest. I catch a glimpse of lime green lacy bra peeking above the neckline of her tank. Interesting. "Bitch Face," she answers serenely.

I laugh. This chick is something else. "Fitting. I'm Shep. Though you already know." I lower my voice. "Since Mommy has a treat for me and all that."

Her cheeks go crimson. Busted. But she doesn't say a word in her defense, which I find admirable.

I turn my focus on her boyfriend. "Hey. Asshole." He lifts his gaze, pale blue eyes staring into mine. He looks petrified. He should be. "What's your name?"

"J-Joel." He clears his throat, his gaze falling to his cards once again. He shifts them around, moving two from one side to the other. Then he plucks one from the five and tosses it out face down. "I need one more please."

Hell. What kind of hand does he have? I'm pretty sure I'm fucked. "You gonna raise the pot or what?"

He meets my gaze once more, trying to school his

expression but I see the flash of triumph. He has a good hand. Fucker thinks he's gonna win. "Uh, I'll raise you fifty." He tosses in the last of his chips.

"Fifty?" I cock a brow and toss in a matching fifty then deal him a single card. "That's all you got?" I rapidly exchange out my cards, discarding the three junk ones and taking three new ones. I don't turn them over. Not yet. The anticipation is half the fun especially when I'm fairly sure I'll lose this round.

Damn it.

"Clearly." The kid waves a hand in front of him, where zero chips remain.

"Hmm." I lift my cards, cupping them in my hand so Bitch Face won't see them. She's as still as a stone sitting next to me but I can hear her breathing, can feel the tension radiating off her in heavy waves. She doesn't like this. She's nervous for her boyfriend especially because she can't look at him. Her body is angled toward mine and I chance a glance at her before I study what I have.

Holy hell. I dealt myself two more queens. Four of a kind.

Beat that fuck stick.

"Let's make this interesting," I say, staring at Joel once more. His expression lights up. Everyone who'd heard of, or who'd come to our little gambling venture in the past know that's the game changer statement. It's the cue that the round is about to take a wild turn.

More like it's one of us—my friend Gabe, my cousin Tristan—bored out of our minds and ready for an adventure. We like to win big. But by winning big, you need to lose big too. That fifty-fifty chance is what always gives me a thrill. I've lost more than I've won but that doesn't really bother me.

"What do you have in mind?" Joel asks, impressing me. He's played this game before. That's the pat question we want them to ask. I don't recognize him but I'm guessing he might've played a night I wasn't here, or at someone else's table.

It doesn't matter. He understands what's about to happen and that's all that matters.

"Let's see." I set my cards down and drum my fingers on the green felted table. We run a semi-professional operation here. Gabe owns the house. Well, his family owns the house. We converted it a little less than two years ago, turning the living and dining room into a mini casino a few miles off campus. Blackjack tables, poker tables, hell we even have a roulette table though I hate playing it. Roulette is a game of total chance. The odds are shit.

At least with poker and my preferred game of choice, blackjack, we use some sort of skill.

"Don't do it Joel." I lift my head at first sound of her voice. She's not looking at Joel though. She's staring straight at me, her mouth hard, her eyes flat. "Show your cards and end the game. Don't let this asshole get you in any deeper than you already are."

"Ouch. So mean with the name calling." I rub my chest, pretending she hurt me. I've been called worse. "You going to let her tell you what to do, Joel?" I say it because I know the question will piss her off. And it does. She's practically got steam coming out of her ears but she says nothing to me. I can't help but be faintly disappointed.

"Shut up, Jade," Joel mutters, shocking the both of us. "Let me do this."

I turn to her. "Joel just grew some balls, Jade. Or should I still call you Bitch Face?"

She grimaces. "I'd rather you call me nothing at all."

"Jade," Joel says, his voice firmer. I can tell he really wants her to shut up. I'm taking this as a sign that he also wants to carry forth on the bet. Meaning his hand is fucking stellar.

Well, guess what? So is mine.

"What kind of name is that anyway? *Jade?*" I make a face, trying to hold back the laughter that wants to escape because I know for a fact that I'm irritating the shit out of her.

"Like you have any room to talk. What the hell is a Shep?"

"I'll have you know it's an old family name." I try my best to remain dignified but I'm failing. This chick amuses me like no other. Her smart mouth is kind of hot. "My mother is a Shepard. I come from a long line of Shepards."

"Well goody for her. My mom happens to like the color green." She flashes me a smile and tosses her head, her ponytail swishing, tempting me to grab it, yank her close and wipe that shitty little smile off her face.

With my lips.

"You two done flirting so we can do this, or what?" Joel asks, sounding furious. And he looks furious too. Interesting. I'm enjoying this more and more.

"We were *not* flirting," Jade says as she starts to turn her head in Joel's direction.

"Ah, ah, ah. Better watch it," I warn and she returns her attention back to me, earning a fierce frown from her for my efforts. "I don't want to have to kick Joel's ass, you know."

"He could probably take you," she mutters halfheartedly.

"Ha. I'd demolish him and you know it."

"I'm sitting right here, you know," Joel pipes up.

"Okay." I look away from Bitch Face Jade and study Joel, who appears much more confident than he did a few minutes ago. This would normally make me nervous. And I normally don't mind feeling nervous during these situations because it amps up the adrenaline and makes everything that much more intense. Life is what you make it, right? I'm all for crazy bets and tense moments. At least I'm actually feeling something while it's unfolding. "Let's bet on Jade. If I lose, I'll pay you some ungodly amount of money."

"What sort of ungodly amount?" Joel asks, never missing a beat.

I ignore his question. "And if I win...I get your girl."

"Joel, if you agree to this asshole's stupid bet, I will kick you in the nuts so hard, you will *never* have children. And that's a promise," Jade threatens, her voice like ice.

Hell, even my nuts shriveled up a little at her words.

"It's a sure thing," he says, never once looking at her. "Don't worry about it. What sort of ungodly amount are you talking about, Shep?"

The kid wants money. No problem. I can more than deliver. "Fifty."

He rolls his eyes. "Big fucking deal."

"Thousand," I add, and those rolling eyes are now bugging out of his head.

Low murmurs erupt from the observers watching the game, startling me. I forgot they were there. Glancing up, I see Gabe standing near the doorway, leaning against the wall with his arms crossed in front of him and an amused expression on his face. He loves this shit as much as I do, maybe even more so. He gives me one of those shit-eating grins of his and I nod once before I resume my focus on Joel.

"What do you say?" I ask nonchalantly, clutching the cards in my hand. I could win this. Not much else can beat four queens, unless the schmuck has four kings or four aces. What are the odds though? Really?

They're in my favor. They have to be.

"I'm not up for barter, you assholes," Jade spits out, her voice laced with venom. "I don't know who the hell either of you think you are, but you just can't *bet* on me. I'm a freaking human being." She pauses. I'm guessing she's realizing her words are having little effect on either of us. "What would you do with me anyway if you won?"

"Wouldn't you like to know?" I slide my gaze over her, imagining the many ways I could have her if she was mine. Though it would be brief. I don't keep girls, never have. Girlfriends want too much. Have high expectations that I can never, ever deliver. I don't even want to deliver, because women? They are demanding as fuck.

And this one I know would give me nothing but endless shit.

"I hate you," she whispers, shooting daggers at me with her…hmm. Hazel eyes? Yeah, they're a mix of colors, green and gray and a hint of brown, so I'm calling her eyes hazel. "Don't think I won't stomp on your balls if you go through with this, because I so will."

"Maybe I like that sort of kink," I say, sitting up

straight. "So what'll it be, Joel? You in?"

"I'm fucking definitely in!" He shouts, then high fives the jackass who's sitting behind him.

"All right then. An extra fifty-k if you win, Jade Bitch Face if I win." I throw a hundred dollar chip into the center of the table, adding it to the pot as a goodwill gesture. "Call."

"Here you go." The smugness in Joel's voice is unmistakable. "Read 'em and weep." He spreads his cards out in front of him. Three aces and two kings.

A fucking nice hand for sure.

"A full house," I murmur, keeping my voice even while deep inside, I'm ready to offer up my own triumphant shout. Hot damn, I've got this fucker. "Aces and kings high."

"Fuck yeah, dude." Joel starts to reach for the pile of chips, coins and dollar bills, looking like a greedy kid who just busted the piñata and has no plans on sharing any of the candy that fell from it.

"Hold it." Joel pauses in his gathering. "I haven't showed my hand yet. There's a protocol to this procedure you know."

"Right, right, dude. Go for it." He releases his hold on the pile of winnings, though his greedy gaze never strays from it. He's not even looking at his girl, who just happens to be staring at me. She hates my guts. I can feel the waves of anger coming at me, heavier and heavier as each minute passes.

She's really going to hate me when I share my cards.

"Ready?" I cock a brow, drawing out the suspense. I'm relishing this moment because it's going to be a good one. There's a vibration beneath my skin, a buzzing that grows and grows until it's a dull roar in my ears and I blow out a long exhale, crinkle the cards between my fingers before I slowly drop them onto the table, one by one.

Six of hearts — the trash card.

Queen of spades.

Queen of hearts.

Queen of diamonds.

And — dramatic pause — the queen of clubs.

The entire room erupts into cheers, choruses of 'no way' and the occasional 'he fucking beat you man!'. Gabe rushes me, shaking my shoulders from behind and offering up his congratulations. Others follow suit and clap me on the back, some chick drapes herself over me and kisses my cheek. A defeated Joel pushes away from the table so fast his chair falls backward with a clatter. He leaves the room in a huff, never once saying a word to anyone, not even his freaking girlfriend.

What a jackass.

And speaking of his girlfriend…

"You don't really think you've won me or anything, right?" She rests her hand on my thigh — Jesus that feels good — and digs her fingernails in so hard, I can feel them even through the thick denim of my jeans.

That doesn't feel so good. At all.

"A bet is a bet," I remind her, wrapping my fingers around her wrist and disengaging her from my flesh. I drop her hand back into her lap, ignoring the tingle I feel in my fingertips from touching her.

"It was all for show," she says, sounding the slightest bit worried. While all hell breaks loose around us, we're having this conversation. Funny how I'm able to tune everyone else out and only focus on her. "You didn't lose your fifty thousand, so everything's good right? You get all that as your prize." She waves her hand toward the pile of chips that Joel so recently abandoned.

"I hate to break it to you, Jade. But *you're* my prize. And I plan on collecting." I lean in close to her, so close I can feel her warm breath waft across my face, see the way her eyes widen the slightest bit. Her lips part, her tongue appears, touching the very center of her upper lip and my skin tightens. "How about a victory kiss for starters?"

"Fuck you," she spits out.

Just before she slaps my face and storms off without another word.

chapter TWO

Jade

S top texting me. I broke up with you. Deal with it.

I toss my phone beside me on the bed and flop back against the pillows with a dramatic sigh. "I hate men."

"You and me both sister," Kelli agrees though I know she really doesn't mean it. She never came back to our dorm room last night and finally texted me at one in the morning to let me know she was staying the night with Dane.

As a matter of fact, she has that after-sex-glow thing going on since she arrived fifteen minutes ago. They must've been doing it all morning. Her hair is a mess, her cheeks are flushed and she moves like her limbs are made of rubber, all languid and easy.

Lucky bitch.

I, on the other hand, had to break up with my boyfriend last night—who was just okay in the sex department—and am now once again single.

If you don't count on me also being the personal property of one Shepard Prescott, thanks to the ridiculous bet Joel agreed to.

God, I hate him so much. Both of them.

"Joel won't leave me alone," I say as I watch Kelli move about the small room. She's gathering up clean clothes, probably going to take a shower and I realize she might still be all sticky sweaty from her sexual escapades.

Ew.

"You *did* just break up with him," Kelli points out as she turns to face me. "I'm sure he's pretty upset."

"Are you saying I shouldn't have broken up with him? He *did* offer me up as part of his bet."

"He didn't offer you up. Shepard Prescott took over the entire situation. You know this." Kelli starts laughing. "You should've seen the look of shock on his face after you slapped him. It was priceless. There was a red handprint on his cheek, Jade. You hit the boy hard."

"Whatever. He deserved it." I glance at my buzzing phone. Another text from Joel.

It's not my fault. Come on Jade.

Please forgive me.

"Ha." I start texting.

I never want to see you again. Quit making an ass of yourself.

"He makes me crazy," I mutter as I discard the phone, wishing he would just leave me alone. I'm probably being a total bitch but I can't help it. He never ran to my defense, he never told Shep to back off, nothing. He let it all unfold and then left me having to deal with the aftermath.

I'm feeling pretty justified in breaking up with him. We'd been growing apart anyway. This was just the final layer of frosting on the gigantic shit cake our relationship had turned into.

"You're so mean," Kelli says, shaking her head. "What was Joel supposed to do? Shep Prescott is a big deal. Very intimidating. Joel didn't have a chance."

"So? He should've defended me, not run away." I shrug, but what she says makes sense and guilt swamps me. "Besides, you're mean too. You treat Dane terribly."

Kelli waves her hand, dismissing my lame accusation. "We're not talking about Dane. And really, I'm not as mean as you. Poor Joel. He thought he had that game won. Did you see his hand?"

"Did you see Shep's?" The way he revealed it too. Smug bastard. One card after another. One queen after another. My heart had sunk with every card that fell onto the table. Until it was in the pit of my stomach and

I knew I lost. Not Joel.

Me.

"You know he wasn't serious." When I say nothing, Kelli continues. "About the bet. About you. He can't claim you as his prize. You're a human being with your own mind. He wouldn't be that much of an asshole to try and collect."

"Please. He's a spoiled rich asshole who can have whatever he wants. I'm sure he believes he has every right to claim me." A shiver moves down my spine and I try to ignore it. The words are kind of sexy when you think about them. Shep "claiming" me as his, like I'm some sort of possession he can take whenever he wants.

Another shiver, this one full body. Those words conjure up all sorts of images, every one of them sexual. Every one of them featuring acts I've never once tried to attempt. The more I imagine them, the more curious I become.

This is so not good.

"Well, he probably hates you now since you slapped him so hard his head reared back. I swear I've never seen anything like that before. It was straight out of reality TV or something." Kelli sounds downright excited by the spectacle I caused, which she probably is. I must admit, I'm pretty shocked by my behavior too. I can't believe I slapped him. I saw the flash of shock register in those dark, dark eyes right before my palm made contact with his skin. Yes, I felt bad. Yes, I shouldn't have slapped him.

But deep down inside, I know he deserved it.

"I shouldn't have hit him," I say, feeling an attack of guilt coming on.

"No, you shouldn't have," Kelli agrees. "You'd probably be head mistress in his harem right now if you'd just been agreeable from the start."

I burst out laughing and shake my head. It feels good to laugh. I'd been tense since we met up with Joel and Dane last night and they'd told us we were going to that stupid poker palace place Shep and his friends run. I'd known from the start the evening would end up crappy. And I'd been right.

"I'm laying low," I tell Kelli. "In case Shep has set some traps in the hopes he can catch me and take me back to the harem."

"I'm guessing he's not interested any longer since you hit him in front of everyone."

Why do her words bother me? I should be glad Shep isn't interested in me any longer. I'm not a toy that Joel can hand over in trade. I don't want to belong to Shepard Prescott in any way, shape or form.

"Good," I say weakly when I realize Kelli's waiting for an answer. "Serves him right, to mess with me." But there's not much force behind my words. I feel…bad for hitting him. And I can't help but have a *what if* feeling too. Like…

What would've happened if I hadn't slapped Shep? Would he have tried to charm the pants off of me? Would I have let him? Despite my still being with Joel at that moment? Would I have cheated on him in order to sample the Shep Prescott goods?

Maybe…

Ugh. That's not good. I'm not a cheater. I'm loyal. Not like I've had a ton of boyfriends — fine, I've had two serious ones — but I don't mess around behind anyone's back. That Shep tempted me, even in my head…disturbs me.

Greatly.

"Well, forget all that." Kelli waves her fingers in a dismissive gesture, clutching her clean clothes to her chest with her other hand. "I'm going to take a shower and then we're going out."

"We are?" I run my fingers through my still damp hair. I'd truly planned on laying low tonight. I have a paper due Tuesday I need to finish. Well, more like start.

"Yeah. Saturday night. Party at one of the frat houses. I got us an in." Kelli grins, looking pleased with herself.

"What about Dane?" I ask warily.

"What about him? We're good. We're solid. He has a birthday party to go to. Guys getting together and eating buffalo wings and drinking beer at someone's house off campus. Bleh."

"Yeah, well we're in for the same scenario. Minus the buffalo wings," I point out.

"Right, but we need to find you a new boyfriend since you dumped Joel."

"That is the absolute last thing I need." I met Kelli a few days before school officially started, when we were moving into the dorms. We hit it off right away and I was so thankful since one of my biggest fears was that I would hate my roommate.

We have a lot in common. We're both sarcastic. We both like to study but aren't fanatical about it. We're both reasonably clean. But where we differ is our attitude toward guys. Kelli likes to keep them coming, one after the other. Not that she's a slut or anything. Far from it. She just ends it with one and picks right up with another.

Me? I take a long time to even find one that I click with. And once I find him, it takes me a while to come around. After I come around and I'm finally ready to say yeah, let's do this, I like to settle in and consider him my somewhat boyfriend.

So now that I've broken up with Joel—my only boyfriend thus far my freshman year and it's already early April—it's going to take me months to get back on the boyfriend train.

Months. Like maybe not until my sophomore year

because school's almost finished and everyone will go home, including me.

"You're no fun." Kelli mock pouts. "Have you ever thought how awesome a quick hookup would be?"

"Ew." I make a face. "I don't do hookups. That's so gross." My body is my temple, damn it.

"You big prude." Kelli throws her clean pair of underwear at me and I dodge them, practically tumbling off my bed. "I'm not talking blow jobs in a back bedroom or a quick screw against the wall—though there's nothing wrong with either of those things. I meant like… flirting with a hot guy. Getting a little drunk. Dragging him to a secluded spot. Running your hands through his hair as he slides his hands down your back and you make out for a solid ten minutes. With lots and lots of tongue." The dreamy look on Kelli's face tells me she's describing a personal interlude. I really hope she's not talking about Dane, because I'll never be able to look at him the same way again.

Not that I'm going to be looking much at Dane. He and Joel are pretty close friends. So I'll be avoiding the both of them, thank you very much.

"Sounds lovely," I say. "If I'm lucky, I'll find some handsome prince type tonight who'll sweep me off my feet and kiss me until I can't feel my lips anymore. I can't wait." I toss Kelli's underwear back at her and the royal blue scrap of silky fabric smacks her right in the face. "Go take your shower already. You reek of sex."

"I do?" She leans her head down and sniffs at the neckline of her shirt. "I can smell Dane's cologne, but that's it."

God. Her sexual afterglow is kind of annoying. More like it makes me jealous. With Joel…I shouldn't fault him. He was eager. He always wanted to please me. And I appreciated that but…okay fine, the problem was me. I had the hang ups. I couldn't let go. I get too nervous during sex. I worry about how I look, how I'm touching him, how he's touching me, do I smell, do I look fat, can he see the cellulite on my butt, oh my God did I just fart?

Do I give good blowjobs or bad? Ugh, does he want to lick me down there? Gross, don't do it. I won't come anyway. I'm sweaty. I'm smelly. I'm tired. My jaw hurts. Can't he just come already and get it over with?

Yeah. I have serious self-esteem issues when it comes to sex. I wish I could just relax and let loose and be free. Like Kelli, or like the rest of the girls on campus who are getting some on a regular basis. Performance anxiety really stresses me out. Sex is supposed to be fun, right? I feel like it's a job. Or worse, I feel like it's a test.

Yes, a giant, everything depends on this moment epic test and I am always, always going to fail. I've gotten quite good at pretending. Faking orgasm. Faking interest. Faking everything.

Maybe I should've become a nun. Bad thing is, I'm not Catholic.

"While I'm taking a shower, you need to do your hair. Curl it like you do sometimes. It's pretty like that." Kelli waves a hand at the bright yellow, very expensive curling iron my mom had shipped to me for my birthday from Sephora. The thing works like magic. Considering its price tag, it should.

Not sure where Mom got the money for it since we are most assuredly middle class, but I do know she's been dating a new guy lately who I think she's getting to foot all the bills. She says she's been remodeling the house lately too, which is kind of strange but hey, he must really like her. And she's a pretty awesome lady, I must say. So if her boyfriend Dex is funding the remodel, then good for her. Good for us. I should reap the benefits of this too since I'm coming home for the summer.

At least there's something to look forward to.

"And wear that cute pale blue top. You know, the one that's sleeveless and has the crisscross in the back?"

"Kell. That shirt shows practically all my goods." I bought it because Joel encouraged me to. I've worn it exactly once and felt so self-conscious the entire night I deemed it unwearable forevermore. "In fact, it's yours now. You're an owner."

"No way. I bought one just like it but in a different

print. You are so wearing it tonight." Kelli grins. "And you're wearing it *because* it shows off all your goods. You have a hot bod, friend! Such a tiny waist and those boobs! Women pay good money for boobs like those."

I glance down at my chest. "You're crazy."

"No, *you're* crazy for not showing those ta-tas off more! You're gonna curl your hair, I'm gonna do your makeup, you'll wear that shirt that shows off your goods and we're gonna get wasted, baby. We're going to have the night of our lives!" Kelli dances out of our dorm room, slamming the door behind her.

I stare at the door for a moment too long before I finally heave myself off the bed with a big sigh and go over to the makeshift vanity Kelli and I turned our one lone desk into and plug in the curling iron. Flopping into the chair, I settle in and flick on the lights of the three-way mirror Kelli brought with her from home, making a face at my reflection.

I look crazy. Hair is whack since I let it dry naturally so it's sort of all over the place. My skin looks pale, the freckles stark and too obvious for my liking. My brows need plucking and…I lean in closer, turn my chin to the right. Great. A pimple. I run my finger over the blemish right on my jawline, knowing that with a few dabs of foundation and one of those magic brushes Kelli's always wielding, she can make it disappear.

Thank God for friends. And moms that splurge on

too expensive curling irons.

Amen.

Shep

"A frat party? That's so déclassé." I'm lounging outside by the pool, soaking up the spring-but-it-almost-feels-like-summer heat. California is suffering a major drought, which means hot women in string bikinis hanging out by the pool comes that much earlier. I should have a poolside party tomorrow afternoon...

"Quit with your bullshit fancy words and just agree to go with me," Gabe gripes good naturedly, like he's wont to do. Because nothing ever gets this asshole down, his life is perfect. Gabriel Walker should be one of those models in a Ralph Lauren ad, where they're all beautiful, wearing perfect clothing and riding horses through a lush green field and laughing with children and a gorgeous woman is clinging to his side.

Good thing he's my best friend or I'd hate his guts.

"And why are we going to a frat house again?" I sound bored because I am. I've been to enough frat parties to last a lifetime. I'm also frustrated. Last night had been...insane. I went from the incredible high of winning that crazy hand and getting the girl to having said girl slap me across the face in front of everyone.

Everyone.

Reaching up, I touch my face, wincing at the hint of pain when I probe my cheekbone. Bitch Face Jade has a solid swing. I'll give her that.

"Because I want to. We need to cut loose, man. I just turned in a major paper and it feels good to have that out of my hair. I'm going to be leaving for the summer and won't see your ass for months. I'll miss you."

"Aw," I interrupt. "We can write each other. Send each other selfies so we don't forget what we look like."

"Shut up," he mutters. "Come on. We need to live it up before school's out. Next year is our last. Then we gotta be all responsible and shit." Gabe sounds melancholy. He has no problem sharing his feelings, getting sentimental. Me on the other hand? I show nothing. I keep everything, every emotion, every feeling, close to my chest.

It's easier that way.

"Besides it's our frat asshole, not that you've been coming around lately," Gabe continues. "They miss you. They want to hang out with the legendary Shepard Prescott."

"Bullshit." I take a sip from my beer, set it down on the tiny metal table beside me with a loud clunk. The late afternoon sun is intense and I'm sweating. I should jump in the pool real quick to cool off, but it's still ice cold so I'll pass. "No gambling tonight," I add. It's Tristan's night to work anyway so I don't have to be there.

"Why? You still mad over how the little redhead burned you?" Gabe laughs.

I'm tempted to throw my phone in the pool but restrain myself. "My cheek still hurts," I mutter.

Gabe laughs harder. "She's a firecracker, I'll give her that. Bet she's an amazing fuck."

"You thought about fucking her?" I feel vaguely possessive. Fine, more than vaguely possessive. More like, I'm venturing into *she's mine* territory.

"Well, yeah. Did you get a good look at her? I know you did. You couldn't keep your eyes off her. She's hot, with all that hair and the tits and her mouth? Christ."

"What about her mouth?" Yeah. He has no business thinking of Jade like this. Talking about Jade like this.

You don't either asshole.

"You sound jealous."

I snort. "Impossible. What could I be jealous of?"

"Exactly. That's why you need to come to the house tonight. Lots of girls will be there. You can have your pick and get that temperamental Jade out of your head for good," Gabe says.

"I won her fair and square. If I ever see her again, I'm collecting," I say, feeling like a jerk the second the words fall from my mouth.

"I think it's in your best interest you never see her again. Right? She's crazy, dude. She fucking *slapped* you. What the hell was her problem anyway?"

Oh, I don't know. Her boyfriend gave her up pretty damn easily. I was being a prick. Granted, she was being somewhat of a bitch and I was just leveling the playing field so to speak but...

It was a tense night. An insane night. One I don't want to repeat.

So why'd I dream about her? About those bee-stung lips clinging to mine, and her tongue. About my hands buried in all that vibrant red hair, tugging on it, making her moan. About her ass filling my palms and her tits pressed against my chest and...

"I'll pick you up at ten," Gabe says, crashing into the middle of my hot thoughts.

"What time does the party start?"

"Nine. We'll make an epic entrance," Gabe reassures me before we end the call.

I'm tired of epic entrances too. I'm tired of... everything. It all bores me. I sound like a dick but I can't help myself. I've been handed everything I could ever want. My family comes from old money. The Prescotts have been around for generations, originally making their money in real estate. Mother is a Shepard and their multigenerational fortune came from the stock market.

Jade had been right. I'm a complete asshole with my rich guy name and my rich guy attitude. I know nothing else. I've never been anything else but the spoiled rich kid. The boy who went to boarding school because his parents were sick of dealing with his shit so they got him out of the house in the most legitimate way. The boy who shoplifted from various stores one too many times when he was thirteen so he got shoved into the back of a police car and questioned at the station in order to be taught a lesson. The high school student who was caught snorting coke in the chemistry lab with a couple of friends and almost got expelled.

Thank God for Daddy who wrote a big check and got all that nastiness swept under the rug.

I don't really do drugs anymore. My vice of choice is alcohol and ever since I became of legal age to drink it, I'm not indulging as much. It's not forbidden anymore so therefore, I'm over it.

Oh, and my other vice—besides women—is gambling.

It's illegal, what we're doing, what we're running at Gabe's. And that's more than half the thrill. If I can't push it to the very edge, then I'm not having any fun.

Sick but true.

I'm fairly sure that's why I enjoyed toying with Jade so much, why I included her in our bet last night. It felt forbidden, asking Joel to bet his girl. I've pushed guys to bet their cars (and I've won two, sold them both on Craigslist), to bet their motorcycles (never won one), to bet their designer sunglasses (won more than my fair share), their gold necklaces, their fucking Nikes, their dogs (never won a pet either).

I've never asked for a girl though. Her anger had fueled me. Her smart mouth had turned me on. Touching the bare skin of her arm…she's incredibly soft. The scent of her hair, those big eyes, those bigger tits.

Christ.

I have it bad. Maybe I need to find another hot redhead tonight and fuck her. Fuck Bitch Face Jade right out of my system so I'll quit thinking about her.

But first, I'm gonna take a shower and jerk off to thoughts of her lips wrapped tight around my cock. Just to take the edge off.

⌒◯

"This sucks," I yell in Gabe's ear.

"What are you? An old man?" Gabe looks incredulous, then flashes a giant smile at me as he clutches his bottleneck beer tight. "Look. How can this even begin to suck?"

I let my gaze cast out to where Gabe is indicating with the wide sweep of his hand. It's mayhem in the backyard. White lights are strung between the trees, zigzagging over our heads. A DJ is at the backend of the yard, his equipment on a stage as he clutches a pair of headphones in one hand and waves his other hand in the air to the beat of the song, his face lit up by his laptop's screen. The yard is jam packed with bodies hopping up and down to the latest by Katy Perry, some sickeningly upbeat song that makes me want to gauge out my ears with extra sharp knives.

Gabe and I stand on the back patio at the top of the stairs, like kings surveying their land. A few stragglers linger up here as well and there's a particular girl watching us from afar, though she seems to only have eyes for Gabe. Fine with me, considering she's not a redhead.

Yeah. The shower beat off session hasn't taken the edge off whatsoever.

"Nothing but girls dressed in their skimpiest clothes as far as the eye can see," Gabe says. "I think we'll find good fortune tonight, my friend."

"What the hell? Have you turned into a pirate?" I take a giant swig of my beer, polishing it off. I need another to make it through the next half hour, let alone the rest of the night.

"Aye, in hunt of gorgeous, sexy women." Gabe squints one eye and makes a variety of pirate noises, causing the girl staring at him from afar to giggle flirtatiously. He turns, notices the girl and leaves me in the dust, not bothering to look back.

Typical.

"You need another?"

I glance to my right to see a girl with strawberry

blonde hair smiling at me, a beer bottle clutched in each hand. She's wearing extremely short black shorts and a white lace top. Without a bra.

Damn.

"Yeah. Thanks." I take the beer she offers and tip it to my lips, keeping my gaze on her the entire time. She weaves on her feet, teetering on the extremely high heel sandals she's wearing. "You all right?" I ask after I swallow.

"Ss' fine." She smiles crookedly, her blue eyes going a little hazy and I reach out, gripping her by her arm before she falls. "You're Shep Prescott right?"

"Yeah," I say warily. I hate it when they already know me. Makes them feel stalkerish even though that might not be their intent.

"I've heard of you." She takes a step closer, her tits brushing against my arm. They're small. She's small in general, doesn't even come up to my shoulder and I'm a solid six-one. "I hear you have a big dick."

Thank Christ I wasn't taking a drink when she said that. "Is that so? And where did you hear this bit of info from?"

She smiles, revealing teeth covered in metal. How old is she anyway? "My name's Manda. Amanda. Mandy. Whatever you want to call me. My sister is Lacy Douglas. You dated her last year."

Lacy Douglas. I don't recognize the name. And I

don't 'date' anyone. If I supposedly went out with Lacy that means I fucked her once, maybe twice, and then never called her again. I guess I made an impression though, what with the big dick remark.

"Lacy said you're a prick." She curls her arm around mine. "I'm more intrigued with the idea of your big dick though. I'm a professional blow jobber."

I try my best to keep a straight face. No way in hell am I letting brace face get anywhere near my dick. "So you're saying you get paid to suck dick?"

She frowns. "Nooo. I'm no prostitute."

"But you said you were a professional," I point out.

Manda, Mandy, Amanda rolls her eyes and releases her hold on my arm. "I said that I'm a professional blow jobber. As in I've given lots of BJs. I have skills. Skills you wouldn't know what to do with."

This chick is super drunk. She'll regret everything she says and does in the morning. Not to mention the hangover. "Are you a freshman?"

"Nooo." She likes drawing out her nos. "I'm a senior in high school. I came with Lacy tonight. She's showing me the college life." She throws her arm up in the air and lets out a whoop. "I'm coming for you next year damn it! I will own this campus!"

Time to go. I slowly back away, offering whatshername a little wave before I turn on my heel and run straight into the redhead of my dreams.

Or nightmares.

Take your pick.

"You have got to be kidding me," Jade Bitch Face mutters, taking a step back, allowing me to see her in her full sexy-as-fuck glory. "Hanging out with children I see."

I glance over my shoulder to see Amanda grinning at me, showing off the braces, looking like a child trying her best to convince everyone else she's a grownup. I wave at her again and she frowns, turns on her wobbly heel and starts down the stairs toward the makeshift dance floor.

"Isn't she a little young for you?" Jade asks.

I return my attention to her, trying my best to keep my eyes on her face but...I can't. She's wearing some crazy shirt that's sleeveless and cropped, offering a teasing glimpse of her flat stomach, the curve of her waist. The pale fabric strains across her chest and the cropped denim skirt she's got on shows more thigh than covers them.

Dayum.

"Come to repay your debt?" I ask, decidedly happy at tonight's turn of events. I know Gabe said I needed to forget her. And I agreed with him. But if she's going to magically appear and drive me crazy with what she's wearing, then I'm going to take full advantage of this.

And collect my payment.

chapter
Three

Shep

"I don't owe you shit," Jade says, her cheery voice at odds with the scowl on her face. It doesn't detract from her beauty though.

She's looking extra gorgeous tonight too. Her hair is down, long past her shoulders and wavy. Her lips are this vibrant pink glossy shade I have the sudden urge to kiss off. And her legs in that skirt...I want them wrapped around me. Naked. Just before I—

"You have a lot of nerve, you know that? Showing up at this party like you own it. I've never seen you before in my life and all of a sudden I see you two nights in a row? If I didn't know any better, I'd think you were stalking me," she says, sending me a withering stare.

"I could say the same for you." I grab hold of her

arm and yank her close, trying my best to ignore the electricity that crackles between our bodies but it's no use. I'm attracted to her. She's attracted to me.

We need to see where this takes us.

"Like I'd stalk you. I think you're an asshole, remember?" She jerks her arm from my hold, her foot on the edge of the deck and where the stairs start. One minute she's standing before me, the next she's falling... falling...

It goes in slow motion but happens so fast, I leap forward, catching her before she goes crashing onto the stairs. I'm holding her in my arms, leaning against the stair railing and bent over Jade, one hand cupping the back of her head, her hair clinging to my fingers, silky soft and fragrant.

Everything about her is perfect. And soft. She's staring up at me, a grimace of what looks like pain crossing over her delicate features. "Are you okay?" I ask, hearing the panic in my voice but not really giving a crap. Her near fall just scared the shit out of me.

"I'm fine. It's just..." Her voice trails off and she winces again. "My ankle. I think I twisted it."

Without hesitation I scoop her up and carry her into the house, ignoring her protests, ignoring how she beats on my chest with her fist to get my attention. I'm focused on taking care of Jade, nothing else. I feel like an ass, driving her away, making her almost fall.

"Put me down," she says for about the twentieth time. "Where are you taking me?"

"To one of the back bedrooms so I can look at your ankle." I angle her to the side and carry her down the narrow hallway, kicking in one of the bedroom doors which is thankfully empty and haul her inside, where I set her carefully onto the bed. "Now let me look at it." I sit on the edge of the bed, ready to reach out and start probing but she jerks her legs away from me, whimpering when she does so.

"Go away," she says with a sniffle.

"Stop being such a baby." I brace my hand on the mattress on the other side of her legs, caging her in. "I'm trying to check out your ankle, not look up your skirt."

Though now that I mention it...

"Yeah right. God, do you think of nothing else or what?" She rolls her eyes and leans back against the headboard, making herself somewhat comfortable.

Which is good. Real good. I hope this means she'll let me make sure she's okay without much protest.

"Think of what?" I ask innocently as I let my hand settle carefully on her foot. She flinches, tries to move away but I circle my fingers gently around her ankle, keeping her in place. "It doesn't look swollen."

She leans over the slightest bit, the scent of her perfume washing over me, a heady mix of floral and citrus. "It doesn't hurt as bad," she admits.

"Yeah?" I lift my head, my gaze meeting hers. We're close. Kissing close. Not that I want to kiss her. Not really.

Okay, I'm a liar.

"Yeah," she whispers, parting her lips, a shaky exhale escaping when I sweep my thumb over the top of her foot.

I drop my gaze, taking in her pale blue painted toenails. "Cute."

"My toes?" She wiggles them. "The color matches my shirt."

Ah, the perfect excuse to check out that shirt again. I love how much of her it exposes without being trashy. Her skin is pale but not ghostly and she has a smattering of freckles on her shoulders. Makes me wonder where else she might have freckles. And why I'm suddenly so attracted to freckles.

I drift my hand up, over her calf, stopping at her knee. Her leg is smooth and if we were both drunker, I'd let my hand continue its search, going higher and higher until I ended up under her skirt. Under her panties...

"What are you doing?" she asks, sounding the tiniest bit breathless.

"Making sure you're not injured," I answer, proud of how under control I sound. Inside, I'm chaos. My heart is thumping hard against my chest and my breathing's accelerated. I grip her knee, and realize my hand is fucking shaking.

"I think you're trying to get your hand up my skirt." Leave it to Bitch Face to call me out. I can't help but find her straightforwardness attractive. No girl is ever straightforward with me. They're always coy. Playing games and flirting and never asking for what they really want. They always defer to me.

After a while, that gets pretty damn boring.

"Maybe I am," I say, moving my hand to rest on top of her knee.

Her lips curve into the smallest smile and seeing it feels like a victory. As if I've just won an extra difficult battle and that tiny curve of her lush lips is my prize. "You're pretty determined, aren't you?"

She's not pushing me away. I need to take this moment. Seize this fucking moment and make it mine. Make *her* mine. At least for tonight. Her scent is making my head spin and just touching her knee has got me sporting wood. "I'm always determined."

"Determined to piss me off?"

I chuckle and her smile grows. "Am I doing a good job?"

"You're an expert at making me mad."

"I think we're having a moment," I tell her. "A bonding moment."

She looks the slightest bit horrified. "No. Way. That is the last thing I want to do."

I raise my eyebrows, let my hand slide up a bare inch more. Then another. I'm so close to getting under that skirt, it's not even funny. "You don't like me very much, do you?"

"You don't like me either. You call me Bitch Face."

"You introduced yourself to me as Bitch Face."

She tilts her head, all that wavy red hair tumbling over her shoulder. My fingers itch to touch it. "I did, didn't I?"

"Yeah. I thought it was an unusual name..." I let my voice drift and she smiles once more.

"Says the man with an unusual name."

"I told you it's an old family name."

"As a last name, not as a first." She makes a little face. "It's not very sexy."

"You don't think?" Interesting.

"I can't imagine shouting out your name in the throes of passion." Her cheeks go the faintest pink. That she's even thinking like this gives me a secret thrill.

Forbidden. Unknown. This is the last girl I should consider getting naked with.

"Throes of passion?" I ask. "Someone's been reading too many romance novels."

"You know what I mean." She waves a hand, dismissing her words.

"I don't." I pull the innocent act, which she isn't falling for but it's still fun. "What are you talking about exactly?"

"You're not going to make me explain, are you?"

"I would love for you to explain. Or maybe I should help you." I crawl my fingers up her thigh, playing with the frayed hem of her denim skirt. "Are you talking about...having sex?"

She nods, her cheeks blazing up. Hmm, she's extra pretty when she blushes.

"And that moment...when we're fucking...and you're so damn close." I lean in and inhale deep, my eyes almost falling shut as I absorb her scent, her warmth and that flush in her cheeks, the way her breathing quickens. "So fucking close as I push deep inside you. You don't think it would be sexy to yell out my name just as I make you come?"

"N-no." She shakes her head, that single word coming out as a squeak.

"Really." I give in and settle my cheek next to hers, nuzzle her ear with my nose before I whisper, "Because by the time I have you coming, I'm fairly certain you'll be crying out my name and begging me please."

"You're a real arrogant prick, aren't you?"

I pull back from her the slightest bit, a little shocked. The girl doesn't mince words. "Merely confident in my abilities." I cup the back of her head, thread my fingers in the silky soft waves of her hair. I'd love to wrap her hair around my fist and tug her head back right before

I kiss her…

"Proud of your man-whore status?"

"I can't help it if the ladies flock to me."

She rests her hand on my chest and gives me a gentle shove. "I'm not flocking to you."

"Even after all that talk about coming and with my hand up your skirt?"

Jade looks down with a sharp gasp, dropping her hand to mine and shoving it out from beneath her skirt. "What are you *doing?*"

"I thought it was obvious." When she says nothing, only glares at me, I continue. "I was going to kiss you and hopefully get you off with my fingers."

Her mouth drops open. Instead of looking aroused, she looks…pissed. Vaguely horrified. "You're disgusting."

I lean back. Move way, way back though I'm not getting off the bed. Not yet. I still have a chance.

Or then again, maybe I don't.

Jade

I almost fell for all of that. The charm, the seductive tone of his voice, the way he looked at me, the way he touched me. Somehow, without me being aware of it, he'd skimmed those too sure fingers up my leg and slipped them beneath my skirt. Nuzzled my face with his. Freaking talked about being inside of me and making me come all while I'd be begging and shouting his name.

What a perv. Worse? I like his perverted side.

A lot.

"Shepard Prescott," I whisper, trying it out. "Shepard. Shep."

He runs a hand through that sexy mop of hair. It's in dire need of a trim. Touched with gold as if the sun reached out and shot her rays directly on those rich brown strands. "What are you doing?"

"Oh, Shep." I smile, feeling like the chick that fakes an orgasm in that one movie from the eighties. Mom loves that movie. I prefer Sleepless in Seattle but whatever. "Touch me there, Shep. Deeper Shep."

He smiles. "See? Is that so hard?"

"Are you hard?" I clamp my lips shut the moment the words fall out of my mouth. Did I really just say that?

He clears his throat, readjusts the front of his jeans. Oh good lord, I did. And I think he *is*.

"You're the one calling my name," he points out.

"I was pretending to try it out." I sit up straighter, jerking my legs away from him. My ankle feels much better thank goodness. "But it's not working for me. Shep is definitely not sexy."

"Says the only female on campus who thinks that."

"Please. You're so arrogant." I dart out my foot and nudge it against his thigh, surprised at how rock hard it is. The man is solid muscle, I'll give him that. I bet he looks damn good with his shirt off. Or even naked.

Yeah. Don't go there.

"See? You're trying to touch me."

"I'm trying to get you to stand up so I can get off this bed."

"Why didn't you say so?" He leaps to his feet, agile as a cat. And he's a sneaky predator too. Scary. "Need help?" he asks, offering his hand toward me.

I ignore his outstretched arm and push off the bed, putting my weight gingerly on my twisted ankle but it's fine. All better now.

I can make my escape.

"Since I just shut you down maybe you should go try and charm the panties off some other innocent girl," I say, blinking up at him.

"You still owe me."

Ugh. He's not going to let this go. "And by *owing* you, are you implying I'm supposed to have sex with you? Please. I'm not your whore."

"I never said that," he says, all calm, smooth and irritating as hell. "But a bet is a bet. A deal is a deal. I won you fair and square."

"Yeah, because my ex put me up for grabs!" I point out, immediately regretting that I yelled at him. It's annoying, how serene he is when I'm all flustered.

"You two broke up?" I refuse to hear the hopeful note in his voice.

Refuse. Refuse. Refuse.

"We'd been headed in that direction for a while." God, I'm trying my best for nonchalant but it's difficult. I lift my chin. "Not that it would matter to you. You were making a play for me, believing I was involved with someone else."

"Give me a break. You were willing. Don't make me out to be the scumbag." He jerks a thumb at his chest. His very broad, very nice chest.

True. Not that I'd ever admit it. And why can't he back away a little bit or better yet, leave the room? He smells delicious. That same earthy, woodsy scent with the hint of citrus, and he looks damn good in those jeans.

"I expect you to pay up. I won that hand. I won *you*," he says, his voice low, his gaze intense. And directed right at me. "If Joel the loser can't come through then you need to."

I gape at him. This entire situation is surreal. Why is Shepard Prescott so determined to—have me? I don't get it. So I guess I should ask him. "Wh-what do you want from me?" I sound like a stuttering fool and I hate it. He unnerves me completely. I swear he was going to kiss me not even five minutes ago.

And I would've let him.

"Your time."

I squint up at him. Man, he's tall. "What?"

"Your time. I won a girlfriend so I expect…a girlfriend." He shrugs. "You'll do all those girlfriend things girls do. Hang out with me. Wash my clothes. Feed me. Rub my back. Go out to dinner with me. Watch TV together."

"Wash your clothes? Feed you? You make me sound like a maid."

"Isn't that what good girlfriends do?"

This guy doesn't have a clue. "So that's what you want from me?" I ask incredulously. "I thought you didn't have girlfriends. That you don't want a girlfriend."

Jeez. Should I have just said that to him? It's a well-known fact that Shep has never dated anyone seriously for the last three years he's been on this campus. He has a revolving door of women and that's it. I don't want to be one of the many.

I don't want to be with him, period.

Liar.

"I definitely don't want one. A real girlfriend would always want something from me. But you wouldn't be a *real* girlfriend. You're temporary. A girl I won in a bet." His face lights up, as if he's figuring out what a great deal this is. Which it is.

For him.

"And what do I get out of this?"

"Me." He grins and spreads his arms out wide, like he's a prize or something.

I want to sock him right in his smug as hell face. "No way."

His smile falters and he drops his hands to his sides. "No?"

"Absolutely not." I shake my head. "You'll need to find Joel if you want him to repay this debt. I owe you nothing."

I start to leave but he grabs hold of my arm, stopping me. His grip is gentle. I could pull out of his hold easily but I don't. There's something about the press of his fingers into my skin, his nearness, the way he speaks, low and steady close to my ear, that makes everything inside of me come instantly, achingly alive.

"You owe me everything. All that you have. And don't deny that you want to give it to me because I know you do," he murmurs, his breath stirring my hair.

God, his words...they *do* something to me. Has any guy spoken to me like this before?

No. Not ever.

We stare at each other, the air charged with unspoken tension. He sweeps his hand down my arm in a gentle caress, causing gooseflesh to rise on my skin and I want to step away. I tell myself to step away. Instead I'm tilting my head back, he's moving his head down and oh my God, he's going to kiss me. Fucking sexy Shep Prescott who knows just what to say to make me light up inside is going to put those perfect lips on mine in three...two...

"Hey." The door swings open and there stands a guy I recognize from last night, his arm looped around the neck of a really short, really pretty dark haired girl who's giggling uncontrollably. "Oh. Shep. What are you doing in here?"

"What does it look like I'm doing in here?" Shep asks tightly as I move away from him. Far, far away, so I can breathe again.

I take in a shaky breath, refusing to look at him. Because he knows. I know he knows I would've given in and I can't give him that power.

The guy grins and holds his hand out toward me as he enters the room. "Gabriel Walker. A friend of Shep's. I saw you last night. You have a most excellent backhand."

Oh God, how embarrassing. "Jade Frost." I shake his hand, momentarily dazzled by Gabriel's good looks. Was there some sort of unspoken law that attractive men must hang out together? "Nice to meet you."

"Pleasure's all mine," he drawls, earning a deathly glare from Shep.

"Quit flirting with her, Gabe," Shep snaps. "You brought your own date."

"I'm Meadow," the brunette chirps. I shake her offered hand as well. Shep doesn't even bother.

Asshole.

"Didn't mean to interrupt," Gabe says, grabbing hold of Meadow's hand and the two of them start backing toward the door. "We'll find another room."

"No need. I have to go find my friend," I say, walking toward them, ready to move past them and make my much-needed escape. "She's probably worried about me." Kelli was probably outside dancing and didn't even realize I'd left her but they don't need to know that.

"You came with a friend?" Shep asks.

"Well, yeah. I wouldn't come to some crazy frat party all alone." How dumb does he think I am? I flash a smile at Gabe and Meadow. "Nice meeting you two."

"Great meeting you," Gabe says, watching me carefully as I sidestep out of the room.

"This isn't over," Shep calls but I don't look back at him. He'll find me. I know he will. We'll run into each other again and he'll demand I owe him something and ask for his payment in the form of sexual favors, which should totally piss me off yet somehow...doesn't.

I get what he wants from me. And for the teeniest, most fleeting moment, I wanted it too.

But as I walk away and head back outside in search of Kelli, I know I can't give in. I can't repay him on this stupid bet. The minute I allow myself to fall under Shep's spell, I'm done for. He sure talks a confident game but could he really make me forget myself and fall into the moment? All that talk about making me come and me denying my feelings for him...

Fine. His words left me hot and bothered. More than once. Big deal. He's all talk and no action. Lots of effort but zero return.

Just like all the rest.

chapter
Four

"Y ou need to buy your mother a gift."

I make a face even though Dad can't see me. I'm driving through town, bored. When all else fails I hop in my car and think. I absently answered my phone via the Bluetooth link in my car, regretting it the moment I heard my dad's voice fill the interior. It's like he's the omnipresent great and powerful Oz. Sucks. "What do I get a woman who has everything?" And what she doesn't have but wants, she runs out and buys. Immediately. Mom waits for no one.

"It's her birthday." Pierce Prescott is one of the richest men in the country. He came by his money the old fashioned way—an inheritance. Me? I'm the same way, since I benefit from the same inheritance and my parents are the old-fashioned types. They encourage my sisters to get married to equally wealthy men so they can leave me all of their wealth, which just bites my sisters' asses. I will never have to work a day in my life if I don't want to. My children probably won't have to either.

The idea of that, of never having to work a day in my life, doesn't always sit well, especially lately. No wonder I caused so much trouble during my younger years. I was bored out of my freaking mind.

"I'll send her flowers," I suggest. All women love flowers.

"That'll be nice." I can tell he thinks that's a terrible idea. "But you need to do more, son. Send her something special. Thoughtful. Straight from the heart."

Mom and I have a special relationship. As in, I'm her only son and she loves spoiling me. I'm her greatest heartache and her greatest joy. She said that to me once in the middle of a massive sobbing fest. Probably right after I got kicked out of school for that coke snorting incident in chem lab.

"I'm not sending her a Hermes bag. Isn't there some special waiting list I need to get on before I can even buy one?" That I even know what a Hermes bag is probably takes the validity of my man card down a couple of notches. But when you're a little kid surrounded by three older sisters and a shopaholic mother, you learn about Hermes bags. Chanel. Prada. Vuitton.

"She already bought herself a new Hermes bag for her birthday. Powder blue." The irritated sigh Dad lets forth tells me what he thinks about that purchase. "She has way too many already."

"Look, I'll go to one of those quirky little stores downtown and buy her some coastal knickknack. Something you can't find anywhere else but here," I suggest. "How does that sound?"

Dad heaves out another, even more irritated sigh. I can't win with this situation and he knows it. Hell, I can never win with him. The guy barely tolerates me most of the time. "Don't forget to send her a card too."

I end the call and head downtown, determined to get this chore done pronto. Hopefully wherever I end up finding Mom's gift, they can ship it directly to her. Or if it's not common store policy, I can convince the employee to do it for me. With enough charm and cash, you can convince just about anyone to do just about anything.

The weather's nice, bright and sunny and in the mid-seventies, making me think I have the wrong idea and I need to be on a beach somewhere. Drinking a beer and catching some rays, scanning all the hot girls in string bikinis behind my shades as they walk by. I bet Gabe's there. And maybe Tristan is with them. If they're not, we should hang out by my pool later and invite every girl we know.

Which is a lot of girls.

There's only one girl on my mind though.

Fuck.

I somehow got my sorry ass out of bed by ten, a miracle but I'd actually gone to bed early after the epic fail of last night. I'd hoped to find a sexy little redhead to get that other bitchy little redhead out of my mind and instead I found the real deal.

The real deal who left me in the dust. Again. Jade Bitch Face isn't interested in me whatsoever. Despite how close I came to kissing her. I would've. I would've kissed the fuck out of her if that asshole Gabe hadn't interrupted us. Some friend. His timing is for shit.

And then Jade bailed. Left me standing there like a loser with my limp dick in my hand. Not literally but man, it felt like it. I thought Gabe was gonna bust a gut laughing at me. His date for the night told him he was mean. I agreed with her.

Didn't stop my best friend from laughing at my expense though.

I went home, jerked off—again—and fell asleep before midnight. Like I was Cinderella and my skin had an orange tinge, I rushed home, disappointed in the party. Once Jade left, I had no interest in staying.

What does that mean? I won't be satisfied until I have her naked beneath me at least once? I hope that'll solve this problem and I hope it happens fast because this case of blue balls I have going on sucks.

Once I find a parking space, I start toward the row of shops, surprised at how crowded it is, though I guess I shouldn't be considering it's a Sunday. Somewhere among all the homegrown shit they sell downtown I should be able to find something for Mom. It might be kitschy and useless, but Mom likes that sort of stuff. Sometimes.

Christ. I may as well just flush my cash down the toilet.

I find a candle store and go inside because hey, she likes candles. What woman doesn't? My sister Victoria almost burned the house down when one of the curtains in her room caught fire, all from a lit candle that sat on a nearby table. She'd planned to seduce her boyfriend that night and lit up her entire room with a bunch of tiny votives, going for the romantic look.

Yeah. Talk about an epic fail.

The moment I enter the building, I'm assaulted by a variety of scents that makes my nose twitch. One of those table fountains that used to be so popular when I was a little kid sits near the door, the sound of running water pleasant if you like that sort of thing.

Which I guess I do. But my family always took it to the next level. I'll see your tabletop fountain and create a rock wall water fountain that takes over the entire family room.

True story.

Slowly I move through the store, cracking a smile at the new age-y music playing in the background, the giant baskets set on a glass table at waist level, full of a variety of healing crystals. I'm starting to suspect this place is a front for a medical marijuana facility when I hear a voice ask if I need any help. A very familiar voice that makes my skin prickle and the hairs on the back of my neck stand on end.

Whirling around, my suspicions are confirmed.

"Oh, you have got to be fucking kidding me," Jade mutters, her hands going immediately to her hips.

I grin at her. I can't help it. This is a lucky streak for sure. "You work here?"

She's wearing a red T-shirt that says Light My Fire across her chest—the name of the store—and there's a nametag pinned to her shirt that reads Jade in swirling, feminine handwriting. "Don't act like you don't know this. Somehow with all your money and connections, you found out where I work. So creepy. Can't you just leave this bet thing alone?"

"You think I hired someone to track you down?" Hell, I can't work that fast. I've been sleeping pretty much the entire time since I saw her last and that was only last night.

"How else would you keep popping up where I am? You've crossed a line this time though, asshole." She turns on her heel and starts heading toward the register counter at the back of the store. My gaze drops to her ass, which looks mighty fine in those khaki shorts she's wearing. And her legs…damn they're long. "I'm calling the cops."

"What? No." I chase after her, grabbing her arm before she can make a grab for the phone on the counter. "I'm not having you followed or whatever you're accusing me of doing. This is total coincidence. I swear." Awesome coincidence for me, not so much for her, I guess.

And really, why does she hate me so much? I don't get it. Any other girl would be falling at my feet, begging me for something. Anything.

Not this one.

She tugs out of my hold and rubs her arm in the exact spot where I touched her. Trying to rub away those sparks? Because yeah, they're there. My fingers are still tingling. "Please. This is the third day in a row. And I've never seen you before in my life."

"Really?" I find that hard to believe. I know her boyfriend, ex-boyfriend, whatever she wants to call Joel the Wuss, has definitely gambled at our place before, which means at the very least, she had to have heard about me.

"God, you're such an egotistical ass." She waves her fingers at me, as if flicking away an annoying bug. "Get out of here. I'm serious. Before I really do call the cops."

"But I came in here to buy something."

She rolls her eyes and flicks her head. Today her hair is in some sort of bun thing on top of her head. She looks like a ballerina minus the tutu. It's sort of a shame, all of that sexy red hair restrained like it is when it should be wild and free. I prefer it wild and free.

I'd also like to take her somewhere more private and slowly pull every pin out of her hair as it falls past her shoulders, piece by vibrant piece…

"What in the world would you want to buy here?"

"Uh, candles." I glance around. "We're surrounded by them, in case you haven't noticed."

She ignores my jab. "And who are you buying this candle for?"

"My mother. It's her birthday in a few days." I start walking down an aisle, scanning the various candles on display. There's some nice ones I spot already, candles I know Mom will like but I'm not about to give up my hand too soon. I say I like something, next thing I know Jade's wrapping it up, I'm signing the credit card receipt and then she's ushering my ass straight out of here.

Nope. I'm going to savor this. Ask her questions. Make her show me different things before I finally, *finally* make my decision. She's established this crazy relationship between us from the start.

I'm just trying to keep it afloat while I plot my way

into her panties.

Great. I sound like a pervert even in my own head.

"You're going to buy your mother a candle from Light My Fire for her birthday?" She sounds incredulous. Like I can blame her.

"I am," I say determinedly, stopping in front of one display in particular. "What the hell is this? Black voodoo magic?"

There's a hammered silver tray covered in shiny black and silver crystals, with three fat black candles clustered together in the middle. Mom would hate this sort of thing but I have to ask.

"Enid is into all that stuff. The crystals, how they heal and ward off evil spirits and the like." Jade leans in closer to me, as if imparting a great secret. I catch her scent, sweet and clean and inhale discreetly, trying to keep it together. She is pure temptation and doesn't have a clue. "I personally don't believe in any of that but I play along."

She's being nice to me. I wonder what's wrong. "Is this really a medical marijuana store?"

I blew it. Now she looks offended. "Ugh, no. This is a legit candle and crystal store. If you think we're selling pot brownies in the back, then you're sadly mistaken."

Huh. Wonder if she's ever tried a pot brownie. It might mellow her ass out when I can only figure she prefers being wound up, so I doubt it. "Sorry. My mistake. So…show me your best candle. Or why don't you show me which one you like best."

"You're being serious."

"As a heart attack." I nod solemnly, shoving my hands in my pockets before I do something stupid.

Like grab her.

"Because you want to buy a candle."

"Isn't that what most people want to do when they come in here?"

She rolls her eyes. If she keeps that up every time she's with me, she's going to give herself a headache. "And you're not following me."

"I already told you this is all some weird coincidence." Or fate. I'm not a huge believer in fate but what are the odds? It's so wild, Jade fully believes I'm stalking her.

"Is everything okay?" A large woman almost as tall as me sweeps down the aisle, coming to a stop directly in front of us. She's wearing a long black velvet dress dotted with clear rhinestones and flowing sleeves, her pitch black hair pulled back into a low ponytail. She looks like a stereotypical witch. "Jade, are you helping this darling young man?"

Ah, her boss. And an ally. I can sense it. "She's trying her best," I say, my voice filled with disappointment.

The look Jade shoots me is the deadliest stare she can muster, which is pretty damn deadly. "I know him," she mutters.

"Doesn't mean he should be treated poorly." The woman makes a tsking noise and holds her hand out toward me, her long pointed nails a sparkly black. "I'm Enid. I own Light My Fire."

"Shep." I shake her hand, smiling at her. She smiles in return. Way more friendly than Bitch Face. "I like your store."

Enid beams. "Thank you. Do you want me to show you around?"

Jade starts backing up, the smug smile on her face telling me she thinks she won.

"Ah, I appreciate the gesture but I'm sure you're extremely busy, being the owner and all. And Jade's not that bad. She just likes to give me grief." I send an innocent smile in Jade's direction and she gives me the finger. Lucky for her, she's standing behind her boss who doesn't even notice.

"Jade, treat this boy right. You hear me?" Enid turns to send Jade a pointed look.

"Of course," Jade says through clenched teeth. "I'll give him top notch treatment."

"I'll hold you to it," I say with a wink.

Jade

He is insufferable. I always thought that word was ridiculous but now? It fits stupid insufferable Shepard

Prescott to a T. How the hell did he find me here? I don't know if I believe him when he says it's a coincidence. I think he tracked me down. I should find that totally creepy. I should be calling the cops, filing a restraining order, whatever it takes to keep him away from me.

The problem is...I sort of enjoy our banter. The way he smiles at me, his dark, dark eyes full of unspoken promises. Promises I wouldn't mind exploring. I like how he always seems to find everything amusing. Like life is just one big joke and he's the only one in on the punch line.

Every time he touches me I feel a spark. A zip of heat just beneath the surface, rumbling under my skin. I tell myself to ignore it. Tell myself it means nothing.

He feels it too though. It's in the way he pulls his hand away from me like I shocked him. It's in that subtle smolder of his velvety gaze. He's aware of it. Just like I'm aware of it.

Chemistry.

Beyond the chemistry bit, which could be totally fleeting, who knows, why would he want to find me? I'm not that special. He could have anyone he wanted. He'll find out quick I'm a boring lay when he has adventure written all over him. I'm the girl who has performance anxiety. He's the guy who probably revels in the performance. I'm the one who runs from it.

Clearly, he needs to move on and forget all about

me.

"Come on," I tell him wearily once Enid heads back to her office. "Let's get this over with."

"Sorry I'm such a drag," he drawls, his deep, delicious voice wrapping all around me, making me feel warm. I tell myself to ignore it.

So I do.

I show him a variety of candles, all the while trying my best to deny the tension between us. Our arms brush against each other by accident and it's like my skin's been lit on fire. I catch him watching me and I feel my cheeks heat. And when he purposely touches me, his voice close to my ear as he grabs my arm, I want to sag into him. Feel his arm come around my waist, his other hand slip beneath my chin before he lifts my head up so our lips can meet...

"I'll take this one," he says firmly, handing me a giant three wick pure white candle. "I think my mother will like the scent."

"But it's white." It's a gardenia-scented candle, which I love but I always prefer a candle with a little color. White is boring.

"It's perfect. Everything in their house is white," he says. "It won't disrupt her color scheme and trust me, that'll make her happy."

Ugh. I bet his parents live in a sterile mansion. I bet they have a ton of servants and the mother never has to leave the house or lift a finger. She probably sits on a pure white velvet couch and lounges with her white dog while eating white chocolate bon bons.

That sounds perfectly awful.

"Where do your parents live?" Okay fine I'm trying to find out information about him because I know next to nothing. And I'm just asking to be polite. That's what good little sales associates do.

"East coast. Connecticut. In fact, I was wondering if your store ships?" He lifts his brows, his expression almost pleading.

I ignore his question. "You don't have an accent."

He lowers his brows into a frown. "Say what?"

"You're from the east coast? I don't detect an accent."

"I went to boarding school for a few years. They beat any and all accents out of their students."

Now it's my turn to frown. "Really?"

"Yeah." He shrugs. "I moved around a lot. I've lived in Europe, Manhattan, Los Angeles, Miami…" His voice trails off. "My parents never like to stay in one place for too long."

I grew up in the same house my entire life. The first time I moved is to come here for school. My hometown is two hours away and it still feels too far. I'm a total homebody, though I would never admit that to anyone. "We ship worldwide," I tell him, choosing not to acknowledge what sounds like a glamorous—though lonely and unstable—childhood.

"Perfect." The relief in his voice is unmistakable. "You do giftwrapping?"

"We have a nice gift box I can put it in but it'll cost extra." I lead him back to the sales counter where I start ringing him up. He flashes a black American Express card and I take it from him, our fingers grazing, causing a tingle to shoot up my arm.

"Cost doesn't matter," he says, acting like he wasn't affected by our touching at all. Jerk. I wish I could be that nonchalant. But no, my fingers are shaking as I hit the buttons on the cash register, then have to punch in all the info on the credit card machine. All while Shep watches me, drumming those long, blunt-nailed fingers on the glass countertop. His scent wraps all around me, that citrusy, earthy smell I'm slowly becoming addicted to.

"Must be nice," I murmur under my breath, reaching under the counter to pull out a few sheets of tissue paper. I carefully peel off the price tag on the bottom of the candle and then wrap it, securing it with a single piece of tape.

"It usually is. Unless I'm dealing with a stubborn female who refuses to pay back her debt."

I lift my head, glaring at him. "I don't owe you anything. I never agreed to that bet. Joel did."

"And you're his girlfriend," he points out.

"*Ex*-girlfriend," I stress, turning my back to him so I can grab the gift box I charged him five dollars extra for. Screw it. I padded his shipping charge too. Enid will be thrilled. Business has been slow lately and she's thankful the weather has finally turned, bringing back the tourists. "I wish you would just leave this alone." I start to put the box together.

"Maybe I don't want to."

"Clearly," I say with a little snort.

"Maybe I want to see you even more." He pauses. "Maybe you're all I think about."

My fingers fumble over the box, sending it flying off the counter onto the ground. I hear him come toward me, see his feet encased in very expensive looking Nikes appear next to me as he bends down at the same time I do, the both of us going for the slightly crumpled box. "There is no reason whatsoever for you to keep thinking about me." My cheeks are on fire I'm so embarrassed. This is stupid. I shouldn't let him get to me like this. He's just saying these things to get under my skin and it's working.

"Despite how much you hate me, I keep thinking about you." He hands over the box and I take it from him with numb fingers. "A lot."

"Like how you want to murder me with your bare hands?" I twist the box within my grip, mangling it further. I owe him a new one. Good thing I overcharged.

"I'd rather do something a lot more fun to you with my bare hands," he whispers, his mouth curving into the slightest smile.

For once, I've got nothing. My throat is dry, my heart rate is going triple time and I'm feeling more than a little overwhelmed at his simple words. "You don't mean it."

"I definitely do." His gaze drops to the box in my hands. "I think we'll need a new one."

We both come to a full stand together, my head just reaching his shoulder. Perfect height for me to tear off his shirt and run my mouth all over his hot, hard skin. "You're right," I say weakly. "Let me put together another one."

He says nothing as I trash the first box and put together the second one with even shakier hands. But I succeed in getting it in place and I settle the candle inside, sealing it before I grab a label and take down his mother's address.

I'm not acknowledging what he said. I'm not acknowledging what I'm thinking either. This is all a big mistake. If I even consider pursuing this...thing between us, I know he'll just use me up and spit me out. I don't want to risk it. I'm not a risky person. I hedge safe bets. Hell, I usually don't bet at all. I test the waters, test them again, then test them yet again before I finally jump in.

Shep is a *jump in without a thought* type of guy. I can't

do it. I can't. I can't, I can't, I can't…

"Go out with me tonight."

"Okay."

I slap my hand over my mouth, which just makes him laugh. Jerk. Smug, gorgeous, hot as hell jerk.

"No taking it back," he says once his laughter dies. Those dark eyes of his go even darker if that's possible. "You're mine tonight, Jade."

"Wh-what exactly do you have planned?" I clear my throat, hating how nervous I sound. The man unnerves me like no other.

"Don't know yet," he answers, not sounding bothered by his lack of planning at all. "I'm sure it'll be something amazing though."

For once, I don't plan on calling him out for his arrogance. I'm actually finding it attractive, which I would never admit to him. "Want to meet here? I get off work at five."

"I am a true gentleman, Jade. I refuse to meet you anywhere." He smiles. "I'll come pick you up."

"And let you see where I live? I don't think so." I shake my head.

Now it's his turn to roll his eyes. "Really? You're still on the Shep is a stalker kick? Because I can reassure you, I am definitely not."

"Fine." I blow out an exasperated breath. He's relentless. Or I just easily give in when it comes to him.

"Hand me your phone."

He does so, purposely touching me again. And there's that spark again, too. Yikes. I start to add my name and phone number to his contacts but hesitate. Should I give him my number?

You so want to. Give it up girl.

I enter my phone number then my address and hand the phone back to him. He takes it, frowning at my entry before he lifts his head, his eyes meeting mine. "You live in the dorms?"

I shrug. "I'm a freshman. Kelli and I are roommates."

"Your friend at the party last night?"

"Yeah."

"Your friend you were sitting with at the poker game?"

I nod.

"How old are you anyway?"

"Nineteen." I cross my arms in front of my chest, my go-to defensive pose. He does the same thing, mirroring me right down to the way I'm standing, one foot sort of cocked out. "Do you have a problem with that?" I ask coolly.

He smiles and shakes his head, dropping his arms back to his sides. "None whatsoever. I don't discriminate. Age is nothing but a number."

I roll my eyes. "What time will you pick me up?" I ask.

"I'll text you later and let you know." He starts toward the front door and I stare, unabashedly admiring that long legged stride of his, the easy way he moves. It's almost overwhelming, how hot he is.

And he's definitely, outrageously hot.

"You didn't give me your number," I shout at him as he opens the door, his broad back still to me.

"I'll give it to you in a minute," he answers from over his shoulder before he leaves, the door slamming shut behind him.

I plop down into the chair behind the counter and let out a harsh breath, resting my hand over my chest. My heart is racing and I swear I'm lightheaded, all from our little encounter.

So crazy. He shouldn't affect me this way. I shouldn't care. He shouldn't matter. But somehow, someway, he does. He's wormed himself into my brain and I can't stop thinking about him. Apparently he feels the same way.

Weird.

My phone beeps and I pull it out of my pocket, unable to stop the smile that curves my lips.

Here's your text. And my number.

I decide to answer him.

Promise you won't stalk me?

Promise.

A pause.

But I can't promise I won't become obsessed with you...

Another pause. Another message.

Because I think that might be already happening.

chapter
Five

"**Y**ou mean to tell me he's coming here to pick you up and take you out? On an actual *date?*" Kelli curls her lip into an undeniable smirk. "Wow. Shep Prescott doesn't date, you know. Ever."

I roll my eyes, trying to tell my overactive stomach to calm down. It's like there are a million little baby tap dancers inside of me, kicking the shit out of my guts and making me hopelessly, horribly nervous. "What do you mean?"

Of course, he dates. He's known to go through girls, one after the other. He has a man-whore reputation. Pretty much every girl on campus wants to drop her panties for him or one of his equally gorgeous friends.

It's sort of irritating, how easily I fell under his spell. Because he definitely knows how to cast one. I was so incredibly irritated when I saw him in the shop. Irritated and intrigued.

My irritation quickly turned to pleasure. Awareness. So much damnable awareness and chemistry and whatever else you call it that brewed between us. I could feel it. Did he feel it? He had to. He's the one who asked me to go out with him.

Though maybe he's doing it because supposedly he won me in a bet and he thinks I'm easy prey. Or more like an easy lay.

Nope. Not going to fall for that. I will not end up naked with him tonight. No. No. No.

And now I can't help but wonder what he looks like naked.

"He hooks up but doesn't steadily date any of them. Sounds like you might be an exception." Kelli sounds surprised.

Hmm. So am I. I shouldn't read too much into what she's saying. This is probably just a hookup. "He claims I owe him a date. All because of that stupid bet. I could kill Joel."

"Right. Kill your now ex-boyfriend for getting you the opportunity to date Shep? That bet might be the best thing that ever happened to you."

"Please." I wave a hand. "I'm pissed that I have to

go out with him. Trust me."

A skeptical eyebrow is raised, one that tells me Kelli's about to call me out on my shit. "Seriously? Do you really think I'm going to believe that?"

I'm trying my best to believe it, so I hope she does too. "I may as well get this over with." I go to my tiny closet and start thumbing through the clothes, pushing through the hangers, one after another. I have nothing good to wear. Nothing pretty and new or flirty and sexy. Not that I want to flirt or look sexy.

You so do.

Okay, fine I do. I want to knock stupid sexy Shep on his ass when he takes one look at me but how? "I have nothing to wear," I moan.

Kelli magically appears at my side, pushing me out of the way so she can have a go at the pitiful offerings in my closet. "Too bad you wore that cute shirt last night. I'd suggest you wear it again but it's too soon."

No way would I wear it. I'd felt too exposed last night in it. I remember the way Shep looked at me. His eyes hot, seeming to see everything, all of me and making me shivery…

"How about this?" Kelli interrupts my thoughts, holding out a cute little black dress I wore to a holiday party last Christmas.

I wrinkle my nose. "That's way too much. I'm not going to prom."

Kelli huffs out a breath. "But what if he's taking you to some fancy dinner? He might, considering he's filthy rich and can afford just about anything he wants. Did he tell you what you're doing tonight? Where you're going? And who goes out on a Sunday night anyway? Don't you have class in the morning?" Kelli asks as she shoves the dress back into my closet.

"What are you, my mother? And no, he didn't tell me where we're going." He didn't tell me much of anything beyond saying that he might become obsessed with me.

Talk about crazy. Is that some sort of line he's trying to use so he can get in my panties? Maybe, because come on. Shep Prescott obsessed with me?

Please.

I shouldn't trust him. I shouldn't believe anything he says, especially when he's in flirt mode, which is all the time. But I can't deny the little thrill that shot through me at his admission. The admission I still have on my phone, that I stare at every once in a while, when Kelli's not looking.

Clearly I've lost my mind.

"Do you have his number?" When I nod she continues, a respective spark in her eye. "Nice. Text him. Ask him what the plan is."

"But isn't that kind of…rude?" I'm not big on dating protocol. My first serious boyfriend I had my senior year in high school, we started seeing each other within a giant group of friends. We always just hung out. And every time we all hung out, David and I naturally gravitated toward each other, until finally we mutually decided to become boyfriend and girlfriend. We broke up before we left for different colleges, deciding that a long distance relationship wouldn't work.

I met Joel because we had a class together. We sat next to each other and we talked and flirted. We saw each other at parties. One thing led to another and then we were going out. Again, we tended to hang with a group. Or Kelli and Dane once those two got together.

Looked like that scenario was dead and gone. Thank God Joel and I had that class together last semester. If we had to see each other three times a week…talk about awkward.

"It's not rude, especially when you're in the dark about what to wear. Guys don't get this." She waves a hand at me. "Go. Text him. Ask him how you should dress for your date."

I grab my phone and settle on the edge of my bed, my fingers poised over the keyboard. What exactly should I say? I feel stupid. Like I shouldn't ask any questions. Like I should already know the answers.

Here I go again, failing the test. I hate this.

"Do it," Kelli practically growls when she sees my hesitation. "Come on. What's the big deal?"

Blowing out an irritated breath, I type out a quick

message and hit send before I can second guess myself.

Kelli's making me ask you how I should dress for tonight.

A couple of minutes pass and there's no reply. Of course. Maybe he's going to cancel. Oh my God, maybe he's never going to answer and that'll be it. I'll never hear from him again. It's over before it's even begun.

What, exactly, is over? Why do you even care? Don't you hate this guy?

Yes. Yes. I do.

No you don't.

"Has he answered yet?" Kelli asks from where she's sprawled out on her tiny twin bed. Guess she gave up on looking for something for me to wear.

"No." I toss my phone away from me so I can't stare at it. But I still do. I look at my iPhone like it's a bug and it's making its creepy way toward me. "I should've never texted him."

"You big baby," Kelli mutters just as my phone dings.

I lunge for it and read his message. It's one word that leaves me a little confused.

Scantily

Frowning, I send him another text.

Say what?

You asked how you should dress. I suggest scantily. As in, wear as little clothing as possible.

Oh. My. God.

My cheeks burn and I can feel Kelli watching me, her curiosity growing like a living, breathing thing. She sits up, perched on the edge of her mattress like she's going to take flight.

"What did he say to you?" she demands.

I shake my head. "Nothing," I mumble as I send him a reply.

You're a pervert.

And you're only just now realizing this? I figured you'd already been warned.

I want to laugh, but don't. I should be mad. He's sort of awful. In a sort of sexy way.

Seriously, should I wear something casual or maybe a dress...

Dresses = easy access

I bite my lip to keep from smiling. I should find that totally offensive, right?

"What's he saying now?" Kelli asks again like the nosy bee she is. She leaps to her feet and starts pacing.

"Nothing important." I furiously type my answer, telling myself I absolutely do not want to wear a skirt or a dress tonight. No way.

Like how you tried to slip your hand beneath my skirt last night?

I didn't TRY anything. I DID slip my hand up your skirt.

And made me mad because I didn't even notice. Because I was too enraptured with his lips.

Ugh.

I'll definitely wear jeans then.

"I'm wearing jeans," I tell Kelli, who immediately heads back to my closet and starts looking through my shirts.

"This calls for a sexy shirt to show off your boobs," she calls from over her shoulder.

Just the idea of Shep looking at my boobs, let alone touching them, sends a warm, tingly sensation through my blood, making me shiver. My phone dings again and I glance down.

Jeans. An unfortunate choice.

Frowning, I continue texting him, dodging the shirt Kelli just tossed in my direction.

Unfortunate for you since you can't slip your hand up my skirt.

I think you liked it when I slipped my hand up your skirt.

No, I really didn't.

Stop denying your true feelings.

My frown deepens. He's a total pain in the ass.

"I'm not wearing jeans," I tell Kelli, who turns to glare at me. "Do you have a skirt I can borrow? The shorter the better?"

The slow grin that curls Kelli's lips makes me smile in response. "Look at you, trying to drive Mr. Prescott out of his mind. I love it."

Hmm. I don't want him to love it. I want him to hate

it. Because my policy tonight is look, but don't touch.

This might be the greatest plan in all the world, or the worst plan ever created.

Shep

I hate dorm halls. They remind me of my not so distant past. When I was a freshman and eager to fuck any cute girl who so much as smiled at me. My first year in college, I snuck my way into more dorm rooms than I can count. I've had sex on more narrow twin beds than you can imagine. And bunk beds? Fuck, I think I almost broke one once.

Lesson learned? Don't have sex on the top bunk in a dorm room. It doesn't matter if the girl weighs a buck-oh-five and you know you plan on only lasting for ten minutes tops. Those bunk beds are made out of sticks.

I told Jade I'd pick her up but I'm wary about actually going inside because that means I'll see a variety of girls. Some of them I might've...been with before. Maybe? I don't know. Most of the girls in the dorms are on the younger side and I haven't fucked a freshman in a while.

That I know of, at least.

I swipe a hand over my face, feeling like a world class asshole. I've never cared about all the girls I've been with. It's not that I use them and toss them away like yesterday's trash when I'm done with them but...okay, yeah. That's sort of how I've always treated women. I'm not mean. They know what they're getting when they hook up with me. After all, those are the key words.

Hook. Up.

Commitment is for sissies. I see the way my parents are. I seriously believe they don't like each other. More like they tolerate one another. They've been together for so long, they don't know how to function without each other. My sisters are all lined up to be involved in the same sort of marriage. Giant, over the top wedding, spit out the requisite kids quick like, get a little plastic surgery to keep the bod and face intact, work out like crazy while the husband works long hours. Or pretends to work long hours. Extravagant house, glorious vacations. Wash, rinse, repeat.

No thanks.

I'm a free agent. It's the best way to be. I've seen enough turmoil and bullshit to last me a lifetime. Girls want to sink their claws into me and I shake them off every single time. They've eventually given up. My reputation precedes me. I usually prefer it that way.

So what's up with the way I think about Jade? I'm freaking myself out. I want her…that much I know. She acts like she hates me most of the time and I fucking love it for some twisted reason. She's a challenge. No girl is a challenge for me.

Ever.

Deciding to hell with it, I get out of my car and hit the keyless remote, locking the doors. I head toward the front of the dorm hall, shoving my keys in my pocket, my steps determined, my thoughts in turmoil. Let's hope she walks out and meets me. That would make my life so much easier. So freaking much easier it's not even funny…

I head up the steps, no Jade in sight. I already have her dorm room number memorized. I know exactly where to go and as I enter the building, I turn right, ready to head in that direction when I hear someone call my name.

And it's not Jade. I'd recognize her voice anywhere.

Slowly I turn to find some girl standing in front of me, her tight T-shirt showing off her small boobs—no bra in sight, nipples everywhere—and tiny shorts that should probably be illegal. As in, one wrong move and I'll probably see her vagina.

Yes, I can think the word vagina like a grown up. Say it out loud? Probably not. At heart, I'm sometimes still a twelve-year-old boy trapped in a twenty-one-year old's body.

"Hey," I say, flicking my chin in her direction.

She rests her hands on her hips, looking pissed off. Her hair is blonde. Like super blonde. "You don't remember me, do you?"

This is the last thing I want to deal with before I

pick up Jade to take her on a date. Jesus. "Refresh my memory."

"Your cousin's party, right before winter break." She glares, her eyes like icy lasers. "Tell Tristan he can go to hell."

Relief sweeps over me, making my legs weak. Thank God this is all about Tristan. "Will do," I tell her cheerily, earning a pissed off look for my efforts.

I turn and get the hell out of there, heading down the narrowed hall that leads to the promise land.

Otherwise known as Jade's room. Jade's bed. Why that gives me a thrill I have no clue. Again, the twelve year old is rearing his immature head.

I hope to hell she doesn't have a bunk bed or I'm screwed.

I find her room and stop just in front of it, my arm raised, hand curled into a fist to rap my knuckles on the thick, old wood. The door swings open before I get a chance to knock, another girl standing in front of me. The girl Jade was with the night of the poker game.

She smiles at me, the look in her eyes full of pure evil. Not the, *I will slice off your head* variety. More like, *you have no idea what you're in for.* She pulls the door close to her, so I can't see inside.

Swallowing hard, I smile at her, deciding to put on the charm. "You must be the roommate."

"And you're the asshole who's trying to collect on

a bet." She sticks her hand out, her smile serene. "I'm Kelli."

"Shep." I take her hand and don't feel a thing. Not a zing, not a zip, nothing. I figured I'd feel something. She's cute, this girl. Not kick me in the balls gorgeous like Jade but she'd do. Normally.

But again, there's no reaction. My body is keyed up all right, full of anticipation over the fact that Jade is mere feet away from me. Mere *inches.*

"Shepard Prescott, in the flesh." Kelli makes a tsking noise, like I've already disappointed her. "Are you as bad as they say?"

I give her my very best, most wolfish grin. "Worse."

Her eyes sparkle. "Good. That's just what our Jade needs." She holds the door open a little wider and calls over her shoulder, "You ready sugar plum?"

"As ready as I'll ever be, sweet cheeks." My mouth goes dry at hearing Jade say the words sweet cheeks, which is the stupidest thing ever because how cheesy can we get?

But then she appears and it's like my mouth turns into the Sahara Desert. What in the holy hell is she *wearing?*

Black skirt that hits her about mid thigh—maybe higher, good God—and black stilettos with thin straps that crisscross over the top of her feet. A tight white shirt that accentuates her chest and nipped in at the waist and ah, shit, she just grabbed a black sweater and is pulling it on, ruining the entire affect.

This is probably for the best.

"Hi," I say, my voice cracking like I'm going through puberty and I clear my throat, pissed that my thoughts are constantly straying to my general immaturity. How the hell am I ever going to impress this girl if my mental state is set back in my middle school days?

She smiles, pushes her wavy hair back so it falls behind her shoulder, exposing her neck and I'm hit with the overwhelming need to kiss her in that exact spot where her pulse throbs. Breathe in the scent of her skin, let my lips linger, maybe even lick her to see if she tastes as good as I think she will...

"Hi." Her voice shakes the slightest bit, as does her smile and I realize she's nervous. Cute. I'd like to put her at ease but hell.

I'm a little nervous too.

"You ready to go?" I ask as she exits her room, coming to stand closer to me. I can smell her now, sweet and clean and I clamp my lips shut, breathing through my nose, trying my best not to inhale her.

I really want to fucking inhale her.

She casts a wary glance over her shoulder at her roommate before returning her attention to me. "Yes, I am."

"You kids be safe," Kelli calls as we start down the

hall. "Use protection. Make good choices!"

"She's seen Pitch Perfect way too many times," Jade mumbles, making me laugh. Her cheeks flush pink. "And ignore her use of protection line."

"Why? I *always* use protection." I shove my hands in my pockets so I won't make a grab for her because having her this close is doing something to me. Making me want to grab her and do inappropriate things to her.

"Right. Of course you do." She glances at me, her cheeks still flushed, her eyes full of fire. "Not that there'll be any need for protection tonight, considering we're not going to have sex."

Disappointment crashes over me and I push it aside. She just threw down the first challenge of the evening. "You've already got the entire night all figured out, huh?"

She nods as we make our way down the hall toward the front entrance. Swear to God the doors swing open as we pass, girls peeking their heads out, mouths agape. As if they knew I was going to make an appearance tonight and all my adoring fans showed up to see me. It's annoying. It's freaking nerve wracking because if one of them is someone I've been with before, and she opens her mouth and says something…I'm screwed.

Jade will leave me in the dust. And I haven't even kissed her yet.

I really, really want to kiss her. Those lips…are the

stuff of fantasies. Plump and full, her upper lip a little puffier than the bottom one, and slicked in a flattering pink color that isn't too glossy. When their lips are covered with that sparkly shiny shit, it's not pleasant to kiss. At all.

But I would love to kiss all that lipstick off her mouth. Breathe deep her scent. Run my lips down the length of her neck. Wrap her hair in my hand and tug the slightest bit, make her gasp, make her moan, make her pull me in closer…

"I don't put out on the first date," she says haughtily, her nose tilting upward. Snobby *you can't touch me* waves radiate off her but I see right through them.

It's a front. A form of protection. A wall she believes will keep me from scaling over and getting to the true Jade.

Yet another challenge. I almost want to rub my hands together and tell her I'm ready to start the climb. Though she'd probably take it the wrong way and slap my face.

"That's a shame," I say with a heavy sigh. She shoots me a look and I smile at her, reaching out to push open the door as I come to a stop. "Ladies first."

She studies me, her gaze roaming all over me and my skin goes hot. What does she see? I wish I knew. Or maybe I don't want to know. "Thank you," she murmurs as she exits the building, giving me a prime view of her ass in that too short skirt and holy shit, I've never been so turned on by the back of a girl's thighs in my life. They're slender and pale and I narrow my eyes, looking for a birthmark. A scar. A mole. Something I can remember those thighs by.

And then I see it. See *them*. A scattering of freckles on the back of her right thigh, they remind me of stars.

chapter
Six

Jade

He took me a to a shack for dinner.

Okay fine, it's by the beach so he gets points for that. The moment I emerged from his car—ignoring his offered arm for me to take after he opened the passenger side door for me, so he could escort me to the restaurant like some old world duke of something or other, all proper and gentleman-like when we all know he's not a gentleman whatsoever. But anyway, I could smell the salty air, the wind whipping my hair in front of my face and I silently gave him points for location choice.

I'm not impressed by the front of the restaurant—shack—that he's brought me to. It's a wooden structure that almost looks dilapidated, like it might crumble at any given moment. The roof looks like it's constructed out of a piece of rippled metal and I think of that stupid song by the B-52s my parents used to play when I was a kid. Love Shack.

Tin roof! Rusted.

Shep is perceptive, I'll give him that. I must've given off an apprehensive vibe because he settles my hand on my lower back, his fingers suspiciously close to that gap where my shirt has ridden up from my skirt. I shed my sweater, my cloak of defense, in his car. It was so hot in there and I swear he planned it, though I never really felt the heater blasting on me or anything like that.

Maybe sitting so close to him in his car made me… hot. Like every other pitiful girl who meets him, who spends time with him alone. In his car. I was halfway disappointed he didn't try and jump me when we pulled into the parking lot and he shut off the engine.

So lame. I don't want him to jump me. I already told him there's no need for condoms tonight since he wasn't going to get a piece of this. Forget it. I'm nervous enough. I don't need to worry about my lack of sexual experience at the possibility of getting naked with a guy like him.

But think of all that experience he has. All the things he could do to you. Teach you. He snuck his hand up your skirt and you weren't even aware of it. Imagine all the possibilities!

I banish the hopeful thoughts running through my mind to the very darkest recesses of my brain.

"This place doesn't look like much but trust me. The food is awesome," Shep murmurs close to my ear as we enter the building.

"What if I'm allergic to shellfish?" I ask, batting my eyelashes at him when he turns to me, horror etched in his handsome features.

He clears his throat, his gaze locked on mine. "Are you?"

Slowly I shake my head, smiling. "No. But next time, you should probably ask."

"Next time I won't need to ask because I'll already know," he says, frowning at me.

"I mean next time. When you bring another girl to this restaurant," I correct, hating the cold ball that seems to have formed in my stomach at the idea of Shep bringing another girl here. A girl that will come after me, because one will, I don't need to fool myself.

But I don't necessarily need to think about her at this exact moment in time either.

He stares at me as if I've lost my mind and for a moment, I wonder if I have. Or maybe I have something on my face. Maybe there's a smudge of mascara beneath my eye (I told Kelli not to put it on so thick) or maybe I have lipstick on my teeth. Crap, I don't know. This guy makes me feel so self-conscious it's almost painful.

Shep doesn't say a word. He shakes his head and steps over to the hostess stand, telling the older woman who's blatantly ogling him that he'd like a table for two.

As discreetly as possible I press my index finger to the corner of my right eye and wipe, then look at it. No black smudge. I do the same to my left eye but there's no mascara there either. Licking my lips, I dart out my tongue, touching the corner before I wipe at it with my thumb, taking away a little lipstick but nothing major.

"What are you doing?"

I glance up to find Shep watching me very carefully. Almost too carefully. I stand up taller and drop my hand away from my face but otherwise I say nothing. How can I explain myself? I'd end up sounding ridiculous.

He leans in closer and bends down, his mouth almost level with my ear and I hear him murmur, "You look beautiful. Stop fidgeting."

Pleasure blooms in my chest, spreads through my limbs at his compliment. I should be offended he said stop fidgeting like I'm a child but I'm too focused on the words that preceded that comment.

You look beautiful.

I know I'm not a hideous troll but it's not easy being a natural redhead with fair skin and freckles. I hated my freckles with everything I had when I was younger but I've come to terms with them now. I used to hate the red hair too. I'd get mean comments from boys, especially in high school, asking if my crotch was as fiery as the hair on my head. Some asshole called Lindsay Lohan a particularly nasty name referring to her hair, ahem, down there once a long time ago and I blame him for starting that whole thing.

Fire Crotch.

Ugh.

The hostess leads us through the tiny dining area toward a small round table draped with a white tablecloth that sits next to a window. She presents our menus to us as soon as we're in our chairs and then she buzzes off, ready to greet the next group of customers that just walked inside.

It's crowded and warm, there's music playing in the background and I glance to my right to find the view of the ocean breathtaking, the sun so low it looks like it's melting into the water.

"Beautiful view," I say as I turn to look at him, startled to find him staring at me blatantly.

Ravenously.

"Definitely," he murmurs with a wicked smile and I feel the flush wash over me, my neck, my cheeks, oh my God even my forehead grows hot. He's not talking about the ocean.

I think…I think he's talking about me.

"You need to stop," I tell him as I open the tiny menu to check out what is a rather limited selection.

"Stop what?" he asks innocently.

Glancing up, I find him watching me still, which only makes me blush harder. I silently curse my fair skin. And overly flirtatious guys. I have zero experience dealing with someone like Shep Prescott. "You're making me nervous."

"How?"

"With the—" I wave a hand. "—the compliments. The flirting."

"You've never flirted with someone before?"

"Of course, I have," I snap, immediately regretting my tone of voice. The man pushes me like no other. "It's the way you flirt."

"And how's that?"

You're good at it. More like, you excel in your flirtation skills. And I don't know how to handle myself. I'm the failure, not you.

"The over the top compliments aren't necessary either," I say, avoiding his question.

"Afraid I'm going to have to disagree with you," he tells me as he flips open his menu and studies it. "My compliments toward your beauty aren't over the top."

There he goes again, saying I'm beautiful. I don't even know how to react. I feel like I want to laugh or tell him to stop like I'm some uncomfortable preteen who doesn't know how to take a compliment.

More like I'm an uncomfortable nineteen year old

who doesn't know how to take one. So lame.

I guess I remain quiet for too long because he's watching me again, his brows furrowed, his mouth, his entire expression serious. "Has no one told you you're beautiful before?"

I shrug, mortified. "Beyond my mom? Who has to think I'm beautiful since she created me?"

He looks shocked. "What about Noel?"

Of course, he can't get his name right. "You mean Joel? What about him?" Why are we talking about my ex on this so-called date?

"He never told you that you're beautiful?" Now he sounds disgusted.

"No." I want to shrink into the smallest ball possible and disappear. I keep my gaze fixed on the menu in front of me but the words are blurry. And I can feel him watching me, examining me bit by bit, feature by feature. What does he see? Or more important, does he like what he sees?

I'm almost scared to know the answer.

"Can I take your drink order?"

I almost faint with relief. Saved by our server. She reminds me of my grandma, with short graying hair and glasses, a friendly smile plastered on her face. "Just water please," I say.

"Hey Barb, can I ask you a question?"

Oh, no. He knows our waitress by name? What in

the world is he going to ask her? I stiffen my shoulders, bracing myself for what he's about to say.

"Hit me with it, sugar." Barb sounds amused but I can't even look at her. Or him.

"Do you think my date is beautiful?"

"Oh my God," I groan under my breath, holding the menu in front of my face.

"I love her hair," Barb says sincerely. "Though I can't see the rest of her, what with that menu hiding her face."

"Come on, Jade. Don't be shy," Shep encourages.

I drop the menu onto the table, where it falls with a loud clatter, and I glare at him, wishing I could silence him with my eyes.

But it doesn't work. He just grins at me, then looks up at Barb. "Even when she's mad, she's gorgeous."

"Very pretty," Barb agrees with a nod of approval. "Considering you don't bring girls around here ever, I can finally say you have most excellent taste. Not that I'm surprised."

Wait a minute. He doesn't bring girls around here? Ever? I don't understand.

"Thanks, Barb. And I'll have a beer. You know what I like."

She smiles and with a promise to be right back, scoots off. I watch her go, turning over what she said again and again. He doesn't bring girls to this restaurant, yet he's a frequent visitor since he knows the waitress. And she knows what type of beer he likes.

What in the world is going on?

"I always come here for lunch, usually with Gabe or my cousin Tristan," Shep explains, like he can read my mind. "Barb owns the restaurant with her husband Jim."

"Oh." I nod and reopen my menu, deciding I need to get the shrimp basket and just be done with it. So it's fried shrimp with fries. So it'll be packed with a bazillion calories. So what. I'll make Kelli go running with me tomorrow morning to make up for my pig out.

"I'm sorry if I made you uncomfortable." He sounds sincere. I don't know why he's acting like this. Being so…

Nice.

That night when he caught me signaling to Joel, he'd been such a jerk. I gave him reason to be angry, I won't deny that, but he'd been so smug, so rude. I could handle him then. Last night and earlier this afternoon too.

But now? With him offering up compliments and behaving like a gentleman? He's throwing me off.

"Um, it's okay." I lift my head but thankfully this time he's not looking at me. Which allows me to blatantly check him out. His head is bent, his golden brown hair falling over his forehead, his eyes cast down and I see that even his eyelashes are tipped with gold. Everything about him is gold, gold, gold. He's gorgeous and rich and the epitome of the perfect golden boy and what the hell is he doing here with me when I am the farthest thing from perfect or golden.

"I can feel you staring at me," he says, his head still bent but I see the smile stretch across his face. Makes me want to throw my menu at him.

Okay, fine. Not really.

"I'm mad at you," I tell him.

He lifts his head, the smile fading. "Why?"

"Because you embarrassed me."

"I was only speaking the truth. You're going to have to get used to people telling you that you're beautiful," he says.

Like that's going to happen all the time. I am nothing special. "I don't even know if I can take what you say seriously. Everything's like a big joke to you."

"What do you mean?"

"You always look like you're ready to burst out laughing. Your life is so easy. Nothing bothers you. It must be nice."

His eyes flicker with some unrecognizable emotion. Could that have possibly been…hurt? Anger? "You have no idea what you're talking about. My life is the farthest thing from easy."

My mouth goes dry and I return my focus to the

menu even though I already know what I want. I feel like a jerk. He's been nothing but nice to me tonight and I've been nothing but a jerk to him. I've probably blown my chance at another date with Shep, even though that was already blown the moment I agreed to go out with him.

He must hate me.

Shep

Why'd I have to get all serious on her? I'm annoying the shit out of myself, let alone Jade.

But she doesn't know who I am or what my life is like. I get tired of everyone thinking I have it easy. I don't. Dad is an asshole, Mom medicates herself to function and my sisters got their asses out of the house as fast as they could. I have no plans on going back either. I chose this college for a reason—it's on the complete opposite coast of where my parents live.

Barb shows up and takes our order, shrimp baskets for the both of us. The moment she leaves Jade blurts out, "I'm sorry. I didn't mean to—upset you."

"Don't worry about it." I wave a hand, dismissing my mood, her words, all of it. "I don't want to talk about me. Let's talk about you."

Her expression goes from contrite to uneasy. "There's not much to tell."

"I barely know you. There's plenty to tell. Where are you from?"

"A small town about two hours north of here." She shrugs, drawing my attention to her chest. If I could will her to take off her sweater with my mind, I'd be working it hard right about now. "I lived there all my life. It's very boring."

"This town isn't much better." Santa Augustina isn't awful but it's a small, typical coastal college city.

"More exciting than where I grew up, trust me." She flashes me a small smile, then turns it on Barb when she shows up to deliver our drinks. "I haven't lived all over the world like some people sitting at this table," she says pointedly after she takes a sip of her drink.

My gaze is now locked on her lips. Those fantasy-inducing, bee-stung lips that look damn good wrapped around a straw and would look even better wrapped around my...

"You have any brothers or sisters?" she asks, her sweet voice breaking through my dirty thoughts.

"Two older sisters," I answer before I grab my beer and down half of it in a few swallows. I need to get my shit together and stop acting like a leering jackass. Considering Jade's strung pretty tight, I don't want to piss her off.

"So you're the baby of the family."

I smile. "The prodigal son." With all the expectations

and bullshit that comes with it.

"Did your sisters dote on you?"

"If by doting on me you mean did they paint my fingernails and toenails and put makeup on my face, all while having me model their clothes? Yes, they totally doted on me." They were mean even when they were young. Not that I was much better. I was a holy terror — direct quote from Mom.

"Aw." She smiles and it's genuine. I can tell because it lights up her face and steals my breath so all I can do is stare at her. "I bet you were an adorable girl."

"Gorgeous," I agree, never missing a beat. "I missed my calling. Maybe I should've become a drag queen."

"Then you could share shoes and clothes with your girlfriends," she jokes, that smile still in place.

"I don't have girlfriends, remember?" The smile fades and I feel like an ass. Way to remind her I'm nothing but a player who only hooks up.

"Then you could share clothes and shoes with your sisters," she suggests with a little shrug. "Makeup tips. Braid each other's hair."

"No braids. Only wigs will do. Those giant ones, made with the finest hair you can buy," I correct, making her lips curl. Now I'm determined to make that smile reappear. "I'm sort of tall for a woman so I'd want to stand out, you know? Add a few inches with a wig. And heels."

"Four inches?" she asks, raising one delicate, perfectly arched, perfectly red eyebrow. I have never had a thing for redheads before. I don't know if I've even hooked up with one before...have I?

I don't think so. What a prejudiced bastard I am, discriminating against redheads. Might make my hooking up with Jade that much sweeter.

Because I will hook up with her. Get her naked. Get her beneath me. However you want to say it, it's going to happen. By the end of tonight, preferably.

"Is that as high as they go? Maybe five inches? With platforms or whatever?" I ask.

The smile is back. Subdued but there, lighting her eyes, lighting up her entire face. "You sound like you have more knowledge about women's fashion than you should admit."

Leaning across the table, I lower my voice, "There are things you don't know about me, Jade."

Her eyes widen the slightest bit. "Like what?"

"Like I'm a kinky bastard who enjoys wearing women's panties in my spare time." The horrified shock that washes over her face makes me burst out laughing. "Kidding. I swear."

She slowly shakes her head, her smile turning into a smirk. "Very funny."

"It was pretty funny, the look on your face," I agree.

"You're just proving my point." She takes another

sip of her water and I die a little inside. Fuck, her mouth. It should be outlawed. "Everything's a big joke. Ha ha, so funny. Har har."

"Better to laugh than be sad all the time?" I ease back against my chair, trying my best to hide the smile that wants to happen but failing. "And did you just har har me?"

Her cheeks turn crimson. I love that I can make her blush. I love her pale skin, something I never found attractive before. I'm struck again with the question — just how many freckles does this girl have? Will she let me spend enough time counting each one?

The thought of her naked and sprawled across my bed as I meticulously count every tiny freckle on her body is exceptionally appealing.

"You're a pain in the ass," she mutters, making me laugh.

Oh, yeah. I like this girl. A lot.

"Har har," I tell her and she looks ready to throw her glass of water on my face. Thank God Barb shows up at that precise moment with our dinner.

"Listen, I don't know why you're putting me through all of this torture, but I'm done," Jade hisses at me the moment Barb is gone. "We'll eat dinner, you'll take me back to my dorm, and that's it. The date is finished. *We're* finished."

I raise a brow. No girl has uttered those words to

me before. Ever. I sound like an asshole even in my own head but it's the truth. I never give them time to want to be finished with me. "You don't mean it," I drawl, my stomach growling. The shrimp and fries smell fucking delicious and I'm starved.

"I definitely mean it. This has been a joke to you from the start. Winning me in a hand of poker. Give me a break," she mumbles just as she plucks a giant shrimp from her basket and sinks her teeth into it. The sound of pleasure she gives at first taste has my cock twitching.

Damn it.

"This is good," she says once she swallows. Her eyes are wide, her expression a little dazed, like she's shocked I'd take her to a place that serves, you know, delicious food.

Her expectations of me seem incredibly low. But I'm thankful for the distraction. At least she's not griping at me about what a shit I am anymore.

"You sound surprised." I give in and start eating, thankful for that first awesome bite. I haven't been here in a while and I always wonder why I don't come more often.

"Well, look at this place. It's kind of run down." She glances around and so do I. She's right. The interior isn't the most impressive but the restaurant has been around for ages and we're right by the ocean. The food and the view are what make this place.

That and the fact it's far away from campus so I'm ensured we won't run into anyone we know. Or I might know, like some girl from my past.

Talk about a mood killer.

"Usually the worst looking places serve the best food," I tell her because it's true. I learned that a long time ago, traveling as much as I did growing up. The hole in the wall is where all the locals eat. It's practically law.

"You're right," she says as she grabs another shrimp and holds it aloft. "Looks can be deceiving."

"Definitely," I agree, never letting my gaze stray from her face. I wonder if she's referring to me. I can only hope she's referring to me. She thinks I'm one thing but *fuck*.

I'm tempted to prove to her that I'm another.

chapter
Seven

Shep

The second we leave the restaurant my phone dings, indicating I have a text from Gabe.

It's out of control here dude.

I type out a quick reply.

I could give two shits. Handle it yourself. I'm on a date.

My phone immediately rings, earning me a dirty look from Jade.

"Please don't tell me it's one of your skanks," she says.

"It's Gabe," I tell her before I answer the phone. "What the hell do you want?"

"A date?" Gabe asks incredulously. "Give me a break, fucker. Who you banging now?"

"Get a life, asshole." I'm about to hang up but I hear

Gabe yelling at me not to. "What?"

"I was serious when I said it was out of control here. Some dude is losing his ass at the blackjack table and he's about to come unhinged."

"Kick him out then," I suggest, already bored. We've had guys lose their shit before when playing our tables. Some don't know when to stop. Some are up so high with a fat stack of chips in front of them and then they lose everything, which in turn, enrages them. We've had to deal with drunken assholes, fights, accusations of theft, and we've always been able to bring everything under control.

More like I've always been able to bring everything under control. Gabe is useless. He'd rather charm everyone rather than deal with angry people. Tristan isn't much better.

"He won't go. He's drunk as hell and literally gripping the edge of the table like his life is depending on it. Making all the other players nervous, including our dealer." Gabe pauses and I hear a guttural roar in the background, like something you'd hear in the jungle. "Did I mention he's about six-foot-five and easily three hundred pounds?"

Exhaling loudly, I let a string of curse words fly, earning a weird glance from Jade. We're standing beside the front of my car and she's watching me with curiosity in her eyes. "I'll be there in a few minutes," I say before

I end the call. Freaking Gabe can't handle the tough shit on his own. He always leaves it up to me.

"You need to be somewhere?" Jade asks hopefully.

I head over to the passenger side and open the door for her. She gives me an odd look, pausing before she slides inside the car. "Yeah. And you're coming with me."

"Oh, no I'm not." She starts to protest, her mouth opening to spew out something else negative but I shake my head, cutting her off. Then I gently shove her shoulder, pushing her into the car so she has no choice but to land in the passenger seat with a plop. She glares up at me, her green eyes shooting daggers, her pale legs at an awkward angle that draw my attention because she has a great pair of legs, damn it. But I don't say a word. Just slam the door shut and round the back of the car, opening my door and getting in so I can get the hell out of there.

"You're taking me back to my dorm," she says as I start the car. "Right?"

"No." I press my foot against the gas, making the engine rev. It sounds good. Fucking great. I love this car. It's fast as fuck and I need that right now because my plan is to go to the house, help drag that gorilla drunk away from the blackjack table and then return my attention to Jade. Fuck this fucking problem and Gabe taking me away from her. Jesus. So much hate for my life right now.

"What do you mean, no?" She sounds furious, which somehow turns me on. I'm fucked. Hearing the anger in her voice actually arouses me and I have no idea why. Angry chicks usually piss me off. Or I walk away from them, not wanting to deal with the drama.

With Jade, every time she gets angry at me — pretty much every time we're together she's angry, I can't lie — all I can imagine is if she's that passionate when she's mad? Imagine what she'd be like in bed.

Or on a couch.

Against a wall.

In the shower.

On the floor.

In the backseat of my car.

Clearly, she distracts the shit out of me.

"I mean, this date isn't over," I tell her as I throw the car into reverse and wrap my arm around the back of her seat, glancing over my shoulder so I can back out. My fingers dangle treacherously close to her shoulder and I'm tempted to touch her. Just a casual brush of fingers, nothing major.

But I'm nervous that once I touch her, I won't be able to stop. More like I won't *want* to stop.

"You took me to dinner. Isn't that enough?" She crosses her arms in front of her chest, plumping up her breasts and I sneak a glance at them, only to immediately regret it because damn, her cleavage. The girl's body is bangin'.

"No, it's not enough." I keep my gaze focused on the road in front of me, speeding but not too much over the limit. "I just need to make a quick stop. It won't take long." Better not take long. I have way more important things to do.

Like Jade.

"Where?"

"There's trouble at one of the tables," I mutter, just under my breath, hoping she won't hear me.

But she must have sonar hearing because she swivels in her seat, her arms dropping to her sides as she stares at me so hard, I bet she's burning holes in my face. "You're taking me back to that—gambling house? Oh God, no. I do not want to return to the scene of the crime."

"The scene of the crime?" She's hilarious. Says the craziest things.

"Yes. Where we met." She stares at me with a look that says *duh.* "Remember?"

"Trust me. I remember every detail about that night."

I can still feel her glaring at me and I'm tempted to say something else but I don't. It's best I leave it alone. Focus on driving. Focus on my anger towards Gabe because what the hell. Why can't he take care of this problem? It's not that big of a deal.

We arrive within minutes and I park the car out on the street, directly in front of the house. We make any and all so-called patrons of our establishment park down the street so as not to call too much attention and so far since we started this little side business two years ago, we've been successful in doing just that.

"I won't be long," I tell her as I put the car into park. "A few minutes, tops."

"I'm staying in the car," Jade says when I turn off the engine.

"Whatever. It's your choice." I don't feel like arguing. We could go round and round in circles wasting precious time. Besides, she might be safer in the car. I have no idea what's going on inside.

The moment I enter the house and see the six-foot-five gorilla sitting at the blackjack table with his meaty fingers curled around the edge of the table, his expression one of pure fury, I know it's a huge deal. This guy is massive. Gigantic. With closely cropped dark brown hair and murder in his pale blue eyes, his face so red he looks ready to explode, all earlier plans of how to approach him evaporate.

"He's been sitting like that for the past five minutes," Gabe says out of the side of his mouth when I come to stand beside him. He's leaning against the wall, his arms crossed in front of him, his gaze never leaving our subject. "Doesn't move, doesn't say a word, just his face keeps getting redder and redder."

"How much has he had to drink?" I evaluate the scene. No one else is currently sitting at the blackjack table. In fact, the entire place is pretty much empty, which is typical of a Sunday night. Business is usually slow. But not this slow.

"Plenty of beer. I don't think that's the problem though. He's been in here before. I recognize him. Name's Stan. Football player." Gabe turns to look at me, his expression serious. "I think he's on something."

I frown. "Like what?" Drinking happens here. We encourage it. Makes everyone looser with their bets. Drugs? Can't necessarily escape it because we're in college and it feels like everyone's doing drugs. Prescription medication, weed, and cocaine seem to be the drugs of choice lately, but we don't usually have a problem with anyone getting out of control while under the influence.

"Coke," Gabe says, shaking his head. "I just spoke to one of his friends. Says Stan here can get real angry sometimes when he's done too much coke."

"Fucking great," I mutter as I start to head over to the table. The dealer—Patrick, great guy, a senior, sad to see him graduate—looks nervous as hell, his gaze skittering to mine briefly before he returns his attention to Stan the Gorilla. "Hey Stan. What's the problem here?" I keep my voice light, my approach friendly. Don't want to rile this guy up any more than he already is.

He blinks slowly, his eyes narrowing as he tips his head forward. "Who the fuck are you?"

I wave a hand at Patrick. "Head on out, bro. I got this handled."

Patrick doesn't say a word, just scurries his skinny ass out of there like his jeans are on fire.

"I own this place," I tell Stan, smiling at him. "And we're just about ready to close down for the night so I'm afraid you're going to have to leave."

I swear Stan's fingers tighten even harder around the edge of the blackjack table. I hope like hell he doesn't break it. "Fuck you," he says, his voice slow and thick. "I'm not going anywhere, asshole. Need to win my money back before I leave."

"Afraid you'll have to come back another night to do that." I reach out to grab his arm but he shrugs me off, his expression tight, his eyes dull. The dude is clearly wasted. "Come on, no need to be stubborn."

"Fuck you and your pansy ass talk. I'm not leaving until I can play enough hands to win back the money I came here with," he slurs, his head lolling to the side before he snaps back to attention.

Hell. How much did this guy drink? And how much coke did he do? Oh and… "How much did you lose?"

Stan smiles, his eyelids drooping. He looks ready to

pass out. "Forty bucks."

That's it? Big fucking deal. I got this. I go behind the table where Patrick stood and scan the various chips before I lift my head and meet Stan's gaze. "Let's play then."

Jade

He is taking way too long and I'm starting to freak out. What if something's gone wrong inside? They won't call the cops to handle their problems. What they're doing is illegal.

God, look at me. Yes, me. Straight laced, good girl Jade Frost is hanging out with a billionaire spoiled sexy brat who runs an illegal freaking casino in a house just off campus. What have I done? Who am I, for God's sake?

Heaving a big sigh, I push open the heavy door and climb out of his luxurious Mercedes, slamming the door behind me. I'm heading up the walk when I spot two girls sitting on a couch on the front porch of the house, the both of them gawking at me like I'm some sort of celebrity who magically appeared.

"Did you just get out of Shep Prescott's car?" one of them asks, her voice full of wonder.

Oh, here we go. Shep groupies. "I did," I say with a lift of my chin. I hope they don't want to beat me up or pull out my hair or whatever.

"Wow," the other one says, drawing out the word so it sounds more like woooooow. "Rumor has it he doesn't let *any* girl get in his car. Not even his mom."

His mom doesn't even live in this state but whatever. "Is that so?"

"Yeah," the first one pipes up. "He won't even fuck a girl in the backseat. Too afraid he'll get his leather interior dirty and sweaty and…wet." They both dissolve into giggles.

Um, this is awkward. Even more awkward? That what they're telling me actually makes me…happy. If what they're saying is true, I feel some sort of strange honor that I'm supposedly the first girl to ride in his car.

"Hey." The second one straightens up, her giggling coming to a halt. "Aren't you in my communications class?"

I tilt my head, studying her. She's cute, with long golden blonde hair pulled into a high ponytail and clear blue eyes. Her boobs are about ready to burst out of the deep V of her pale pink T-shirt and she's wearing extremely short denim cutoffs. "I think so," I tell her though truthfully, I don't recognize her. That class is ginormous though so there's a good chance she's right.

"I knew it!" She smiles brightly, her ponytail swishing. "My name is Emily and this is Emma."

Emily and…Emma? Oh good lord. "Nice to meet

you," I say with a smile.

"We like to call ourselves Em and Em." Emma smiles and nudges Emily with an elbow. "Get it?"

"Oh yeah," I say as they start giggling again. "I definitely get it. That's...cute."

"We thought so! So hey, are you going inside?" The giggles are gone again and Emily leans in close, like she's about to confess something big. "I wouldn't if I were you. There's some freak sitting at the blackjack table who refuses to leave."

"We know that freak, you bitch," Emma says, slapping her arm.

"Right. I think that's why Shep is here," I tell her, my gaze going to the window. The blinds are cracked but I can kind of see through them and I try to peer inside, hoping to catch a glimpse of Shep. But I don't see him.

"Ooh, so are you two fucking exclusively or what?" Emma asks, all perky and cheerleader like. I can imagine her as a cheerleader too. Her dark hair is pulled into a high pony just like Emily's and she's wearing a black V neck T-shirt with denim shorts. Just like Emily. In fact, Emma has a pink bow in her hair and Emily has a black bow. As in, they match.

Weird.

"We're not...fucking," I tell them, earning disappointed looks from the both of them. I'm tempted to apologize for letting them down. "I barely know him."

"Honey, you don't have to know Shepard Prescott to fuck him," Emily says sarcastically. "I mean, look at the man. He's fucking gorge."

I've heard of girls who talk like this. I've witnessed them in class and even Kelli slips on occasion. Shortening her words, talking in code, tossing out crude words like they're no big deal. It's so odd. With my friends back home, we never talked like that.

Of course, we were pretty nerdy.

"Want a drink?" Emma waves a silver flask at me and I blink, wondering where it came from. "Vodka and Redbull. It'll give you wings." Emily bursts out laughing and I figure she already found her wings.

"Sure," I say, because why not? I have no idea how long Shep's going to take and I could be out on this front porch all night. Besides, Em and Em, they seem harmless.

Emma hands over the flask and I take a sip, then another, wincing as the liquid slides down my throat. It's sort of awful. I've never liked Redbull. I prefer vodka and cranberry juice. But hey, when in Rome…

Within twenty minutes we've polished off Emma's flask and are starting in on Emily's. Shep still hasn't come out of the house, I'm giggling like the Em and Em girls and we're all three relaxing on the couch—because all houses close to the university have a couch on the front porch, duh—passing the flask back and forth between us, careful not to spill a drop.

"Can I confess something to you?" Emma asks me as she wipes the back of her hand across her mouth but somehow she misses. Her lips are still shiny with vodka and Red Bull and her eyes are dilated. She looks spun.

I start to laugh because my head is fuzzy and damn it, I'm a happy drunk. "Sure," I tell her as I take another sip. Emily's flask is hot pink. I like it. I need a flask. I'm going to ask for one for my birthday. Or maybe Christmas. It would make a great stocking stuffer. I'm sure my parents won't mind.

"I thought you were a total stuck up bitch when I first saw you in class." Emma slaps her hand over her mouth the moment the words tumble out.

"Em!" Emily yells, nudging her so hard Emma goes toppling into my lap. We all start laughing, though deep down, I'm sort of hurt.

She thought I was a bitch? Why? Why do so many people think that? God, even Joel said the same thing to me once we started dating. He admitted he was afraid to approach me and ask me out on a date but somehow worked up the courage. At the time I thought it was cute.

Now I'm thinking maybe I give off some sort of bitch vibe or something. Ugh.

Fucking Joel. Fucking Shep. Fucking everyone in my

life.

"You're not a bitch though," Emma says once we've all calmed down. "You're very sweet. I like you. We should hang out more." Her head is still in my lap and she reaches up, tapping me on the tip of my nose. "Want a bump?"

"Huh?" I'm confused.

"Em," Emily hisses before she sends me an apologetic look. "Forgive her. She's super drunk. And when she's super drunk, she wants to do all the drugs she can find."

"Like a mountain of cocaine sounds sooo good right about now," Emma says, laughing as she taps my nose again. "You have a perfect nose, you know that? I'm jealous." She taps her own nose. "I had to get a nose job to fix my honker."

The word honker sends the three of us into another fit of giggles and I push Emma off my lap, clutching at my sides. "It hurts to laugh," I protest.

"I know what'll fix that right up." Emma whips out a vile containing a small amount of white powder. "Want some? Stan hooked me up."

"Wait a minute." Emily shoves at Emma's shoulder, earning a dirty look for her efforts. "You mean that asshole who won't leave the table? That Stan gave you coke?"

Emma shrugs, a smile curling her lips. "I might've offered up my—cock sucking services for some. He readily agreed. I figured he'd be too wasted to remember and looks like I was right."

I stare at the both of them like they've totally lost their minds. What in the world have I gotten myself into? These girls…are hardcore. Flasks and vodka and fucking and Redbull and bumps and vials of coke? Blow jobs for drugs? What in the hell?

"You gonna try some?" Emma waves the vial at me, a sweet smile on her face before she twists the lid off and dips her pinky finger inside. She holds it up to her nose and gives a delicate sniff, a shiver moving through her. "Stan always has the best shit," she tells me with complete authority.

Without a word Emily hands me the flask and I gulp from it, not even tasting the Red Bull any longer. Not tasting anything. I'm not just buzzed I'm drunk. Stuck waiting for my so-called date to finish up his so-called task so he can take me back to my room and tuck me into bed and kiss me and touch me and…

No. I shake my head. It's the alcohol talking. I absolutely do not want Shep touching me and kissing me and stripping my clothes off, piece by piece…

"Pass it over bitch," Emily says and Emma hands her the vial. I watch in fascination, feeling like I'm in a movie. A movie that's about the perils of college, a glimpse into the seedy dark side where sweet college students have gone hopelessly wrong. Where underage freshmen girls drink from flasks and snort coke in public. "You want some, Jade or what? Because if you don't, I'm going to snort the rest."

"Don't be so greedy Em!" Emma yells and they both laugh. Like they do this all the time.

"Um." I hesitate, watching Emily dig into her purse and pull out a compact mirror and her student ID. She taps out a thin but sloppy line of white powder onto the mirror, then straightens it out with the edge of the ID card, the mirror resting haphazardly on her knees.

"I created this line just for you," Emily sing songs as she thrusts the mirror in my face. "What do you say, new friend?"

I look from Emily to Emma, the both of them watching me, matching smiles on their faces. They look harmless. They look like they're having fun. When was the last time I had fun? School has been driving me nuts. I'm sort of depressed over my breakup with Joel (lies). I'm confused by Shep and what he wants from me (absolute truth). I'm confused in general.

"Okay." I smile brightly. So brightly, my cheeks hurt from the strain. "Let's do this."

"Yay!" they both yell, Emily almost dropping the mirror, making Emma yell at her not to waste a fucking drop — and I quote.

"Just press your finger here." Emma demonstrates by touching the left side of her nose. "And inhale like so." She gives a short sniff with her right nostril.

Taking a deep breath, I tell myself I'll be okay. It's just a little coke. Emily lifts the mirror higher, so it's practically in my face, and I tuck my hair behind my ear, lean over the offered mirror with my finger pressed against my nose and…

Yeah. You know what happens next.

"Come on, dude." I slap Stan's massive back as I lead him out of the house. I'm irritable. Frustrated. But trying to put on a good game face—something I'm most excellent at doing. We went round and round, playing hand after hand, me trying to give away the game yet he still managed to somehow fuck it up. Over an hour later and he finally got his forty bucks back.

Gabe left when he realized I had everything under control, the asshole. I've ditched Jade all this time and I'm sure she hates me but what the hell could I do? I sent her a quick apologetic text but she never replied. I sent another text asking her to come inside but she didn't reply to that one either. Didn't make an appearance so I figure she's long gone. I fucking blew it with Jade.

Business comes first though. It couldn't be helped.

Imagine my surprise when Stan and I step out onto the porch and I see Jade sitting on the couch with two girls, Jade holding a mirror covered with a white line of power up to her face, the other two watching her raptly as she presses her finger to her nose, about ready to… what? Snort a line of fucking cocaine?

I don't think so.

"What the hell are you doing?" I yell, causing all three of the girls to jump. The mirror goes flying, landing face down on the porch and one of the girls leaps to her feet, her ponytail swishing indignantly.

"Fuck! You made her drop it!"

The dark haired one jumps to her feet as well. "Such a waste of good coke!"

The both of them fall to their knees and pick up the now shattered mirror, their fingers scurrying all over the ground as they try and salvage the powder.

"Jesus," I mutter, running my hand through my hair in frustration. My gaze snags on Jade's. "Are you all right?"

She studies me for a long, quiet moment, as if she's not sure whether she's all right or not, her teeth sinking into her lower lip, her expression pure sex kitten.

Huh. Jade has never given me the sex kitten vibe.

"Em! What the actual fuck?" Stan bellows, garnering

the attention of the other girls. One of them beams as she hops to her feet, rushing toward Stan. He gathers her into his arms and swings her around, her feet nearly nailing me in the gut as she goes flailing.

I take a step backward to get out of their way and look at Jade again, who just stepped closer to me. Like real close. Everything within me tightens when I hear her whisper close to my ear.

"I guess I'm all right. I thought you might've forgot about me." Jade's staring at me. More like she's staring at my mouth. She's smiling. She looks…happy to see me.

Okay. Something's not right.

Like I could forget her. And the way she's watching me, like she wants to eat me up with that sexy mouth of hers? Fuck, that is so right I can barely pull my gaze away from her. "Yeah, uh sorry about that," I say as I turn around and reach out to pat her shoulder awkwardly like a complete idiot.

She swallows visibly, her gaze still locked on my mouth and, holy shit, what is she doing? What are *we* doing? She's not protesting but come on. This is Jade. The girl who so sweetly introduced herself to me as Bitch Face. Who accused me of being her stalker. This is the girl that slapped my hand away when I snuck it up her skirt. And no girl ever does that.

"Are you really okay?" I ask. "I didn't mean to keep

you waiting."

"It's okay." She sounds like she means it. "I made new friends. Em and Em." I turn to look at the girls who tried to give her cocaine for God's sake and she's suddenly there, pressed up behind me, nuzzling her face against my back. "You smell fucking amazing," she breathes.

The gust of her warm breath on my skin makes everything within me tighten. Yeah, something is definitely not right. I can appreciate her new attitude but it's so completely opposite of her usual mood, I'm on guard. Grabbing her hands, I remove them from where they're resting on my hips and turn in the circle of her arms, not quite ready to end the physical contact just yet. "Were you really going to snort that line?"

She smiles and tosses her head a little, all that glorious red hair falling down her back. The black cardigan has disappeared, thank God, and I let my gaze drop to her equally glorious cleavage on display with that tight white shirt she's wearing. I'm tired, pissed that I had to deal with Stan the freak for so long but all that's forgotten in the midst of Jade. "Probably not. I've never done coke in my life. So don't worry, you're not getting involved with a drug fiend or anything like that." Her smile fades and her cheeks color the faintest pink. "Not that we're getting involved or you know, *dating*. Since you don't do involvement. Or date. You don't even allow girls to *ride* in your precious car."

What the fuck is she talking about? I let go of her hands and they immediately find themselves on my chest. I could get used to touchy feely Jade real quick. Rambling Jade is another story. "Okay. So what else have you been up to with your new friends?"

"She found her wings, Shepard Prescott!" the girl still crouched on the ground yells.

Jade giggles and steps closer to me, her hands moving up and down my chest slowly. Extra slow. And she's watching her hands move too, like she's fascinated with the idea that she's actually touching me. I know I am. "I might be a little drunk," she admits.

"Ah." That makes sense. And unfortunately for me, I refuse to take advantage of a drunk Jade. I do have some standards. "A little? Or a lot?"

She giggles again and this time, plasters her body against mine so I can feel just about every inch of her pressed into every inch of me. "A lot. Vodka and Red Bull is dangerous. I'm feeling…loose."

"Loose," I repeat, taking a deep breath when her hands continue to roam up, curling over my shoulders, sliding around my neck and up into my hair. My lids waver because Christ, her touch feels good but I need to stop this. I've fucked plenty of drunk girls before in my life. I've been plenty drunk myself while fucking too.

But I want Jade to remember this. Remember us. A

quick drunk lay is not on my agenda tonight.

"Oh, yeah. Real loosey goosey." She's whispering, her fingers tighten in my hair and she tries to tug my head down to hers but I resist. Barely. "I'm feeling horny, too."

Get the fuck out.

Did she really just say that?

"Jade." My voice comes out gruff because holy fuck if I'm not feeling horny too. I try to get out of her grip but she's surprisingly strong. The little growl of frustration she gives is sexy as hell and when she stands on tiptoe, her mouth pressed against my neck, I swear to God I'm this close to losing it. Forget my good intentions and just give her everything I've got. "I don't think you know what you're saying," I mutter.

"Why? Don't you like it? I thought you wanted this sort of thing. Not in your car though." She kisses my neck, her lips damp and so fucking soft. Everything about her is soft and curvy.

But I don't get why she keeps mentioning my car. "Someone could see us." Not that it matters if anyone sees us or not. I'm not trying to hide her. But I am trying to get her under control.

"So?" Her lips move across my neck and I grunt when I feel a little sting.

Did she just bite me? I think she did.

I rest my hands on her hips to push her away, but I

don't. It's like I can't do anything but enjoy this. "Your friends are right there. We should go."

"I don't want to go." She withdraws the slightest bit so our gazes meet. Her pupils are huge and her cheeks are flushed. She looks beautiful and…wasted. "Kiss me, Shep. I've been dying for you to kiss me all night."

Well, drunk Jade is definitely honest Jade and I love that. "Jade…" I touch her cheek, mesmerized by the way she tilts her head back, her bee stung lips slightly parted, her lids lowering as if she's expecting me to kiss her at this very moment…

Instead I cup her shoulders and set her away from me, needing the distance. Hating that I did that because I'd much rather kiss her. Devour her.

Drown in her.

Her eyes flash open, full of fire. Now there's the Jade I know. "What are you doing?"

"Taking you home." I grab her by the arm and steer her off the porch. "You're tired."

"No I'm not," she protests, trying to jerk out of my hold but I tighten my fingers.

"You're drunk," I say instead as I escort her down the stairs.

"What, Shepard Prescott can't close the deal?" one of the girls calls after us. "Jade honey, you need to find someone new if you can't get him to give it up for you. You know nothing's going to happen in that car!"

Jade presses her lips together, her head averted as she blinks furiously. Everyone on the porch is laughing, both of the girls and Stan, so I hurry my steps, practically dragging her with me.

She's embarrassed. And I feel like a shit because I'm the one who embarrassed her.

I hit the unlock button on my keyless remote and she hurries to the passenger side, throwing open the door before I can get it for her and climbing inside. She slams the door as I approach, glaring at me through the tinted window, her arms crossed in front of her chest, plumping up her breasts.

Staring at her, I blow out a harsh breath, push the hair away from my face and then round the car, sliding into the driver's seat and starting the engine so I can get us the hell out of there.

"This is all your fault, you know. You left me there," she says the moment I pull away from the house. "I got bored, I started hanging out with Em and Em and next thing I knew we were passing flasks around."

Flasks? Not just one but multiple flasks? "Em and Em? Like the candy?"

"Like Emily and Emma. They're sweet. They're like surround sound. You know what I mean? It's like they talk at once, coming at you from all sides." She drops her arms and turns sideways in her seat to look at me.

I chance a glance at her, see the hurt still lingering

on her face. "I'm sorry if I embarrassed you in front of them, but I didn't want things to get out of control."

She smiles, the sight of it sending surges of pain to my heart. Like there's a miniscule baby in a diaper sitting on her shoulder zinging a constant stream of arrows right at me. "I thought you liked it when things got out of control."

I return my attention to the road, clutching the steering wheel hard. "You're drunk, Jade." I don't know if I'm reminding her or myself. Probably both.

"So?"

"So I don't take advantage of drunk girls."

She starts laughing. "I find that hard to believe."

Jesus. This whole having a reputation thing is a real pain in the ass. "Maybe I don't want to take advantage of you."

The laughter stops. "Why? Am I that disgusting? A few hours with me and you realize your mistake?"

"I never said that."

"You may as well have. I should be happy about this turn of events, right? I hate you. I don't want you." She dips her head, I see all of that gorgeous red hair fall forward out of the corner of my eye, obscuring her face. "I guess you don't want me either."

Without thought I hit the brakes hard and pull the car over to the curb, my tires squealing. She lifts her head, her wide gaze meeting mine, her lips parting to come up with some quick protest or quip, I'm sure, but I cut her off.

"You really think I don't want you?"

She gapes at me, appearing at a complete loss for words. A miracle moment I should note.

"Really?" I goad, wanting to hear her answer so I can prove her wrong.

So fucking wrong.

Jade

I stare at Shep, shocked by the incredulous anger in his thunderous features. God, he looks good right now. Like, extra good, all angry and sexy and intense. His hair is a mess from running his fingers through it—and it's super soft, I know this because I touched his hair, sunk my fingers in all that incredible softness. Rubbed myself all over him like a cat in heat, kissed his delicious neck.

Who knew a neck could be so delicious? And smell so good? Who knew that delicious neck could belong to someone like Shep? A guy I supposedly despise.

"I—I don't know w-what to th-think," I stutter, pressing my lips together and feeling stupid. He's making me so freaking nervous. The air in the car is charged, filled with electricity that seems to bounce between us and I feel like I'm about to jump out of my skin when he touches me, his fingers drifting across my knee and making me shiver.

"Then you're drunker than I thought because I want you so fucking much it's killing me," he murmurs, his voice low and so incredibly deep I feel it between my legs where I'm throbbing.

For him.

"But I'm not going to do anything to you tonight," he continues, crashing all my hopes and dreams with a few choice words. "You won't remember it and that would be a fucking shame. Or worse, tomorrow you'll regret it, tell me you were drunk and you would've never let me touch you or kiss you or fuck you. So screw all that. I want you just as into this as I am. Nothing less."

His little speech lights up everything inside me, making me ache. I ache so bad for him, I don't remember ever feeling like this for anyone else. No other guy. No one.

He wants me just as into this as he is. What does that mean? That he's into me? That he likes and wants…me? After everything I've said and done? I told him I hated him only minutes ago. He should be beyond frustrated with my immature antics.

I may as well keep it up though, right? Stay consistent?

"So you won't even kiss me?" I ask, my voice small, my humiliation knowing no bounds. It's like the words fall from my lips without thought. No way would I ever say something like this to him sober. I totally blame the vodka.

He sends me a heated look, one that completely steals my breath. "You want me to kiss you?"

Yes, yes, yes. A million times yes, pretty please with your sugared lips on top of mine.

I shrug, wishing I could tear my gaze from his but I...can't. "Well, yeah. If you want."

The man actually has the nerve to laugh. "If I want, she says." He shakes his head and looks down, the sight of the wry smile curling his perfect lips making me feel a little wild, a little out of control. Like I want to throw myself at him and see if he'd catch me. I think he would. Scratch that. I *know* he would. I can feel it in my bones. "You just said you hated me."

"Um." I swallow hard, feeling twenty times the fool for making that statement. "I didn't mean it."

"Uh huh." He inhales deeply, his chest rising and falling in this magical way that has me staring. His chest is really broad. And hard. His entire body is hard. I should know, since I tried to climb him only a few minutes ago. "I shouldn't."

Ugh. His refusal of me is starting to give me a complex. His speech about wanting me to remember everything is ringing false. Maybe he finds me repulsive. I was a total bitch the entire night so I can't blame him. Besides, isn't this what I want? To be rid of Shep Prescott once and for all?

No. Don't bother lying to yourself. You want him. And it makes you crazy.

"Why shouldn't you?" I ask.

"I already told you why." He removes his hand from my knee and I feel the loss of his touch. "Let's get you home."

"No." I give in to my urges and lunge at him, throwing my body on top of his. He lets out a surprised grunt, his hands landing on my waist as I readjust myself so I'm straddling him in the driver's seat, my knees on either side of his hips, my skirt riding up so high I'm probably flashing my panties.

But I don't care. I'm drunk and my head is spinning. Being in such close quarters with Shep is a heady feeling. His big hands slide to my hips, our panting breaths mingle together. I brace my hands on the seat just above his head and look down at him to find he's staring in fascination at my chest, which is mere inches away from his mouth.

Oh, God. His mouth. I want it on me. On my skin. I want his tongue on me too…

"Jade." He tilts his head up, his gaze meeting mine and then he shuts his eyes on an agonized groan, his fingers slipping beneath the hem of my shirt and touching my bare skin. My breath catches at first contact and all I can think is *more please*. "What the fuck are you doing?"

"What does it look like I'm doing?" Oh, this is fun, torturing Shep. I release the seat to touch his hair once more, curling a soft strand around my finger, watching with breathless anticipation as he slowly opens his eyes, the mysterious dark brown depths drawing me in, hypnotizing me.

"I won't kiss you," his perfect lips say.

I slump against him, letting my forehead press against his. Now I'm the one who's tortured. "You're being ridiculous."

He squeezes my hips. "There's something to be said for anticipation."

"What, that you're trying to drive me out of my mind?" God, he's so warm, so solid beneath me. I remove my hand from his hair and rest it on his shoulder. His broad as a mountain, very muscular and perfect shoulder.

Everything about this man screams perfection.

"Think of how much better this will be when we finally do kiss," he murmurs as he reaches out and gently cradles my chin, his index finger drifting across my lips in a ghostly caress. "Fucking hell," he mutters under his breath, his eyes sliding shut for a brief moment and a surge of power rushes through me.

His other hand tightening around my hip, he caresses my skin with his thumb and all the power drains out of me, just like that. I want to scream. I want to press my mouth to his and end this torturous moment. I could. It would be so easy. Just lean in and do it. Settle my mouth on his and force him to kiss me.

But I don't. Something inside me makes me hold back. Instead I lift my forehead away from his and lean back, studying him. Look my fill since this is the first time I've had Shepard Prescott so close. Like I can see every single one of his pores close or I can count every single one of his eyelashes close.

He has a lot of eyelashes. And those dark, dark eyes that reveal nothing. He watches me as intently as I watch him, his lips slowly parting as he works his jaw, drawing my attention to the stubble that grows there.

It's tipped with gold too, just like his eyelashes, his hair, his fucking bank account. I bet he has a secret stash of gold bars buried deep somewhere and again, I'm hit with the notion that I'm nothing to this guy. He's just a player and I'm most likely setting myself up to get played.

"It'll be worth the wait," he finally says, his deep voice breaking the silence.

I raise a brow. "Are you saying you're worth the wait?"

He smiles and shrugs. "You tell me. You're the one who's on top of me."

It's the way he says it, his words layered with all

sorts of sexual innuendo. I'm both irritated and aroused. Irritated more at myself for being aroused.

How I feel about Shepard Prescott is ridiculously confusing.

With an exaggerated sigh I lift away from him, noting the way his hands suddenly become involved as I tumble back into the passenger seat. His fingers tickle along my back and drift across the inside of my thigh in the move and I yelp, falling into the seat like an idiot, breathless and frazzled by his sneaky touch.

Shep doesn't say a word. He barely even looks at me. Merely puts the car into drive and pulls back into the street, turns up the music as we continue our drive back to the dorms. Like what just happened between us is no big deal.

But it's a huge deal. I almost kissed Shep. I threw myself at him and he refused. Talked like he plans on doing this with me again. And again. That in the end, we will end up naked together and oh my God, I can't freaking wait.

chapter
Nine

Jade

"So what happened, you big ho? You totally
fucked him, didn't you?"

I barely crack my eyes open at first
sound of Kelli's voice. When Shep dropped me off at
the dorms a few hours ago, I'd found my room empty. I
figured Kelli was out with Dane.

I'd been thankful for the alone time. My head still
spinning from too much alcohol, I'd stripped down to
my panties, threw on an old tank top and collapsed
into bed. But I couldn't sleep, too wound up from my
weird date with Shep, going over and over in my mind
everything that happened. The way he looked at me.
How he touched my lips, his fingers light, the tortured
sound of his voice. The things he said.

You're drunker than I thought because I want you so fucking much it's killing me.

I want you just as into this as I am. Nothing less.

There's something to be said for anticipation.

Unable to stop myself, I slipped my hand beneath my panties, feeling sneaky. When was the last time I touched myself like this? It was sort of difficult, what with a roommate and all. So I took advantage of my opportunity and proceeded to bring myself to orgasm with my fingers, imagining they were Shep's fingers instead. Then immediately fell asleep to dreams of Shep actually completing that kiss. His mouth soft and firm as it took command of mine…

"Wake up, slut bag," Kelli insists, her voice shrill.

"Leave me alone," I tell her, rolling over on my side so I'm facing the wall.

She doesn't leave me alone. Instead, she plops her ass on my bed and shakes my shoulder again, her voice insistent. "Come on, J. Tell me what happened with Shep. Is his dick big? Oh wait, more important, does he know what he's doing with that big dick? I'm surprised you're back so soon. I figured you'd at least spend the entire night with him. I know I would've."

Oh God, her rambling is going to drive me insane. I squeeze my eyes shut, my head throbbing already. I need water. Hydration. And fries. Fries sound good. Maybe I'm still drunk. "What time is it?" I keep my eyes tightly closed, anticipating Kelli's reaction when I tell her nothing happened, not even a kiss.

She's going to blow up. Worse, she's probably not going to believe me. We are talking about Shepard Prescott, after all. King of the Hookup. I wonder if they have a crown for that title.

"Just after one. I made Dane bring me back. I have class in the morning."

I roll over, cracking one eye open so I can look at her. "Like you care about your classes all of a sudden?"

Kelli shrugs and looks away. "I wasn't feeling it. We haven't been getting along lately."

I sit up, yanking the sheet up over my chest. It's cold in our room and my nipples are probably full on headlights right now. "Is everything okay?"

She waves a hand, dismissing my concern. "Don't worry about it. Tell me about you. About Shep. And you. And his dick in your vagina."

"Stop." I shove at her shoulder but she hardly budges. Looks like she's not going to budge on wanting the details either. "Fine," I sigh. "Nothing happened."

Her jaw drops open. "What?"

"I'm serious. Nothing happened. I got drunk on vodka and Red Bull and I almost did a line of coke but otherwise, nothing."

"What the ever loving...are you fucking serious?" She leaps to her feet. "Where the hell were you when all this went down? Did he take you to a party?"

"No. He took me to dinner, then we had to go to his little underground casino because there was a problem. Some giant guy wouldn't move from the blackjack table. So we drove over there and I was pissed. I didn't want to go back to that place. That's where it all happened, you know?" I twist the edge of the sheet in my hands, mulling over my rotten behavior. God, I'd been so cranky. I didn't even want to go inside with him. I sat outside like a little kid pouting.

"I do know." Kelli nods. "Then what happened?"

"Well, he was taking too long and I was waiting in the car. So I got out and met some girls hanging out on the porch. They were sweet. We started drinking, and then they got me drunk. When they offered up a line of coke, I was tempted to snort it." More than tempted. I was giving about zero fucks at that moment until Shep yelling at us scared the crap out of me.

I'm really, really glad he yelled at us and stopped me from doing something I'd probably regret.

"But you didn't."

"No, I didn't. Shep came out at that exact moment and stopped me."

"Aw…" Kelli drawls but I shake my head, cutting her off.

"Then he dragged me out of there, practically pushed me into the car and drove me back to the dorms." I flop back down on the bed, my head sinking into the too soft, extra cheap pillow. "That's it."

Kelli studies me, her gaze narrowed, her lips pursed. She looks full of disbelief. Not to mention disappointment. "That's really all that happened?"

How can I tell her I threw myself at him and he rejected me? That he refused to kiss me? Talk about humiliation. "That's it."

"So he was a perfect gentleman." The sarcasm is thick in her voice.

"Really. He was." Sort of. I distinctly recall his hand landing on my ass when he escorted me to the front doors of my dorm hall. A discreet touch, nothing major and when I turned around to glare at him, he smiled, saying, *Just making sure it's real.*

What did he mean by that? Like my fat ass is fake?

My phone buzzes at that precise moment, making my pillow vibrate and I pull the phone from beneath it, frowning when I see who's texting me at one in the morning.

Shep.

Silently acknowledging the butterflies bouncing in my stomach, I read his text, ignoring Kelli's repeated requests asking who is it.

Are you asleep?

"It's Shep," Kelli says. "I can tell by the way your cheeks are turning pink."

"Shut up." I catch my lower lip with my teeth, wondering what I should say. Telling myself I shouldn't be happy that he's texting me. It's no big deal. He does this with lots of girls.

He so does not.

Not asleep. Roommate woke me up. Wanted to hear all the dirty details about tonight.

Did you tell her?

There's nothing to tell.

"Now he's texting you in the middle of the night. Booty call? Thanking you for an epic blow job? I think you're holding out on me, J," Kelli accuses.

"Nothing happened, swear to God," I stress, anxiously awaiting Shep's reply. I can see he's typing. The little bubble is there on the screen, indicating he's responding. What does he want? Thank God I wasn't asleep or I might've missed this.

You could tell her that you jumped me.

I press my lips together, wanting to laugh or die of shame, I'm not sure which. Yes, I jumped him. And then he did absolutely nothing about it.

What happened next is too humiliating to admit.

No response. Glancing up from my phone, I see Kelli watching me.

"If he's texting you in the middle of the night, it means he wants something to happen with you," she states, like she knows all. But she so doesn't. I'm probably not sophisticated enough for him. I don't know any sexual tricks. I'm pretty basic. The missionary position is my standard sexual operating procedure and I've been on top not even a handful of times. One experience is especially vivid with Joel—the single time we tried it with me on top, his dick kept slipping out. Blow jobs…ugh. I don't really want a dick in my mouth. And there's that pesky orgasm issue I have.

God. Why would the campus sex god be interested in me?

"I think one night with me turned him off completely. He's just being polite," I say, sending a quick glance to my phone's screen. No reply still.

Figures.

"Whatever." Kelli rises from the edge of my mattress. "I'm going to bed."

She moves about the room, changing out of her clothes and I roll back over on my side, my back to her, facing the wall, my phone still clutched in my hand like a stupid, ridiculous girl waiting for her dream man to text her back. My head is still fuzzy from alcohol and I really wish I had a bottle of water on my bedside table but I don't.

I need to just go to sleep. Forget this night ever happened. Forget that moment with Shep when our faces were so close and he muttered fucking hell under his breath, like I was torturing him or something. I'm sure that was the farthest thing from the truth. I'm sure he was irritated he had to deal with such an inept little girl who threw herself at him and he wasn't about to get involved in that sort of mess.

My phone vibrates in my hand, startling me so much I let out a muffled squeal. I check the screen and see it's a text from Shep.

A long ass text. As in, that's probably what took him so long to reply.

Giddy with excitement, I open my phone and read the text, my gaze skipping over the words, hurrying along to the end and I blink hard, resuming my attention to the first, heart stopping sentence so I can savor this moment, damn it.

I regret not kissing you. I should've. Having that sexy mouth of yours so close to mine, I should've gone for it. But I meant what I said. I don't want you to forget everything when it does happen. Because it's going to, that I can promise. All I can think about is your lips. You have the most amazing fucking lips I've ever seen. Has anyone ever told you that? Because if they haven't, or worse, they haven't noticed, they're fucking idiots. I have fantasies about those lips. I'm having one right now. Fantasies and regret because holy shit, Jade, I really wish you were in my bed with me.

Oh. Wow. Is he sexting me? This feels like he's sexting me. I should answer him with some witty, scorching hot reply, but what do I say?

I decide to go for it. Make it funny, not necessarily scorching hot because what if I screw that up? If I try for serious it'll end up funny but the wrong kind of funny.

So are you saying my lips provide you plenty of masturbation material?

My finger hovers over the send button and I press it before I chicken out. He immediately responds.

Hell. Yes.

I don't know whether I want to laugh or die a little inside. That I'm Shep's beat off material is just so... weird.

And exciting. Definitely exciting.

Well our conversation just turned awkward. Good night. Sweet dreams. ☺

I wait for his reply, my eyelids drooping, my entire body relaxing. My phone buzzes one last time in my hand and I check the message, smiling as I read it.

Sweet dreams sexy lips.

Shep

"So. The redhead." Gabe studies me after shoveling a forkful of waffle into his mouth, chewing with narrowed eyes. "I thought you had no interest in her," he says almost accusingly after he swallows.

I shrug, not willing to explain myself. I *can't* explain myself. Worse, I don't know what possessed me to send those texts to Jade last night, like some sort of lovesick boy waxing poetic over a girl's lips. Granted, her mouth is what a man dreams of finding wrapped around his dick, not going to lie, but there's more to it than that. More to *her* than that.

I just can't put my finger on it.

"He likes the challenge," Tristan says after taking a giant gulp of coffee. He's already cleaned his plate and is probably itching to leave. We meet on occasion at this breakfast house not too far from campus, especially on Mondays when all three of us don't have class until later in the morning or early afternoon.

Or not at all, like Gabe. That we were able to drag his lazy ass out of bed on a Monday morning says something about his need for a greasy breakfast.

"What do you mean?" I ask defensively, setting my fork down. The small restaurant is busy, the waitresses hustling to and fro, the booths filled with locals and the occasional group of college students like us. There's a cluster of five girls sitting in the booth directly across from us, all of them making eyes in our direction.

We ignore them. They look young. I usually don't like them young as I get older, but somehow Jade is an exception.

Breathing deep, I finish off my coffee, pissed at myself. I need to stop thinking about Jade all the fucking time. One night with her — I barely touched her and didn't even kiss her — and I act like I'm completely sprung.

"She's not interested in you. Or, she is, but only when she's drunk," Tristan explains, a giant smile on his face. The asshole. Should've never told them what happened last night between Jade and me. "And they're all interested in you. Interested in us. You want the challenge. You want to prove to her that you can get her to fall under your spell just like the rest of them."

I don't say a word. Maybe he's right? No female has ever challenged me before beyond my mother and my sisters and that just comes with the family territory.

"Valid point," Gabe says, like we're having some sort of scientific discussion in class. "When I saw them together a couple nights ago, she was putting out some pretty hateful vibes."

"That's because you interrupted us." I almost had her that night at the party. Hell, I could've had her last night, but she was drunk. Behaving strangely. I meant every word I said to her. I didn't want her to forget, or full of regret afterward. I wanted her into me. Into us.

"And so you pushed her off last night, why?" Tristan asks, turning to look at me. His gaze is razor sharp as he waits for my answer. "Because you were trying to be a gentleman or some such bullshit?"

I push my plate away, smiling up at the waitress when she stops by and pours me another cup of coffee before she darts off. "She was too drunk."

Gabe snorts. "There is no such thing as a girl who is too drunk to fuck."

"Are you even listening to yourself right now? You sound like a complete asshole." He sounds like me approximately four days ago, before I met Jade.

Has it really only been four days? Unbelievable.

"And so do you," Tristan quickly adds, jabbing a finger in my direction. "All panties look the same once they hit the floor, bro. Or when they get lost in a tangle of sheets in your bed. There is nothing special about this girl's panties. Trust me. They're all the same."

"Damn, simmer down, T. Who burned you to make you so bitter?" Gabe asked, making me crack up.

Tristan shrugs then leans over and snatches a piece of toast off my plate, taking a bite. "My motto is to keep my heart out of it."

"Right, making you a heartless bastard," Gabe says with a slight sneer. "It's all about fun while we're in college. Nothing serious. If you're upfront with a girl, they get it right away."

"Oh yeah? And how's Meadow?" I ask Gabe, making him frown in confusion.

"Who?"

"Meadow. The girl you were with Saturday night when you so rudely interrupted me and Jade," I remind him. I knew he'd answer like that. They're giving me a bunch of shit? Gabe is the epitome of the love 'em and leave 'em guy.

"Oh, yeah. Meadow." Gabe smiles fondly. "She has a great rack. Decent kisser."

"Right," I say sarcastically. "Surprised you can remember. You didn't even know who I was talking about until I reminded you."

"Hey, at least I closed the deal with her, unlike you and your redheaded babe," Gabe throws back at me accusingly. "I'm not here to find my future wife or anything like that. Real life's barreling down on all of us and we'll have to face it sooner or later. May as well enjoy our time here while we can, right?"

"I'm not looking for my future wife," I say, ignoring the panic rising within me at the word *wife*. Fuck no, that is the last thing I want. Gabe is seriously reminding me of my mother right now. And that's not a compliment. "I barely know this girl."

"You've never, ever wanted to spend more than one night with a girl," Tristan points out. "And you always close the deal, as Gabe so aptly described. You're all about closing the deal. I've always admired your abilities in being able to close the deal with every single girl you encounter."

"Maybe I'm not ready to close the deal with Jade yet," I mumble, feeling under attack. What does it matter? Since when did these two care so much about my sex life?

"And there's where it gets strange," Tristan says, Gabe nodding enthusiastically in agreement. "One and done. Isn't that something you've said countless times? Hasn't that been your philosophy when it comes to girls?"

One and done. Yeah, it definitely was.

"Them's the rules man," Gabe says, his expression serious. "Three little words. One. And. Done."

I throw my napkin across the table and it hits Gabe in the chest. "We don't have rules or any of that bullshit. So fuck you both. I don't want anything serious with Jade. Trust me. She'd probably wrench my balls off and hand them to me with a smile if I tried to make a move on her."

Lies. I'm lying through my teeth. After the way she acted last night, the things we said to each other, I don't think she'd mind me making a move on her. I should text her. Find out what she's doing today. See if we can get together soon, maybe tonight…

"You're thinking about her right now," Gabe says, pointing at me. "You want her. Holy hell, I think you actually *like* her."

I slide out of the booth as they laugh at me, sending them both a dirty look. Reaching for my wallet, I peel out a ten and throw it on the table, then shove my wallet back in my jeans. "Have a nice day, pussies."

Their laughter follows me out of the restaurant but I don't look back, though I'm tempted to give them the finger and tell them to fuck off only because they're getting too close to the truth.

I like this girl. I *was* thinking about her. I want to see her again. I don't care if I'm breaking the so called rules or whatever. I don't want anything serious.

I'm thinking spending time with Jade beyond the one and done variety could be worth it.

Pausing at the streetlight, I wait for it to turn green so I can cross and get to my car. I pull my phone out and send her a quick text, shoving my phone back in my front pocket and not waiting for her to reply. She could be in class or still asleep. It could be hours until she responds. She might play hard to get. Worse, she might hate me. I never know with Jade. She keeps me on my toes.

I think that might be my favorite thing about her. Oh, that and her fucking incredible mouth.

My phone dings and I check it, surprised and pleased to see her answer.

Tonight? Are you serious?

Shaking my head, I answer.

Yeah. Are you busy?

I have class.

The light changes and I start crossing, typing as I do, earning a few dirty looks for my effort.

What time are you out?

Ten.

I wonder if she's lying to me. Maybe she doesn't want to see me.

I can pick you up after.

Really?

Yeah.

She makes me wait and in turn, makes me sweat. Just a little bit. Not much. And it pisses me off. Girls don't make me sweat. Nothing makes me sweat beyond my old man.

Finally, my phone dings with a text alert.

Okay.

chapter
Ten

Jade

The second I walk out of the building I see him in the near distance, leaning against the front of his car. I'm walking with a friend from class, listening distractedly as she rambles on about the assignment for next week, my gaze never leaving him though he doesn't notice me, not yet. She catches me staring though and stops short when she spots Shep.

"Ooh, he's pretty," Nicole breathes. "Looks like he's waiting for someone too."

I pretend for a moment he's not waiting for me and I try my best to observe him objectively. It's tough because I'm totally hot for him and I can't blame it on alcohol, not tonight. He's wearing a black T-shirt that molds to his chest and shoulders, the sleeves tight around his biceps.

Dark rinse jeans, a baseball cap on backwards, his face lit in shadows from the lamppost just to the right of him. He looks...amazing, bent over his phone, the glow of the screen highlighting that gorgeous face.

My phone buzzes and I check it.

You're staring.

I laugh and he lifts his head at the sound, the upward tilt of his lips just for me. Even from such a long distance, I feel the impact of his smile all the way down to my bones.

"Wait a minute." Nicole touches my arm, stopping me. "Is he waiting for *you?*"

She sounds surprised. I guess I can't blame her. "Yeah, he is," I say proudly, hitching the strap of my backpack higher on my shoulder.

"Wow." She squints, studying him as we draw closer to the parking lot and Shep. "Is that Shep Prescott?"

"Uh huh," I tell her, bracing for some *what a player, he's a total man whore* remark from her.

But she remains blissfully silent. I can only assume she's so stunned Shep would be waiting for me she doesn't know what to say.

"Hey." He lifts his chin when I draw closer, his gaze going to Nicole by my side. She's gawking at him unabashedly and I'm almost embarrassed for her. Almost.

Really, I can't blame her. I would totally gawk at

him myself. Which I am.

"Hi," I say as I nudge Nicole in the side. This helps stop the gawking. "Shep, this is Nicole."

"Hello," he says with a nod, his gaze immediately returning to me. "You look good."

Those three simple words spoken in that low, seductive voice just about melt the bones in my legs. "Um, thanks." I'm wearing my tightest jeans as per Kelli's instructions and a blue and white plaid button up shirt over a white camisole with a built in bra, though that went against my better judgment, Kelli insisted. I'm definitely dressed up compared to my usual yoga pants and a sweatshirt outfit I normally wear for this Monday night class.

"You need a ride?" he asks Nicole and for some strange reason, my heart warms because he's considerate enough to think of her and make the offer.

"No, I drove." She shakes her head and flashes me a knowing smile, one that says *you lucky bitch.* "Nice meeting you, Shep. See you around, Jade."

She walks over to her car, I can see one of the security guards that watch the parking lot nearby and I know she's safe. We always walk in pairs or groups out here at night because you never know. Too many campus rape horror stories across the country and we don't want to risk it.

"Are you two close?" he asks once Nicole is out of

earshot.

I shake my head, and tuck a strand of hair behind my ear. "She's more like a class friend. Not like we hang out, but we always talk before class, walk out together. Most of the time she gives me a ride."

"You don't have a car?"

"No, I can't afford one. When school's out I'll go back home and get a job for the summer. I'm trying to save up for a cheap used car." My mom can't afford to just buy me a car. She drives an '01 Jetta that's a European heap of crap she's constantly taking to the shop. What I make at Light My Fire pays for the extras but I couldn't manage a car payment on my part time wages. I have no idea what it's like to be outlandishly wealthy like the Prescotts.

Worry knots my stomach and I try to push it away. Just thinking about the wealth, the legacy Shep comes from makes me nervous. What is he doing with me? Half the time I wonder if he's just trying to torment me.

The other half wonders if he really could be in to me. Nah.

"You won't stick around here for the summer?" he asks, knocking me from my thoughts.

"There's no point. The dorms close and I can't afford rent anywhere, not even if I had a bunch of roommates." A breeze washes over me and I shiver, wishing I brought a sweater. I forgot my cardigan last night at the casino or whatever they call it. I should ask for Shep to look for it. I hate losing clothes, more so because I don't want to have to replace them.

"That's too bad," he says, his voice soft, his expression pensive. He pushes away from his car and approaches, stopping directly in front of me. "You ready to go?"

"Yeah." I tilt my head back so I can look into his eyes. He's so tall. And broad. He looks cute with the backward baseball hat on. I wonder if he used to play sports. If he works out constantly or maybe his body is naturally that amazing. "Where are we going?"

He smiles and the sight of it sends a zing of electricity through my veins. "It's a surprise."

"Your house?" I ask incredulously as he pulls into the driveway and waits for the garage to open. "If you think you can get me into your bed that easy, you're sadly mistaken." My voice comes out shaky and I clear my throat. What if that's his real intent? Would I refuse him? I should.

I should, I should, I should.

He gives me a look. "Do you think I have a one track mind or what?"

"Well, you are a guy." And all they think about is sex.

But here's the problem. The more time I spend with Shep, the more *I* think about sex. *With* Shep. Only him. No one else.

What's he like in bed? Fast and intense? Slow and methodical? Does he joke as much naked as he does clothed? Just imagining him stripping off my clothes, his mouth blazing a path along my skin, makes me uneasy. In a great but nerve wracking way. What if I don't measure up? I don't have any secret sexual tricks. When it comes to sex, most of the time I feel like an utter failure.

Yep, off I go. My performance anxiety is at it again.

"Right," he practically snorts as he pulls into the garage and shuts off the engine. He turns to look at me, his hands loosely gripping the steering wheel. "And only guys think about sex."

"Most of the time," I agree quietly.

"And girls *never* think about sex." He starts to chuckle and it's this deep, rich sound that makes me warm inside. "I should be offended by your generalizations."

I'm a hypocrite is what I am. I was the one who threw myself at him last night. Who agreed to see him again. Who can't help but think about him. Naked.

"And you do realize you can have sex in places other than a bed, right? I mean, why limit yourself? You can do it against a wall. On the floor. In the back seat of my car." He flicks his gaze to the back seat while he says that.

And instantly fuels my imagination, especially with the way he said *my* car.

As if he's thinking of the two of us together. In the backseat. Right now...

"Don't you think a bed is more...comfortable?" I can't believe we're having this conversation and that I'm actually encouraging it.

He stares at me quietly, his gaze dropping to my mouth, lingering there. My heart starts thumping extra hard and I lick my suddenly dry lips.

I swear he just groaned.

"Sometimes, it's not about the comfort," he finally says, his voice scratchy. Husky. Sexy. "Sometimes... you're so overcome, you can't wait to get your hands on her."

I look at his hands, see the way they flex and shift as they still cling to the steering wheel. His palms are wide, his fingers long. They've touched me before and I wish they were touching me right freaking now. "Overcome?" No guy has ever acted like he's had to have me, no matter what the cost. I wonder what that's like.

More than anything, I wonder what that's like with Shep.

"Well, yeah." His fingers curl around the steering wheel tightly and he turns his head, his smoldering gaze meeting mine. "Don't tell me you've never felt like that."

I'm feeling like that right about now. Not that I can say so. "Not really," I confess, my voice barely a whisper.

He's quiet for so long I want to squirm in my seat I'm that uncomfortable. I look away from him, staring at my hands as I clutch them in my lap. I should've never said that. He must think I'm hopeless. He'll probably start the car and drive me back to my dorm hall, drop me off and hit me with a casual, "Nice knowing you," before he speeds off.

I know I would if I were him. I don't measure up in more ways than I can count.

He makes a strangled sound in the back of his throat and I lift my head, my gaze going to his hands as they drop from the steering wheel and he starts to move.

Toward me.

I lean back, my shoulders bumping against the passenger door, my breath catching in my throat. I look at his face, taking in his determined expression, the spark in his gaze. He looks...intense.

Serious.

"Prescott! What the fuck man? Are you jacking off in your car or what?"

"Who's that?" I practically scream, fear sending my heart into my throat. Shep falls back into his seat, muttering curse words under his breath as he reaches for the door handle and opens it, climbing out of the car.

"Fuck off, Tristan. Jesus." Shep slams the door, leaving me alone in the car.

Taking a deep, shaky breath, I smooth my hand over my hair, then rest it on my chest, my heart throbbing against my palm. I think Tristan is his cousin. Kelli gave me a run down of the people Shep's known to hang out with and I already met Gabe.

A sharp knock sounds directly behind me and I shift away from the passenger door with a squeal, turning to find an extremely good looking guy peering at me through the window. He knocks again on the glass, flashing me a friendly smile and I try to smile back but it feels wobbly.

Shep appears by Tristan's side, glowering at him so Tristan has no choice but to back away from the door. Shep opens it for me and I climb out of the vehicle, casting a nervous glance in Shep's direction before I turn to Tristan. "Hi."

Tristan smiles lazily, his perfectly straight, perfectly white teeth flashing. "What's your name, gorgeous?"

"Jade." I feel my cheeks flush as Shep sends Tristan a deathly glare.

"Tristan." His deep voice is a warning.

"I'm just being polite." Tristan extends his hand, his expression neutral though his eyes are sparkling with mischief. "Nice to meet you, Jade. You must be the redhead Shep and Gabe keep going on and on about."

I gape at the both of them, too stunned to say a word. They've been going on and on about me? What in the world? Why?

I'm dying to know why.

Shep

My cousin has the biggest mouth on the planet. I hate that guy. And I especially hate the way he keeps staring at Jade like he wants to gobble her up.

Only I get that privilege damn it.

"Where's your restroom?" Jade asks, glancing around the giant kitchen that is perfectly clean because we never use it. Granite countertops gleam beneath the lights and the stainless steel appliances are spotless. It helps that we have a housekeeper.

Jesus, we sound spoiled even in my thoughts.

"There's one right back there," Tristan says, pointing the way we just came from the garage. "First door on the left."

"Thanks." She flashes me a look, one that says she's petrified, before she leaves.

I turn toward Tristan. "What the hell are you doing here?" I ask him quietly. We share the house that we've lived together in since we came here for college.

Family sticks together and all that bullshit. Our dads are brothers, meaning Tristan is a Prescott too and he's even more irresponsible than I am. Or at least, he used to be. Lately he's actually been concentrating on school and getting decent grades, versus partying all the time.

"Uh, I live here?" Tristan scratches the back of his head, his gaze going to Jade's retreating back. The bathroom door closes with a soft click.

"I know that, dickhead. I just thought you'd be somewhere else tonight." It hadn't been my intention to get her in my bed. Not really. I'd hoped to just hang out and…talk to her. Get to know her.

But the minute she started accusing me of being able to think of only one thing, I could only think of…one thing. Sex. With Jade. Hot and sweaty fucking with my name falling from her lips as I make her come over and over again.

Then Tristan had to show up and ruin everything.

"A few people are coming over." At my death glare he shrugs, totally unfazed. "Nothing big. Gabe is bringing a couple of chicks so I wouldn't be lonely. We were going to watch the Giants game I DVR'd. Drink beer. Smoke a bowl. You in?"

I don't want to be in. I want to spend time with Jade. Alone. But I don't want her to be uncomfortable either. Would she care if I smoked a little weed? I'm amped up. Feeling a little edgy.

I blame it all on sexual frustration.

"I'll see what Jade wants to do," I start, then clamp my lips shut when I see the shit eating grin on Tristan's face. "What?"

"You're going to consult with the redhead first? When do you ever consult with anyone? You always do whatever the hell you want." Tristan's smile somehow grows wider. "You like this chick."

There's no use denying it. "Don't call her that. She has a name. And didn't we already have this conversation?" I ask irritably as I walk away from him and head for the fridge, opening it so I can check out what's inside. I should offer Jade something to drink but all we have is beer and bottled water. Oh and a fifth of vodka in the freezer.

"Yeah, but now I'm seeing it in action. You looked ready to maul her in your car, man, which is stupid when you have a perfectly good house you can put to use."

Couldn't put the house to use with his ass in it. "You didn't see shit," I mutter, slamming the double doors of the refrigerator. I turn and face him. "Just...lay off tonight, okay? She's skittish enough."

"What do you mean, she's skittish? Around you?" Tristan asks incredulously. "Give me a break. You usually have them tearing their panties off within minutes."

I say nothing. He's right. But Jade's proven different from the moment we first met. She's unlike any girl I've ever been with. Hell, I haven't even *been* with her yet. I haven't kissed her. We haven't done shit but torture each other.

And it's been pure torture. I had my chance and denied myself. Tonight that's the last thing I want.

"So tell me." I glance up when Tristan approaches. He leans against the kitchen counter, contemplating me. The smile is long gone, his expression serious. "What's so different about this girl compared to the others? Is it only about the challenge? I can understand the appeal. She's beautiful. And there's something to be said for wanting what you can't have."

"I've always gotten whatever I wanted my entire life. So have you," I tell him and he nods in agreement. "But there's something about this girl that I think... might be worth waiting for."

"Really." Tristan's voice is flat, downright disbelieving. "But what makes her so different, man? I don't get it."

I don't either. I'm about to tell him that but then I hear the bathroom door open and I clamp my lips shut, not about to let Jade overhear our conversation about her. I turn to face her, watching as she enters the kitchen, her gaze everywhere but on mine.

"You all right?" I ask, looking over my shoulder

real quick to discover Tristan is gone. Like a ghost. He's good at that sometimes. Other times, his timing is for shit. Like out in the garage.

She smiles but she still won't look at me. She seems fascinated by the oven that's just behind me. "Your kitchen is gigantic."

"Yeah, it is." I try to see it through her eyes but it's hard. I've lived here three years. I've come in and out of this kitchen every day to get to the garage and I don't pay attention to shit. I don't really ever hang out in the kitchen, beyond rushing in for a bag of chips or a beer. "You like it?"

She goes to the oven, her fingers drifting over the burner knobs. "It's a professional range."

"What?"

"The oven and stove. It's professional grade. Like, out of a restaurant." She touches one of the burners. "It looks like it's never been used."

"Probably, because it really hasn't been. Tristan and I don't cook much," I admit.

"Such a shame." She sighs, her gaze finally lifting to meet mine. "I like to cook," she admits.

"Really?" I'm surprised. But then again, I'm not because I don't know anything about this girl. Nothing.

Jade nods. "I really like to bake. Growing up, my grandma used to bake all the time and I would help her. I'm sure I was more a pain in her butt, but she was always so patient with me." She smiles but it's sad and her eyes get this far away look in them. "It's one of my favorite memories of her."

"What's your favorite thing to bake?" Her grandma must've died but I don't want to ask. The memories might be too painful.

"Homemade cookies. Cakes. My grandma made this chocolate cake that's to die for." Her smile grows. "I can bake a mean apple pie too."

"A mean one versus a nice one?" I tease, wanting to make her laugh. I don't like thinking about her sad.

She rolls her eyes. "You know what I mean. My grandma's recipe is the best apple pie I've ever tasted. I even make the crust from scratch."

"Wow, I'm impressed." I take a step closer to her, catching her scent, warm and sweet. "So tell me. What's a guy gotta do to get you to make him a chocolate cake from scratch?"

"You don't like apple pie?" she asks, her eyes going wide when I draw even closer to her.

"I prefer cake, especially ones that are to die for." I smile. "I like the frosting part best."

She laughs. "I bet you were the kid who always stuck his fingers in the frosting bowl when your mom wasn't looking."

"My mom has never baked a thing in her life. Besides, I wasn't allowed in the kitchen when I was a kid. I'd just get in the servants' way."

Her laughter dies and she stares at me as if I've sprouted three heads. "You had servants? As in plural?"

"My family still does." Hell, we have the housekeeper here, not that I want to admit it to her. Nadia comes in twice a week and cleans this place up. Once a week, she shops for us, keeping the fridge and pantry full. I don't know what we'd do without her.

"Wow." She edges away from the oven, away from me, her hand sliding across the smooth granite countertop. Her nails are short and painted a deep red and her fingers are slender. I imagine them on me. Touching me. "I can't even wrap my head around what that's like."

No one can. Tristan gets it since he comes from the same world. Gabe's family is wealthy too. It's why we're such close friends. We understand each other, what it's like to be us. Not many people can wrap their heads around it.

The doorbell rings, startling us both, and I turn toward the living room, listening as I hear Tristan answer the door, Gabe's voice ringing through the house.

"I've brought the party, motherfucker! So gimme a beer!"

Jesus, he's obnoxious when he wants to be.

Jade sends me a look. "Your friends?"

"Yeah," I admit. "Look, I didn't invite them. This is

all Tristan's thing. I had nothing to do with his plans."

"What did *you* plan for tonight?" She raises a delicate brow.

"We were just going to hang out," I say innocently. The way she's looking at me...she makes me sweat. And not necessarily in a good way. "Maybe have some ice cream."

"Ice cream?" she asks incredulously.

I sound like the biggest idiot ever. This girl makes me say stupid things. "Well, yeah. Or whatever you want. We have a pretty full pantry." I wave a hand toward the living room, where I hear more people entering the house through the front door. How many people did Tristan invite anyway? "Or we could go hang out with everyone and watch the baseball game. You a Giants fan?"

"I've always been more of a Dodger fan," she admits with a wince.

I clutch my chest. "That's it. Sorry. This won't work. Giants and Dodger fans don't mix."

Laughing, Jade shakes her head. "Fine then. I'm out." She makes like she's going to leave but I grab her right at her elbow, curling my fingers around her arm, smoothing my thumb over her skin.

"Kidding," I say, my voice soft, my gaze locked with hers. "Let's go see what everyone's up to."

She nods. "Okay."

Pleasure ripples through me. She didn't try to pull out of my touch once, and she's sober.

We're making progress.

chapter Eleven

Jade

There are six girls in this living room, including me, and only five guys. Meaning the odds are off and they're all glaring at me because I'm the one sitting next to Shep Prescott. He doesn't pay attention to any of them, despite them constantly trying to get his attention. They call his name, they ask him questions, they offer to grab him another beer, did he want anything from the pantry? Or they keep trying to pass him a joint.

He took a couple of puffs when Gabe offered him a hit but other than that, there's been no smoking on his part. Not that I care. I'm not a big smoker of weed. I've tried it a few times but it's harsh on my throat and always makes me cough no matter what I do. So I tend to avoid it.

I do sip from my second beer as I sit next to Shep on the couch, hyper aware of his close proximity. Our thighs touch. His arm is slung around the back of the couch, his hand dangling precariously close to my shoulder and I swear I feel the occasional brush of his fingers in my hair. He's extremely focused on the game. Yelling when there's a bad play, a good play, it doesn't matter. He's really into it.

Me, on the other hand? I'm really into watching him. He's very…relaxed, and I figure it's from the weed. He keeps asking if I'm okay, if I need anything, if I want another beer.

He's treating me like the girls are treating him. And it's kind of awesome.

Fine, it's really awesome. I swore to myself I wouldn't fall for his act. I thought he was a world class player. In fact, I *know* he's a world class player. But for some reason, he's into me and I'm going to enjoy this for as long as I can.

I think this might be the beer talking.

Gabe sits next to me on the couch, making his moves on some innocent girl who has no idea this is most likely her one and only chance with him. On occasion, he says something to me. Something silly and funny that makes me laugh. I like Gabe better than I do Tristan, but I think it's because Gabe is so easygoing, even more so than

Shep, and that's saying a lot.

There are other friends there. Two guys who are doing tequila shots and brought a bong with them that they keep passing back and forth. They're friends of Tristan's and they sort of keep to themselves.

Weird. This entire night is weird. And confusing. I don't know what Shep wants from me anymore. I know what I want. I sneak a glance at what I want, staring at his face, his perfect, full, sexy lips. I want those lips on me. Yes, that's what I want. I want my hands all over him and his mouth on mine and his hands on my butt, pulling me in closer and…yeah. I want all of that. Every last drop of it.

Clearly, the beer is talking.

I drink the last of it and lean forward, setting the bottle on the coffee table. One of the girls—I can't keep track of their names and I swear to God, they all look the same, blonde, fake and blonde—glares at me from where she's sitting, her eyes narrowed, her lips pursed.

If I could flip her the bird, I so would but instead I lean back against the couch, yelping in surprise when I feel Shep's arm come gently down upon my shoulders. I stiffen up, my breath lodges in my throat as I wait for him to say something. To do something.

But he doesn't. He keeps his arm firmly in place as he and Gabe discuss the last inning, his long fingers curling around my shoulder and gripping it lightly. His touch is possessive without being obvious and I want to lean into him. Rest my head on his chest and go to sleep. I've been going all day and I had a late class. I'm suddenly tired.

Yep, beer is the culprit again.

I wish everyone would leave. Just magically disappear so Shep and I could be alone on this couch. I wonder what he would do then. I would love whatever he wanted to do to me because *oh my God*, the only thing I could possibly want at this very moment is to feel his hands on me. Possessing me. His mouth on mine. Soft and sweet at first. Then firmer, more insistent. I bet he's an excellent kisser. I bet he knows just how to use his tongue too. I've fantasized about his tongue and his lips for days. Since the moment I first saw him, truthfully.

"What are you thinking?" he asks, his voice low so only I can hear, his mouth right at my temple. "I can just see the cogs turning in your brain."

My cheeks are hot. My entire body is hot. Should I tell him the truth? Probably not. That's too risky. Being honest is not always the best policy, or something like that. "Nothing," I tell him.

"Liar."

I look up at him, ignoring whatever's happening on TV, ignoring what Gabe's yelling about. Forgetting about the girls' glaring at me, not paying attention to Tristan as he yells he'll be right back before he dashes into the kitchen.

"You don't want to know what I'm thinking," I admit.

Shep's gaze smolders again and it sets my body on fire. He's really good at that. "Now I definitely want to know."

"It's too embarrassing," I say, shaking my head.

"Come on, Jade. Don't be shy," he coaxes.

It's the beer, I tell myself yet again. Otherwise I would never do this. Never say this. "I was wishing everyone would just…go away."

"Why?"

"So…we could be alone." Worry buzzes through me but it's too late now. I've said it. It's out there.

"And why do you want to be alone with me?" he prompts.

I want to roll my eyes but restrain myself. This is do or die time. I'm about to play true confessions with a guy for the first time in my life. "Because I want to kiss you," I admit in a soft whisper. Not that he doesn't already know this, because he so does. I tried to kiss him before but he rejected me.

If he rejects me again? I don't know what I'm going to do.

He's leaping off the couch in a flash, his hand reaching out for mine. I let him take it, squealing when he pulls me to my feet and we start heading down the hall toward…oh my God, his bedroom? I don't know but I'm letting him pull me helplessly behind him and no one's batting an eyelash, asking where we're going, nothing.

Shep stops in front of a door and pushes it open, dragging me inside, his hand never letting go of mine. He slams the door shut, turning me so my back is against the door, as he stands directly in front of me. He takes off his hat and tosses it across the room. I hear it land on the ground somewhere but I don't care. I'm too enraptured with watching Shep as he takes a step closer, so close, our chests bump, and he rests his hands on the door above me, caging me in.

I slowly lift my head, our gazes meeting, both of us never saying a word. I'm holding my breath, waiting for him to do something, say something and then his head starts to descend, his face drawing closer before he whispers against my lips, "Are you sober?"

My breath leaves me in a stuttering gasp. "Y-yes." I have a little buzz on but nothing like my vodka and Red Bull moment from last night.

He pulls back the slightest bit. "You're not going to forget this?"

I shake my head, my hair rubbing against the door. He reaches out, curling a thick strand around his finger, and I want to die. Just…die.

All from him touching my freaking hair.

"Good. Because I'm never going to forget this either," he murmurs just before he settles his mouth on mine.

It's electric, that first moment of our lips connecting. His hand is in my hair, his fingers sifting through until they're touching the side of my neck, his thumb streaking along my jaw. He softly captures my bottom lip between his, giving it a gentle tug before he releases it and a sigh escapes me. It feels so good, so deliciously, wonderfully good and he smiles against my lips. I want to smile back but then he tilts his head to the side, his mouth on mine again as he deepens the kiss.

He drops his arm to slide it around my waist, his hand settling at the small of my back and bringing me forward. I go willingly, curving my arms around his neck, my hands in his hair because so far, it's one of my favorite places on him to touch. His tongue circles around mine, teasing it, making me crazy and I press my chest to his, silently marveling at how hard his body is.

Because he is. Hard. Everywhere. I can feel him beneath his jeans. He already has an erection and I rub against him shamelessly. Just like I did last night, only this time, he's just as turned on as I am.

A groan escapes him and the deep masculine sound pulses through me, making me yearn for more. More touching, more kissing, more wanting his hands on me, all over me. I slide my hands down to curl them around his shoulders, then along the front of his chest, all the way down to his jeans before I slide them back up. I feel emboldened, uninhibited as I lightly nip at his bottom lip with my teeth, and I moan in delicious surprise when he sucks my tongue into his mouth.

He says my name against my lips and he sounds tortured. I break the kiss first and open my eyes to find him watching me, his chest moving rapidly, his lips swollen, his eyes dark. He leans in again and I close my eyes on a sigh when I feel his mouth land on my neck, his damp lips blazing a fiery path along my skin. His tongue darts out for a lick, his teeth nibble and I clutch him close. My brain shuts down, shuts out everything else happening. The faint roaring coming from the television in the living room, everyone yelling when someone scores — those sounds I heard only moments ago are gone.

All I can see, hear, taste, focus on is Shep. And it's so good, so perfect I'm almost scared. How can it get any better than this?

Shep

I knew it would be like this between us. Jade's mouth is perfection. The way she tastes, the sounds she makes, how she feels in my arms…

Again. Perfection.

Gripping her ass in my hands, I lift her up and she goes willingly, her legs wrapping around my hips, her arms sliding back around my neck. I continue kissing her as I turn and head for the bed, sitting down first with her in my arms and she presses against me, sending us both toppling backwards onto the mattress. Laughter huffs out of me when her thick hair lands in my face and I push it away just as she lifts up so she can stare down at me.

Her hair creates a curtain over us as it falls around her face, shutting out everything else so she's all I can see. "What are we doing?" she asks breathlessly.

I let my hands drift back down over her ass. It's as perfect as she is. Round and soft and I'm fucking dying to see it without the jeans on. Without any panties on either, though catching a glimpse of Jade in a pair of sexy panties and nothing else is high on my list. "What does it look like we're doing?" I shift upwards so I can press my mouth to the spot where her pulse throbs at the base of her throat, breathing deep her intoxicating scent. My eyes close and I exhale against her skin, making her shiver.

Her hands sink into my hair as she holds me in place, right against her neck. I know she likes what I'm doing. "I'm guessing this probably won't work between us."

"Why do you say that?" I murmur against her skin.

I took a couple of hits off the joint Gabe had earlier and I got a good buzz on but now I feel like I'm high on Jade. On the feel of her in my arms, her body nestled close. Her scent, the sound of her voice, the taste of her skin, her lips, her tongue…

Fuck. I should run. Push this girl off my lap, pay someone to take her back to her dorm and be done with her. She's dangerous, but worse?

She doesn't even know it.

"We don't like each other." Her breath hitches when I lightly graze her skin with my teeth. "We fight all the time."

"We didn't fight tonight." I lift up and brush my mouth with hers, enjoying the little hitch of her breath when our lips connect. "The last thing I want to do is argue with you, Jade."

After I make that statement, there's no more talking. Our mouths are fused, our tongues tangled, our hands everywhere. Her hips thrust against mine, subtly at first, driving me fucking insane with wanting her. My cock is hard, my skin is hot and then I'm rolling her over so she's beneath me, her vibrant hair spread all over my pillow, her head tilted back, her lush mouth swollen and red from my kisses. Our ragged breaths mingle as I study her, my knees on either side of her hips, her chest rising and falling rapidly.

Reaching for her, I settle my hands on the front of

her shirt, my fingers slowly undoing the buttons. She doesn't utter a word of protest, just stares up at me with those big hazel eyes, her skin flushed, her freckles... Christ, I want to kiss every single one of them.

But my gaze falls from her face so I can see the prize I'm slowly unveiling. The last button comes undone and I spread her shirt apart, staring in fascination at her chest. She's wearing a white tank with one of those bogus built in bras or whatever they're called and I can see her nipples. Small and tight, protruding against the thin fabric of her shirt.

I want to suck them into my mouth.

Her breasts raise on a deep inhale and I wonder if she's pushing them into my face on purpose. There is a faint smattering of freckles across her creamy skin and I bend down, pressing my face into her cleavage like some sort of pervert. Some sort of tortured pervert because holy hell, she smells good. And feels good. Her skin is so damn soft.

She wraps her arms around me, one hand curling around my nape and I brush my lips across her collarbone lightly. I'm afraid if I push too hard, too fast she'll shove me off her and end it. And I can't have that. Not when I'm so close.

I hadn't planned on this but I'm not about to blow my chance either.

"Tell me to stop," I whisper against her skin, handing

over the control. She's got it. I refuse to do anything she doesn't want. She needs to tell me how far she'll let this go or give me a hard limit.

Because right now, having her like this, open and warm and so fucking sexy, I'll take her as far as she'll let me.

"I—" She sucks in a breath when I kiss the very top of her left breast. "I don't want you to stop."

Triumph surges through me. That's exactly what I wanted to hear—what I needed to hear. I grip her waist, my fingers slipping beneath the hem of her camisole to touch bare, smooth, soft as a cloud skin and I shift lower. Ready to slowly take her shirt off so I can finally see her…

The door plows open and I lift my head, ready to tell whoever it is to fuck off when I see a girl standing in the doorway, her eyes wide, her mouth dropped open. "Uh, sorry." She smiles. "I thought this was the bathroom."

The exasperated sound from Jade matches the way I feel. "Clearly, it's not," I say as coldly as possible because fuck me, this chick just ruined everything.

Everything.

Jade shoves at my shoulders, trying to get me off of her and I refuse while the girl is still standing there, looking smug as shit. Like maybe she did it on purpose? She'd been trying to get me to talk to her all night and I'm not interested. You'd think she'd realize this, especially with Jade beneath me on my fucking bed but whatever.

"Sorry, I'll leave you two fuck birds alone." She waggles her fingers at us and starts to shut the door. "Toodles."

"Get off me," Jade murmurs the moment the door closes and I roll over so I'm lying by her side, staring up at the ceiling as I try to calm my breathing. "Did she really call us fuck birds?"

"You should be more irritated by her use of the word toodles." I grimace. "Because that sucked."

With a sigh she turns to look at me and I do the same, staring at her pretty face. She's so close I can practically count her freckles and I mentally start doing just that. "You should take me home."

I flub up at the fifteenth freckle across the bridge of her nose when I hear her request. "You really want me to?" *Please say no. Please say no.*

She nods, her thick hair rustling against my pillowcase. "It's late. I have class tomorrow."

"I thought you didn't want me to stop." I reach out and touch her hair, testing the silky strands between my fingers.

Her cheeks flush and her gaze skitters away from mine. "I think Miss Looking for the Bathroom just ruined the moment."

"We could pick up where we left off if you want." I need to respect her wishes because right now, I sound desperate. What the hell is wrong with me? I never do this. I should just attack her again. She can't resist me. I heard the little sounds she made, the way she moved against me. She was into it. I can get her right back into it with a few choice words and determined kisses.

"I don't think so." She winces. "Sorry. I really... should head back to my dorm. Sorry to make you drive me back. I bet I could get a ride or —"

"Hell no," I say vehemently, rolling over so I'm sitting on the edge of the mattress, my back to her. Damn that stupid chick for interrupting what was building up to an amazing moment. "I'll take you back. I don't mind."

I stare at the wall, willing my erection to calm down. I can tell she's standing, can hear her fixing her clothes, buttoning up her shirt, smoothing out her hair, whatever. When I finally turn back around she's standing in the middle of my room, looking a little lost, a lot embarrassed.

Without thought I go to her, pull her into my arms and drop a soft kiss on her upturned lips. "This is going to happen again, you know."

"Who says?" One delicate brow rises and I'm relieved at seeing that tiny glimpse of the Jade I'm used to return.

"Me." I kiss her again, my lips lingering on hers. Damn, they're soft. And plump and delicious and *fuck me*, I need to get a grip before I lose all control. "I say. So tell me. Are you game?"

A shuddering sigh escapes her, her breath wafting across my lips. "Okay," she whispers shakily.

chapter
Twelve

Jade

That girl's interruption broke me from the Shep spell he'd been weaving. And what a spell he can weave. Holy crap, he knows how to kiss. His lips, his tongue…there are no words. My mouth is still tingling.

He's sort of bossy. I liked how he shoved me against the door. I loved it when he picked me up and carried me over to his bed. I'm no petite little girl and he hauled me around like I weighed nothing.

Which means he's super strong. I felt his biceps. They were the stuff of dreams. *He's* the stuff of dreams.

But see, that's the thing. Dreams are just…dreams. They're not real. So what Shep and I are experiencing? It's not real, not at all.

That's what I keep telling myself so I don't end up hurt when he dumps me out of nowhere.

We're on our way back to my dorm hall in his precious car, neither of us saying a word. It's so quiet I can hear him breathing. How he shifts in his seat like he's restless. I swear I can hear him freaking blink and it's making me slowly insane.

"That was probably a mistake," I blurt out, clamping my lips shut the moment the words are out. I bang the back of my head against the seat, pissed that I said it.

Because I don't mean it and I'm just proving to him yet again that I really am a Bitch Face. Or an immature idiot, take your pick.

He chuckles, the rich, warm sound slowly unfurling in my belly and making me tremble. "Liar," he murmurs.

Now I'm sort of pissed at him for calling me out. "I mean it. We should've never…kissed."

He glances at me, dark eyes flashing, his perfectly kissable lips curved into a perfectly adorable smile. "I'm calling bullshit, babe. Sorry."

"What do you mean, you're calling bullshit?" He called me babe. What an asshole.

Fine. I liked that he called me babe. A lot. Not that I'd ever, *ever* tell him.

"We definitely should've kissed. Because it was fucking amazing before we were so rudely interrupted by Miss Bogus I'm Looking for the Bathroom, Whoops

My Bad, Toodles."

I start to laugh. I can't help it. His frustration is so palpable. He hated how that girl interrupted us. I hated it too. I'd had freaking Shepard Prescott on top of me on his *bed*. He'd been this close to taking off my shirt. And I was going to let him. I desperately wanted to feel his hands on my bare skin. I *still* want to feel his hands on me.

The interruption helped me realize that what I'm doing with Shep is bad for me. As in, he's going to leave me in a bad state. More like wreck me. He's not the lasting kind. More like the fuck 'em and leave 'em type. I know this. My logical, very smart, very cautious brain knows this.

But my body lights up like a burst of flame every time he so much as looks at me with those sexy, full of mystery eyes. He touches me and I melt. And when he kisses me? Oh good lord, all of my very logical, very smart brain cells evaporate into thin air and I'm left wanting more. More, more, more.

"Why are you laughing?" He sounds cranky, which makes me laugh even harder. "It wasn't funny. We were making progress, Jade. Before she had to ruin it."

"You call what we were doing progress?" I call it delicious.

Wait. I so didn't think that.

"Fuck yes, I call it progress." He slows at a stoplight,

turning to look at me. His hair is an absolute mess, sticking up everywhere. I really love his hair. And I'm the one who made that mess because I kept tugging on it while he kissed me. "Stop trying to act like you hate me. I know you don't."

"How do you know?" I ask warily, crossing my arms in front of my chest.

"You wouldn't have agreed so readily earlier if you hated me."

I don't want you to stop.

The words I said to him ring in my brain. At that very moment, the last thing I wanted was for him to stop. And that makes me feel a little crazy. A lot on edge.

God, he frustrates me. He makes me nuts. He's so… arrogant. So sure of himself and full of bravado. Plus, it's not right for a guy to look so deliciously hot. More like it's unfair.

And why is he interested in me? I don't get it. Because he supposedly won me in a bet? Does he think I'm easy? I'm so not. I'm difficult. Extremely difficult. I think I'm sexually broken and I have no idea why.

None.

"You don't hate me." He settles his hand on my knee and his touch warms my skin, even through the denim of my jeans. "Just admit it, Jade."

The light turns green and he removes his hand from my leg, turning left onto the street that leads to my dorm hall. My skin is still buzzing from his touch and I'm anxious to get out of this car. Away from Shep so I can hole up in my room, crawl into bed and yank the covers over my head where I'll try my best to collect my thoughts. Go over what happened tonight and analyze everything.

We're quiet again as he pulls up in front of my dorm hall and cuts the engine. I undo my seat belt, about to reach down to grab my backpack when he grabs me first, yanking me into him with so much force I have no choice but to scrabble across the center console and collapse on top of him. It's an exact replica of our position Sunday night and I stare down at him breathlessly, my brain flailing to come up with something to say when he slips his hand across the back of my head and pulls me down to his mouth.

And then he's kissing me. Again. His other hand is at my waist, sliding beneath my shirt and my cami to touch bare skin, burning me with his fingertips. His lips devour mine, his tongue playing a wicked game within my mouth, making me moan, making me shiver, making me wet.

God, he's awful. He doesn't play fair. How can I resist him when he's kissing me like this? Touching me like this? I grind my hips against his, I can feel his erection straining beneath his jeans and I suck in a harsh breath when his hand wanders up…up…until it's stopped by the elastic band of my shelf bra.

Stupid, stupid shelf bra.

"You still think it was a mistake?" he mutters against my mouth just before he takes my lower lip between his and sucks on it.

Holy wow, I really like it when he does that.

"Well?" he prompts when I say nothing. It's like I can't speak. He slips his hand out from beneath my cami and now he's touching my chest, his fingers delicately tracing the neckline of my camisole, skimming across the tops of my breasts and I'm trembling. God, his touch feels so incredibly good...

"Answer me, Jade." His voice is deeper. Firmer. Like he means business. "Do you still think this was a mistake?" His fingers drift lower, across my right nipple and I suck in a gasp.

"Y-yes. No. I don't know." His mouth stops the flow of my stupid words and I fall into the kiss, squishing myself against him so tight you couldn't slip a piece of paper between us. I'm full on making out with Shep Prescott in his car, right in front of my dorm hall and I couldn't give two shits about it. I've clearly lost my head.

Clearly.

Within minutes though he's shoving me away from him, frustration written all over his handsome face. I whimper in protest, trying to grab onto his shirt, his neck, his shoulders but he won't have it.

"I'm not fucking you in my car. No matter how badly I want to." He sets me away from him. Literally picks me up, and plops me back down in the passenger seat like it was no problem and I marvel yet again at how strong he is. He looks completely unhinged. His T-shirt is wrinkled, his lips are swollen and his eyes are so dark they look almost black.

I love it. Oh my God, I love how he's looking at me at this very moment. Like he wants to consume me. I feel the same. Exactly the same.

"Is it because you don't want to get your leather seats dirty?" I ask, remembering what Em and Em told me. I tentatively touch my lips with shaky fingers, marveling at how swollen, how tingly they still feel. Damn him and his magical lips. I wonder if Shep would let me just make out with him for hours. Kissing is the best thing ever. Eventually, it always just leads to sex and considering I'm no sexpert, I'd rather just make out. Feel each other up. Sex always complicates it.

Kissing is the only way to go.

He starts to chuckle and I decide right there he has the sexiest laugh on the planet. "Is that what you think?"

"I've heard rumors."

He raises his brows. "Rumors? About me not having sex in my car because I don't want to ruin the leather interior?"

"Um, yeah?" I feel stupid. Again. I blame the kissing. His lips are like weapons, zapping brain cells with a single touch.

"It has nothing to do with my leather seats." He leans over the console, dropping a kiss on the tip of my nose. "And everything to do with the fact that when I fuck you, it's not going to be in the backseat of a cramped car. I want you naked, in my bed. So I can kiss you. Everywhere."

"Oh." My voice is small but my thoughts…they are filled with all sorts of images. Of me lying beneath Shep in his room. On his bed. Only this time, we're naked. Oh my God…

He smiles and touches my cheek, his fingers drifting across my skin. "Now get out of my car, go inside and lock your door before I reconsider and throw you in the backseat."

Wait a minute. He'll throw me in the backseat and have his way with me if I don't leave soon? "Really?" I ask hopefully. It's weird, how I momentarily forget all about my sexual hang-ups with him.

Shep laughs again and shakes his head, giving me a gentle shove. "Go, Jade. Now."

I open the door and crawl out of his car on shaky legs, grabbing my backpack and slinging it over my shoulder as I slam the door. I stand there at the base of the steps that lead to the double doors of my dorm hall, staring at his beautiful car, at the beautiful man sitting behind the steering wheel. I'm so freaking confused. I should hate him. But I don't. Not really. Not when he kisses me like he does and talks to me like he does and is so…sweet.

The passenger side window rolls down and he leans forward, peering at me through the open window. "Stop looking at me like that."

"Like what?" I frown.

"Like you don't want to me to leave."

"But I do want you to leave," I say, the words sounding so incredibly lame I want to punch myself in the mouth.

"Yeah right. Keep fooling yourself." He starts the car and waves at me. "I'm not leaving until you go inside so…"

I turn on my heel and run up the steps, grabbing my key card and waving it in front of the keypad. The door springs open and I hurry inside, turning to watch as he pulls away from the curb. I stay there until his red taillights are swallowed up by the darkness before I start toward my room.

My phone dings just as I reach my door and I pull my phone out of my pocket to see it's a text from Shep.

You're in your room?

Aw, he's concerned about my safety. That's sweet.

Just got here.

Tell me when you're tucked into bed.

I smile. Where is he going with this?

Why so you can ask me what I'm wearing?

Of course. I need more masturbation material.

A groan escapes me. He's so…awful. And funny. And sexy.

You're gross.

Don't lie. You think it's hot.

I smile. Fine. He's right.

I'll call you tomorrow.

My smile fades. He's also extremely bossy.

Maybe I don't want you to.

Stop lying. You know you'll be on pins and needles tomorrow waiting for my call.

Ugh. He's so annoying. Worse?

He's right.

Shep

"You fucked her didn't you? Finally. Jesus. This whole thing was starting to get on my nerves."

I glare at Tristan as he shuffles into the kitchen, headed toward the coffeemaker. I'm on my third cup, hopped up on caffeine and memories of the taste of Jade's lips. I hardly slept last night, spent most of the time tossing and turning, thinking about her.

"What was getting on your nerves?" I don't bother

arguing over his assessment. He's wrong. I didn't fuck her. I'm dying to fuck her, but there really is something to be said for anticipation.

Who knew?

Not me, and the anticipation is slowly killing me inside. I jacked off again last night to thoughts of Jade. Her soft, plump lips. The sounds she made when I kissed her neck, when I touched her...fucking hell. She makes me insane.

"You walking around like a lovesick puppy. At least now you look satisfied. Like you got that girl out of your system once and for all." Tristan grabs a mug out of the cupboard above him and pours himself a cup of coffee, dumping a pile of sugar and a gob of vanilla creamer into the mug before he stirs it. "So how was she?"

"What do you mean?" I ask warily, knowing exactly what he means.

"In bed. Is she any good? Is she a natural redhead? Come on, I need deets."

I scowl at him. Fucker. I can't answer that question because I don't know. Though I'd bet big money on it that she is a natural redhead. "I'm not going to answer that question." And I used to, all the time. I had no problem telling Tristan and Gabe all about my hookups. We swapped stories. It's what we do.

Now, I can't imagine giving Tristan or Gabe any details about Jade and the way she tastes or the sounds she makes. And once I see her in her full, naked glory—because I will, you can count on that—I'm not going to tell them shit about that either.

She's like my little secret. And I'm not willing to share. She belongs to me.

Tristan makes a noise and approaches the counter I'm sitting at, standing across from me, clutching his coffee close. "Redheads usually aren't your thing."

"You've said that before." And he's right. There's always an exception to the rule though. Jade is my exception.

"Well, I'm saying it again. Though you two didn't seem to last long in your room. I'm guessing it really was a one and done? Please tell me you've moved on. Got her out of your system."

I clench my hands into fists. I'm pissed. I hate how he's talking about Jade. But what the fuck do I say? I'm in a no win situation. He'll mock me no matter what. "I haven't got her out of my system," I mutter, hanging my head, staring at my phone. Which isn't lit up. Meaning I'm staring at a black screen.

"What did you say?" Tristan doesn't wait for my answer. "Are you serious right now? Wait a minute… you *didn't* fuck her last night, did you? What the hell are you waiting for?"

"I'm not waiting for anything." I look up so I can glare at him only to find he's glaring at me too. "We were interrupted last night."

"And when has that ever stopped you before?" Tristan asks incredulously.

It hasn't. But I never actually respected another girl's opinion before either. "Jade didn't want to stick around. So I drove her back to her dorm," I admit, feeling like an idiot because I didn't close the deal, as Tristan so fondly likes to put it.

"She didn't want to stick around? More like she didn't want you to stick it in her. What the hell is wrong with this chick anyway? Is she a lesbian?"

"Aw, fuck you Tristan." I snatch my phone off the counter and slide off the stool I was sitting on, making my escape. But he's right behind me, carrying on like the dick he is.

"I'm serious, man. What's her prob? More like, what's *your* prob? Why are you pursuing this chick so hot and heavy when she's clearly not interested in you? If she's not a lesbian, then what's the deal? Is she a virgin?"

I stop in my tracks, dread filling me. Holy shit. What if she is? Yeah, she had that weenie boyfriend of hers, Noel or Joel or whatever the fuck, but that didn't mean shit.

She didn't kiss like a virgin. But how does a virgin kiss? There are a lot of virgins out there who are saving it for Jesus—I swear, that line has been used on me before—but they'll do everything else. And when I say everything else, I *mean* everything else.

"That's it, huh. She must be a virgin."

I turn to stare at Tristan, who's sipping on his coffee, looking like he doesn't have a care in the world. And he doesn't. He's a rich fuck who skates through life and uses women like they were Kleenex. Just like I used to be until I met Jade.

It's really hard for me to believe I've known Jade for only a few days. It feels like an eternity. And not in a bad way either.

"I don't think she's a virgin," I say slowly.

"Aha! And that's the problem." He points a finger at me. "You don't know if she's a virgin or not. Meaning you don't know anything. She's stringing you along and she's eventually going to give you a major case of blue balls for your trouble."

Sighing, I toss my head back and stare at the ceiling, struggling for patience. If he weren't my cousin, I would've kicked him out of the house a long time ago. Guy never knows when to shut up.

"I'm serious dude. Stop wasting your time on that ice queen. One and done, remember? Those are the rules," Tristan stresses.

"Who came up with these so called rules anyway, huh?" I look at him again, ignoring my buzzing phone, wanting to hear Tristan's answer. "Because they are seriously fucked up."

"*You're* the one who came up with them, asshole," Tristan reminds me just before he turns and stalks back toward the kitchen, muttering the entire way.

I run a hand through my hair, tamping down the frustration that's rolling through me. I'm so sick of everyone telling me what I'm supposed to do. It's been that way my entire life. My sisters bossed me around. My parents. Hell, now even my freaking cousin and my best friend are supposedly offering me advice about my sex life.

But what the hell do they know? What does anyone know? I have no idea what's happening between Jade and I, and I'm not going to stop pursuing her either. I want her. Badly. One shitty interruption by an obnoxious girl who yells *toodles* isn't going to stop me. I can be patient when I want.

With Jade, I'm willing to do just that. Be patient. Coax her into this. I know she's reluctant. I think...I scare her. Hell, she scares me too. I don't do this sort of thing. I'm not a believer in relationships. My parents cured me of that. They have one of the most fucked up relationships I've ever seen.

Then again, maybe I'm coming on too strong, though I've behaved like a freaking saint most of the time when I've been with her. I could've fucked her the night she was drunk but I was respectful enough not to.

I almost want to laugh. Me, respectful? That's all kinds of hilarious.

My phone starts buzzing in my hand again and I glance at the screen to see that it's my mother calling.

Hell. I don't want to talk to her. She's bound to give me an endless bunch of shit, like she usually does.

"Thank you for the birthday gift darling," she coos when I answer.

Great. I forgot to call her on the most important day of her life. I'm never going to hear the end of it. "Happy Birthday, Mom."

"Ah, thank you, Shepard. I do adore that candle. It will go perfectly in the house. And it smells absolutely divine."

I think of Jade. How she thought it was so boring that I bought my mother a white candle. "Glad you like it. Are you having a good day?"

"Well, your father isn't around, but that's par for the course so his absence hasn't disappointed me yet. Though he claims he'll be here tonight to take me to dinner." I wonder sometimes why they're still married. They hate each other. Reminds me yet again that marriage is a complete farce, forced upon us as the right thing to do.

"I'm guessing you're going out with your friends then?" I ask.

"Yes. A late, martini soaked lunch is on the agenda.

I can't wait." She laughs and I wince. I don't want to hear about Mother and her martini soaked birthday lunches. Bad enough I feel like a shit for forgetting to call her. Though thank God my father reminded me of her upcoming birthday a few days ago.

"Listen, I need to go to class." Lies. "But I hope you have a great day, Mom. You deserve it."

"Thank you, darling." She sighs, sounding wistful and just before I end the call she says, "Trust me, though. The older you get, the harder these birthdays are to face."

Huh. I guess that's why she wants to get drunk on too many martinis. When I celebrated my twenty-first, I got drunk because I finally was legally able to. Mom's getting drunk because she wants to forget she's getting old.

And this little realization is exactly why I have zero desire to get serious about…anything.

chapter Thirteen

Jade

You've been avoiding me.

I drop my phone after reading Shep's latest text and press my face against my pillow so I can groan into it. Can't he be like every other shitty guy out there on the planet and leave me alone? Guys have ignored me pretty much my entire life and I was used to it, thank you very much. The first gorgeous one who comes along has for some reason set his sights on me and now he won't leave me alone. I should be thrilled.

And I am, I swear. I'm also scared. He makes me so incredibly nervous it's stupid.

It's been three days since the kissing incident— or as Kelli likes to call it, the fuck birds moment. Yes, I told her about Miss Toodles and my roommate and tormentor found the entire story hilarious. I'm glad she can laugh at my pain.

Anyway.

Shep called me as promised the next day, but not until the late afternoon. Yes, he kept me on pins and needles, just like he predicted. He made me laugh. He flirted heavily. He asked what I was doing. I told him I was writing a huge paper that was due the next day. Eventually he ended the call but not before murmuring in that sexy, melt all my bones voice that he would call me again tomorrow.

And he did. I mean, what the hell? I don't get his fascination with me. I really, truly don't. I'm a bitch toward him most of the time and it's like I can't help it. I think he brings out the worst in me. He's been so sweet though. Calling me, making me laugh. Sending me silly texts. Asking me if we can get together again and I keep putting him off with lame excuses.

I don't want to tell him the truth. Not only does he scare the crap out of me because he so does, but there's also that pesky little monthly issue that I'm currently dealing with.

As in, Aunt Flo is making a visit. And she's a real nasty bitch sometimes.

It started with the small migraine headache the morning after the kissing incident (aka fuck birds moment). I knew when I woke up I was in trouble. By that afternoon I had major cramps. I really did have to write a huge paper that night so the excuse was legit. But since then?

Nope. It's been all about the period.

"Your misery is making me crazy." Kelli slams her laptop shut, startling me. I glance up from my pillow to find her glaring at me. We're usually in sync. It's that weird female hormonal thing that causes women who are together a lot to be on their periods at the same time, which is just…odd. But she finished last week and is all perky and happy while I'm drowning in my grouchy mood.

"Sorry," I mumble, not sorry at all. My phone dings again, reminding me of my text from Shep and I inhale deeply, wishing I could answer him. But what could I say?

Oh hey, Sheppers I wish we could hang out tonight but I'm surfing the crimson wave at the moment and there's no way you want to get near that so…toodles!

Yeah. That wouldn't go over so well. And I bet no one in his life has ever called him Sheppers.

"We're going out," Kelli announces as she stands, stretching her arms above her head and making her spine crack. I really hate it when she does that. "So put on some shoes and let's go."

"I don't want to go out." I sit up in bed and glance down at myself. Favorite faded pink T-shirt that has a hole in it, black leggings, no makeup on and my hair pulled back into a sloppy braid, I look like a train wreck.

"We're just going down to the field. The summer soccer league has started practicing there every Tuesday and Thursday night."

Hmm. Well, it is Thursday. And what's the big deal about soccer? Blech. "Why do we want to watch them?"

"The dudes on the summer soccer league team are hot. And they always take their shirts off halfway through practice." Kelli grins. "So throw on some flip flops or whatever and let's go. It'll take your mind off your womanly problem."

"Fine," I grumble as I grab my phone and stare at Shep's text yet again. Should I answer him?

"Just answer him," Kelli says like the total mind reader she is.

"What do I say?"

"What did he say?"

"He accused me of avoiding him."

"He's right. You are avoiding him, which is silly because even though he's a guy, of course, he knows about periods and all that stuff." She rolls her eyes and rests her hands on her hips.

"Yeah, he's a guy who doesn't know what the word commitment means so he's probably never been with a girl long enough to have to deal with her period." I ignore my phone and stand, slipping on my flip flops that are under my desk. I grab my small purse—the one I keep a couple of tampons in—and shove my phone inside, then sling it across my body. "I think I can get away with putting him off for the next few days."

"Playing hard to get does seem to work," Kelli points out.

"See? Then that's what I'm doing. I'm playing hard to get." This entire situation is ridiculous. I'm not a game player. I never have been.

"No, you're avoiding him because you have cramps. That's a whole different scenario," Kelli says. "You should take birth control pills. It would make your periods shorter and less crampy."

I shrug. There's been no point. I haven't had frequent enough sex to warrant birth control. Besides, what's wrong with making the guy wear a condom? "Let's just go," I mumble, feeling grumpy. I don't want to talk about birth control and sex. I could probably be having sex with Shep right now if I wasn't dealing with my current issue.

My entire body flushes hot just at the thought of being with Shep like that. Naked. Having sex…

"Come on." Kelli hooks her arm through mine. "Let's go ogle hot guys without their shirts on. It'll make you feel better."

"I don't know how," I say as she drags me out of our room.

"Don't you feel hornier when you're on your period? Seeing dudes without their shirts on is just the fix you need," Kelli informs me.

"God, you're gross," I say as I start to laugh. Though she has a point. I have been feeling a little…hotter lately. I just figured it was from my constant rehashing of the kissing incident with the hottest kisser on earth. Shepard Prescott.

If they handed out medals for kissing, he would most definitely win the top prize.

"You won't think I'm gross when you see those shirtless hunks out on the field. Trust me," Kelli says firmly.

I don't bother to protest. I figure she's probably right.

∽

I'm just sitting down on the bottom bench of the bleachers, sucking in a breath as my butt connects with the cool metal when I catch a flash of a certain someone running by. My body goes on instant high alert.

Freaking Shep. Shirtless Shep. Running like a madman out on the field while chasing a little black and white ball Shep.

I turn an accusatory eye on Kelli, who holds her hands up in mock innocence. "You knew he'd be here."

Kelli drops her hands and shrugs. "I was hoping for it."

"Damn it, Kell. I look like terrible." I glance down at myself. Ah crap, my leggings have a hole in them too. Right at the knee. I feel bloated and still a little crampy. My hair is falling out of the braid slowly but surely, and my pedicure is for shit. Chipped Kiss Me I'm Brazilian coats my toes. Sort of.

"You look fine. He won't notice you anyway. He's way too focused out on that field," Kelli says nonchalantly.

"Thanks for the uplifting speech," I mutter as she bumps her shoulder into mine.

"Please. You whine when you're afraid he'll see you, you whine when you think he won't." Kelli shakes her head. "Just watch him. It's fun. Trust me."

"You've done this before?" I'm almost afraid to turn my attention back to the field. What if watching Shep run around in shorts and no shirt for too long makes me do something stupid? Like…drool?

Hey. It could happen.

"By complete accident. I was out here last week and stopped to watch because, hello. Who wouldn't? While you were writhing around on the bed clutching your stomach earlier, I knew I needed to do something to help perk up your mood. I figured you might want a covert glimpse of your precious Shep, so now you're here. You're welcome."

"I didn't say thank you." Though I guess I should be thankful for a glimpse of shirtless Shep. I can't even look yet, I'm so afraid I'll be dazzled to death.

"Well, you should because the man is a sex god. Seeing him without a shirt on makes me want to weep with joy." She turns to stare out at the field, tipping her head to the side. "We need to figure out which one has the sexiest back. He's a strong contender."

"Sexiest back?" Slowly, carefully, I turn my head, my gaze snagging on him immediately.

Of course. It's like I'm automatically drawn to him no matter what.

"Mmm, hmm. Haven't you ever noticed how sexy a man's back is? All sleek and full of muscle and covered in smooth, smooth skin." She sighs dreamily, her gaze riveted on the field. "They're *all* contenders. Look at them."

I study them. Him. Damn it, just him. It's like my eyes refuse to look at any of the others scrambling out on that field. He's wearing black shorts that hang to his knees. That's it. Oh, and shoes of course. But they don't count because he's not wearing a shirt and just like Kelli said, all I can see is sleek, smooth, smooth skin. His shoulders. His chest. His abs. Good lord, his *abs*. Defined with ridges of muscle and covered in the faintest sheen of sweat, accentuating every dip and curve of his body.

He slows down some, resting his hands on his hips, lifting one bent arm to wipe the sweat off his brow, his hair a haphazard, damp mess.

I clamp my lips shut hard to prevent the drooling.

"Please tell me this isn't the first time you've seen him without a shirt on," Kelli says out of the side of her mouth.

"It's the first time," I admit, not bothering to look at her, afraid she'll mock me.

She sighs. "You two seriously blow my mind. Why haven't you done it yet? This goes against every *Shep is a man-whore* story I've ever heard. And I've heard a lot of stories about his man-whore status."

I hate hearing about his man-whore status. It depresses me. He has all of this experience and I have so little. Worse, what if I don't measure up? There's a distinct possibility that could happen. "I don't know what's going on with him. And I have no clue what he wants from me."

He starts to jog across the field, his head turning in my direction and I shrink into myself, dropping my head, hoping he doesn't notice me.

"Uh oh," Kelli murmurs and I know. I just *know* he spotted me.

It's like I can feel his gaze on me, hot and intense. Awareness prickles over my skin, making every tiny hair on my body stand on end and slowly, I lift my head to find him staring at me. His mouth curls into this half smile that's way too fucking cute and his eyes light up as he makes his way toward where I'm sitting. I smooth a hand over my hair, tuck a few wild strands behind my ears and pray to God he has a secret thing for girls who wear no makeup and holey clothes while out in public.

He stops just in front of us, his breathing accelerated, the now familiar scent of him surrounding me and I try my best to inhale as discreetly as possible because wow, he smells good. I can actually see sweat *glisten* on his belly and oh my God, I think my ovaries just exploded.

Or that could just be cramps.

I can't really tell.

Shep

I couldn't miss her if I tried. She's the last person I expect to see sitting on the sidelines while I'm at soccer practice—shit, I don't even think I'm going to stick around town this summer to play, though I did last year and had a blast—but there she is. You can't hide all that glorious, vivid red hair from me. I'd know that pretty head from a mile away.

Jade. Looking flustered with her hair falling out of a braid. I don't think she's wearing any makeup and her freckles really stand out against her creamy skin. Her lips are this peachy pink color that I'm dying to kiss.

I can't stop staring at her and I try to catch my breath, calm my racing heart, which had started out racing because of the exercise. But is now racing because the girl I want more than anything I've ever wanted before in my entire fucking life is sitting right in front of me.

"Hey." I take a deep breath, wipe at my forehead again with my arm. Fuck, I'm a mess. I bet I stink too. "What are you doing here?"

"I brought her." Her roommate sends me a serene smile and a wink, like we had this planned all along. Which we so didn't, but now I owe her one. "She's been grumpy lately."

Jade jabs her in the ribs with her elbow. "Shut up."

"She's been avoiding me," I say, deciding to just lay it all out. Fuck it. Any other girl who didn't reply to my texts, I would've said good riddance. Hell, I don't think I've ever texted another girl much unless it's to say the following:

> *Wanna hook up?*
> *Got any weed?*
> *Aren't you the girl I kissed in the men's bathroom last night?*

You know. Along those lines. This makes me sound like a shallow asshole and I'll agree wholeheartedly. I've been a shallow asshole most of my life. A product of my environment, I'd say. But there is always that defining moment when a man decides he wants to change his ways.

Meeting Jade, spending time with Jade…has become that defining moment for me. Wild but true.

"I've been…" She sinks her teeth into her lower lip and I want to groan. It's like she's so incredibly sexy and doesn't even realize it most of the time. "Busy."

That's the lamest excuse I've ever heard. I'm not going to give her any grief for it though. I'm walking a delicate line right now. I can feel it. "Totally understandable."

The roommate frowns at me, as does Jade. "Really?" she asks.

I nod, glancing over my shoulder to see what's going on out on the field. We called a break a few minutes ago and I should be chugging water so I don't collapse from dehydration when I get back out there but…I can't walk away from Jade. I'd rather suffer and pass out than miss this opportunity to talk to her. "What are you doing right now?" I ask when I return my gaze to her.

Jade's cheeks turn pink. Almost as pink as the shirt she's wearing, which happens to have a hole in it. A couple of them actually—one at the neckline and another that's just below her left boob. "Um…"

"Nothing," the roommate supplies for her. "She's absolutely free." That remark earns her another elbow jab.

"Kelli right?" I smile down at the roommate who beams back up at me like I just made her day. "I owe you. Big time."

"I'll collect too. Just saying." She breathes deep and stands, smiling at the both of us. "My work here is done."

"You're not leaving are you?" Jade asks, her voice low and vaguely threatening.

"You're going out with Shep after he's done, right?" Kelli asks.

"That's the plan," I confirm.

"I can't go out like this." Jade waves a hand at herself, the frown she's wearing so deep I swear she's going to give herself permanent wrinkles. "I look…"

"Beautiful," I finish for her, which only makes her cheeks turn pinker.

"You're so full of it," she mutters and I chuckle, moving so I can sit in the spot her roommate just vacated.

"Just telling the truth." I take hold of her hand, my arm pressed against hers and I'm ultra-aware of her scent, the way she feels next to me, her fingers curling around mine. "Hang out with me tonight, Jade. You've ditched me all week. I've missed you."

She turns her incredulous gaze upon me, those big hazel eyes eating me up, I swear. "You *missed* me?"

Nodding, I bring our connected hands up between us and drop a light kiss to her knuckles. "Yeah."

"You don't even know me," she whispers.

"I want to. Get to know you." I kiss her knuckles again. Her skin is so soft. I want to kiss more than her knuckles. Hell, I want to kiss her all over. "Come over. I'll ditch practice right now. We can leave together."

"But Kelli." She waves a hand at the spot where her roommate once stood.

"Is gone." I need to send her flowers or something as a thank you for bringing Jade to me. "Come on, Jade. Let's go."

"Don't you need to finish practice?"

"They'll survive without me." I stand and pull her up along with me, releasing her hand. There are a few stragglers sitting on the bleachers, most of them female and gawking shamelessly at the field. I'm guessing they're here for the shirtless show. Speaking of my shirt…"Let me grab my stuff and we'll go?"

"Okay." She nods, a bunch of strands of wild red hair falling around her face and I give in to the urge, reaching out so I can tuck all that silky soft hair first behind one ear, then the other. I skim her face with my fingertips, hear the shuddery breath she sucks in and I know I'm not the only one buried deep in this.

We're both feeling it. The chemistry that crackles between us, that's been there from the start, from that first moment our gazes met in the mirror. I touch her chin, smooth my thumb across her lower lip and her eyelids waver.

"Stay here," I murmur. "Don't leave this spot, okay?"

She nods silently, her gaze dropping from mine to stare at my...chest.

Right. Because I'm not wearing a shirt. And I'm all sweaty and I probably smell and whoa, is that interest flaring in her eyes because that's the first time I've ever seen Jade look at me like *that.*

"Five minutes," I tell her, leaning in so I can press a quick kiss to her surprised lips. Who knew lips could be surprised? And they would taste so damn good? "Give me five minutes."

"Okay," she whispers.

I walk away from her backwards, like I can't stop looking at her and truth be told, I can't. Her lips curl into this mysterious little smile and she shakes her head. "You're going to hurt yourself," she calls right as I fucking stumble.

I right myself, quickly glancing over my shoulder before I look at her once again. "It would be worth it."

Her cheeks go pink again and I swear to God, I'm going to make it my life's mission to make her blush as much as possible.

I turn and head back to the field, snatching my T-shirt from where I flung it on the ground, then grab my phone and car keys. We're so casual out here, I know none of these guys are going to take my shit. Gabe's standing nearby, polishing off a bottle of Gatorade and I approach him.

"I'm out," I tell him. He's never been part of the summer soccer league. He just comes out here to practice when he has nothing else to do. I think he likes feeling like he belongs to something. "Tell the rest of the guys, okay?"

Gabe frowns. "Where you going?"

I slip my shirt on and shove my phone in my pocket. "Home." The less I tell him the better. Tristan's not home tonight. It's his turn to manage the tables. I'll be working Saturday night. Gabe's on for tomorrow. We've decided to close on Sundays for the rest of the semester. Business is down and school's almost over.

This means I have Jade all to myself tonight. No interruptions, no nothing.

Gabe scans the bleachers, his gaze snagging on Jade, no doubt. "You found the redhead." He sends me a look. "Did she come here to tempt you or what?"

"She didn't know I'd be here." And I believe her. She'd looked too surprised, too mad at her roommate, for this to be a planned visit.

"Right. What a coincidence." Gabe rolls his eyes and I clench my hands into fists. "You're confusing me, bro. I don't understand what's going on here with you and the redhead."

"Her name is Jade," I bite out.

"Okay. Then I don't know what's going on with you and *Jade*." He shakes his head. "Are you actually trying to pursue a relationship with her?"

Am I? I don't know. "What does it matter?"

"I guess it doesn't matter. It's just weird to see you so twisted over a girl. A girl you don't even know," Gabe explains.

"Yeah well, that's the thing. I want to get to know her. And fuck all that one and done crap, and it's the rules and I'm breaking the rules or whatever. I don't care about any of that. I just..." The words die in my throat and I glance over my shoulder, my gaze going unerringly to Jade. She hasn't moved, just like I asked, and she's watching me. I feel her eyes on me and I smile, my stomach tumbling when she smiles back.

Fuck. I've got it bad.

"I just like her," I say to Gabe when I turn back to face him. "I can't explain why and I can't explain what exactly I'm doing, but I like her and I want to spend time with her."

"No one and done?" Gabe asks, sounding genuinely — confused? Sincere? Perplexed? All of the above?

I shake my head. "I think I'm sick of that shit."

"You think?"

"Yeah." I start to laugh. "I think. We'll see. I'm

testing this out. One day at a time."

"And that's all you can do, man." Gabe takes a step closer and slaps me on the back. "That's all you can do."

chapter
Fourteen

She's waiting for me when I return to the bleachers and she stands without a word, approaching me with hurried steps, her gaze filled with unspoken…urgency. An urgency I've never seen before, but I'm not about to question it.

Instead, I settle my hand at the small of her back and guide her away from the bleachers, the field, the campus. We're headed to the parking lot, toward my car and it's so fucking deep in, practically at the end of the row in the middle of the lot. It's like what you see on TV or movies, when the path stretches out for an eternity, and it seems endless, like you'll never be able to find what you're looking for.

That's what it feels like. We keep walking, the

silence between us stretches on and holy hell, I hope I don't screw this up.

As discreetly as possible I try and sniff my pits to make sure I don't smell and she catches me, sending me a small smile. "You don't stink."

I frown. "I don't?"

She slowly shakes her head, all those wayward strands of hair tickling her cheeks. Her hair is like fire. Vibrant and bright, wild and free—I sound like a fucking poet in my head. Jesus. "You smell...nice," she says.

"Nice?" My frown deepens and I scan the lot, spotting my car waaaay down there. I press my fingers into her waist, steering her toward the row where I'm parked.

"You smell good." She pauses and I glance at her, see that her cheeks are yep, rosy. "Like sunshine and the outdoors. Like...grass."

"As in weed?" I'm joking and she knows it.

"No. God, you're awful." She bumps her shoulder into my chest and it's the most casual thing in the world but it feels like a victory. They're so few and far between, those victorious little moments I earn when I melt Jade's resolve. Slowly but surely I'm tearing down her walls and she's actually letting me. I can't forget what happened Monday night. The kissing. Her hands all over me. Her hips subtly thrusting against mine as I rolled her beneath me.

"You don't really think I'm awful," I tell her, sending her a heated look. One that says, *I know the taste of your lips. The sounds you make when I kiss your soft, soft skin.*

She looks away, a faint smile still curling her mouth. "I think you're awful for parking your car so far away."

I laugh. "Couldn't be helped." I slip my arm more firmly around her waist and pull her in close, pressing my nose to her hair. It smells like wildflowers. "You don't mind going back to my place, do you," I murmur.

"No, as long as you don't mind that nothing's going to happen tonight."

"What do you mean?" I stop walking, as does she and we both stare at each other. Why is she throwing up a roadblock so soon? "Did I do something to uh, make you mad?"

She shakes her head. Doesn't say a word.

"I don't ever want to push you into doing something you — don't want." I need to be careful. I'm treading on unfamiliar ground. I've never really been with a girl who doesn't want to do, ahem, *anything* with me. And when I say anything, I mean sex. Or activities of a sexual nature. Since I prefer to spend time with girls who want the same thing I do, you know? A casual hookup. A quick blowjob. A few hours involving consensual sex with a hot girl who has zero expectations.

This is new to me, what I'm doing with Jade. She's a hot girl who most likely has expectations. A girl who doesn't want anything to do with me most of the time yet I've somehow worn her down. Who's now telling me that she wants to spend time with me tonight but nothing's going to happen.

I'm almost tempted to tell her, "I don't understand."

Because I sort of don't.

"I'm glad you said that," she's saying, knocking me from my thoughts. "I've heard stories, you know."

"What, that I push girls into doing something they don't want?" I shake my head, incredulous. Even a little mad. "That's so not the case. They're all willing."

"And you're saying I'm not?"

"No, *you're* saying you're not." I start walking toward my car again and she follows along beside me. She seems irrationally angry. "I'm trying to respect your wishes."

"I know. You're such a gentleman," she mutters, her mouth twisted into a grimace.

We're finally at my car when I turn to look at her. "Are you okay? Be honest."

She rests her hands on her hips. "Why do you ask?" The evil eye is strong in this one. She's giving me a look right now that could slay just about anyone dead. I'm standing my ground though. This isn't just about me. Something else is annoying her. She's acting awfully moody. Like maybe she's...

Realization dawns and everything clicks into place. I

have older sisters. Granted, it's been a while since we all lived under the same roof, but I should've recognized the signs.

I have a feeling it must be Jade's time of the month.

Not that I've ever dealt with that sort of thing with a girl I'm seeing. Living with the rage monsters known as my sisters was like surviving a war once a month because for some freakish reason, they'd be on the rag at the same damn time. When it first started I'd been too young to know what was going on and their moodiness had scared the shit out of me. And pissed me off. As I grew older though, I figured it out. Started to recognize the signs. It's usually best to ignore a woman when she's like this.

At least, that had been my past motto. But I'm interested in this girl. I need to be able to handle all of her moods. Is this some sort of test? Is God upstairs laughing at me, throwing me one obstacle after another in the hopes that I'd fail?

I'm not going to fail. Hell no. I know what I need to do. Sweet talk her. Treat her right. Maybe give her a massage. Definitely offer up some chocolate. That shit is like a cure all.

She's glaring at me, waiting for me to answer her no-win question and I offer her a smile. "No reason. Never mind." Best not to poke the dragon. I decide to change tactics. "Are you hungry?"

"I seriously need some caffeine." She tucks a few vivid strands of hair behind her ears, sinks her teeth into her lower lip. I withhold my groan that wants to escape because damn it, she's fucking sexy. Like at the most inopportune moments too. "I'm, um…I'm sorry I got all weird just then."

"Don't worry about it." I hit the button on my keyless remote and unlock the car. Yeah, I can tell this could be a long night or a freaking test. More like a little bit of both. If I can pass this, I'm in. And she's in. We're in this together. "Come on. Let's go get you caffeinated."

Jade

He's being so sweet he's melting all the resistance within me. I'd been chock full of resistance too, from the very start when he sauntered over looking good enough to — *lick.* Not wearing a shirt, all those muscles on blatant display, that smile he seemed to flash just for me. That smoldering look in his eyes that again, seemed just for…

Me.

I still don't get it. Somehow, with me looking terrible and bloated and acting like a PMS'ing crazy woman, he still wants to be around me. Took me to Starbucks and bought me a venti iced white chocolate mocha, nonfat, no whip, thank you very much. He presented it to me like a prize, an endearing little smile curling his perfect, sexy lips and I took it gratefully.

The ultimate though, is he brought me back to his place, searched through his freezer and found a giant tub of rocky road ice cream. He then proceeded to make me a bowl of it so now I'm stuffing my face with ice cream while sitting at the kitchen counter, sipping the last of my white chocolate mocha.

The combination of my favorite caffeinated drink and chocolate ice cream with those frozen little marshmallows inside it—yes, marshmallows are the best thing ever, I hope you realize this—I'm in heaven. Even cramps can't get me down.

Not that I'm having them anymore. Though if I don't watch it I'm going to give myself a stomachache. In fact, I'm sort of disgusting, eating ice cream and drinking Starbucks. I gaze down at the near empty bowl, irritated with myself.

"You need to stop licking that spoon." Shep's suddenly in front of me, his expression pained, his mouth thin.

I drop the spoon into the bowl, startled by his reappearance. He'd left the kitchen right after giving me the ice cream and I'm embarrassed to admit I sort of forgot about him, I'd been in such a chocolate/caffeine-induced haze. "Why?" I ask warily.

He leans across the counter, his dark, smoldering gaze never leaving mine. "I keep seeing your tongue."

Everything inside me goes warm and liquid. I grip the edge of the granite countertop, praying I don't slip off the barstool like an idiot. "You don't like seeing my tongue?" My voice is small, my chest light and full of something...unfamiliar. This flirtatious game we've been playing has been mostly one sided. I always feel like he's the one with the power.

But right now, at this very instant, I feel like I'm the powerful one—and I like it.

"I fucking love seeing your tongue. But considering the rules you laid out for us, it's nothing but a tease." He leans even further across the counter, his hands drawing closer, like he's desperate to touch me.

"What rules?" I lean away from him, needing the distance. He's pure temptation. The way he looks, how he smells. I think he changed clothes. In fact, he looks like he just came out of the shower. His hair is damp and he smells fresh and clean.

Fresh and clean and so freaking delicious it's taking everything within me not to just leap across the counter and grab him.

"You established right from the start that nothing's going to happen between the two of us tonight," he reminds me.

Oh. Right. Nothing can happen. I stare at his lips, study them really. They're perfectly formed. His lower lip is full and has the slightest dent in it. A dent I'd like to trace with my tongue...

Shit.

His upper lip is thinner but not by much, and at this very moment, his mouth is formed into this sexy pout that's not really a pout at all but I don't know how else to describe it. All I know is I like it. Memories fly at me, one after another. When he kissed me against the door. On his bed. In his car. His taste. The way he touched me, the things he said...

I'm regretting what I said to him. Rules were made to be broken, right?

Right?

"I'm having second thoughts," I murmur, my gaze still locked on his mouth.

He raises his brows. "About what?"

"About those rules I established. Though really... they can't be helped." I pause, feeling awkward. How do I broach the subject of my period? I'm thinking he must be a mind reader. Buying me coffee, giving me a giant bowl of chocolate ice cream, then staying away for a few minutes while I devoured it all...he must know. Or have a suspicion.

"I know what you're referring to. And...I get it." His voice is low, so incredibly deep that I can feel it vibrating within me.

Oh God, I really love his voice, and the fact that he's making this so easy on me. I feel like such a dork and I seriously don't get what he sees in me. What he wants from me.

But I'm running with this. I'm sick of fighting it. He's persistent and I'm giving in. As much as I can, due to the circumstances.

"You get it?" I ask. More like squeak.

He nods. "Yeah."

Hope lights a tiny flame deep within me. This guy blows my mind. He's nothing like what I thought he'd be. "Okay. So maybe we could just…make out instead."

His eyebrows go up even further. "Make out?"

I nod, liking the spark in his gaze. "You know, kiss. Where it leads to nothing else but…kissing. For hours." My favorite thing in the whole wide world, where there are no expectations beyond kissing.

"You want to kiss me for hours." He appears perplexed, which is a good look for him, no doubt, but still. He also seems surprised that I'd suggest such a thing.

"Sure." I'm starting to feel like maybe this wasn't a good suggestion. He's staring at me like I'm crazy. I'm starting to feel a little crazy and I blame him. He could have any girl he wants. Could be with any girl he chooses and she'd drop her panties for him so quickly his head would spin.

And then he'd get right down to business. He's a guy who doesn't waste time. Who knows exactly what to do when he has a willing female in front of him. But I'm not a willing female. I'm willing to take it only so far and that's probably a disappointment.

So the fact that pitiful little me is suggesting to him we make out for the night is really just...extremely lame. He's going to turn me down. He *should* turn me down, and go to a bar or a party and pick up on some hot drunk chick who'd do whatever he wanted.

That's the easy route. I'm the difficult route. The route not worth taking. I stiffen my shoulders, prepare for the blow that I know is coming and when I catch a glimpse of his perfect lips parting, I close my eyes and wait.

"If we're going to make out." He pauses and I crack open my eyes. "For *hours*." A shiver runs through me at the pointed look he sends me. "Then I need to do something first."

I frown, blinking up at him. "Like what?"

He rounds the kitchen counter so he's standing beside me, towering over me really. He's so tall. And broad. I want to climb him like a mountain. I *have* climbed him like a mountain and had a great time doing it too. "Stand up," he commands quietly.

Without protest I do as he says, surprised at myself. Usually I'd offer a flippant remark. Maybe tell him to go fuck himself. But I'm too curious to see what he wants from me. Too excited at the prospect that in mere minutes, I'll be in his arms, kissing him.

Shep steps closer and settles his hands at my waist. His head is bent, as if he's staring down the length of my body and I want to shrink into myself. Disappear. Do I meet his approval? Not that I need it but I want him to be attracted to me. I want him to find me attractive.

Or is he actually seeing me—the real me—for the first time and realizing that maybe he doesn't like me after all? With the old T-shirt and leggings, my chipped nail polish and ratty flip flops, I can't hardly blame him. I'm sure the girls he's normally drawn to are perfectly put together. Beautiful and smart and flawless.

I know deep down inside I'm none of those things.

My heart is racing and I exhale on a shuddery breath, my stomach clenching with nerves. What does he want from me? What will he say? Oh my God, what is he doing…?

He lifts me up as if I weigh nothing and settles me on the edge of the counter, kicking away the barstool I was sitting on only moments before. When he steps forward, I have no choice but to spread my legs so he's standing in between them. I keep my head bent though I can see him as he reaches out and grabs hold of the end of my braid.

And slowly pulls the band off, setting it on the counter.

"I don't know what I like most about you," he says

conversationally as he methodically begins to undo my braid. His fingers sift through my hair, gently tugging and pulling, and it feels so good that my eyelids waver. Unable to help myself, I lean into him. "Your hair, your freckles or that fucking mouth of yours."

I say nothing. The ability to speak has left me completely. The way he's touching me, the words he's saying...I'm undone. No other guy has ever had the ability to make me feel the way Shep does with only a few choice words and seemingly innocent touches.

No one.

My hair falls in heavy waves around my face, past my shoulders and then he's smoothing it out, untangling it with his fingers and I want to die from bliss. Nothing feels better than someone playing with my hair.

And when that someone is Shep? It's like pleasure overload. If I were a cat, I'd be purring and rubbing against him. Maybe even writhing around on my back, begging for more.

"I don't like it when you pull your hair back or put it up," he says, his voice this low, velvety whisper that washes over me, leaving goose bumps in its wake. "It shouldn't be restrained. I like seeing it wild."

He cups my cheeks with his hands and tilts my face up so I have no choice but to look at him. He studies me with those mysterious eyes, his expression serious, all traces of Shep the joker, Shep the charmer, gone. "I want to count your freckles."

I'm frowning again. Is he for real? "That'll take all day."

His smile is faint, just a curve of lips, nothing else. "That's the plan. You have so many. One in particular drives me crazy."

I suck in a deep breath when he leans in close and presses his lips to the farthest left corner of my mouth. "This one on your lip," he whispers, kissing me again at the same exact spot. His lips are so soft it's like I can barely feel them touching mine. "Right there."

Never in my life have I loved my freckles more. "I hated them when I was a kid."

"I love them," he says without hesitation. "And I love this mouth of yours too." Another kiss. Tentative. Sweet. He's saying the word love so casually and I don't know what to make of that. "For all the sarcastic things you say." He shifts, his mouth covering mine fully now, and his lips cling. "For the way you taste." He draws my lower lip between his and sucks gently, making me whimper. I think he already knows how much I like that. "I fucking dream about these lips, Jade."

"Y-you do?" I close my eyes when he kisses me deeper, his tongue darting against mine, retreating like a tease. Returning like a promise.

He pulls away from my mouth and I open my eyes to find him studying me, his gaze glittering. "Yeah." His voice is more whisper than words—deep and dark and pulling me in, pulling me closer. I settle my hands at his sides, gathering the fabric of his T-shirt between my fingers. I'm fearful that if I don't hold on, I might slip right off the counter. "More than once I've dreamed that you're...I shouldn't say it."

People who do that sort of thing make me insane. I grip his T-shirt harder, tighter. "Tell me."

He shakes his head, his thumbs streaking across my cheeks. "You'll get mad."

I can only imagine what he's about to say. "Shep..."

His smile fades. "You never say my name enough."

"Tell me what you dream about and I'll say it so much you'll want me to shut up."

He laughs. God, I love his laugh. "You have to promise you won't get mad."

"I won't get mad," I immediately say.

"Promise." He gives my face a gentle shake. "And say my name again."

"I promise. Shep," I whisper, tingles sweeping over my skin when he studies my mouth intently before returning his gaze to mine.

He exhales loudly and presses his lips together. "You're going to hate this."

"I probably won't." I'm sure I will, but I must know. I have to know what I do to him in his dreams.

"Oh, you probably will." Another exhale before he

tilts my head up as he leans his down. Our mouths are so close I can feel his warm breath waft across my face and I want more. It doesn't matter that he's about to say something incredibly offensive. More like it'll just turn me on, I'm sure. Maybe there's something to what Kelli said, about being hornier when you're on your period. I'm starting to firmly believe it. I'm on fire for Shep and I've never felt this way about a guy ever. "I've dreamed of you on your knees in front of me."

My lips part on the softest gasp at his words and I swear his eyes go even darker. "Go on," I whisper.

Shep doesn't even hesitate. "And you're giving me the most unforgettable blowjob of my life." He closes his eyes and swallows hard. "And I warn you to stop, that I'm going to come in your mouth but you don't stop."

I can see it. Oh God, I can actually see this happening and I have never been a fan of giving blowjobs. But with Shep…I think I'd get off on him getting off.

My cheeks warm at the mere thought.

"Wh-what happens next?" I clear my throat, my eyes fluttering closed when he touches his mouth to mine in the barest kiss.

"You keep going," he murmurs against my lips. "And I can't stop watching you. Your hair is…everywhere. And your face is flushed and those pretty eyes of yours are wide as you stare up at me." He releases his hold on my cheeks and nuzzles my face with his, his mouth at my ear when he whispers, "You lick the tip of my cock with your tongue, then wrap those fucking sexy lips around just the head and that's it. I'm coming. And you don't move, you don't pull away. You just take it, swallow every bit of me and then..." His words trail off and all I can hear is his accelerated breathing and mine. I want more. I need to hear what happens next.

"And then what?" My voice is hoarse and shaky. I'm trembling. He's so warm and solid and I cling to him, my hands falling to the waistband of his shorts, my fingers slipping just beneath to feel hard, hot skin.

"And then I wake up."

chapter
Fifteen

I should've never told Jade about the blowjob dream. One of the best dreams in recent memory, to be sure, but now she might think I'm not so subtly asking for one and I'm not.

Not yet, in any case. Though it'll happen, mark my words. It'll happen and I'll probably fucking blow my wad at first touch of those magical Jade lips on the tip of my dick after all the dreams and fantasies I've had about them, but it'll be worth it.

So fucking worth it.

She's trembling. I can feel her shaky fingers as they dip beneath the waistband of my shorts and just her hands touching me so innocently have me sucking in a deep breath as I mentally tell my dick to calm down.

I can't begin to express just how disappointed I am we can't take this any further tonight.

Wasn't I the one who said there's something to be said for anticipation? That night when I refused to kiss her because she was drunk? I was trying to be noble. Respectful. Two words no one would use to describe me.

I'm a total asshole for even uttering the word anticipation, for believing it's a good thing. Anticipation fucking sucks.

"Come here." I don't give her a chance to answer or do anything. I take over, grabbing her ass and hauling her into me, her body flush with mine. She tips her head back, our gazes meet and I stare at her, fascinated with her pretty face. I notice something different every time I look at her and this moment is no exception. "Your eyelashes are red, like your hair," I tell her, like she doesn't know.

She tears her gaze away from mine. "Usually I have mascara on to darken them."

"But you're not wearing any makeup." I touch the side of her face, the tip of her nose. Her skin is pale, the freckles like little flecks of cinnamon across her flesh and I drag my thumb across her plump bottom lip, liking how it catches right in the center.

"Half the reason why I was so mortified to run into you. No makeup. Sloppy hair," she admits. "I'm wearing my oldest, most favorite T-shirt and ratty leggings. I'm a mess."

"I noticed the holes." I touch the one at the neckline of her shirt, then decide the hell with it and touch the one that's just beneath her boob, my finger brushing against her ample chest. I am fucking dying to get a look at her tits naked. Does this make me an asshole? Probably, but I don't care. Not at the moment. "You're not a mess, Jade. I like you like this. You look...real."

"Opposed to me looking fake all the other times we've seen each other?"

Ah, there's my sarcastic girl. That smart mouth of hers is such a fucking turn on. There's gotta be something wrong with me, that I like it so much. "I didn't say that. Honestly? Seeing you like this makes my imagination run wild."

Her brows draw together. How did I never notice they're red too? Well, more like a deep auburn color. Very dark and perfectly arched. "How?"

I think I'm trying to seduce her with words. Not like I planned this but since we're not going to do anything tonight, I should at least talk about it, right? What I want to do to her. With her. What I want her to do to me. With me. How I want to see her naked and flushed and moaning my name all while I'm buried deep inside her. I want to know what she looks like when she comes.

Yeah. More than anything, that's what I'm dying to

see.

"I imagine this is what you'd look like in my bed after you spent the night." I push away the little tendrils of hair that curl around her cheeks. "No makeup, no pretense. Just you."

Her lips part and she blinks up at me. "Kiss me. Before you say something awful and ruin it," she whispers, her eyes falling shut when I lean in and do exactly as she asks. Her arms move so they're wrapped around my neck and I grip her ass harder, pulling her in as close as I can get. I take the kiss deep in an instant, thrusting my tongue against hers, swallowing the moan that escapes her.

Christ, she tastes good. Sweet and seductive. She scoots closer to me, her legs clamping tight along my hips and I keep one hand on her ass, with the other I reach up and touch her cheek, tilt her face to the side to deepen the kiss further. She whimpers and I draw her lower lip between mine and suck—I know she likes it when I do that.

"You make me crazy," I murmur against her mouth when I release her lip. "I'd fuck you right here on the kitchen counter if you'd let me."

"Oh God," she says on a gasp. "Say that again."

"Say what again?" I drop kisses along her jaw, down the length of her neck, moving her heavy hair behind her shoulder so I can kiss the spot behind her ear. "You're always accusing me of saying something to mess it up."

"Just…repeat what you said. What you want to do to me if I'd let you." She swallows hard, I feel the movement beneath my lips and I pause there, knowing exactly what she wants me to say.

Does this mean Jade likes dirty talk? Who fucking knew?

"I said, that if you'd let me." I press my mouth to the spot where her pulse thumps erratically, inhaling her heady scent, humming against her skin. This is like torture. Touching her. Kissing her. Talking to her, all while not able to do exactly what I want to her. "I'd fuck you right here on this kitchen counter."

"God, this is absolute torture," she whispers as I continue to kiss her neck. She's reading my mind. "I should…probably go."

Everything within me skids to a stop at her words. "Hell no," I practically growl, lifting my head so I can stare at her. "You're not leaving."

"We can't—" She whimpers when I nibble on her earlobe. "But we can't do anything."

"We're making out," I remind her as I pull away from her fragrant neck. "Tristan's gone tonight. He won't get home until late. So we have the entire house to ourselves." I wish I could fuck her on every available surface but since that's not happening, we'll have to make plans to do it another night.

That I'm thinking of future nights with Jade is freaking unbelievable.

"Your cousin is gone?" She sounds hopeful.

"Yeah." I brush my thumb back and forth across her ass, tracing the band of her panties beneath her leggings. Teasing is fun right? I might come close to giving myself a heart attack and a massive case of blue balls by the end of the night but I'll survive.

Barely.

"So it's just us." She trails her hand down the front of my T-shirt, her nails lightly grazing and my dick twitches. Well, it's been twitching for a while but I want her hands on my bare skin. This clothes on business is for the birds.

"Just us." I kiss her once, then slip both of my hands under her ass, indicating that I want to pick her up. She grabs hold of my shoulders, her shocked gaze meeting mine. "Come on." I heft her up into my arms and turn, heading toward the living room.

"How is it that you're able to carry me so easily?" she asks in wonder.

"You don't weigh that much."

She snorts. Actually snorts. It's kind of cute. "You don't need to lie to keep me here. I'm sort of trapped and at your mercy."

I like that at my mercy part. She should've never said those words. Now my imagination is going absolutely wild, thinking of all the things I could do to Jade while she's at my mercy.

More like I'm at her mercy, considering she's drawn the line in the sand for tonight. Look, look, touch, touch, but don't touch me *there,* kiss, kiss…that's it.

Fucking misery.

"I'm respecting your wishes." I sit on the edge of the couch with her straddling me and lean back slowly, enjoying the way she leans in with me. Her knees are on either side of my hips, her hands still on my shoulders, my cock nestled between her legs. An ideal position that's going nowhere. "We're just going to kiss. Nothing more."

"Right." She sounds hesitant. Almost… disappointed? "Nothing more."

I reach for her, settling my mouth on hers, kissing her before she has a chance to think, to say something else, to remind herself that maybe she doesn't want to be here after all. I trace the seam of her lips with my tongue and she opens easily, a moan sounding low in her throat when I circle her tongue with mine. I cup her nape, holding her still, not wanting to let her go and she starts doing this circling of the hips thing that I know is going to drive me absolutely crazy.

This entire night is driving me crazy. Jade makes me lose my fucking mind. Is it because she's so resistant yet…not? That she only lets me take it so far before she withdraws or we're interrupted? I don't know what to think. The theory behind wanting something you can't have plays heavily on my mind. I think that's my problem. I think once I finally have her, I'll be done. Able to walk away without a backward glance.

What scares me worse is that might not be the case at all. That I'll finally fuck her and only end up wanting more. Want her all the time. She makes me feel completely out of control with just a few kisses and innocent touches. What will happen when we finally get naked together?

Fuck I almost don't want to find out.

Jade

My thoughts are running rampant, coming up with all sorts of solutions to this—problem Shep and I are currently facing. I can't do anything with him tonight. Well, I suppose I could, but ew. I don't want to. My first time with Shep is not going to be when it's my time of the month. That's just too much, too soon.

But there are other things we could do. Things I could do *to* him…

That I'm even contemplating this shows just how wrapped up I am in him. Normally I wouldn't do this sort of thing. Offer this sort of thing. The other guys I've been intimate with always asked for it. Almost demanded it. I did as they asked, never fully comfortable with it. One even told me my skills were lacking and that totally put me off of blowjobs pretty much forever.

It's different with Shep though. I don't know why. I like how he touches me. The things he says, spoken in that sexy as hell voice. He says he wants to fuck me and it's like I melt. Just thinking about how he said it earlier, his mouth on mine now, his tongue working some sort of magic, his hand gripping the back of my neck, his other hand at my waist...I give in to my instincts and just let go.

Slowly I thrust my hips against his and I feel his erection straining beneath his basketball shorts, brushing against me, making my eyes practically roll back in my head. He's so...big. I can tell. And so incredibly hard. He groans when I move against him and power flitters through me, making my head spin. Without thought I reach down, drifting my fingers along his length in a feather light touch and he rips his mouth from mine, staring at me with hungry eyes.

"What are you doing?"

My insecurities come rushing back, one on top of the other and I jerk my hand away from him while answering, "Touching you?" Though I phrase it more like a question. The way he's looking at me makes me feel unsure.

His chest lifts and he exhales roughly. "We can't

do anything tonight. You already established that boundary."

I can appreciate his respecting my boundaries. He's more of a gentleman than I ever thought. "I won't let you do anything to me," I point out to him, shocked that I'm even about to say this. Here I go. "But I could do something for…you. *To* you."

He stares at me, his gaze dropping to my lips, lingering there for a moment as he starts to shake his head. "No way."

"Why not?" Now I'm offended. I reach for him again, about to wrap my fingers around him, shorts and all but he grabs hold of my wrist, stopping me.

"I don't want you to think you—have to do this." He drops his head against the back of the couch and closes his eyes. "I can't believe I'm doing this."

"Doing what?" I try to wrench my wrist out of his hold but he won't let go. Damn it, he's strong. I'd really like to see him naked. Everything within me goes molten at the mere thought and I squirm against him, his erection brushing against my sex and making me whimper.

"God, stop moving. Please." He drops my wrist and grips my hips, holding me still. So still that I swear I can feel his cock throbbing against me. That's so freaking hot. "I can't believe that I'm turning down your offer. I *never* turn down offers like the one you're making."

Ugh. And this only reminds me that he's a complete man-whore. "So why are you turning me down?"

"Because I can't return the favor. You won't let me tonight. I don't want you to think that you have to do this as some sort of obligation." He lifts his head so our gazes meet once more. "You confuse the hell out of me."

I frown. "You confuse me too. My feelings for you confuse me."

His lips quirk into this adorable little smile. Ugh, he's just too cute. And sexy. And hot. And huge. "You have feelings for me?"

Great. Last thing I should've ever admitted to him. "Not like that," I say as I start to swat his chest.

He grabs hold of my wrist again. His reflexes are impressively fast. "Then like what?" he asks quietly.

I can tell that this is A Moment. A time for me to be honest. It could go either way. Disastrous or momentous.

I'm hoping for momentous.

"I like spending time with you," I admit in a whisper. His eyebrows lift in surprise. "You make me laugh. You make me feel good. You make me…"

"I make you what?" he urges. He's whispering too and I realize that our position, how close we are, the way we're watching each other, it feels so intimate. Almost too intimate.

"Want things I shouldn't want." I reach up and touch his hair, smoothing it away from his forehead. He closes his eyes, his lips parting and I lean in, my mouth level with his, inhaling his soft exhale. "Like you."

And then I'm the one who's kissing him, our mouths fused, my hands busy. I slip them beneath his T-shirt, coming into first contact with his firm abdomen and holy smokes, he's hard there. I trace the ridges of muscle, feel his skin quiver and contract beneath my touch and I push his shirt up, wanting to feel more. Wanting to feel all of him.

"Jade." The word is gruff, as if he's trying to stop me but I feel like no one and nothing can stop me. I slide off of him, landing on my knees on the floor and he spreads his legs to accommodate my new position. "What are you doing?"

I almost want to laugh. He looks pained. The front of his shorts are tented with what appears to be a very aggressive, very large, erect penis and I seriously cannot wait to yank his shorts off so I can see this wonder in the flesh. "What does it look like I'm doing?"

"You don't have to—" He hisses out a breath when I slip my fingers beneath his shorts and touch the inside of his thigh. It's muscly and covered with soft hair— very masculine and big.

Everything about him so far is masculine and big.

"I don't have to what?" I push the leg of his shorts up and start to kiss the inside of his knee, his thigh. He smells delicious. All fresh and clean, like soap and just beneath, the scent that is unmistakably Shep.

"Do this." He chokes the words out, his head falling back against the couch again and I take my advantage. Rearing up on my knees, I reach for the waistband of his shorts and slowly start to peel it back, discovering that he's not wearing underwear beneath those shorts.

I come face to penis within a few shocking seconds.

"Wow," I whisper, since it's now turned into a whisper-worthy moment. I have never before in my life thought a penis beautiful. They're sort of funny looking. I'm definitely not into dick pics and no guy has ever sent me one, thank God. And most guys let their penises do all the thinking, which means they're idiots.

But Shep's is…long. Smooth. With a thick head and arcing toward his stomach in this incredibly appealing way. I lick my lips, anticipation filling my blood, making my body pound with need and I reach out, drawing my index finger down the length of him, making it twitch.

"Fuck me, Jade. You should stop." But he doesn't look like he wants me to stop. He's sprawled in front of me, his arms loose at his sides and not touching me, his head still leaning back on the couch. He's staring up at the ceiling and that sort of pisses me off because I want him to watch when I do this.

Right? I mean, I may get performance anxiety but I still want him to see. Guys like to watch. They're visual beings. Hello, porn.

"I don't want to stop." I wrap my fingers around the base of his erection and hold him like that for a few long, anticipation filled seconds. Carefully I stroke him, all the way up, curling around the head, before sliding all the way back down.

The groan that escapes him does something to me. Makes my heart race, my breath shallow. I do it again, pleased when he tilts his head down so he can finally watch and the look on his face, the glow in his eyes, fills me with pleasure.

"I'm not going to last long," he warns me. I glance up, our gazes meeting and I smile, leaning in close so I can drop a light kiss to the very tip of him. He moans and triumph fills me. "Do that again," he demands hoarsely.

So I do. I rain kisses all over the tip of his erection, my tongue darting out to trace the flared head. He tastes clean and the slightest bit musky, velvety soft skin covering steel. Shep is cursing up a storm, like he can't help himself and his words only encourage me to keep going.

I tug his shorts down, past his knees, until they fall at his feet and he kicks them off, spreading his legs further, allowing me in. I scoot closer, resting my left hand on his thigh, wrapping my lips around the head of his erection. He thrusts his hand into my hair, cradling the side of my face and I glance up at him, his cock still in my mouth, my body flushed and hot over what I'm doing.

This is…so unlike me. I can hardly wrap my thoughts around it.

"That. Right there. The fucking stuff of my dreams." His voice is strained and rough, his features pulled almost into a grimace. He's studying me intently, his fingers gripping my hair, his thigh tense beneath my palm. "Holy. Shit."

I take it that he likes what I'm doing.

The weird thing is? I'm liking it too. I'm deriving pleasure from giving him pleasure and it's a heady feeling. I grip the base of his erection firmly and suck him as deep as I can go, withdrawing almost all the way before I draw him back in again. His hand hasn't left the side of my face and he's holding my hair away like he doesn't want to miss a thing. The farther I take this though, the more inept I'm starting to feel and I hope I don't screw it up.

Please, please, please don't let me mess this up.

I withdraw him from my mouth and continue to stroke him, going on instinct as I lean in and trace the veins with my tongue. A choked sound comes from him and I glance up to find his gaze glued to me, his lips parted, his chest rising and falling in time with his accelerated breaths.

"I'm close," he whispers. "I'm warning you."

"Tell me what you want me to do." Oh, I'm really

feeling bold now, asking for directions. But I want this to be good for him. I want him to never forget the night I gave him a blowjob. Really? I'd like to obliterate all of those other girls who've done exactly this from his mind. So all he can remember, all he can fantasize about is me.

Me.

His eyes flare with heat at my words and he readjusts his position, sitting up straighter. "Grip me tighter."

I do as he asks, liking how he doesn't hesitate. How can I know what he wants if I don't ask for it? Not that I'd ever had the courage to ask any other guy what he wanted before but there's something about Shep that makes me feel different. In a good way.

In an I-will-own-my-sexuality-and-make-it-mine way.

"Suck just the head of my cock into your mouth. Ah, fuck. Yeah, just like that." I follow his request, sucking him so hard my cheeks hollow out and from his panting breaths, I can tell he really likes that. I begin to stroke him, increasing my pace, encouraged by the dirty words that fall from his lips. Who knew Shep could be such a dirty talker? I should've known, but it still comes as a surprise.

A very pleasant one.

My body is tense, my nipples tight beneath my bra. I'm almost painfully aroused and I wish like crazy I didn't have this period problem happening. Though he was the one who praised anticipation that night when I was drunk and I thought he was crazy then.

Maybe he was right after all.

"Jade." His voice is a warning, dark and low. I glance up, sucking him deeper, loving the way he's watching me like he's just about to attack. "I'm gonna come."

I don't stop. I keep going, *wanting* him to come. I want to see this. To—taste this. I've never been in the situation before where the guy is actually going to come in my mouth so I'm curious. Really curious.

And perfectly willing to let Shep be the one to come in my mouth for the first time.

He says my name again, deeper this time, his eyes sliding closed, his mouth falling open, the cords in his neck straining beneath his skin. I stare in fascination, my lips tightening around him just as I feel the first eruption of his semen on my tongue.

"Fuck," he groans as he lifts his hips, his length going deeper inside my mouth. I don't move, I just take it like he described in his dream, swallowing him down, shocked that I would even do this. That I'm actually… enjoying it.

But holy hell, it's super-hot watching him lose all control, feeling him come inside my mouth, knowing that I'm the one who did that to him. For him. His entire body is tense, his expression one of agonized pleasure as he lifts his hips one last time. I finally pull away from him, letting go of his still very hard erection and I wipe at the corner of my mouth, draw my thumb and index finger along my lower lip, making sure I'm not a mess.

"Damn." I glance up to catch Shep rest both hands over his face, his chest still moving rapidly, his mouth pursed as he blows out a harsh breath. He runs his hands up, over his eyes, into his hair and then he's watching me, his face like a mask, his eyes full of…something I can't quite figure out. "I should take you home."

I nearly fall backwards at his words. Take me home? It's not even that late. We have the entire night together since Tristan is gone. Why would he want to take me home?

I meet his gaze again, see the unfamiliar light in his eyes and realization dawns on me.

I think what I'm seeing might be regret, mixed with a major dose of guilt.

Great.

chapter

Sixteen

Jade

"I hate Shepard Prescott."

Kelli rolls her eyes, sending me a look that says *here we go again.* "We're back to that? Really?"

"Kelli." I grab hold of her arm and glance around, making sure no one can hear us before I whisper, "I had his *dick* in my *mouth.* And the minute it was over, he took me home. Never to be heard from again." It stings just saying it. Why do I keep reliving it? It's like pure torture yet I can't stop thinking about it. Thinking about him.

God, what a jerk. How could I be so stupid? The one time I actually want a dick in my mouth and I end up with a whole lot of dick all right. A dick who got off and then ran like a dog with his tail tucked between his legs.

"Maybe he got busy." She shrugs, trying to look positive. When I continue to glare at her, she gives up the pretense, her shoulders slumping. "Fine. He's an asshole. Just like you always said. You had good reason to throw up all those walls. The minute he got what he wanted, he bailed."

Ouch. Hearing my predicament spelled out so simply is painful. But Kelli's right. Shep is a total dick. He got what he wanted and left me without a backward glance.

It's been a week since I last saw Shep—an entire week. No calls, no texts, no nothing. Not even a glimpse of him on campus. It's late April, final exams are coming, I'm working on a final project for my communications class that's keeping me extra busy and we're down to the wire. School will be over in May. I'll head home pretty soon after that and won't return until classes resume in August.

Meaning I most likely won't see Shep again, if ever, which should thrill me right? The asshole ditched me. Just like that. As if I don't matter.

But it hurts, damn it. I'm confused. Was I that awful? Did I do it wrong? I followed his exact instructions and he seemed to enjoy himself. I mean, my God, I made him come in freaking minutes. I let him come in my mouth and I *never* do that. I really got into it, but he left me in the dust. Like I don't even exist.

If I wasn't so pissed off, I might've cried over this.

We're at the cafeteria, eating salads for lunch while I lament over my Shep problem. Again. It's all I've talked about since it happened. The BJ Experience. Why I name all of my moments with Shep, I don't know but it sort of makes it fun.

Again, it's either laugh or cry over this mess. Take your pick.

"I hate him," I tell Kelli. "Seriously. If he were to come up to me at this very moment I'd probably knee him in the balls and tell him to go to hell."

Kelli's nods sympathetically, her gaze lifting to a spot above my head. Her eyes widen and I see her visibly swallow. "Uh oh," she murmurs.

Panic sweeps up my chest, settles in my throat. Oh my God, what if it's Shep? Yes, I want to knee him in the balls but I also want to…throw my arms around him and ask him where it all went wrong. Damn it that makes me want to punch myself in the face for even thinking that.

"What's wrong?" I ask her, ducking my head so my hair falls in front of my face, like I'm trying to hide.

"You'll never believe who's headed this way." I watch from beneath the veil of my hair as she sits up straighter, her smile bright. "Dane! Hi."

Oh no. I can only assume who's with Kelli's

boyfriend. My *ex*-boyfriend.

Joel.

I lift my head to find Dane and Joel standing by our table, Dane bending down so he can drop a kiss on Kelli's upturned lips. Joel watches me, his hands shoved into the pockets of his jeans, his expression hopeful. "Hey Jade," he murmurs.

"Hi." I try and give him a smile but it feels more like a twist of my lips so I let it fall. "How are you?"

"I'm good. Glad the semester's almost over." He rocks back on his heels, a habit he has when he's nervous. So I make him nervous. Great. "I uh, I'm glad you're here."

"Oh?" My voice goes high and I clear my throat, irritated with myself.

"Yeah. I wanted to apologize for how everything went down between us. It uh, didn't end well and I'm sorry."

Oh. Well, I didn't expect that. Though I wasn't very nice to him either. "It's okay." I shake my head, offer him a genuine smile this time. "We all just got—caught up in the moment I guess."

"Yeah, that's one way to describe it." He blows out an irritated breath. "I was an asshole for letting Prescott bet on you though. Guy thinks he can do anything he wants and I let him."

Just hearing his name makes me yearn for him. So

freaking stupid. "He can be pretty persuasive. And really, he's the asshole for coming up with the bet in the first place."

"I guess. What really makes me mad is that I thought I was going to win. I figured it was a sure thing, what with the hand I had." Joel shakes his head, his face etched with regret. It's really kind of sweet of him, that he's still so upset over what happened. Granted it was over two weeks ago and I'm the whore bag who forgot all about him in my hot pursuit of Shep, but I'm letting bygones be bygones.

I wave a hand, dismissing his words. "Let's not rehash it, okay? What's done is done."

Joel glances toward Kelli and Dane, who are cuddled up together in their own little world. He indicates the empty chair beside me. "Can I sit?"

"Of course." I watch as he settles his lanky body into the chair. He looks good. He's cute, I always thought he was with his close cropped brown hair and his blue eyes. He's tall—though Shep is taller—and leanly muscled. Guess he used to be on the swim team at his high school. He still looks like a boy though, while Shep is all man.

Ugh. I really, seriously need to stop comparing Joel to Shep.

"It's just that...I can't stop thinking about you, Jade," Joel says the moment he pulls his chair close to mine. "I feel bad for how it ended between us. I hate that it ended." He pauses, his gaze meeting mine, his expression deadly serious. "I miss you."

I can't even believe he's saying this. I don't know how to answer him either. Have I missed Joel? Not really. I've been too preoccupied by Shep. But if I'm being honest with myself, Joel is more my speed. He's the type of guy I *should* be with. Shep is too much, while Joel is just right.

"I feel bad for how it ended too." Now that's the truth. I'd been a total bitch to him after it all went down, not giving him a chance to explain but I was so angry over the entire situation. Angry at Shep especially.

Now I'm even angrier with him and I have good reason to be.

"Listen." Joel scoots his chair closer to mine, resting his arm on the edge of the table so he can lean into me. "There's a party tomorrow night. I want you to go with me."

I stiffen in my chair, my gaze automatically going to Kelli. Like she can feel me looking at her, she nods her encouragement when her gaze meets mine, and I know Dane has already told her Joel's plan.

"What kind of party?" I ask carefully, praying he doesn't say the gambling house or whatever the hell it's called. The illegal casino Shep and his cousin and friend run out of that house. That's the last place I want to go.

"It's at a frat. One of our friends invited us. Dane and

Kelli will be there. I figured we could all go together." He smiles that cute little boy grin of his I used to find so appealing. I still sort of do. "Come on, J. Say you'll go with me."

I don't want to give him the wrong idea. But why should I sit home miserable on a Friday night when Shep's already forgotten about me? If he can push me right out of his life, I can do the same. "I'll go with you," I say, smiling when Joel hugs me. I pat him on the back, my gaze meeting Kelli's once more. She offers me a thumbs up and I roll my eyes, noticing the way Dane's watching me, like he's just waiting for me to screw over his best friend again.

I don't plan on screwing anyone over. That hurts too much.

Pressing my hand against Joel's chest, I create some distance between us, and his arms fall away from me. "We're going as just friends, okay?"

"Sure." His smile doesn't fade. I don't know if he believes me. "I get it."

"I'm glad." I pat his shoulder. I need to quit patting him. I'm acting like a mom or something. "I'm glad we can be friends again." I mean it too.

"So am I." His smile fades. "But you need to know I still...want more. I want what we had before Jade. Like I said, I've missed you. A lot."

Oh, crap. My smile freezes on my face and I laugh

uneasily. I don't know what to say to him.

So I don't say anything at all.

"I didn't want to tell you this," Kelli says conversationally as she curls her hair, her gaze meeting mine in the mirror. "But the party we're going to tonight? Is at Shep's frat."

We're crowded around my makeshift vanity in our room, fighting for the mirror as we get ready for the stupid, *stupid* party. I drop the mascara wand that I'd just been using, thankful I didn't stab myself in the eye. "You're serious."

She nods, her expression somber. "I bet he won't be there though. I hear he doesn't hang out at his fraternity house so much anymore."

"Last time we went to a party at the house, he was there." I turn to look at her, dread filling my stomach. That was the time he slipped his hand under my skirt. The pervert. The sexy as hell, rotten, horrible, most excellent kisser I've ever met, absolute *dickhead*. God, I loathe him. I love that word. Loathe. It describes my feelings for Shep perfectly. "I don't know if I should go now."

"Oh come on, you have to go. You don't want to disappoint Joel, do you?" She sets the curling iron down on the table. "Jade, you can't let Shep win. If he's going to be a dick, then you're going to turn into his worst nightmare come to life. I'm serious. Wouldn't it be awesome if you show up at that party looking smokin' hot and he sees you? He'll be salivating after you and you can tell him to go fuck himself. He'll regret everything and you'll get some satisfaction by telling him off."

Is it wrong that I sort of like this idea? Looking sexy as hell and watching Shep's eyes bug out of his head as I walk into the house on Joel's arm? Yeah, he'd look at Joel like he was nothing, but it wouldn't matter. I'd look at Shep like he was nothing.

Because he is. He's nothing to me.

Absolutely, positively nothing.

"You can wear that cute little denim skirt like you did last time or…oh! I know what you can wear." Kelli dashes off toward the closet and throws it open, digging around until she pulls out a tiny pair of denim cutoff shorts. "I just bought these. I want you to wear them."

Kelli's shorter than me. I could probably shove myself into those shorts but I'd be all legs. "Don't you think my butt cheeks will hang out of them?"

She shoves the shorts into my hands, a giant smile on her face. "Yes. Isn't that the point? You'll drive him out of his mind."

"Who? Joel?" More like give him the wrong message.

"No, not Joel." She rolls her eyes. "Shep."

I shake my head. "I can't wear these. I'll look like I'm trying too hard."

"You're wearing them. And you're going to look fucking amazing in them. I know it." She waves a hand at me. "Try them on."

"Seriously?" I hold them up, examining the frayed edges. Oh, these are short. My ass cheeks will definitely hang out the back of these shorts.

"Do it. Right now." Kelli snaps her fingers and with a sigh I shove off my cotton shorts, grab the cutoffs and slip them on.

They fit perfectly. Crap. I go to the full-length mirror that hangs on the wall and examine myself. My makeup is half on, my hair is in a sloppy bun on top of my head and I look like I have legs for miles.

Miles and miles and miles.

"Oh yeah." Kelli comes up just behind me, beaming. "You are definitely wearing those shorts."

"Were you going to wear them?" I ask weakly, turning to the side. Oh my God. "Because I don't want to take them from you. And my ass is practically hanging out. Look at me." What the hell am I doing? Trying to impress Shep who probably won't even be there? So I'll end up wasting all of this time and a perfectly good outfit for nothing. And I might end up setting Joel on fire too, the very last thing I want to do.

I like Joel, but I have no plans on dating him again.

Even though I consider him more my speed, it wouldn't be fair of me to pretend I'm interested in him when I… am interested in someone else.

"Fucking Shep Prescott." I turn to face Kelli, who's practically bouncing up and down and clapping her hands. I've changed my mind. I am so wearing this. Fuck him. "We need to find the skimpiest top in this closet. Whether it's mine or yours, I'm wearing it tonight."

"On it." Kelli salutes me before she starts skimming through the closet. "How about a tank top? That's sexy without trying too hard."

"Perfect." I reach up and take the band from my hair, shaking it out so it tumbles past my shoulders, almost to the middle of my back. He likes it best when my hair is down. He likes to see my freckles too so I won't wear any foundation or powder tonight. I'll play up my eyes instead. Wear a pretty pink lipstick that makes my lips look big. Give him exactly what he wants.

And then walk away from him without a second glance.

chapter
Seventeen

Shep

"I can't believe you convinced me to come to this fucking party," I mutter as I glance around the room, watching everyone with disdain. Yeah, I'm acting the prick. Reveling in it really because fuck me, I'm frustrated. Frustrated with everyone, but especially myself.

"You've been such a dick, I figured a night of drinking would do you some good." Tristan points at the red cup I'm holding. "So bottoms up dude."

I chug the weak beer, wishing for something stronger. Harder. Preferably vodka. Tristan's right. I've been a total dick. I need to get wasted. Drown my problems with booze and hope to hell I'll black out by the end of the night.

Anything to help me forget Jade.

"You need to find a girl too," Tristan says, scanning the room, whistling low. "We definitely have our pick tonight."

I don't bother looking. Instead, I stare at the bottom of my cup, which is now disappointingly empty. "No chicks," I mutter.

"What?" I glance up to find Tristan staring at me like I've lost my damn mind. "Are you serious? You definitely need a chick. Fuck the pain away. Isn't there a song called that?"

I have no idea what he's talking about. "Women are trouble. Every single one of them," I mutter, thinking of one in particular. Though she did no wrong. She was fucking perfect. Sucking my dick like she practically got off on it and instead of showing my eternal gratitude — what I should've done, I'd been dreaming of those fucking perfect cock sucking lips from the moment I first met her — I pushed her away. Took her home, dropped her off without even a kiss to remember me by and never called her again.

The truth? She scared me. My reaction to her scared me. Instead of being a man and talking to her like a responsible adult, I ran like a little kid. Not that she called me or texted me in return. Knowing Jade, she's most likely furious at me.

Not that I can blame her.

She's all I can think about. All I want. I screwed this up royally and I don't know how to make it right. But I freaked out. Freaked out so bad when all those overwhelming emotions came rushing at me...

Regret washes over me now, and I blow out a harsh breath, tell myself to get a grip. I'll get over her. I will. I swear I will.

"You're still twisted up over her, aren't you?" Tristan shakes his head, his eyes full of...is that concern? Get outta here. "What the hell did she do to you anyway?"

Everything. She blew my mind. Rocked my world. Made me smile. Made me laugh. Made me want something I never considered possible.

A chance with a girl. A chance at a committed relationship, something that usually scared the hell out of me, and with good reason. Look at my parents—worst example of a supposed solid, loving relationship ever. They can barely tolerate each other. I don't want that. I'd rather be alone.

Or so I thought. A few weeks with Jade and I want... more. Too much. I can't do it. Can't face it. Face her. So instead...

I pretended she didn't exist like I'm some sort of callous, heartless asshole. Guess I'm just following in the steps of my dear old dad.

Inhaling deep, I clench my jaw, my fingers squeezing the cup so hard it crumples under my grip. I freaking hate myself for falling into the same old patterns. For not being man enough to face my fears and go for it.

Instead I'm alone as usual, at a stupid frat party and drowning my sorrows in cheap ass beer while hanging out with my stupid cousin who's as much of a commitment-phobe as I am.

Life sucks.

"I don't want to talk about her," I finally say, offering Tristan a grim smile. "Is there anything harder in this house? I'll need to drink an entire keg to get a buzz."

Tristan laughs. "Yeah, man. I know where the secret stash is. You want something in particular?"

Would asking for an entire bottle of vodka seem too greedy? "Vodka. As much as you can find me," I tell him instead.

"Got it. Give me a couple minutes." Tristan tilts his head toward the crowd. "Why don't you go mingle? It might do you some good."

Mingling sounds like the stupidest idea ever. "I'll hold up this wall, thanks."

Tristan shakes his head, muttering something about dudes with no balls as he walks away.

Whatever. I can't take offense. I *am* acting like a dude with no balls. All over a girl. Since when do I let a girl have so much power over me?

You've never met a girl like Jade before.

Isn't that the truth?

I start to drink out of my crumpled cup when I remember it's empty and I leave it on a nearby table. Hopefully Tristan remembers to bring me a cup along with that bottle of vodka. If he even brings a bottle. If not, I'm bailing. Seek out a liquor store and buy my own bottle of vodka I can nurse for the rest of the night.

Shit. I sound like a hopeless drunk.

Girls approach, one after another and I remain stoic. Bored as they try to talk to me, seemingly desperate to engage me in conversation. But I'm not having it. I'm cranky. Not interested. I shut every one of them down, one after the other, until they stop approaching and I'm alone once more, holding up the wall, waiting for Tristan, jonesing for a drink.

That's when I think I spot her. It has to be her. I'd know that glorious fucking hair anywhere. I push away from the wall, my gaze locked on the spot across the room where I swear I saw her. Jade. The front room is packed full of people and the music is deafeningly loud. I start to push through the crowd, making my way toward the beacon that is her. I catch another glimpse of red hair, long and wavy, hanging down her back. Unbound, unrestrained, and my hands literally itch to touch it. Touch her.

It's as if the crowd parts, like I'm Moses or some such shit, and there she is. Standing near the entryway of the kitchen, a red cup in her hand, her sexy-as-fuck lips stretched into a giant smile as she laughs at something her roommate Kelli says.

Not that I notice Kelli or anyone else for that matter. All I can see, all I can focus on, is Jade.

I stare at her like a starving man who just caught his first glimpse of a meal after going so long without. She's wearing...good fucking lord I don't know where she found those shorts but all I see is legs. Lots and lots of legs. Pale and long and firm, the denim cutoff shorts she has on barely cover her.

They should be fucking illegal.

The black tank top reminds me of the first time I saw her. She wore a black tank that night too and I fucking approve. Her tits look amazing — unbelievable I still haven't seen them in their naked glory and that is one of the many serious regrets I have when it comes to Jade — and she pushes her hair off her shoulder, turning in my direction, her gaze meeting mine.

I stand up straighter, releasing a shuddering breath, trying my best to appear cool. Like I've got this. If I smile at her I'm afraid she'll throw a fucking dagger at my chest. Hell, I already feel like a thousand daggers are stabbing me right in my heart just seeing her again like this. She's so close yet so very, very far away.

She lifts her chin slightly, my ever defiant, ready for a fight Jade. Her eyes narrow the slightest bit — damn they look good, all dark and shadowy and sexy as fuck — and her lips curve downward for the briefest moment.

Then she's smiling as she turns away from me, hooking her arm through some guy's that's standing next to her and realization dawns slowly, making my head spin.

Holy shit. She came here tonight with another *guy*. I deserve this. Fuck me, I deserve this for shutting her so completely out but it's only been a week. Does she move that fast? Though how can I judge? I've moved that fast—faster—for years.

Working my jaw, I watch as she leans into the guy and he turns to smile down at her. I recognize him. The ex-boyfriend. The asshole who lost her in a bet. Noel or Joel or whatever the fuck his name is.

No way can Jade be serious about that guy.

"Hey." I turn to find Tristan standing in front of me, clutching what looks like a jug of vodka. Damn, he's good to me. It's like he knows exactly what I need. "It's cheap but better than foamy warm beer, right?" He hands me a cup with a couple of cubes of ice inside and I take it gratefully.

"Pour it." I hold the cup out and Tristan undoes the cap, then fills the cup almost to the very top. "Thanks man," I say before I swallow half of it and hold out the cup again.

"You're gonna get wasted fast on this," Tristan warns me and I ignore him, waving my cup at him.

Frowning, he refills it.

"That's the plan," I mutter as I take a couple of more swallows, slowly turning to see if Jade is still standing there.

She is. The guys are gone. She's with Kelli and the both of them are watching me, their lips curled like I'm a bug buzzing around their heads and they're dying to kill me. Squash me dead.

Feeling brave with vodka coursing through my veins, I start to approach them, ignoring Tristan as he calls my name, ignoring the girls who giggle and offer up squeaky greetings as I pass by. I hear no one else, see no one else with the exception of Jade.

I stop just in front of her, my gaze dropping to her legs. Good God, they're long. Why did I never notice this before? I can only imagine having them wrapped around me as I fuck her deep.

You blew that chance asshole.

"What do you want?" she asks snidely. No hi, no what's up Shep. Not that I deserve anything more.

"You," I tell her like an idiot. I swallow hard, ignoring the buzzing sound swarming in my head that's most likely vodka-induced. "I want you, Jade."

Her eyes flare the slightest bit and then narrow. Like she had a glimmer of hope there for about two seconds before she realized oh that's right, I'm a total asshole. "You had your chance," she whispers as she steps closer to me. Was she always this tall? I let my gaze drop to her feet, see that they're encased in wedge sandals—I know about wedges, don't forget I have two older, very fashion conscious sisters—that make her impossibly tall.

Impossibly sexy.

"And you ruined it," she continues, her eyes sparkling and full of anger. I've never seen her look prettier.

Well, that's a lie. I loved seeing her with no makeup, just bare skin covered in freckles.

"Yeah. I did. I'm sure you won't accept my apology and I totally understand why," I start, clamping my lips shut when her roommate appears at her side.

"Is this asshole giving you trouble, J?" Kelli sends me a look, one that says she'd like to poke me in the balls with an extra sharp stick.

"No." She tears her gaze away from mine to smile at Kelli. "He's harmless." She looks at me once more, her lips curling in distaste. "Like a rat."

"Rats are disgusting, dirty creatures," Kelli says, sneering at me.

I say nothing. I deserve their shitty words, Jade's hatred. She hates me. She has to. I'd hate me too. I *do* hate me.

"Sometimes you can keep them as pets," Jade points out, like maybe she has hope I could change. Does she?

God, I wish. "They can be really sweet."

"Yeah, but they're all beady eyed with pointy little noses and long, disgusting tails." Kelli visibly shudders. "They're awful."

"Hey." Noel-Joel reappears on the opposite side of Jade, turning to look at me. His eyes go wide when he recognizes me and I don't smile. I don't react at all. This guy can go suck a dick for all I care. "Prescott. What's up?"

I nod, still not saying a word.

"You remember Joel, don't you?" Jade asks me sweetly. Too sweetly.

Joel. I knew it was one or the other. Hmm, Joel and Jade. Don't they make a cute couple? I think I'm going to throw up. "Hey," I tell him, lifting my chin in greeting.

Jade rolls her eyes as Joel asks politely, "How are you, man?"

He appears uneasy and he should. He's got his eye on my prize. Hell, I'm fairly certain he brought my prize here tonight and while I'm tempted to thank him for bringing Jade to me, I know she wouldn't appreciate that.

And I bet he wouldn't either.

Speaking of bets...

"I'm good. Sort of pissed at your girl here for reneging on her part of our bet," I say, earning a pissed off glare from Jade.

"Trust me, we're paid up on that stupid bet," she mutters, crossing her arms in front of her chest.

Big mistake. I see her cleavage, remember how I've had my mouth there, kissing along the tops of her breasts and I break out in a sweat.

"You're really going to hold her to it?" Joel asks incredulously. "That was all talk, bro."

"Yeah, well I'm sure if I'd lost and didn't pay you your fifty grand, I could offer up the *it was all talk bro* excuse and you'd go for it?" When Joel frowns I continue. "Didn't think so."

"Let it go." Jade steps closer to me, her gaze pleading. She doesn't look mad anymore. No, she looks…sad. It kills me that I put that look on her face. I hate this. What I've done to her, what I've done to us. If there ever really was an us. "Please?"

"You owe me fair and square," I murmur, wishing I could touch her. Having her this close, I can smell her, see the freckles on the bridge of her nose, watch as those perfect, juicy peach colored lips part, as if she's searching for words and can come up with nothing.

I understand the feeling.

"I owe you nothing," she whispers fiercely. "Go away."

I stand my ground. "No."

An exasperated breath leaves her and she turns to look at Kelli. "This was a mistake," she tells her.

"Wait a minute," Joel says, touching Jade's arm. I see red. He can so casually touch her while I can't makes me want to rip his fingers off, one by one. "Did you come here with me tonight in the hopes of seeing *him?*"

Jade sends me a look that reminds me of a death sentence before she turns to face Joel. "Of course not. I came tonight so I could hang out with you."

"Doesn't look like it to me. More like you just wanted to see this asshole again." He waves a hand in my general direction, not bothering to look at me. I take a step back and sip from my cup, enjoying the show.

I only have hopes the evening continues playing out in my favor.

Jade

Okay this is backfiring big time and I don't like it. I wanted to drive Shep crazy with lust, but I certainly didn't expect him to approach me. And I didn't expect him to say that he wanted me either. God, that had been all sorts of hot, how serious he sounded, the forlorn look on his stupidly handsome face.

You. I want you, Jade.

I shake the words out of my brain and try to focus on reassuring Joel. I've already half lost him though. He looks angry, with a little bit of butt hurt to add for good measure.

"I didn't know he'd be here," I tell Joel quietly, taking his arm and guiding him a few steps away so no one can hear us talk. And when I mean no one, I'm referring to Kelli and Shep. They haven't really budged. Kelli's scowling at Shep and he's drinking continuously from the cup he's holding, like it's bottomless. "I swear."

That's the truth. I'd hope he'd show up and he didn't disappoint. But I didn't come with Joel to hurt him. I came here to hurt Shep. And maybe I did, maybe I am hurting him, but I'm also taking Joel down along with him.

And that's not cool.

"Do you like me, Jade?" Joel asks, his voice low, his expression earnest.

I sigh, unsure how to answer. "I do. But just as a friend, Joel. I already told you this. I don't—it's not going to work between us anymore. I don't want to lead you on," I explain, biting my lower lip. I feel like a jerk. I knew he wanted more and I came to this party with him anyway. All in the hopes of seeing Shep and making him jealous.

I'm awful. I deserve Joel's anger.

Joel studies me for a long, quiet moment, his jaw tight, his gaze narrowing. Then he does something so unexpected, so un-Joel-like, I have no choice but to take it for a few brief, mind-numbing seconds.

He's kissing me. Like he's trying to push my lips off

my face, kissing me so hard and so ferociously I have to shove at his chest to get him to stop.

Joel springs away from me, his expression hard, his lips damp. "You'd rather have him than me," he says accusingly, though he's not asking, he's stating it as fact. There's no use denying my feelings. Though I'm not going to give them all up. Shep doesn't deserve them.

"I don't want either of you." Lifting my chin, I try my best for haughty, aloof ice queen and I think it's working. At least Joel is falling for it. But then I catch sight of Shep, see the way he's studying me with a mixture of disgust and arousal, his mouth grim, his jaw tight. He's angry, most likely because Joel kissed me, but it couldn't be helped.

In fact, I'm glad he saw that. Maybe he'll realize that I *am* desirable, that I *can* find someone else. I don't need Shep.

I don't need any stupid guy.

Without another word I leave them all where they stand, pissed at Kelli for not trying to get me out of there sooner. Pissed at Joel for calling me out on my crap. Pissed the most at Shep for saying such sweet, sexy things and looking so damn good and sad and wonderful and sexy that I want to both punch him and kiss him, though I haven't decided yet what I'd do first.

Most likely kiss him. I miss those stupid lips of his. I could get around to punching him later.

I shove through the crowds of people, angry that I left my cup of beer back at the stupid table next to where Kelli's standing and I glance in the direction of the open kitchen, see that it's incredibly packed with a ping pong table set up in the middle of the room, a bunch of people surrounding it playing beer pong.

Whatever. I'm so glad everyone can have a great time while my world is crumbling around me, thank you very much. I hate boys. They're the worst. Either they make you feel like an incompetent loser, or they ignore you like you don't even exist. Or even worse, for whatever reason you suddenly come back into existence in their pitiful little worlds and now they won't leave you alone.

This is my life in a nutshell.

"Jade."

I don't bother turning around, though my stomach dips when I realize that it's Shep calling me. "Leave me alone," I toss over my shoulder, never slowing my pace. I should walk right out of this house and let the night swallow me up. Not like I'd do anything exciting. More like I'd stumble back to my dorm room on these stupid wedge heels, praying Shep wakes up with a massive headache and a case of herpes because he let some other dumb girl fuck him into oblivion.

God, my thoughts are so bitter, it's pitiful.

"Jade, stop."

I continue to ignore him, coming to a stop when I see a giant group of guys standing in front of the door leading out to the massive wrap around porch. A few of them pick up a smaller guy who's wearing the fraternity T-shirt, holding him upside down as he struggles and begs them to put him down.

Yeah, I'm not getting past that crowd anytime soon. Deciding to deviate from my plan, I turn a sharp right and head up the stairs, hoping like crazy I can hide out for a bit until Shep disappears. He won't be persistent. I don't think he has a persistent bone in his body and how am I going to make him change?

I'm not. I need to face that.

The stairs seem incredibly steep and I'm practically out of breath when I reach the top, glancing around before I start down the hall. I throw open the first door on the left to find a guy and a girl writhing on the bed half naked. They're so into each other, they don't even notice me.

I don't bother saying sorry as I quickly close the door.

It's like this in practically every room I peer into. If they're not having sex, they're passing a joint and in one room, I found one of the Ems—I'm not sure which one—and I wave at her as she smiles and taps the side of her nose, the guy with her holding a mirror in front of her covered with tiny white lines.

Looks like someone is about to get a bump.

I still can't believe I'd almost done one myself. I'm not one to cave in to peer pressure but I'd been so drunk, feeling so unsure…I can't explain it. Since the moment I met Shep, I can't explain my behavior.

The man makes me crazy. Makes me do crazy things. Makes me want even crazier things.

Giving up, I find an empty bathroom and shut the door, turning the lock and going to the sink, where I wash my hands, then splash cool water on my cheeks. It doesn't help. I'm still flushed, most likely from anger, but also from…arousal. I'd actually enjoyed that little encounter with Shep. Everything between us is always heightened. The colors brighter, the sounds louder, our words intense, the way I want him…overwhelming. Whenever we snip at each other, it usually turns me on.

What this says about me I'm not sure but I'm not going to question it at the moment.

The door handle turns this way and that, the actual door starting to move and I call out, "Occupied, give me a minute," as I grab a towel and start drying my hands.

But the jerk on the other side of the door is persistent. The handle rattles again, harder this time and then the door swings open, leaving me standing there with my mouth hanging open, so thankful I wasn't sitting on the toilet when this particular moment happened.

Especially when I see who's standing in the doorway. Shep.

chapter Eighteen

I gape at him, pissed that he'd invade my privacy so easily, secretly thrilled that he was so dogged in his pursuit of…me.

"What are you doing?" I ask, my voice shrill, my emotions going haywire. On one side I'm pissed that he had the nerve to just bust in on me like this. On the other side, I'm thrilled he's proven persistent after all.

Typically confused. That's normal when it comes to my feelings for Shep.

"Looking for you," he says simply as he strides into the bathroom and turns to lock the door, and then the deadbolt above it. "The lock in the handle doesn't really work," he explains as he turns to face me.

"Yeah, just realized that." He would know this,

considering it's his frat house and all. How could I be so stupid, thinking I could escape him? He's everywhere. "I don't want to talk to you. And I definitely don't want you locking us in here together."

"We have to talk." He leans against the door, looking freaking amazing. God, I hate him. It's like he didn't even try and he looks like pure sex. Wearing a charcoal colored T-shirt that stretches across his broad shoulders and chest, accompanied by dark rinse jeans that mold to his thighs, reminding me exactly how strong and thick they are.

Not that I need to remember. The sensation of his hairy thigh is forever imprinted on my palm, thank you very much.

"There's nothing to talk about. Trust me, it's over." I back up a step, my knee nudging against the toilet seat and I step away, grossed out by the thought of all the male butts that have sat on that thing. "Go away."

"I'm not some trained pet you can send away at your every command, Jade." He takes a step closer, like he knows he has me cornered and knowing his asshole tendencies of late, I bet he *does* know this. Has he kept tabs on me? God, I hope not. I'm infinitely boring, especially by Shep standards.

I take another step back, glancing over my shoulder to see the hideous floral printed shower curtain directly behind me. If I don't watch it I'm falling ass backward into the tub and wouldn't that be a sight?

Not that I care any longer what this man thinks of me.

"I wish you were so I could get rid of you once and for all," I retort. "Stop chasing after me, Shep. There's no use."

His eyes light up and I wonder if it was my use of the word Shep. I rarely say his name and I know he realizes it. "I'm sorry." He's approaching, slowly but surely and I have nowhere else to go. Nowhere to escape. He's got me well and truly cornered. "For what I did to you. I was a total dick."

An apology. Again, not what I was expecting. "Do you even realize what you did?"

He nods solemnly, looking downright contrite. "I shouldn't have run."

Ah, so he considers it running. I figured he'd found another girl and that was the end of Shep and Jade. "So you ran away from me?" *After I gave you a blowjob?* I want to say exactly that but I'm too embarrassed. I'll be humiliated if he hated it.

And he must've hated it if it made him run.

"Yeah." He nods, lifts up his hand to run it across his cheek. I don't think he's shaved and it's like I can feel the rasp of his whiskers. As if I'm the one who's touching him. "It's what I do. Run. I'm real good at it. Should've been on the cross country team when I was in high school. Or track. Yeah, definitely track. I would've kicked ass at both of them but I was too busy lighting up bombs and trying to burn down the chem lab."

I frown. He's not making any sense. And he has that ever-present red cup in his hand. "Hand it over," I tell him, wagging my fingers at him, indicating I want to see it. He offers it to me and I lift the glass to my nose, sniffing at the contents.

Nothing.

Though aren't some liquors hard to smell? As in they're odorless. I've heard that about vodka…is that what's in Shep's cup? I wouldn't put it past him.

"Are you drunk?" I hand him back his cup, thankful that he moves away from me. Even though it's only by a few inches, it's still enough to make me feel like I can breathe again.

He smiles and the sight is fucking dazzling. He has the best smile ever. I'm breathless all over again just looking at him. "That's my goal."

Ugh. Men are pathetic. "I think you're close." I sigh. "Just tell me what you're drinking." Why I care I don't know. He should be drinking cheap beer like everyone else but nooo. He's Shepard Prescott, special snowflake.

"No way. You'll steal it from me." He brings the cup to his lips and swallows. I watch unabashedly as he drinks, his lips curved around the red plastic, his throat working as he swallows. My mouth goes dry and he offers the cup to me once again. "Thirsty?"

I step closer as does he, and we meet in the middle of the tiny bathroom, Shep holding the cup out toward me as I take it. He doesn't make any sense, not wanting me to steal his cup but then hands it out to me. Of course, this is probably a ruse so he can get closer and silly me I fall for it.

I take a sip, my gaze never leaving his as I swallow straight vodka on the rocks and I wince at the taste of it. He's watching me so intensely, his expression softening, his eyes darkening, his mouth falling open ever so slightly.

"Thank you," I whisper as I hand him his drink back.

"Jade…" His voice trails off and he sets the cup on the bathroom counter, turning to face me fully. He looks serious. Too serious.

I need to get out of here.

"I should go." I try to push past him but he grabs hold of my arm, his fingers curling around the crook of my elbow, keeping me from leaving.

"Don't go," he murmurs, his voice so low I almost don't hear him. "Please."

I turn my head to look at him, our gazes locking. I'm shaking. Can he feel it? I should hate him. What he did to me is unforgiveable. I'm self-conscious enough already. His seeming rejection only made it worse. Made me *feel* worse. "I can't," I whisper, trying to withdraw my arm from his grip but he only clamps his fingers tighter. "You hurt me, Shep. I refuse to put myself through that again."

He looks shocked at my admission and I use his shock to my advantage. I pull out of his hold and lurch toward the bathroom door, reaching up to undo the deadbolt when he's suddenly there, pressing his big, warm body against mine, trapping me between the door and him.

"Let me explain." His hand is at my waist, slowly sliding down, over my hip, my thigh, along the edge of my cutoff shorts, sending a spark of heat everywhere he touches me. I close my eyes, hold back the whimper that wants to escape at his assured touch and I press my forehead to the door. His fingers dance along my thigh, stroking upward, beneath the denim and I buck against him, trying to get him off me but it only makes things worse.

Because I can *feel* him—hard and hot, his erection nudges against my butt and now I'm the one who's shocked. Did I do that to him? Do I still have that much power over him?

"There's nothing to explain," I say to the door, keeping my eyes tightly closed. It's bad enough I can smell him, feel him, hear him. I don't want to see him. If I look in his eyes, stare at his beautiful face, I'll give in. And I don't want to. I don't want to take the risk of getting hurt again.

How's that old saying go? Fool me once, shame on you. Fool me twice, shame on…

Me.

"I didn't mean to hurt you." He pushes my hair away from my shoulder and I can feel his breath on my neck right before he kisses it. My knees threaten to buckle at first touch of his lips on my skin and I grip at the door, grasping at nothing but smooth, painted wood. "I swear, Jade. It kills me to know that I ruined this."

See, there's the thing that bugs. He *did* ruin it. But I'm so weak, so attracted to him still, that I would let him back in. Easily. I know I shouldn't. I'm only asking for trouble. Hearing the pain in his voice, feeling him strain against me though, I want to give in. Right now.

I need to remain strong. Ignore his mouth on my neck…oh God, on that one spot just behind my ear that makes me shiver. I'm shivering right now as his hand slips beneath the hem of my tank, his other hand smoothing my hair back. He's everywhere, surrounding me with his scent and his touch, his heat and his body. I press closer to the door, plastering myself to it and he follows my lead by plastering his body to mine.

"Let me make it up to you," he whispers close to my ear just before he kisses it, his mouth lingering, making me shiver even more. I swear to God I'm going to melt into a puddle if he doesn't stop doing this. "Turn around, baby."

No. No, no, no. I can't do it. To turn around would be to give in. And I can't…

"Jade." He cups my face with one hand, his long fingers curling around my chin as he turns my head toward him. I keep my eyes tightly closed as he tilts my chin up and I can feel his eyes on me. "Look at me."

I shake my head, which is difficult considering the grip he has on me and how I'm positioned. "No," I whisper.

"Please."

It's the tone of his voice that breaks me. Reluctantly I open my eyes to find his face in mine, his lips so close…

And then they're on mine, soft and gentle, tentative and sweet. Again and again he brushes his lips against mine, never pushing. Just simple little kisses that make my skin tighten, my blood languid, my head swim. He relaxes his hold on my chin, moves away the slightest bit from my body and he rests his hands at my hips, slowly turning me around until I'm facing him.

He pulls away and I open my eyes, our gazes locked, the only sound in the tiny bathroom our accelerated breathing. I can hear the party raging on downstairs, the throb of the music, the low roar of voices. It reminds me I can go if I wanted to. My friend is downstairs, probably worried about me. I can run to Kelli right now and ask her to take me home and she would, no questions asked.

I reach out to rest my hand on the door handle, determined to make my escape when he grabs me, his hands on my face, cupping my cheeks, his mouth on mine once again.

Though this time his kiss isn't gentle or sweet. It's hard and demanding, his tongue thrusting deep. I force myself to remain impassive, as if his kiss doesn't matter but I can keep up the pretense for only so long.

Because his kiss does matter. His hands on me matter too and I release the door handle, rest my hand on his chest, tempted to push him away. Until I feel the erratic thump of his heart beneath my palm and I realize he's just as affected by this, by me, as I am by him.

Everything else falls away and all that matters is me and him in this stupid bathroom, wrapped up in each other's arms. I slide my hand up until I'm cupping the back of his neck, pulling him into me. Our mouths are busy, tongues busy, hands busy and I know without a doubt that I'm going to give in.

Please. I need to be honest with myself.

I've already given in.

Shep

I feel like I just won the most awesome prize I've ever wanted in all my life. That prize is Jade. Soft and warm in my arms, her mouth responsive, her entire body leaning into mine. This is what I'd missed more than anything in the last week that I'd gone without her. The connection, the attraction that links the two of us together, we can't deny it. She may hate me but her body doesn't. She wants me.

And I want her.

Her tongue tangles with mine, a whimper sounds low in her throat when I slide my hands up, tunneling my fingers through her hair. Fuck I could touch her like this all night, kiss her like this all night…

But I've already done that. I've already withstood the make out session with her and almost didn't survive it. When she dropped to her knees in front of me, pulled off my shorts and proceeded to give me the best blow job of my life, I…panicked.

I refuse to panic again. Panicking results in losing Jade. And I can't afford to do that.

Releasing my hold on her face, I reach for her ass, curving my hands beneath it and lifting. She breaks the kiss first, staring up at me like I've lost my mind. "Put your legs around me," I whisper.

When I lift her again her long, bare legs wrap around my hips, her feet digging into my ass. I grip the back of her thighs and press her into the door, rubbing my cock against her like an animal raring to fuck and her eyelids flutter when I make direct contact with her denim covered pussy.

"Feel that?" I thrust against her again, her lips falling open when I do, and she closes her eyes. "That's what you do to me. Look at me, Jade."

Her eyes pop open, hazy and full of hunger. Shifting closer, I press my mouth to hers, keeping my eyes open and she does the same. Slowly I shift my hips to hers and she moans, her eyes shutting again. I grip her chin. "Open your eyes."

She does as I ask, blinking up at me.

"I'm sorry," I whisper. "I was an idiot."

Her perfect lips curve into the tiniest smile and my heart expands at the sight of it. "Yes, you are."

"I need your forgiveness." I touch her cheek, press my fingers to her mouth. She parts her lips, draws the tips of my fingers between them and when she starts to gently nibble them, I swear I see stars. I remove my fingers from her mouth before I completely lose it.

"I need to think about it," she says and I kiss her before she can say anything else.

That's enough for me. At least for now. I lose myself in the taste of her lips, the feel of her in my arms. I'm hard as steel, eager to tear off her clothes and fuck her but I can't do it here, not in the bathroom of my frat house with a party raging on downstairs.

Talk about classless. Jade deserves more than that. She's worth more than that.

"Come home with me," I whisper against her lips.

She sucks in a breath and I pull away slightly so I can gauge her reaction. Her eyes are wide and she sinks her teeth into her lower lip in that innately sexy way she has. She drives me fucking crazy. "I don't know…"

"I want you there. I want to be alone with you." I lean in and whisper close to her ear. "I'm not going to fuck you against this door, Jade. I want to take you home so I can fuck you properly. In my bed."

"You always say that," she whispers.

"Because it's true. You deserve so much more…" I clamp my lips shut, afraid I might say something that'll ruin it. Like usual.

She's trembling when I withdraw from her and I touch her face, press my hips to hers and wait for her answer.

"I'm scared," she whispers.

Well, Christ. That's the last thing I expected to hear her say.

"Why?" It's what I did to her. She gives me a blowjob, makes me come like a geyser and I never contact her again. I'm a dick. I know this. I can't explain why I ran like I did beyond offering up the scared explanation too.

But I can't admit that to her, not now. She'd probably laugh at me.

"I'm not—" She releases a shuddery breath and tips her head down, her hair falling around her face, obscuring her from my view. "I'm not very good at this," she admits in the barest whisper.

I frown. "At what?"

"At...sex."

I don't believe that for even a minute. "Are you serious?"

Her expression turns wounded. I swear she looks like she's going to cry. "Don't make fun of me."

"I'm not," I say quickly. Fuck, I'm walking a delicate line right about now. One wrong word and I could mess up everything. "It won't be bad between us, Jade. I promise." I lean in and press a light kiss to her lips. "It'll be so fucking good you won't ever want to leave my bed."

She starts to laugh. "Awfully confident in your abilities, aren't you."

"Merely stating what I believe is true." I kiss her again, my lips lingering, hers parting so I slip my tongue between them for the quickest moment. I need to convince her that this could work for us. "I'm not saying it's going to be good because of me. It'll be good between us because of...*us.* The connection we share." I touch her. Cup her breast, run a thumb across the front of it, her nipple rising beneath the lace of her bra.

"I don't know..." She sighs when I circle her nipple with my thumb, the sound going straight to my dick. "I don't know if I can fully trust you, Shep."

I go completely still, shame washing over me. I

deserve that. "Let me prove it to you."

"Prove to me what?" She's frowning, her eyebrows draw together and damn it, I love every look she wears. When she's happy, when she's sad, when she's mad, when she's aroused, confused...

All of them. Every single one. I want every expression, every sound, every word she says. I want to know about all of them, I want to share these moments with her, I want them to be all for me and no one else.

Selfish. I sound like a selfish asshole and I've always been one. But I desperately want to be selfish with Jade. I want all of her. I need to convince her that I'm worthy to stand by her side. To be a part of her life.

"Prove that I'm worthy of you. That I can earn your trust back. That I'll be there for you no matter what," I tell her, noting the way her eyes go wide at my words. She probably doesn't believe me.

I can't wait to prove her wrong.

chapter
Nineteen

I got Jade the hell out of that frat house as fast as I could. She wanted to tell her roommate she was leaving and I could respect that. I didn't much appreciate the dirty looks Kelli kept shooting my direction as Jade explained where she was going — my house — and who she was going with — me — but I figured I deserved those evil looks. After all, I'm the one who ditched her friend after an epic blowjob.

Meaning, I'm a complete idiot.

Thank Christ Joel wasn't around when we made our escape. I didn't want to deal with that kid. I'm still pissed at the way he kissed Jade right in front of me. Just fucking kissed her like he had the right to do so and holy hell, I'm seeing red just thinking about it.

"I have a question," I say nonchalantly as we're

driving back to my house. It's been oddly quiet the entire drive and I wonder if she's having any regrets. I hope not.

"What is it?" she asks, sounding wary.

"You and Joel." I take a deep breath, contemplating if I should ask her or not.

"Yes," she answers before I can say another word. "I've had sex with Joel."

What the fuck? This mind reading thing is freaky as hell. "You have." My voice is flat and I exhale loudly, gripping the steering wheel.

"Yeah. We were together for months, Shep. I thought…" She shakes her head. "I sort of thought I was falling in love with him at one point, but I think I just liked the idea of being in love, not necessarily being in love with *Joel*, you know what I mean?"

I have no idea what she's talking about. Liking the idea of being in love? I can hardly wrap my brain around it. All I can focus on is that Joel's seen her naked. He's touched her. He's fucked her, the lucky bastard. I hate that he's been with Jade in such an—intimate way that I haven't.

Yet.

"Does he want you back?" I sound like a croaking frog and I clear my throat.

"Yeah. He admitted as much yesterday when we talked." My gaze cuts to hers and she's staring at me, her eyes wide, her expression serious. Too serious. "I don't want to be with him. I told him that from the very start."

"Yet you went to the party with him." Dressed like... fuck, like that. All sexy and shit. I can hardly focus on the road ahead of me. All I want to do is run my hands over her bare legs.

"Kelli wanted me to go with them so I agreed. She knew it was at your frat and she was banking on you being there."

"Were you banking on me being there?"

"Why do you think I wore these shorts?"

Surprise filling me, my gaze meets hers again and she's smiling at me, looking rather pleased with herself.

"So you wore them for me."

"In the hopes that you'd be there...yeah."

"You about gave me a heart attack when I first saw you in those shorts," I mutter, my gaze going to her pale thighs. I want to touch them. My fingers are fucking tingling, I want to touch them so bad.

"The shorts are Kelli's. They're way too short for me," she explains.

"They're perfect." I give in and reach out to rest my hand on her thigh, sliding my fingers between them and she shifts beneath my touch, trapping my fingers. Her skin is silky soft and so fucking smooth. "You're a tease."

"I think you like it when I tease you," she whispers.

No use denying the truth. Removing my hand from her legs, I clutch the steering wheel and press harder on the gas. Eager to get back to my house so I can drag her up to my bedroom and end this night on the right note. Nothing is stopping us. No drunken Jade. No random girls bursting into my room and calling us fuck birds. No period issues. No Shep issues.

Well. I can't guarantee I won't have an issue but I gotta ignore it. No panicking allowed. No worry over what she wants from me. No worry over what I might want from her. I need to focus on the here and now. That Jade is willingly in my car and is going home with me — again, willingly. This is major. I can't mess it up.

I refuse to mess this up.

Within minutes I'm pulling the car into the garage and I practically leap out of my seat, going round to the passenger side so I can open Jade's door. All I see are her legs as she climbs out of the car, my mouth going dry as I drink them in.

I am in serious trouble tonight.

Taking her hand, I tug her into the house, through the kitchen, the living room, down the hall, heading straight for my bedroom. She's been there before. I had her pinned to my bed that one night when we finally kissed for the first time. How long ago was that? It feels like months though I think it's really only been weeks.

How can I feel so connected to a girl I've known for only a short time? I want to learn everything about her — and not just what gets her off. I want to know what makes her tick, what she wants out of life.

This is the sort of thing that scares the crap out of me so I push the crazy thoughts from my head as I pull her into my bedroom and shut the door behind her, turning the lock, watching as she stops at the foot of the bed, slowly turning to face me.

There's no light on in the room but my blinds are still open and slivers of moonlight spill into the room, illuminating Jade in shadow. I say nothing and neither does she and I wonder for a panicked moment if she can hear my heart racing. It's like all I can hear, the rushing sound filling my ears, filling my head.

She sits on the edge of the bed and takes off first one sandal, then the other. They both fall to the floor with a solid thump and she pushes her feet into the floor, her toes curling as I hear them crack.

"Those sandals were killing my feet," she murmurs.

Relief floods me. God, she's so normal. So…regular. And not in a bad way. In a wonderful, perfect way. Any other girl would've tried to jump me the second the door closed. Or she would've offered up a strip tease, ending up sprawled across my bed looking nothing like I imagined. Push up bras hide small tits. Excess makeup hides regular features. Teased, blonde hair lies when the pubic hair is revealed to be pitch black. Or worse, there's no hair, nothing but a very bare, very pubescent looking pussy and that just turns me off.

I'm starting to realize I don't mind regular girls. Everyone has flaws, including me. Lies are just that. Lies. With Jade, everything I see is what I get. The vivid red hair. The freckles — so many fucking cute freckles. Her breasts are real. I've felt them enough to know there's no padding in that bra, those tits are one hundred percent Jade's. Pale, creamy skin, no spray tan in sight. She's natural.

Beautiful.

Real.

I approach her, stopping just in front of her. She tilts her head back, all that red hair spilling down her back and realization dawns.

"Did you wear your hair down for me?" I ask, keeping my voice low, not wanting to break the spell that's slowly forming between us. Everything's quiet in this room, the only sound our breaths and I wonder if I should put on some music but I'm afraid that'll ruin the mood.

She nods. "Yes," she whispers. "Everything I've done tonight, has been for..." She presses her lips together for a brief moment, like she doesn't want to offer up this bit of information. Makes me want to hear it that much more. "It's all been for you."

"Why?" I don't deserve her trying to do anything to impress me. I damn near ruined this.

Jade starts to laugh, the sound light and pretty and making my skin tighten in anticipation. "I wanted to look amazing so I could knock you on your ass, tease you into wanting me again and then walk away from you without a backward glance."

Okay yeah, she was setting me up but I'm stuck on one tiny bit of her admission. "Wait a minute. Did you say tease me into wanting you *again?*"

She gives me a funny look. "Well, yeah. Because clearly you…"

"Clearly I nothing." I touch her, slip my fingers into her hair and push it away from her forehead gently. She leans into my touch, her eyes sliding to half-mast. "I never stopped wanting you, Jade," I murmur. "Ever."

"It felt like you did," she admits softly. "I thought I didn't…please you. After what happened, it's like you didn't want to have anything to do with me ever again. I figured that was all on me."

I close my eyes for a brief moment and breathe deep. Guilt settles over me heavily. That she's in my room at this very moment, giving me another chance…I should get on my knees and thank the lord above. "I'm an asshole. I — panicked."

She frowns up at me, appearing genuinely confused. "Panicked? Why?"

How do I explain that she scares the hell out of me? How my feelings for her scare me even worse? "I don't know." I shrug. I'm such a liar.

Slowly she stands, her body rubbing against mine, her gaze intent. I don't back up, don't move away from her and she's so close, I absorb her body heat, inhale her sweet, clean scent, and my hands automatically settle on her hips.

"I'm probably going to regret this," she whispers as she settles her hands on my chest. Her fingers are hot, burning through my T-shirt, branding me and I wait in anticipation of what she's going to say next. "This won't end good for us, I know it. But—"

I don't even give her a chance to finish the sentence. I don't care about the explanation, the worry or fears she might be experiencing. All I can concentrate on is how she's looking at me, how good she feels pressed next to me. I bend my head and kiss her, cutting off her words, thrusting my tongue in her mouth, triumph surging through me when she melts into me, her hands slipping beneath my T-shirt to touch my bare skin.

I've got her.

And I'm not about to let her go.

Jade

He's kissing me. I'm in Shep's bedroom—again—

and he's touching me, kissing me, seducing me. Again. And I'm letting it happen. I'm giving in gleefully, as if what he did to me only a few days ago doesn't matter any longer.

It doesn't. At least, not tonight. I'm taking my opportunities where I can find them and if he ends up hurting me, tossing me aside and forgetting all about me, then so be it. I like this guy. I *want* this guy.

For some wild and crazy reason, he seems to like and want me too.

"I'm sorry," he whispers as he runs his mouth along my jaw, down my neck. I like that he keeps apologizing too. Makes me think he really does regret how he treated me the night of the blowjob fail. Though is it really a fail when the guy comes in your mouth? I don't think so. "I don't know why I acted like such a prick that night."

I say nothing. Just revel in his mouth on my skin, his wandering hands. Oh, I love it when he touches me like this. He just takes completely over, there's no hesitancy, no awkwardness. My past sexual experiences were all about hesitancy and awkwardness. That part sucked. Most of it sucked. I always got performance anxiety and felt like I couldn't measure up.

Oh, and orgasms? Forget it. I seriously don't think I can come with a guy. On my own, yes, but otherwise? No can do.

With Shep, I tend to forget my hang-ups. All I can

concentrate on is his lips on mine, his busy hands, his hard body...

"I want to make it up to you," he continues, his fingers tugging on the hem of my shirt. Slowly he pulls it up, past my stomach, the fabric catching on my breasts before I lift my arms over my head and he tugs the tank completely off my body, letting it fall to the floor.

His gaze lands on my bra-covered chest and he stares blatantly at my breasts, his eyes lighting up like a little kid who just caught sight of the pile of presents beneath the tree on Christmas morning. I'm tempted to cross my arms in front of my chest but he'd only make me drop them so I don't. I stand there, letting him look his fill, eager for him to say something, anything to move this moment along.

"You're beautiful," he murmurs, his eyes glowing as they lift to meet mine. "Take off the shorts, Jade."

Shock and arousal rushes through me at the tone of his voice, the command of his words. Here he goes being bossy again and without hesitation I do as he asks, shedding the shorts and kicking them off, so I'm standing in front of him wearing nothing but my black lace bra and the matching panties.

That I picked out and wore tonight just for him, in the hopes that he'd see me like this. Matching bra and panties is so not my style.

I'm bad. I planned for all of this. I wanted him to

see me, to chase after me, to beg me for forgiveness. I wanted to give in and have him take me back to his place and strip off my clothes and…

"Lay back on the bed." He swallows hard and works his jaw, his eyes never leaving me. He rests his hands on his hips, standing at the foot of the bed, foreboding and sexy and oh my God, I can't believe this is really happening.

In fact, I'm starting to freak out just the slightest bit. Frowning, I ask, "Why?" Worry trickles inside of me and I tell myself to get over it.

But I can't help it. Old habits die hard.

"Just do it," he commands, his voice softening the slightest bit, as do his eyes. "Please."

Is it wrong that I really love it when he says please? When he looks so tortured by my mere presence on his bed? Do I really have that much power over him? Because if I do?

That's heady stuff.

Without a word, I do as he asks, lying back on his giant bed, scooting up the mattress so my back and head are leaning against the fat pile of pillows. They smell like Shep, spicy and clean. I close my eyes and turn my head, inhaling deeply, my nose practically buried in the pillowcase.

"Damn, you look pretty," he murmurs, his voice husky. "Spread your legs for me, baby."

I'm supposed to hate it when he calls me baby, but I don't. I freaking love it. His gaze races over me, from the top of my head to the tips of my toes and I bend my knees, place my feet flat on the mattress before I slowly open my legs, sliding my feet across the bed.

His eyes flare with heat but he doesn't speak. Feeling emboldened, I rest my hand on my stomach, my fingers perilously close to the waistband of my panties. I could just slide them beneath the black lace and sink them deep. I'm that wet, I can tell. All from him only watching me.

But it's the *way* he watches me. He looks ready to pounce. Ready to take and conquer and make me his. That's...exciting. My skin tingles in anticipation and then he's there, climbing onto the bed with me, climbing over me, his face in mine, his arms braced on the mattress on either side of my head. I bring my legs closer together, his knees resting on each side of my hips and I release a shuddery breath when he presses his face to my neck, his mouth on my skin.

"Tonight is all about you," he whispers close to my ear just before he kisses it. I close my eyes, my heart racing as he starts to slide down my body, his mouth never leaving my skin. He blazes a trail with his lips, across my collarbone, my chest, kissing along the tops of my breasts, over them, licking first one nipple, then the other, his tongue dragging over the lace of my bra.

A shock of heat pulses through me, settling between my legs and I swear to God, all the oxygen leaves my lungs when he shifts lower, his mouth drifting across my stomach. I'm so sensitive I almost want to laugh, or at the very least squirm away from his mouth. I bite my lip to keep myself under control.

"You have freckles here," he murmurs, his fingers coming into play. He touches my stomach, pressing his fingertips into my flesh as he oh so slowly kisses around my belly button. "You have freckles everywhere."

He's fascinated with them and I sort of don't get why. All these years I've silently — and not so silently — cursed their existence and now I have the hottest guy on campus running his lips all over them.

His *freaking* lips. God, I'm weak just thinking about it, let alone actually feeling those magical lips on my skin, his fingers drawing little circles on my stomach, making goose bumps rise. I shiver when his mouth shifts lower, his tongue teasing along the waistband of my panties. His long fingers curl around the sides of my underwear at my hips, as if he's going to pull them off and he goes completely still.

"What's wrong?"

I open my eyes to find him watching me, his brows furrowed together, his big body nestled between my legs. I go weak just looking at him, assuming what he plans on doing, worried that he's going to be sorely disappointed when he realizes that I just flat out…

Yeah. I can't come. The ever-elusive orgasm will slip right out of my fingers like usual when I'm with a guy and disappear into the ether. Ridiculous, because I have Shep freaking Prescott between my legs, his mouth right there, like he's about to go down on me or something— holy crap does he really plan on going down on me? My girly parts are lighting up like crazy at the possibility of that mouth going ahem, *there*—yet I'm freezing up. Silently freaking out.

He's waiting for me to say something and I don't know how to answer. I don't know what to do. Tell him the truth? Yeah, I'm sure that'll excite him.

Oh hey, Shep. Did I happen to mention I have a hard time um…finding release? Yeah, it's most likely a waste of your time to focus all of our energy—there. You could go downtown on me all you want, but you'll probably just end up spraining your tongue. And it'll be all for naught! So go ahead and skip that part. There's really no point.

"Uh," I start and he sends me a look. A look that makes me snap my mouth shut and wait in breathless anticipation as he slowly starts to tug my panties down, exposing me. He pauses, my panties halfway down my thighs, his face mere inches from my lady bits and then he presses a light kiss on my thigh, a mere brush of his lips against my extra sensitive skin. Yet a jolt runs through me at first contact, settling in my core, and I close my eyes on a whimper.

Hmm. Maybe he *can* make me come with that magical mouth of his...

chapter Twenty

Shep

"Let's take these off," I murmur, keeping my eye on Jade's face as I slowly remove her panties. That little sound she made in the back of her throat when I kissed her thigh was hot. I want to hear that sound again.

Desperately.

She looks a little dazed at the prospect of me stripping her naked and I like that, too. I like it a lot. I want her dazed. I want her open and willing and receptive and eventually, I want her falling apart in my arms—or against my mouth. Around my fingers. However I can get her, I want her. I'm determined to make her come. Give her the orgasm she deserves. I *still* think about that blowjob she gave me and I need to return the favor.

I slip the delicate black lace down her long, pale legs, run my fingers along her silky smooth skin, until the little scrap of fabric is dangling off her feet and she's kicking them onto the floor. She inhales sharply when I place my hands on the inside of her slender thighs and I can feel her tremble beneath my palms.

Fuck. My hands are shaking too. I've waited for this moment for what feels like an eternity and now that I finally have her where I want her, I'm nervous. And I'm never nervous. Girls are just girls. You fuck one, you've fucked them all. Some are a little more up for adventure, some are better cock suckers—crude but true—and some are screamers. But really? They're all pretty much the same.

At least, they have been for me.

Until Jade.

Trying to get my mental shit together, I spread her legs wider, revealing her to my gaze. And it is a damn pretty pussy. She's a natural redhead, though that's no surprise and she's the first natural redhead I've ever been with, which is actually a total surprise. I don't usually discriminate. Blondes, brunettes—I even fingered a chick with pink hair once—but I guess I've never been with a redhead.

Wild.

I run my fingers down the inside of her thighs, my gaze never leaving the spot between her legs. I can smell her. She's turned the fuck on and I am too, so what am I waiting for? Slipping my hands under her, I grip that plump ass of hers in both of my hands and lift her up, kissing first one hipbone, then the other. Teasing her. Wanting to drive her insane because holy fuck, she's been driving me crazy since the very first moment I met her. I set eyes on her in that mirror, heard that smart mouth running a mile a minute as she sat behind me and I was hooked.

If anything, I'm more hooked now. Addicted. Desperate to have her. Desperate to make her mine.

Make her yours? Are you fucking nuts? What, have you gone caveman now?

I shove the nagging voice in my head—it sounds suspiciously like Tristan—to the farthest corner of my brain.

Shifting a little, I readjust her position, ready to lower my mouth to all that pink, wet goodness when she pipes up, her voice more breath than sound.

"I should warn you."

Our gazes meet, hers apprehensive. "Warn me about what?"

"I um, I don't normally uh…" She closes her eyes and swallows. "You know."

I frown but she's not looking at me. She's too wrapped up in her own head. "No, I don't know. Explain it to me."

Her eyes pop open. "I don't usually have an... orgasm." She makes a little face. "It's um, difficult for me."

Huh. Seriously? Does she know what sort of challenge she just dropped? And I'm always up for a challenge, especially a sexual one. "No guy has been able to give you an orgasm?"

She nods, her teeth sinking into her lower lip. That lower lip I fucking adore.

"Can you give yourself one?"

Her cheeks go red but she nods. Just barely. The idea of Jade touching herself, making herself come with her fingers, maybe with a vibrator, is a great one. Something I'd like to see someday, but I have other, more important matters to tackle first.

Like Jade. And her supposed orgasm issue.

"So tell me." I bend my head, nuzzling the soft skin of her lower belly. "What do you like?"

"Huh?" She sounds confused.

"Do you like it when a guy goes down on you? Fingers you? Or is straight sex more your speed?" Me? I enjoy going down on women. Some assholes are selfish and only want a blowjob while giving nothing in return, but I'm a firm believer in reciprocation.

She throws an arm across her eyes. "This is the most embarrassing conversation ever."

"Tell me Jade. If I'm going to make you come, I need

to know what you like." I kiss her hip again, letting my lips linger. I'm eager to put my mouth on her. Lick her into oblivion. I'm positive I can make her come in a matter of minutes.

Positive.

She removes her arm and stares down at me. "You won't be able to make me come. I can almost guarantee it."

Challenge officially thrown down. "Watch me," I murmur as I dip my head and drop a chaste kiss right above her pubic hair.

Christ, she just made that whimpering sound again and that's it. I remove my hands from her ass and push her legs open wider, my fingers biting into her thighs as I lick the length of her slit. She gasps, I feel her quiver beneath my tongue and I do it again, covering every inch of her. I circle her clit, going round and round, sucking it deep in my mouth before I resume teasing her folds with my tongue.

Yet another one of those choked, sexy sounds falls from her lips and I lift my gaze to watch her, never slowing my efforts. She's thrown back her head, her eyes closed, forehead furrowed in concentration, lips parted as she alternately breathes and moans. Her hips lift in natural rhythm, as if seeking my lips and I gather her closer, my hands on her ass once again, holding her to my mouth as I devour her.

Because I am. Devouring her. She tastes fucking amazing, she's so wet and warm. I fucking ache to slip my cock inside her. If I don't watch it, I swear I could come in my jeans and I haven't done something like that since I was a kid. I'm not one to actually get off on going down, but hell.

This is Jade we're talking about.

I watch her, fascinated with her response, curious if she's close. She appears close. She's giving off all the right signals. Her features are strained, her legs and arms tensed…

Wait a minute.

I lift my head and she cracks open her eyes, a frown marring her beautiful, flushed face. "Relax, baby," I tell her, making her frown harder.

She shakes her head once, all that red hair strewn across my pillow. "I told you, I can't come."

"I think you're trying too hard." I dip down to press my lips to the top of her pussy. "Tell me what you like, Jade," I murmur against her. "Do you like it when I do this?" I lick her clit, flick it with the tip of my tongue and she closes her eyes, an agonized groan sounding from deep in her chest.

I'll take that as a yes.

"Open your eyes," I demand and they flash open, staring at me. Her cheeks are pink, her lips damp. She's fucking gorgeous and I want her to watch me do this to her. Maybe watching will help get her there faster. Hmm, maybe using particular words will get her there faster too. "Do you want me to fuck you with my fingers?"

She bites her lip and nods, her gaze never leaving mine.

I remove my right hand from her perfect ass and streak my fingers across her pussy, then slide my index finger deep inside her. Fuck, she's tight. And hot. All that velvety skin clasps around my finger like it doesn't want to let go as I start to move. Her eyelids waver when she sucks in a sharp breath.

"Keep watching me," I practically growl against her and her eyes go wider. My gaze is locked with hers as I start to lick her, swirling my tongue around her clit, drawing it back into my mouth to give it a gentle suck. Her hips shift and I add another finger, shallowly pumping, curling them inside her so I hit that particular spot that drives a woman wild.

"Oh my God," she gasps when I hit my mark. So I rub it once more, lingering over the spot, satisfaction rushing through me when she thrusts her hips, practically grinding her pussy against my mouth. "Right there, right there, right there," she chants mindlessly and I give it to her right there, right where she wants it, sucking her clit, fingering her pussy, until she literally screams my name and falls apart.

As in, she falls *completely* apart. Her entire body shakes with the force of her orgasm, her inner walls grip my fingers in an orgasmic rhythm and her clit throbs beneath my tongue.

Yep. Mission orgasm completion accomplished.

Jade

Oh. My. God.

I can't even.

Oh.

My.

God.

Seriously, did that just happen? Did Shep really just make me come? And did I really just *scream* his name? I've never screamed anyone's name before. Ever. I don't scream. I also don't have orgasms, at least with a guy. Even when I give myself one, it's never like — *that.*

No way. Not like that at all. Not even close.

I'm quivering. My entire body feels like a bowl of Jell-O. The throb between my legs is like *whoa* and my head is spinning.

Spinning.

God help me, his perfect, orgasm-inducing mouth is still on my extra sensitive, twitching flesh and I settle a hand on his head, threading my fingers through his soft hair. I can hardly take it and I'm desperate to push him away. Unfortunately—or fortunately, depends on how you look at it—he still has a firm grip on my butt, meaning that I'm pressed up against his face like it's no big deal and this is a huge deal. A huge, crazy deal because holy shit, I just came and it was the most momentous occasion of my life.

He's nuzzling me between my legs and I finally work up the strength to carefully shove his head away from me and he gets the hint. I'm almost embarrassed to look at him, especially when I catch sight of the smug expression on his face.

Oh yeah, he looks proud. I'm sure he's just thrilled he proved me wrong.

"So," he starts nonchalantly as he moves up to lie beside me. "Was that good for you?"

I turn to look at him, realizing that he's still fully dressed while I'm pretty much naked. "I don't think you need to ask that," I mumble, embarrassed.

Shep reaches out and touches my cheek, his fingers light on my skin. "You're right. I'm fairly certain that I made you come. Hard."

I stare at him. Rear back a little when he leans in and drops a kiss on my lips. Then another. I can taste myself on him and I should be freaked out. Or the slightest bit disgusted…right?

But I'm not. Instead, I wrap my arms around his neck and pull him in closer, molding my body to his hard form, letting my mouth linger on his for a long, delicious moment. "You're wearing too much clothing," I murmur against his lips.

"Take them off me then," he murmurs back, nipping my lower lip with his teeth.

Resting my palms on his chest, I give him a shove so he rolls over on his back. I tug his T-shirt up, revealing his mouthwatering abs and I lean down, running my lips over his hot skin. The muscles tense beneath my mouth and I rest my hands on his belt buckle, slowly pulling the leather strap out as I start to undo it.

"You never did tell me," he says. I glance up at him to see he's watching me, his lips curled into an arrogant smile, his arms folded behind his head, as if he has all the time in the world. "You did come, didn't you Jade?"

I grab hold of his belt and pull it from his jeans, letting it drop to the floor with a clank. "What do you think?"

His smile grows. "I'm guessing with the way you screamed my name, that would be a yes."

"I didn't scream your name," I mutter, curling my fingers around the waistband of his jeans before I get busy undoing the snap and sliding down his zipper. I'm such a liar. I so shouted his name. My mind goes back to the time we talked on the bed at his frat, after I hurt my ankle. When I told him it wouldn't be sexy to yell his name in the so-called throes of passion.

God, what a dork I'd been, saying that to him.

Having his mouth on me, his fingers inside me, when he stroked that particular spot deep within, I'd reacted like I had no control over my body. I'd never felt like that before. He has magic hands. Oh, and a magic mouth and tongue. Just thinking about what he did to me makes me shiver all over again.

So, of course I'd yelled his name. His sexy, ridiculous name, though somehow, it fits him. He's sort of ridiculous—but in the best possible way.

"You most definitely did." He hisses in a breath when I spread his jeans open and streak my fingers down the length of his erection. It strains against the fabric of his black boxer briefs, thick and long, reminding me of when I gave him the blowjob and how much he enjoyed it.

Right before he ran.

I push that unpleasant memory out of my brain and focus on the task at hand.

"Come here," he whispers just as I'm about to tug off his underwear. He reaches for me, gathers me up in his arms, pulls me up so I'm sprawled on top of him, my aching center rubbing his rigid erection. I squirm against him, a shuddering breath escaping me at the delicious friction that sparks between us and then he's rolling me over so I'm beneath him, my back flat on the mattress, my breaths coming hard and quick when he starts to kiss a path down the length of my body.

"This needs to come off," he murmurs as he reaches behind me and deftly undoes the clasp on my bra. He helps me pull it off, baring me completely to his gaze and he leans back, taking me in, his eyes dark and totally unreadable.

I'm self-conscious. What else is new? I need to get over this. The way he looks at me, the things he says…I know he likes what he sees. Which is mind blowing, I can't lie. I mean, this is Shep Prescott. He's been with a bazillion women—at least that's what people say. He's a campus legend.

And here he is with me. Silly freshman, nobody special, little old me. I can barely wrap my head around it.

"Beautiful," he murmurs as he dips his head and kisses my nipple. I inhale on a moan, closing my eyes when he envelops my nipple into his mouth and begins to suck. I touch the back of his head, thread my fingers through his hair, holding him to me, my core tightening with every pull of his mouth. His erection is heavy, pressing against my thigh, and I spread my legs wider, needing him pushing against me, creating that delicious friction once again.

He doesn't comply. The man has a mind of his own and I have to admit, I like it. I reach for the waistband of his boxer briefs but he shoves my hand away. I moan with frustration, startled when he moves up, his mouth at my ear, his hands wrapped around both of my wrists. How he grabbed me so quickly I don't know.

"You get me naked and I won't have any choice but to fuck you," he murmurs close to my ear, his hot breath and warm lips making me shiver. Oh, and his words. I really love how he tosses out the word fuck so casually. "My boxers are the only barrier that's keeping me from diving straight into that hot, tight pussy of yours."

I want to fan myself. His words make me hot. The way he's holding me down makes me hot too. My arms are bent, my hands curling into fists on either side of my head, his fingers wrapped firmly around my wrists. "I want you to…" My voice drifts and he smiles, dipping his head so his mouth hovers right above mine.

"You want me to what? Fuck you?" He drops the lightest kiss on my lips at the same time he thrusts his hips against mine. "I'm trying to be a gentleman."

"I don't want a gentleman," I confess, my voice low, my body weak from the way he's looking at me. Like he wants to gobble me up.

He lifts his brows, looking surprised by what I said. "You don't?"

I shake my head, sucking in a sharp breath when he presses his mouth against my neck, his hips working mine. Oh God, I can feel him. Thrusting against me, rubbing the tip against my clit, like he knows exactly where it is. Every other guy I've been with needed a roadmap to find the damn thing and even then there were no guarantees. Not that I pointed it out or anything. More like I suffered through the too rough fingers, the sloppy kisses, the really bad fucking.

I have a feeling Shep is going to be nothing but really *good* at fucking.

"You're a constant surprise," he murmurs with a smile, just before he kisses me. "Tell me what you want," he whispers against my lips.

"I want…" I want all sorts of things. I love it when he kisses me. When he touches me. He releases one of my wrists, his hand going to my waist and drifting downward, until it settles between my legs, his fingers working my flesh. I'm so wet I can actually hear it as he searches my folds and I'm sort of mortified.

But I'm also so turned on I don't care.

"Tell me, Jade." He slips a finger inside me just as he thrusts his tongue in my mouth. It's sensory overload. He surrounds me, he's inside of me and I can hardly think straight. "Tell me what you want."

"You," I choke out when he presses my clit with his thumb. "I want you inside me."

He's gone in a whirlwind of movement and I blink my eyes open to find him standing at the side of the bed, yanking open the drawer of the bedside table and pulling out a condom. He shucks his underwear and my eyes go wide at the sight before me. Yes, I've had his cock in my mouth but seeing it again like this, hard and flushed and looking rather determined — can a penis look determined? I think it can — the ache between my legs only intensifies. I'm dying to feel him slide inside me for the first time.

"You gotta stop looking at me like that," Shep murmurs.

I glance up at his words, our gazes meeting, his dark and completely unreadable. "Like what?"

"Like you want to swallow me whole. I'm not going to last if you keep that up." He tears open the wrapper and rolls the condom on that monster cock of his — and when I call it a monster, that's a good thing, trust me.

I'm so excited my body is tingling with anticipation. A sigh escapes when he rejoins me on the bed, his big body on top of mine, hands braced on either side of my head, his erection probing my sex. He reaches for me, readjusting my position so we're more face to face, his arm around my waist, holding me to him.

"Put your arms around me," he whispers and I do as he asks, my arms going for his neck just as he starts to enter me. It's a tease though. He removes his arm from my waist and grabs the base of his erection, brushing the head through my folds, against my clit, making me close my eyes and moan in agony. Or ecstasy.

Take your pick.

All I know is, he's driving me insane. I lift my hips, trying to get him to slide inside me, and he chuckles. Yes, he actually chuckles as he continues to torture me, a groan replacing his soft laughter when I tip my hips up further, desperate to make the contact I want.

"You want it?" he asks, sounding like a smug, confident jackass.

A very sexy, smug, confident jackass.

I nod, my hair brushing against the pillow, falling into my face. "Yes."

"Beg for it," he whispers, going still. "I wanna hear you say please."

God, he's awful. He's also starting to pull away and we can't have that. I'm stuck and he knows it. "Please," I murmur, my gaze fixing on his. I reach for him, my fingers curling around his forearm as I try to guide him in. "I need you inside me."

The little smile curling his lips is both wonderful and terrible, all at once. As if he knows how much he's driving me out of my mind. "Say the dirty words, Jade. I want to hear them."

He's pushing me past my comfort zone. I stare into his eyes, my chest rising and falling so rapidly my breasts brush against his chest. I can feel him, thick and long and ready to push inside me but also waiting for my words. Words that are so difficult to say.

"Please," I whisper, my voice strangled and high

pitched. "Please fuck me."

The moment I say it, he pushes inside, just the head, pausing as he stares down at the spot where we're almost joined. "Is that all you got?" He sounds strained, like he's as tortured as I am and I close my eyes, my hips wiggling as if I have no control over my body.

"Fuck me with your cock," I say in the barest of whispers, "Oh God, I need it. Please."

He rewards me with the very thing I asked for, his cock sliding deep inside my body, filling me completely. I go still beneath him, holding my breath, and all I can hear is the roaring of my heart. He doesn't move for a long moment and his cock pulses deep inside me, making me moan. Making him moan.

And then he starts to move, withdrawing almost completely before pushing back inside, establishing this amazing rhythm that has me clinging to him, my arms wrapped tight around his neck, my face buried in his chest.

"Put your legs around me," he demands and I do so, the both of us moaning when the new position sends him even deeper. "Fuck, Jade. You feel so fucking good."

His words send a current of electricity through me, settling in my sex. I might come again. As wild and outrageous as the idea sounds, I'm so worked up, I think it's possible. My clit is tingling in that way it does when I get close and oh God, he's actually touching my clit with his fingers at this very moment. Pressing against it, his thrusts increasing, his mouth seeking mine. The kiss is sloppy, our tongues tangling, and we swallow each other's groans as he increases his rhythm.

It feels so good. *He* feels so good inside me, thrusting hard. Harder. Harder still, until he's pushing me up the mattress. My legs shake as they cling around him, my hands buried in his damp with sweat hair at the back of his head. I'm whimpering, he's moaning, and then his mouth is at my ear, asking if I'm close, he sounds desperate to know if I'm close because he's going to come, he warns me. He's going to come so hard and it's all because of me. All because of me, and the way I make him feel, how badly he's wanted me from the very first moment he saw me…

And then he truly is on the brink of coming, and so am I. He goes still above me as he hangs his head, his lips parted, his hair a disheveled mess as it falls around his face. I'm clenching around him, my orgasm upon me out of nowhere, like it can't be contained. I'm just coming and coming and he shudders above me, my name falling from his lips as he thrusts and thrusts hard inside me, until, finally he's not moving at all.

He's a slumped wreck as he falls on top of me, his big body pressing me into the mattress, his mouth at my ear as he groans one last time. He's as hot as a furnace, sprawled all over me and I scratch my nails lightly down the length of his smooth, damp back. His heart is racing as fast as mine and I close my eyes, trying to calm my breaths, desperate to get my shit together but it's no use.

I just got fucked by Shep Prescott and lord help me, I think he's spoiled me for anyone else.

chapter
Twenty-One

Shep

"You need to quit smiling," Gabe growls irritably.

His grumpy request only makes my smile grow. "What's up your ass, man? And why can't I smile?"

"You look too damn happy." Gabe scans the room, his gaze assessing, his mouth thinned into a firm line. I'm the one on duty tonight but he's more on top of it than I am. My mind is elsewhere. All thoughts directed on one specific person.

Jade.

Jade naked. Jade in my arms, snuggled up so close I can feel every inch of her pressing into every inch of me. Jade in my bed. Her sexy mouth fused to mine, her legs wound around my hips, heels pressed against my ass as I sink my cock deep inside her wet, tight heat. Fuck… we did that a lot. Lots and lots of fucking last night. Best night of my life.

I'm desperate to do it again. Now.

"I can't help myself. I'm in a good mood." I shrug, deciding to scan the room too. It's quiet, despite it being a Saturday night. As we draw closer and closer to the end of the semester, things wind down, especially right before summer. Everyone would rather be outside, on the beach, enjoying the weather. Or everyone's lost all the money they can stand to bet and won't be returning until the fall semester starts. We'll shut down during finals week and resume business about a week or two after the fall semester starts.

We have a system and it works. I never minded divvying up the duties before. We trade off monitoring every Thursday through Saturday night. Sometimes one of us has to pull double duty, when we used to stay open on Sunday night too. I'm thinking with the new semester, I'd rather close on Sundays permanently. I might be busy and not want to deal. You know, because I'll be a senior. And I'll be hanging with Jade.

You are running waaaay ahead of yourself asshole.

I lean my shoulder against the wall, wishing Gabe and I could hide out—or I could leave. Honestly, I'm resentful. I'd rather be anywhere but here. It's slow tonight, the tables aren't even close to being full and Gabe is with me. Why do we both have to be here?

"You finally fucked her, didn't you." Gabe says it as a statement, not a question and I turn to look at him, ready to throw down those, *you better not talk about her like that* words. Though really he didn't say anything rude.

So I keep my mouth shut.

"I did," I say quietly, my gaze meeting his. I really don't want to talk about this, not here. Anyone passing by could hear us and I don't want Gabe giving me a bunch of crap.

Besides, I don't want to share any dirty details with my friend. I have before. Not gonna lie. Hell, we've compared notes, given each other high fives, toasted our good fortune and discovery of good pussy.

But I can't say anything like that about Jade. She... means something to me. What, I'm not quite sure yet. No way can I tell Gabe how much I love the way she smells. How the sound of her moans makes my body quake. The way her pussy clasps around my dick and squeezes so tight I swear I'm gonna blow like an inexperienced kid...

I have a boner just thinking about her. Jesus.

"You really like her." When I offer a jerky nod, Gabe continues. "That's good, man. I'm glad."

Okay, I didn't expect that response. "You're glad?"

"Sure." Gabe shrugs. "If she makes you happy, I'm happy. I've never seen you pursue a girl so aggressively like this one. I figure she must be something special."

My heart squeezes. Look what she's done to me. I'm such a fucking sap. "She is," I agree quietly. "I can't even put my finger on why."

I'm a liar. I like how she looks at me. The things she says to me. She's feisty one minute and sweet and sexy the next. I like pushing her beyond her boundaries. I fucking love the way she tastes. She makes me smile. She makes me laugh. Yes, she's a challenge and I like that too. She doesn't care who I am or what I have. She's never once asked me about my family or how much money we have. Nothing like that. Sometimes it's like she can barely tolerate me and I sort of like that too. It's weird.

But it works. I don't want to mess it up. We're still too tentative, our relationship is still too new. One wrong move, one wrong thing said, and I could seriously screw this up. I can't afford to do that.

"I'm happy for you man. This is fucking tremendous." I wonder if he's been drinking. Tremendous is not a normal part of Gabe's vocabulary. "Me? I'd rather bang a bunch of chicks through college and then deal with real life when I've graduated. A relationship can wait. I never thought I'd say this but with the way you're acting about this girl, I'm thinking you might be ready.

Which is fucking unbelievable but whatevs dude. What the fuck ever," Gabe explains, a crooked smile on his face.

Yeah. I think he's been drinking. We have our own self-imposed rules. We don't get trashed while on duty during gambling nights. But a few beers are usually harmless.

"You really think you're happy banging a bunch of chicks through college?" I ask incredulously. I'd pin him as lonely but maybe I'm wrong. Maybe he's not. Perhaps he likes the man-whore rep he has going on, the one I'm now dying to shed.

"Real life is barreling down on me. I have one more year of college and then it's responsibility time." Gabe's voice and expression are grim. "I need to have as much fun as possible my senior year. This one is pretty much a bust. It's been good, don't get me wrong, but it's over and done with. This summer I'm stuck with the fam, hanging out with them." He snorts. "And that's gonna suck."

"Where you going anyway?" His family started in oil, though they've moved on to a variety of investments that has yielded them extremely high returns. He's originally from Texas, though I don't know when Gabe last spent any specific amount of time in Texas. He hates it there. He much prefers the climate of the central California coast, not that I can blame him. I like it too.

He rolls his eyes. "Practically down the damn road. We'll be staying in Santa Barbara for the summer. My parents rented a house there."

"Nice." The Walkers never do anything half assed. If they're going to summer in Santa Barbara, they'll do it in style. "Big mansion right on the beach?"

"Probably. I don't know. I assume it'll be some obnoxious house with fifty rooms and twice as many servants." He hangs his head, talking down to his shoes. "I'm sure I'll find some rich bitch to fuck for the summer. What else is new, right?"

Damn, he's sort of bringing me down. I remember last summer when he spent it with his family in the Hamptons. That's exactly what he did—found some lonely housewife whose husband only came to visit for the weekends. Gabe regaled us with stories about fucking the chick every which way he could get her throughout the summer. Blonde and stacked, in her thirties and lonely as hell, he claimed he'd had a great time.

I don't know though. It sounded sort of…sad. Not that I ever said that to him.

"Why do you go?"

Gabe lifts his head. "I don't have much choice. They force me. Claim that we're one big happy family and we need to spend as much time together as possible before I go off and get married." He makes a face. "My mother already has a few girls lined up that she thinks are perfect candidates. Like they're running for political office or something."

They are. Anyone who marries Gabe will need to have the most pristine reputation ever. He'll probably need to find a virgin to meet his parents' approval, like that'll be easy.

"That's why you're lucky," Gabe continues, his tone wistful. "You like a girl, you go after her until she's yours. Now you're going out with Jade and you don't have your family breathing down your neck, asking what her bloodline is, who she's related to, if she's up to their standards. This is why I fuck around, dude. I will never measure up. The girl I might fall in love with someday? Swear to God, I'll pick out a chick I know they'll hate just to piss them off."

"My parents are just as big of snobs as yours are," I reassure him, and it's the truth. Mom won't be truly happy unless I'm dating a girl with a perfect pedigree. If Mom doesn't come from old money, then by God I should find someone who does so at least she'll become *related* to old money.

My family sucks balls.

"Seriously. It's bullshit. You ever think of running away? To like, the Virgin Islands or some such shit? Or maybe New Zealand? Yeah, New Zealand works, because that's about as far as I can get from my parents.

They'd never come see me out there," Gabe says, staring off into the distance. "I came into my trust fund. I have my own money. They can't control that."

But they control every other part of his life. I think my parents are bad—and they are, there's no denying it—Gabe's are ten times worse.

My phone buzzes and I check it, a smile curling my lips when I see who it's from.

Hi. ☺

I shake my head, typing my reply.

That's all you got for me? No hey big stud? No can I come over later and fuck your brains out?

No response for a while. Makes me wonder if I made her mad. Though how can she be mad with me? I'm the one who made her come three times last night.

"Are you sexting your girl?" Gabe asks.

"Of course not," I scoff, though I'd like to.

You really want me to call you big stud?

Hell yeah. Don't you wanna stroke my ego?

Isn't your ego big enough?

Then maybe you want to stroke my cock instead?

Again, there's no reply for a few minutes. I think I push her too hard. Hell, I *know* I push her too hard. It's like I can't help myself with her. I love getting a reaction. And she's always good for a reaction...

"I'm gonna grab another beer," Gabe says, pulling my attention from my still unanswered text. "You want something?"

"Nah." I'm loopy enough as it is. Drunk off Jade. Tired from last night. The minute I'm off duty I should go crash out in bed and catch up on sleep.

But sleep is for the dead. I'd rather try to get Jade to come to my place later.

Gabe takes off and I check my phone, pleased when a text appears at that very particular moment.

Didn't your cock get enough stroking last night?

I smile. Glance around, make sure no one's paying any attention to me. Hell, my cock is twitching right now just reading her response.

There's no such thing as enough cock stroking where you're concerned. What are you doing?

I'm in bed.

My cock doesn't just twitch. It happily rises to the occasion.

What are you wearing?

Shorts I got for free at VS and a tank top.

VS?

Victoria's Secret. They say PINK across my butt.

I think I'm breaking out into a sweat.

What color?

God, you're a perv.

Tell me.

Pink shorts, white tank. No bra. Thin material. As in you could probably see my nipples if you look close enough.

I'm definitely sweating. Her next text makes me laugh.

I can't believe I just said that.

I love that you just said that. Let me pick you up when I'm done.

Won't that be too late?

It's never too late for us to get together, right?

She's contemplating my suggestion. I can tell. I glance around the room again, notice that absolutely nothing is happening at this very moment and I wish like hell I could just walk out of this place. Despite Gabe being here too, it's definitely my night for duty so I need to stay. Fucking sucks but I'm here and not about to shirk my responsibilities.

Damn, just thinking that sentence, I know would make my father proud. Well, as proud as he can be with me running an illegal gambling house. He'd shit his pants if he knew. He'd never believe my explanation that it's a practice run for me to take over the family business later.

But I'm already in bed.

All thoughts of my father evaporate as I imagine Jade in bed. All cozy and warm, her hair a mess and all that soft, smooth skin exposed.

You don't have to change on my account. I'll text you before I come over.

What time do you think?

Around one? Is that okay?

Please say it's okay. God, please say you don't mind.

Gabe approaches, a beer bottle dangling from his fingers, irritated look on his too pretty face. The guy needs to be punched square in the nose to mess up all that beauty he has going on. He is way too good looking for his own good. "You should get the hell out of here. There's no point in the both of us staying."

My jaw drops open. Golden opportunity has just landed in my lap. "No way dude. It's my night."

"I have zero plans and from the way you've been tapping on your phone, I'd guess you have an eager girl dying to see you." My friend isn't too far off the mark, though it's more like I'm the eager one dying to see her. "Just go. I owe you. How many times have you bailed me out before?"

Too many to mention, but I don't keep track of all that shit. "Are you sure?"

"Positive," Gabe says firmly. "Now go."

I check my phone to see I have a message from Jade.

But that's so late. Maybe we should do something tomorrow...

"Thanks G," I tell him sincerely, reaching out so I can pat him on the shoulder. "I definitely owe you for this."

"Then I'll definitely come collect." He grins. "Go have fun getting naked with your girl, you lucky bastard."

I tap out another text before I exit the house.

Change of plans. Can you be ready in ten minutes?

Jade

I pop out through the double doors of my dorm hall as soon as I see Shep's car pull up in front of the building, running down the steps in my furry slippers Mom gave me for Christmas. It's almost eleven o'clock on a Saturday night but no one is really around and I'm glad. Last thing I want to do is draw attention to myself, especially in this get up.

Jogging toward his car, I open the passenger door and slide inside, slamming the door behind me. I drop my cell phone in the cup holder in the center console and glance up to find Shep staring at me with a look on his face that can only be described as unabashed hunger.

"Did you just run all the way to my car while not wearing a bra?" he asks, his voice hoarse.

I start to laugh. Boys. They're such pigs sometimes. "Yeah, I did. Do you have a problem with that?"

He reaches for me, his hands going directly to my boobs, kneading them, brushing his thumbs across my hard nipples and making me whimper. "Not at all. Keep up the good work, Frost. If I had my way, I'd make sure you never wore a damn bra."

I shove his hands away and point at the steering wheel. "Drive."

"So demanding," he mutters, flashing me a knowing grin before he throws the car into drive and pulls away from the curb.

I settle back in my seat, trying to calm my accelerated breaths, resting a hand over my chest. I'm sitting in this luxurious car that reeks of Shep in the best possible way, wearing the clothes I normally wear to bed. Not only am I braless, I'm panty-less too and I'm sure Shep will appreciate it when he makes that little discovery.

"So you got off, uh, work early?" I ask, trying to make conversation, anything to fill the tense silence in the car. Not that we're uncomfortable with each other, no way. But there's this awareness between us that's like a low hum, and it pulses through me, comes alive in my blood, vibrates just under my skin. It makes me itchy and anxious, like I want to lunge across the center console and grab him. I can't do that though. I could cause a freaking car accident and kill us both. All for what? Because I can't resist his kissable lips? His gorgeous face? His oh-fuck-me-I-need-more-of-it-now body?

Yeah I need to get myself under control.

So talking. Making conversation is good. Keeps me focused, and him too. That way we don't make a grab for each other and put our lives at risk.

"Yep. Got off so I can assist in getting *you* off," he says with a leer.

I laugh. I can't help it. He says the cheesiest things sometimes. "Who says I want to get off?" Ha, all I can think about is getting off. Specifically, Shep getting me off.

He sends me a look. "You come into my car looking like that? Wearing hardly any clothing? Trust me, before the night is over, you'll be getting off. Most likely more than once."

A thrill runs through me, settling like a pulse between my legs. "Sounds promising."

"Oh, it is. I can guarantee that." He resumes his attention on the road, his fingers curled tight around the steering wheel. "Gabe was there tonight. He said I could go, that he would cover me."

"Oh. That's nice of him," I offer, my voice soft. I chance a glance at him, checking out his outfit. He's wearing black shorts that hit him at the knee and a pale blue button down. Preppy looking, without being too over the top. I can only assume he dresses up a little for the job? I guess they take that place pretty seriously, which is insane because what he's doing is illegal and truly, I shouldn't be involved with someone like that.

But here I am, sitting in his car. Gladly. Knowing he's going to take me back to his place and get me naked in minutes.

I can't freaking wait. I'm so excited I'm practically bouncing in my seat.

"Gabe's a good guy. One of my best friends," he says.

"You've known him a long time? Or only since you came here?"

"Since high school. We went to the same prep school. Miss Derringers School for Wayward Boys." He starts to laugh and shakes his head. "It really wasn't called that but it should've been. We were both troublemakers."

"I'm not surprised," I say dryly. I'm sure he was the epitome of trouble when he was younger. Sometimes he still is. He has a devilish streak inside of him that I can't help but find appealing.

"Enough about me and Gabe." Shep reaches out and settles his hand on my thigh, sliding his fingers between my legs. His touch is like a brand, hot and possessive. "I've missed you."

I can hardly believe he's saying such a thing. He's really missed me? "You saw me this morning." When he drove me back to my dorm room at the crack of dawn, giving me such a warm, wet, spine tingling kiss I'd hardly been able to walk up the steps of my dorm hall, my knees were so weak.

"That was hours ago." He gives my thigh a squeeze and I feel it everywhere. "How was work?"

He would've made me stay with him all day, but

I had to go in to Light my Fire at noon. I had a five hour shift and normally they go by fast, especially on Saturdays. The weather was perfect, which usually means a beautiful day draws in a lot of downtown shoppers and tourists eager to explore the little shops.

But all I did was mope around and think about Shep. Mull over what happened between us the night before. Daydreamer extraordinaire, that was me, to the point that my boss Enid called me back into her office and asked what the hell was wrong with me — direct quote.

How could I tell her that I was sick? She'd think I was crazy if I told her I had Shep flu. Though really it was a Shep hangover but that doesn't make any sense either...

"Work was fine," I say, not really wanting to talk about work at all. I have a shift tomorrow too. I usually work all weekend, every weekend but now I'm thinking that's too restrictive. I won't see Shep as much. Though am I really making future plans with Shep in my head? I must be losing it. Clearly. I need to remember to take whatever it is we're doing here one day at a time.

That's about all he can give me, I know.

"Thinking of me the entire time?" He scoops up my hand in his and brings it to his mouth, dropping a warm, lingering kiss on my knuckles. I swear I feel the touch of his lips in the deepest, most secret part of me.

"Don't flatter yourself," I tell him, my breath lodging

in my throat when he sends me a smoldering look. One that says he's mentally undressing me.

"I'm just stating a fact. At least, for me it's a fact." He kisses the back of my hand, his gaze going back to the road. "You're all I've thought about since I dropped you off this morning."

I shouldn't like his admission so much. More like I shouldn't read so much into it. This isn't the first time he's said this sort of thing to me though. I'm starting to think maybe Shep and I could date and see each other like two normal people, versus just having the occasional hookup.

Ugh, why are you even thinking like this?

Deciding it's best I say nothing, I remain quiet, disentangling my hand from his and resting them both in my lap. I avert my head, staring out the window, nervousness coursing through me the closer we get to his house. We're going to do this again. And it's going to be good. How can it not be? Though I'm dying to do it with Shep again I'm also…scared.

Scared I'll enjoy it too much. Scared I'll want him even more. Scared I'll start to fall for him. Scared I'll believe we could really have something. Scared he doesn't feel the same way about me, about *us,* whatsoever.

I clutch my trembling fingers together and will myself to keep my shit together.

The moment he cuts the engine after pulling the car

into the garage, he reaches for me, our bodies separated by the center console, his mouth fused with mine. He kisses me long and deep, his tongue searching, his hands in my hair, tugging and pulling. When he breaks the kiss first we're both breathing hard, and he's looking at me like I totally confuse him.

The feeling is mutual.

"I couldn't wait any longer." He touches my bottom lip with his thumb, drags it slowly back and forth and I release a shuddering breath. "I get near you and it's like I lose all control."

I feel the same exact way, but no way can I admit that.

"Let's go inside," he murmurs as he cups my cheek. His gaze is zeroed in on my mouth and I lick my lips, pleasure rippling through me when he closes his eyes and exhales loudly. "You're trying to kill me, aren't you?"

"Yes," I whisper, making him growl.

Making me smile.

chapter Twenty-Two

Jade

"I can't move," Shep murmurs, his deep velvety voice washing over me. I shiver at the sound, my skin hot and damp with sweat, my muscles loose and languid.

"Me either," I whisper back, keeping my eyes closed. My heart is...still racing. Third orgasm of the night, best one yet if that's even possible. I have to give credit where credit is due.

Shepard Prescott has a magical mouth. And the most perfect, long fingers ever created. Ohhh, his fingers. And his lips. His tongue. Holy crap, his tongue. I could write a poem praising his oral skills. Though that would probably be in bad taste.

We're lying in the middle of his giant bed, facing

each other. We're both naked and warm and I'm still a little shaky, though I have no idea if he is or not. He's watching me though. I can feel his eyes trail over my skin and for once, I don't feel self-conscious. I flat out don't care what he sees. I'm sure I look a wreck. But he's the one who wrecked me so he may as well take a good long look at what he's done.

"You are so pretty right after you come." His fingers are in my hair, right along my hairline, smoothing it back from my face. I keep my eyes tightly closed, not wanting to open them, afraid it might ruin the moment. Worse, that *I* might ruin the moment. I don't do well with praise. It always embarrasses me, and when that praise has to do with the way I look after he makes me come? Um, mortifying. "Your cheeks are always so pink. Your entire body is. You're fucking glowing."

There's a reason I'm glowing. He's lit me up from the inside. I'm completely wrung out. Just a heap of liquid limbs and warm skin, a pounding heart and tingling bits—and it's all his fault.

"And the sounds you make," he continues, his voice going deeper. He scoots closer, the mattress dips and I roll closer to him, like I have no control of my body. "They make me fucking insane, Jade."

The sounds I make? I try my best to be quiet but he encourages me to say things. Whisper things. Moan and groan and whimper and cry out and…

Oh, God. I make a lot of sounds.

"Um, I think I have that sort of effect on guys, and not in a good way," I joke, my eyes still closed, my voice but a mere whisper. I'm sort of fading. Three orgasms will do that to a girl, especially a girl who was given three orgasms the night before too. It's some sort of record in my book. I go from zero to six within twenty four hours with a guy.

Shep is the overall gold medal winner in making me come.

"Mmm, in the absolute best way." He tangles his legs with mine, wrapping one around the back of my thighs and drawing me closer so I have no choice but to run smack into him. I automatically slip my arms around his waist and press my cheek against his chest, concentrating on the sound of his thumping heart. He rests his chin on my head, his arms around me, hands on my butt.

This is good. Comforting. I feel...safe wrapped up in his arms, nestled close to his naked body and that's stupid, right? I'm just putting it all out there and I'll only get hurt in the end. That's what scares me. He has power and I have none. Not that I've handed over any power to him, he came into this...thing between us holding all of it right off the bat.

I hate it.

"I'm made of boy repellent," I tell him sleepily,

wondering why I even opened my mouth. Yeah, convince him how much boys dislike you. Way to keep him interested. "They never want to get too close for fear I might take them out."

"Take them out? I agree you're pretty damn tough. And you know how to throw a hell of a slap, Frost." I really like it when he calls me by my last name. Is that weird? It's weird. "But deep down inside, you're just a softie."

Well, maybe I am with him...

"Besides, you haven't met the right one yet," he says, sounding completely logical. "You're dealing with the wrong kind of guys. Hence the words boy repellent."

I open my eyes and shift, and he moves away so I can lift my head to stare up at him. "Did you just say *hence the words?*"

"Yeah. I'm trying to prove to you that I'm a man, not a boy." He kisses the tip of my nose, then my cheek. Oh, then my other cheek. Like he can't stop. "By using fancy phrases and stuff."

"You don't need to prove to me you're a man with your stellar vocabulary. I already..." I clamp my mouth shut. I can't continue on with what I was going to say can I? No way.

His fingers are on my lips, as if he wants to pry them open and force me to speak. "Finish that thought."

I shake my head.

"Jade…"

"No," I murmur against his fingers. Oh God, I can smell myself on them. These are the very fingers that were just inside my body, bringing me to a magical orgasm along with that very magical mouth and tongue and…yes, his teeth. Who knew teeth could be so sexy? Clearly I haven't been living a full life, I swear to God.

"Yes." He cradles my jaw and leans in, his mouth on mine once more in a brief kiss. "Tell me how you already know I'm a man."

"That wasn't what I was going to say," I deny and he smiles against my lips. That wonderful, wide, he doesn't give a crap about anything smile Shep is so good at giving.

"Stop lying." He kisses me again, his tongue tangling with mine lazily. I can taste myself on him too and just like last night, arousal courses through me, heady and strong. His cock rises between us, ready to rejoin the action and a moan falls from my lips. I'm tired, my limbs feel heavy but if he rolled me over right now, it would be so easy for him to slip inside me…

"Tell me," he whispers when he breaks the kiss. "Is it because I can make you come so hard your legs shake?"

I say nothing. Don't bother denying his words because they're the truth.

"Or maybe it's the way I fuck you. There's no fumbling, no denying you your satisfaction." He kisses my neck, licks my skin and I tilt my head back, giving him better access. "You get what you deserve every single time."

What I deserve. I like that. "Maybe it's because you're the most arrogant man I've ever met," I murmur.

"Confident," he corrects, shifting away from my neck so he can meet my gaze once more. "Maybe you liked that I knew what I wanted and I went after it with no hesitation."

I frown at him. "What did you want?"

His smile returns, cocksure and bright in the dimness of the dark room. "You, baby. You."

And then he's kissing me again. Stealing all my words, stealing all my thoughts. Stealing away everything that is me, until all I can focus on is the glide of his tongue against mine, his big hands roaming my body, his erection brushing against my belly. He flips me around so my back is to his front and I feel him reach for one of the condoms that's resting on the bedside table, I can only assume.

The next thing I know his hand is on my breast, his warm, slightly rough palm rubbing my sensitive nipple. He's kissing and nibbling my neck, his other hand is spreading my legs and then he's inside me, taking me from behind, his thrusts slow and shallow, like he has all the time in the world.

Oh God, and it feels so freaking unbelievably good. I

close my eyes, my head falling back on his shoulder, the position arching my chest so my breast fills his hand. His other hand is at my hip, holding me in place as he takes me. Which is exactly what he's doing — taking me. Fucking me gently — a term I never believed in before but that's exactly what he's doing.

"Hot and wet," he whispers against my neck. "I can feel you trying to suck me deep, baby. Already eager for this to be over?"

I have zero control of my body. If I'm trying to suck him deep, I'm not aware of it. I readjust my hips, squirming against him and his fingers press into my flesh almost painfully.

"Stop moving," he grits through his teeth, his mouth right at my ear, his breath hot. "Relax. No need to rush it."

I calm my breathing, trying to do as he says. He's right. There's no need to rush. I savor the drag and pull of his cock sliding in and out of my body, how both of his hands are now on my chest, my breasts filling his palms, his mouth at my neck as he kisses me there.

"You ever been fucked from behind?" he asks gruffly.

"N-no." I shake my head, suck in a harsh gasp when he slides his hand down to my stomach, his fingers splayed across my skin as he holds me in place.

"It's best just like this," he murmurs, his husky voice

lulling me into a trance. "Slow and easy, when you're not in a big hurry. When you just want to feel each other. Enjoy each other."

I'm trembling at his words, at the shallow strokes of his cock. His hands are on my hips now, holding me. Unable to help myself, I wiggle against him, sending him deeper, and he groans, then sinks his teeth into the side of my neck. The pleasurable sting is like a direct link to my clit and I press my lips together to keep from crying out.

"Bend forward," he urges, one hand at the center of my back. I do as he says, moaning when that hand strokes down my back, coasting over my butt.

It all feels so amazing, I don't know if I'm going to be able to withstand this much longer.

Shep

The girl is trying to kill me. Her smooth as silk, pale as cream body is driving me out of my mind. I demanded she bend forward because I can see my cock disappear inside her body when she's positioned like that and fuck, watching as I sink into her again and again is making me want to come.

I clench my jaw and pray I can keep my shit together for at least a few more minutes. I've already come twice. You'd think it would be no big deal, that I'm already so wrung out I should be able to make this last as long as I want, right?

But with Jade, it's different. What do I know about slow, leisurely sex when I fuck a girl from behind? Every other chick I've fucked like this, I do it so I don't have to look at her face. I'm just using her, plain and simple.

Not with Jade. I'm getting off on the slowness. How I can feel her pussy grip my dick. The way she trembles in my arms when I push forward, her butt pressed against me as I completely surround her.

It's a totally new experience. Slow sex isn't my style. This though…it's like a fucking wonder. I've just had my eyes opened to a whole new world thanks to this girl.

Unbelievable.

I settle both of my hands on her ass, squeezing and kneading her plump flesh. She groans at my touch and I grip her hips, holding her steady as I start to increase my strokes. The need already claws at me, scraping up my spine, settling just under my skin. I have no control when it comes to her. She makes me insane. I keep telling her that but I don't think she believes me.

She should. One minute between her legs and it's like she's all I want, all I can think about. I was already completely sucked in just spending time with her but now that I've actually had her? I don't want to let her go, don't want her out of my damn sight. I crave her constantly. It's fucking nuts. With her, I'm insatiable.

Completely and totally insatiable.

I'd fully planned on relaxing tonight. Hang out with her, talk a little bit or watch a movie, maybe grab a snack considering I'm always hungry. I'd eventually get her into my bed, get her naked and fuck her. Then we could fall asleep in each other's arms.

Nope. Not even close. I practically jumped her in the garage. Dragged her up to my room, stripped her naked and barely got out of my shorts before I had my cock inside her and she was begging me to fuck her harder. We went another round right after that. She slowly undressed me, seemingly fascinated with unbuttoning my shirt, her shaky fingers fumbling with the buttons, brushing against my skin and making me fucking insane. I let her have her way with me, demanded that she be on top and that had been hot. Watching her move and sway, her breasts in my face, her hips working as she slid up and down my cock.

She'd looked so smug afterward, so pretty and flustered yet confident—a look I haven't really seen her wear when we're involved sexually—I couldn't resist her. I had to show her I could make her come as many times as possible. So I went down on her, licked that delicious little pussy until I had her writhing beneath my mouth and screaming my name.

See? I can't resist her. Like, ever. I'm a goner. I make

fun of assholes that are like this with a girl. Now *I've* become one of those assholes.

And I'm okay with it.

"Shep," she whispers, her soft voice echoing through my head, making me fumble. That's another thing. I'm a smooth motherfucker with girls. But not with this one. She makes my hands shake and my brain scramble and sometimes I'm at a loss for words and that never happens.

Ever.

She whimpers my name again and I reach for the ends of her hair, lightly tugging on it so she lifts her head, bringing herself closer to me. "Yeah, baby?" I press my cheek to hers, inhale her addictive scent, closing my eyes as I lift my hips and give her an extra hard thrust.

"I like it better when you're closer," she admits, reaching behind her so she can wrap her arms around my neck. The position gives me a great view of her tits, her perfect pink nipples and I stare down the length of her body, my eyes cataloging every freckle I can see.

Still haven't had a chance to count them all yet. Need to make more of an effort, but it's so damn difficult. Every time I get her naked the last thing I'm thinking about is counting her freckles...

"Nothing better than having you in my arms," I murmur as my hands roam over her silky soft skin until I'm cupping her breasts, playing with her nipples.

Damn, with her arms around me, her chest thrust out, my dick buried deep in her tight, wet warmth, I'm gonna blow. Soon. I thought this slow and easy stuff would be just that—slow and easy.

But that's not happening. Without thought I increase my pace, tightening my hands on her breasts, making her whimper. She tosses her head back, resting it on my shoulder and I lean down, pressing my mouth to her cheek. "You close?" I ask.

She nods frantically, strands of red hair falling into my face. "Y-yes."

I should've known. She gets close and her voice starts to shake. Her entire body trembles and there's a little hitch in her breath I find impossibly sexy. That I'm the one who can make the snarky, feisty Jade Frost fall apart like this, makes me feel like a fucking God.

No girl has ever affected me like this.

Ever.

Twenty-Three *chapter*

Shep

"So what's it like?"

I turn to glare at Gabe who's watching me with a neutral smile on his face. I don't like that smile. It looks suspicious. Reeks of suspicion actually. "What's what like?"

Monday morning, nine a.m. and we're at the diner for breakfast as usual. It's packed. As the semester winds down, there are less people on campus and more people…everywhere else.

"Banging the same chick every night for over a week straight. Curious minds want to know." Gabe shoves a piece of toast in his mouth and chews, his gaze never leaving mine.

After a few seconds of irritation at his shitty question,

I realize the bastard is serious. He genuinely is curious. Because everyone knows Gabe hasn't been with a girl beyond one day, let alone a week. Same with Tristan.

Fine, same with me. But I'm a changed man, damn it. Thanks to Jade.

Hmm, Jade. Thinking of her immediately has my dick twitching. The shape of her mouth and the way it stretches when she smiles. How the color of her lips is the same pale pink shade as her nipples. The taste of her nipples, the way she moans and writhes beneath me when I suck on them. How slick and wet she is every time I slip my fingers between her legs. Every time. Always wet, only for me. Drives me out of my fucking mind.

Just thinking about her like this, with my friends in the middle of a very busy restaurant, is driving me out of my mind. I need to stop.

So I do.

Tristan is unusually quiet this morning, shoveling food in his mouth, his head bent as if he's staring at his plate. He's not very talkative. None of us have been. Hell, I'd considered skipping our traditional breakfast meeting and I never do that.

When you have a warm, naked girl in your bed, you're willing to skip just about anything to spend a few more minutes with her.

"It's...good," I finally answer somewhat lamely. It's

beyond good but I don't want to sound like a starry-eyed kid. What exactly does Gabe want to know? If it's dirty details, forget it. That's between Jade and me. We have plenty of dirty details. Lots of them. But those are ours and no one else's.

"Really? *Good?* That's all you have to say?" Tristan lifts his head, his gaze zeroed in on mine. He looks tired. Skeptical. Irritated. I know this semester has been kicking his ass and he can't wait for it to be over. We've all been ready to make our escape from this town these last few weeks, especially Tristan and I since we spent the entire last summer here.

But now? For me? There's no rush. I want to savor every moment with Jade before school's done and she leaves. I don't know what's going to happen after we leave. And I'm almost afraid to ask.

"Well, it's definitely not bad," I say irritably, pushing my plate away from me. My appetite is gone. I hate it when they corner me, question me, act like I'm crazy for wanting to spend time with Jade and not them. I think they're just jealous.

"Tell me what it's like though," Gabe urges, his expression...sincere. "You aren't bored yet?"

"Not even close," I mutter, grabbing my cup of coffee and taking a big swig. It's lukewarm at best and I put too much creamer in it so it tastes like absolute shit.

"She must know some real magic tricks in the

sack then, huh? Let's not forget she has that amazing mouth…" Gabe's voice drifts and when I send him a dirty look, he immediately appears contrite. "Sorry dude. You know what I'm talking about."

I know exactly what he's talking about. Her mouth is the stuff of my every wicked dream. She knows how to use it too. But I don't need to hear my best friend go on about Jade's mouth like he wants to sample it.

The mere thought of him only *looking* at her lips makes me want to rip his eyes out of his head. I've turned into a possessive caveman when it comes to Jade and that makes no fucking sense whatsoever.

"Listen." I lean forward and rest my elbows on the edge of the table, staring at the both of them like I mean business. Which I do. "Jade is…off limits. We don't need to talk about her. Not like we do with other girls."

"You mean the ones we hook up with?" Tristan asks, both eyebrows raised.

"Yeah. Those ones," I say slowly, irritated that I even have to make this new rule. But hell, they don't get it. Any other girl, I'd be talking about her, because I'd already be done with her. How good she was in bed — or how bad. What sort of kisser she was. Hell, sometimes we'd rate them, especially back in the early days when we were young and total shitheads.

If I had to rate Jade now, she wouldn't even register on the scale, she's that good. But no way am I going to say that out loud. They wouldn't get it. Hell, I barely get it. Why exactly has she become so important? What is it about her that makes her so different from the other girls I've been with? It's like the minute I kissed her, touched her, everything changed. I want no one else. Need no one else.

Just her.

Worse? I have no idea if she feels the same way. The uncertainty kills me and I don't know how to deal with it. I've never had to deal with it and that's my problem. She makes me straight up crazy. In both the worst and best possible ways.

"So you get serious about a chick and you're suddenly no fun." Gabe shakes his head, his disappointment palpable. "That sucks, bro."

"Never thought I'd see this day happen," Tristan adds as he balls up his napkin and tosses it on top of his empty plate. "I just lost my appetite."

I decide not to remind him that he'd already eaten all his food. "What, are you in mourning now? Give me a break. You are both assholes."

"This is college," Tristan says, stressing the last word. "The land of opportunity. Not a time for you to get serious about some young chick. Dude, she's a freshman, barely out of high school! The girl doesn't know shit. She hasn't even lived. What do you think will happen when you bring her home to mom and dad, huh? Your mom is gonna chew her up and spit her back out in seconds."

I push the worry out of my head that Tristan's words bring. He has a point. But I don't care what my parents think and it's not like I'm bringing her to meet them. I'm not that serious about Jade, not yet. It's only been about a month. Granted, the best month of my life but still.

"Screw all this Shep's got a girlfriend talk," Gabe says irritably. "We have more pressing matters to discuss."

"Like what?" I ask.

"Like when are we going to close down the house? Business is slow. Attendance is down. The semester's almost finished and there's no point in stringing this out." Gabe nods once. "I vote we shut her down right now."

"Without one last weekend blowout event? Hell no." Tristan shakes his head. "We'll shut it down after Saturday. Let's organize something, put together an end of the season event or whatever."

"End of the season?" I send him a look. "I didn't realize gambling had a season."

Tristan shrugs. "It does when your clientele are college students. "

"Do we have enough time to organize an event?" Gabe asks.

"Absolutely. I'll get started on the deets today. Trust

me. It'll be awesome. But we'll all have to work Saturday night. Even you, *Mister I'm in a Real Relationship*," Gabe says, pointing at me.

Great. I was hoping to spend Saturday night with Jade. Maybe I could convince her to come. She hates that place—and I guess I can't blame her—but I'd like her with me that night.

"I'll be there," I reassure the both of them. I'm not about to shirk my responsibilities, though I know they both believe I'll blow them off first chance I get. Not with this though. The house is business. I don't do it for the money but we're so caught up in it now, no way can I abandon it. It's a project that took on a life of its own and I'm one-third responsible for it.

My phone buzzes and I pull it out of my pocket, eager to see if it's Jade.

Imagine my disappointment when I realize it's Mom.

What are your plans this weekend?

My heart starts to thump erratically and not in a good way. Why the hell is she asking me that?

Don't tell me you're coming to see me.

Gabe and Tristan are talking big plans for Saturday night. Free beer (need to put a limit on that). Special two-for-one deals (that needs a limit too). All sorts of special crap to draw people in before we shut down.

My phone buzzes again.

That's exactly what I was going to tell you. Only for one night though. Your father has business in Los Angeles this weekend. Thought we'd drop by and see you for dinner Saturday.

Fucking great.

"My parents are coming this weekend," I mutter to no one in particular, still staring at the screen of my phone.

"Get out," Tristan says. "Why?"

I lift my head and glare at him. "Not joking. Mom just texted me. They'll be here Saturday night. They want to have dinner."

"But you have plans," Gabe points out.

Plans for the illegal gambling house I run with them that my parents know nothing about. If they found out, they'd fucking flip.

"I can work the later shift. No way will she let me skip out on dinner," I say grimly.

"That fucking sucks," Gabe says. "Maybe you should take your girl. Get that whole scenario out of the way."

Say the fuck what? Why does Gabe keep talking about my parents and Jade? Like I'd want to subject Jade to them anyway.

"Tell me about it." I shake my head and glance down at my phone, deciding I need to answer her.

Sounds good. Call me when you get in.

Will do, darling. Maybe you should bring a friend. Bonus points if she's a girl.

Is my mother a mind reader or what? I break out into a cold sweat just reading that latest text.

There's no one special in my life.

I throw out a bogus answer in the hopes it distracts her.

That's not what I heard.

Glancing up, I send a hard glare in Tristan's direction until he can feel my eyes on him. He turns his head, his eyes going wide. "What's up with you gossiping with your mama? And mine?" I ask.

Tristan at least has the decency to look embarrassed. "What are you talking about?"

"Somehow my mom knows there's a girl in my life?" Hell, did Tristan set me up or what? The asshole.

Now he's blushing. And I've never seen him blush. "I was bored. Mom called. I kept talking. One thing led to another and..."

"You told her about Jade," I finish for him.

"Yeah. Sort of." He nods. "Sorry. She worked it out of me."

Great. It's not that I don't want to bring Jade to dinner with my parents. It's more that I don't want her to meet them. Yet. Shit, I don't know what I want. It feels too soon. We don't know each other that well. I mean yeah, I'm feeling pretty head over heels for her, which is fucking crazy but to bring my family into it makes everything seem so damn serious.

And I'm not sure if I'm ready for that.

Jade

"So I have some news!"

I wince at Mom's too loud, too excited voice in my ear. I haven't really talked to her in weeks, not since I started hanging out with Shep and I'd been feeling guilty. Mom and I are close. It's been the two of us against the world for a long time and when I went away to college, she was a little sad. I knew she'd miss me but I didn't want her miserable while I'm off becoming an actual adult.

But then she met Dex and they started going out pretty steadily. We haven't met yet but she's told me enough about him and I can sense he's a pretty cool guy. He treats Mom well and that's all I can ask for.

He also occupies all of her time. Not that I have any room to talk. The minute Shep walks into my life, he's all I can think about. Forget anyone else. Forget my freaking mother, which is awful. So yeah, I haven't called her lately, but she hasn't really called me either so I guess we're both totally preoccupied with the men in our lives?

The fact that I even have a man in my life—a man

like stupid sexy Shep—is a thrill that I still can't get over. I'm freaking pathetic, I swear.

"What's your news?" I ask cheerily as I walk across campus. I just left class and I'm feeling good. School's almost over. I'm confident about my finals. Oh, and it's a perfect spring day. The sky is so blue it looks fake, and the cool breeze brings with it the salty tang of the ocean. I sort of hate that I have class until late tonight. It's my last one of the semester and we turn in the final next week.

Hmm, I bet I could ditch if I wanted. I might. I might text Shep and see if he'll pick me up early so we could go back to his place and get naked and…

"…so it sold! In less than forty-eight hours! Can you believe it? Let me tell you, it was about the most exciting thing that's happened to me in a long time, I swear!" Mom yells.

Wait a minute. What did she just say?

"Back it up, Mom. I think I missed the first part," I mumble, dread creeping over me, settling like a cold lump in the pit of my stomach. I don't know if I'm going to like what she's about to repeat. To say I'm quietly freaking out would be apt.

"I sold the house, sweetie! And I sold it for such a huge profit you would be shocked. Thanks to the remodel, we were able to ask for a much higher price and it turned into this crazy bidding war. I've never seen anything like it." She laughs, sounding shocked and dazed and confused and so incredibly happy, I sort of want to bite my tongue so I don't say anything at all to ruin her good mood.

But I can't help myself. Because I'm sort of pissed. So here I go.

"Um, why didn't you tell me you were selling the house?" I ask incredulously as I come to a full stop in the middle of the sidewalk. A guy walking right behind me runs into me, his backpack plowing into my arm with a heavy thud and I send him a dirty look when he glares at me from over his shoulder.

Yeah, yeah it was my fault but still.

"Well, I thought I *did* tell you," she says tentatively and I glance around, spotting an empty bench nearby. I rush toward it, tossing my backpack on it before I sit. "I swore I did. Didn't I mention it to you the last time we talked?"

That would be a hell no. I think I'd remember something as important as my mother selling the only home I'd ever known. "No, you didn't."

"I didn't tell you that's why I was having the remodel done? It wasn't for my enjoyment, though I wish I would've done it sooner." Her voice lowers. "You should see the kitchen, sweetheart. Beautiful appliances, granite countertops, and the new cabinets… it's like kitchen heaven. It's gorgeous."

I sigh. "Mom, focus. You *never* told me this, I promise. I wish...I wish you would've consulted with me first before you put it up for sale." Not that she needed my permission, but that was my home too, and now she sold it in less than forty-eight hours. Like it meant nothing to her.

"I swear I did, sweetie. Oh, I feel so terrible." She makes a tsking noise and I know she's fretting so of course, I feel terrible too. "Trust me, this was the best thing for me to do. With you out of the house, I realized I wanted something smaller. Dex helped me out with the remodel, got me the right financing so I took a little equity out of the house and now I have enough money that if I'm really lucky, I'll be able to pay cash outright for the next one!"

The way she keeps talking, I can envision an exclamation point after every single sentence she says. It's rather unnerving. I don't want to squash her excitement but crap. She sold my house. Where's all my stuff going to go? "I'm not necessarily out of the house, Mom. I planned on coming home this summer. And the next few summers after this one."

"Yeah..." Her voice trails off and my stomach clenches, that cold lump of dread turning even colder. This doesn't sound good. "About that."

"What about it?" I clutch my phone tight, glancing around the campus. Everyone looks happy. Carefree.

Like they've got no problems. I feel like my entire world is about to cave in on me, all because of a house that really shouldn't matter but somehow, it does.

"Is there any sort of student housing you can look into over the summer? I know it's so last minute—"

"It's beyond last minute," I interrupt, trying to contain my anger, but it's right there, just bubbling beneath the surface. It's almost May and she's asking about summer student housing? Is she out of her mind?

"I know, I know." She sighs. "I've been so caught up in everything and I only just realized you still planned on coming home when you have no home to come home to. I'm not sure what we can do about that."

I'm stunned. It's not like my mom to be so...flighty. I blame the new guy. If Shep can evaporate my brain cells with a sexy look and a long kiss, I can only imagine Mom is suffering from the same thing with her new man. "How long is your escrow, Mom?"

"Thirty days, but I'd planned on staying with Dex while I look for another house." She pauses. "We could do that, I suppose. The two of us stay at Dex's house together. He has a guest room. We can put the majority of your stuff in storage along with everything else. That sounds fun doesn't it?"

No, it sounds freaking awful. No way do I want to stay at Dex's house. I don't even know this guy. "Let me look into other options," I say, trying my best to keep my temper under control but I gotta admit. I'm super pissed about this. And worried. Where will I live? How will I be able to afford it? What in the world am I going to do?

"Aw honey, don't be mad! We'll figure this out. We always do. I have some money so I can help." She's prattling on, telling me to think positive, that I can come home just like I planned but my decision has already been made.

I'm not going back there. How can I?

But how can I stay here?

Twenty-Four

chapter

Jade

Stress makes me extremely bitchy.

This is not a new realization. I discovered this little fact back in middle school, when I had a huge science project due and the group I worked with was full of incompetent a-holes who didn't care if they got a good grade or not. Being the obsessed with grades girl that I was — and still am, sort of — this made me insane. It pushed me to the point that I yelled and screamed at my stupid group, took over the entire project, completed it all on my own and turned it in. All while informing my teacher that I was the one who did everything and the rest of them did nothing.

I received an A on that project. Everyone else failed. They hated me. I didn't care. They got what they deserved in my eyes. Yes, I know this makes me a bit of a stress monster but I've relaxed since then, thank goodness.

That was the first of many blowouts. I've contained them over the years. Learned how to control myself. I have a temper. People blame my red hair, which is so incredibly stupid but hey, maybe they're right. I can get so flipping mad over stuff sometimes, it's ridiculous. As I've gotten older, I've calmed down. It's not worth getting so worked up, you know? All it does is stress me out.

But I'm so mad right now, I could scream, and I think the emotion is warranted. Though maybe mad isn't the right word. More like I'm super irritated. At my mom and the situation she put me in. Oh, and worried. Like, mega worried.

What am I supposed to do? Where am I supposed to go? I spoke with Kelli earlier and she has no plans on staying here for the summer. She's back to her hometown, where she'll be working fulltime and hooking up with dudes she went to high school with — direct quote.

A little over two weeks left until we finally must move out of our dorm and I have nowhere to go. I'm screwed.

Absolutely, totally screwed.

Thanks Mom.

I skipped class. It's the last one of the semester and I should really be there but come on. My mind is a little preoccupied. I asked my friend Nicole to take notes for me and I know she'll keep me informed if there's any changes to the final project that's due next week. I'm halfway done with my project anyway.

Instead of listening to my professor drone on for two hours, I'm trolling Craigslist on my laptop, looking up roommate listings, nibbling on my lower lip so much I swear I'm going to gnaw a hole in it. Shep texted me earlier, pretty much demanding we get together tonight, but I don't know. I'm all stressed out and worried and he doesn't want to deal with my shit.

So I ignored his text. He thinks I'm in class anyway so it's no biggie.

Sighing, I run my hand over the top of my head, frustration swimming in my veins. The roommate listings either sound too good to be true or creepy as hell. There are quite a few expensive ones too. I stopped by Light My Fire earlier and talked to Enid, asking if she could hire me on fulltime for the summer. She said there was a possibility but she couldn't guarantee it, which means I need to go in search of another job in addition to Light My Fire.

With every bit of information I discover, my summer is going up in flames, pardon the pun.

"Hey, what are you doing here?" Kelli asks as she enters our room.

I barely glance up from my laptop. "I skipped class."

"But it's your last one."

"I know. I didn't think I could concentrate, what with everything going on. So I'm searching for a roommate instead." I refocus my attention on the laptop.

Kelli stops beside my bed to peek over my shoulder. "By trying to find one on Craigslist? Ew, Jade. You'll probably end up with a psycho."

"They're not all bad on here." I hope. "Besides, what else am I supposed to do?" I'm bristling. My shoulders are stiff and my tone is the slightest bit screechy. I wish this day would just end.

"I don't know, go look on the community board? Ask friends? People in class? Spread the word that you're looking for a temporary room for the summer? There's gotta be a better way." Kelli flops on top of her bed, lying on her back as she stares up at the ceiling. "I can ask around for you if you want."

"I would really appreciate it." I slam my laptop shut and drop it on the mattress beside me, then stretch out on my bed. "I'm freaking out, Kel."

"I know. I'd be freaking out too." She pauses. "Maybe you should come home with me. We can share my room. We're already used to each other. We survived an entire school year together. It wouldn't be such a hardship."

I'm tempted to say yes. Kelli and I get along great. I met her parents when they came to visit once and they're nice. But I don't think I could impose myself on her family like that. I'd need to find a new job too. "I don't know…"

"Think about it," she says firmly. "I'll talk to my mom tomorrow. I'm sure she wouldn't mind."

What if she did mind? I don't know how my mom would react if I asked to bring someone home for the summer. She's a private person and she has her routine. A routine that's probably totally changed since I left for college.

Not that I can bring anyone home. I don't even have a home…

"You'll figure this out," Kelli says, her soft voice breaking into my thoughts. "Don't freak out. You're smart. Resourceful. Ooh, and you have connections."

"What connections?" I frown up at the ceiling.

"Shep connections. That guy knows everyone. Have you told him what happened yet?"

I don't want to dump my problems on him. He didn't sign up for them and I refuse to be a burden. I can figure this out on my own. I have before and I will again. "I haven't talked to him."

"Well, what are you waiting for? I know he'll help you. The dude is completely head over heels," she says slyly. "I think he'd do just about anything for you."

"He is not head over heels," I mutter, ignoring the giddy pace of my heart. He likes me. I know he does.

But would he really do anything for me? I'm not so sure.

"He so is. Have you seen the way he looks at you? Shepard Prescott doesn't go out with a girl for a long stretch of time. He's a love 'em and leave 'em type of guy. I don't know how many times I've told you this."

She tells me this all the time and fine. I know it's the truth. It doesn't mean he's changing his ways just for me. "I don't expect him to drop everything and help me during my time in need."

"Isn't that what a boyfriend is supposed to do?" Kelli asks incredulously. "Dane is so up in my business sometimes, I swear I need to tell him to back off."

"Shep isn't my boyfriend," I insist. I don't know what he is. That guy I'm banging constantly? The one I also like to hang out with? I have no idea what to call us, what to classify our relationship as. It's confusing. He confuses me.

"Of course, he is." Kelli makes an irritated sound. "You two are ridiculous. Tell him what happened with your mom and how you have nowhere to go. I'm sure he could come up with an easy solution and solve all of your problems."

"I doubt it," I say with a snort. No one works that quick, not even perfect Shep.

"Please, you know what he's like. Don't underestimate him. He's crafty. And made of money. He can get whatever he wants."

"So you're saying he could pull a roommate and a place for me to live out of his magical hat?" I start to laugh. It sounds crazy. Possible but crazy. Shep *is* filthy rich. He could probably buy me a house without even blinking an eye. No way would I ever want him to do that but I bet he could.

I refuse to take a handout from him though. I'd feel like I owe him and no way do I want to deal with that. Especially if we don't...last. Because this can't last, whatever it is I'm experiencing with Shep. It's fun, it's a lot of hot sex and cute teasing and I have a good time with him, even when we're not naked. I enjoy his company. He makes me laugh. He makes me think. He challenges me.

But he's leaving the minute school is done so I figure once he's gone we're done too. So I'm trying to mentally prepare myself for the inevitable.

"I'm sure he could help you figure out something. The guy knows practically everyone on campus. Plus he comes from one of the richest families on the planet. He could probably buy a mansion for you to live in like it was no big deal," Kelli says.

My stomach cramps up at hearing her say he comes from a rich family. I always forget that. Yes, I spend time at his outrageously gorgeous house with the kitchen that makes me drool. Yes, we drive around in his mega expensive car that probably costs as much as my house

Mom just sold. He doesn't flaunt his riches and I've never met any of his family so it's easy to forget that he's a gazillionaire.

"I would never expect him to buy me anything," I mumble.

"Of course. I'm just saying it would be so easy for him, you know? The guy has everything at his fingertips. So why not let him help you? I'm sure he'd love to."

I say nothing. If I told her I didn't want to owe Shep anything—and that's the truth—she'd argue I was being silly. And maybe I am. Plus, it's not his job to help me. We hook up. That's it. There's no real romance here involved at all. Yes, he says sweet, romantic things but I think that's just because he wants to get inside my panties. And it works. I love all the things he says to me. The way he looks at me. How he touches me. It's like I'm trying to convince myself there's nothing between us, though it's getting harder and harder to deny…

My phone rings. Like, actually rings, which never happens and I practically jump off the bed.

"Who in the world is calling you?" Kelli asks as I scramble to grab my phone.

"Probably my mom," I say as I bring the phone up, the air clogging in my throat when I see whose name is flashing on my screen.

Shep.

I answer tentatively, surprised that he would

actually call. When we communicate we usually only text. "What did I do to deserve this call?"

"Considering I have no idea where you are and you never answered my text, I thought I'd go straight to the source and hope like hell you'd answer." He sounds irritated. Sort of pissed. Maybe even a little worried. "Why weren't you in class?"

"Are you checking up on me?" Uh oh. I'm getting a little screechy again.

"I was waiting for you in the parking lot. I planned on picking you up but you never came out of the building. I started to…" His voice drifts and he's quiet for a moment. "Panic."

My heart flips over itself. "Well, I'm fine. I'm in my dorm. I never went to class."

"Why not?"

I glance over at Kelli to find her watching me with rapt fascination. Ugh. I hate that I have an audience. "I've sort of been having a bad day."

"I can change that," he says swiftly. Confidently. His voice full of that sexy Shep swagger that only he can seem to pull off.

"How so?" I ask.

"I can come over right now, pick you up, take you back to my place and proceed to go down on you for the next two hours." He pauses and my heart beat pulses between my legs, I swear to God. He knows it's my absolute, all time, favorite thing. There is nothing better than Shep's mouth between my thighs. Well, his cock runs a close second. In fact, they're probably in a tie. "You game?"

"Um." I glance at Kelli again, hoping she doesn't notice my blush. I can feel it so I know my cheeks are pink. "How soon can you get here?"

"Ten minutes." I hear him start his car. "Be waiting outside for me, baby."

"I'm going over to Shep's," I say after I end the call.

"I figured that," Kelli says wryly. "You're going to tell him about your little problem?"

"Sure." I nod as I push myself off the bed, though I doubt I'm going to talk about my problems tonight. I'd rather just lose myself with Shep. Maybe I should change. I'm in a T-shirt and shorts, my hair is in a braid and I have no makeup on. But I think Shep likes me this way. Though he won't like the hair. He prefers it down. Maybe I should…

No. I shouldn't have to change myself for this guy. I don't believe he wants to change me either. I think he likes me for who I am.

That's sort of mind blowing.

Shep

The second she slips inside my car, relief settles

over me, leaving me weak with wanting her. Without thought I reach for her, cup her cheeks as I bring her face to mine and kiss her with all the pent up intensity I've been keeping inside me for the last, I dunno, six hours? Maybe more?

I haven't talked to her all damn day. Since we've started seeing each other, that's never happened.

"Well, hello to you, too," she says breathlessly once I finally break the kiss.

I'm still holding her face, my forehead pressed to hers and my eyes still closed. I decide to go ahead and be honest. "I missed you. A lot."

"You just saw me this morning." She pulls away slightly so our gazes meet, her brows lowered in a frown. "Everything okay?"

"Kind of a crazy day," I confess. How can I admit to her that I was worried when she didn't come out of that building earlier? That I seriously fucking panicked when I realized she never texted me back? I sound like an old married man but damn it, my mind immediately leapt to the worst possibilities.

After being a guy who had zero interest in relationships or spending any extended time with a girl, it's like I've done a complete one-eighty. The craziest thing? I'm okay with it.

She chews on her lower lip and I brush my thumb across the plump flesh, tugging a little. A silent order for her to stop. I hate it when she hurts herself. "What happened?"

I lean in to kiss her forehead, her cheek. "I'll tell you about it on the drive home." I say home on purpose because seriously, without her there, it doesn't feel like one. A home. Craziest fucking thing ever but I'm rolling with it. Reveling in it. This girl, it's like she belongs with me. To me. Not sure if she realizes it yet but I'm fairly convinced.

After doing a lot of thinking and worrying over the last few hours while waiting for Jade to get out of class, I believe I've come up with a solution to our summertime problem. Now I just need to get Jade on board.

That's not going to be easy. I'm not sure how I'm going to approach her. And I really don't want to talk about it tonight…

"So tell me what's up," she says as I pull away from the curb and head back to my place.

I let her know we're closing the gambling house this weekend. How we're having one last blowout event on Saturday night and then it's dark until the fall semester resumes. She didn't really seem to care all that much, not that I can blame her. She hates that place. Weird considering it's how we met but the circumstances weren't the best.

After all, I did win her in a bet. Something I don't mention anymore.

"My mom called," I drop nonchalantly as I turn onto my street.

"Oh?" she asks just as nonchalantly. I never talk about my family with her. And she really doesn't talk about hers either, though I know it's just her and her mom. Family has turned into one of those off the table subjects for us.

"They're in Los Angeles for business this upcoming weekend and they're stopping by here Saturday night." I pause and slow down, turning into my short driveway and hitting the remote so the garage door opens. "They want to go to dinner."

"How nice. Though won't that interfere with your gambling plans?" she asks, with just a hint of snark.

I choose to ignore the snarkiness. "I was wondering if…you wanted to go with us. To dinner."

She's so eerily quiet. I pull into the garage and shut the engine off, turning to look at her to find her staring straight ahead, an impassive expression on her pretty face. And damn, she really does look pretty. No makeup, hair pulled back into a braid, little wisps of red floating around her face. Painfully gorgeous.

"Jade?" I urge when she still hasn't said anything.

Slowly, she turns to face me. "You really want me to go to dinner with you and your parents?"

I shrug. "Yeah. I mean, I don't necessarily want to subject you to them because let me tell you, they kind of suck. My dad's a narcissistic asshole and Mom only cares about booze and shopping but she uh, made a special request."

Jade frowns. "What do you mean?"

"She asked me to bring my new female friend."

"And how did she know about me?" She's frowning harder, which I thought was impossible.

"Tristan told his mom about us and so his mom told mine." I smile, trying to make a joke. "We're just keeping it in the family."

There's no smile, no reaction whatsoever from Jade. "This sounds…serious."

I take her hand, slide my fingers between hers so they're clasped. "It's as serious as you want it to be."

She squeezes my hand. "We haven't known each other very long."

"I know."

"So dinner with the parental units already feels… serious." She turns her head to look at me, her eyes wide, lips parted.

My heart is thumping so hard in my chest I swear it's trying to burst free. "I've never introduced a girl to my parents," I admit.

"Why not?" she whispers.

"I've never been with one long enough to warrant an introduction." I lick my lips, hoping like hell I say this right. "I know we haven't been seeing each other for very long, but for me, this is…something. And maybe it freaks you out to meet my parents, but I'd really like it if you came with me Saturday night. I want you there. By my side."

She's staring at me, her eyes still so wide. She presses her lips together, her expression unsure and for one horrific moment, I think she's going to refuse me.

"I'll go," she finally murmurs, squeezing my hand again. "If it means that much to you to have me there."

"It does. It means a lot to me, baby." I lean in and kiss her again, like I can't resist her, and the truth is, I can't. I touch her cheek, drift my fingers across her soft skin and when she sighs, the softest, sweetest sound I've ever heard, I feel it right to the very depths of my soul.

That's my cue to get her the fuck out of this car and into my bed, stat.

Tristan's home but in his room and we sneak through the quiet, dark house, Jade giggling and trying to swat my hand away when I pinch her perfect ass. I put my hands on her hips, slowing her down and she leans into me with that perfect ass nestled close to my dick, making it stand at attention. She does this little wiggle move that has me gripping her hips too tightly and then she's pulling away, practically running down the hall and slipping into my bedroom.

I have no choice but to chase after her.

She's leaning against my dresser when I enter the

room, her hands propped on the edge, her legs looking impossibly long as they're stretched out in front of her. A mischievous smile curls her full lips and I stare at her as if I'm in a daze, captivated by the sight of her, shock and lust racing through my veins at how flirtatious she's being. Since we've been together, she's really come out of her shell but she's still shy about some things.

When it comes to us, I don't want her shy about anything.

I approach her without saying a word, my gaze never leaving hers. I reach out, curl my hand around her neck, and stand directly in front of her. "You disappoint me," I murmur.

Her flirtatious look falls and I hate that. I'm teasing. Can't she tell? "Why?"

"Your hair. It's all bound up again. You know I don't like that." I slide my hand further into her hair, tugging at the strands at the base of her neck. "Turn around."

She does as I ask without protest, offering her back to me and I admire her for a quick second, my gaze sweeping down the length of her, lingering on the curve of her ass, the graceful arc of her back. My fingers literally itch to get her naked.

But I need to do something else first.

I reach for the end of her braid and tug the band off slowly, letting it fall to the ground. She remains stiff before me, her shoulders ramrod straight, and I swear she's holding her breath. Carefully, I start to undo the braid, flipping the thick strands of her hair undone, letting the silky softness slide over my hands. Up, up I go, stepping closer to her with every part I undo, until my mouth is on her neck and my other hand is beneath her shirt, fingers pressing into the skin of her waist as I finish taking apart the braid.

Her hair falls around her shoulders, spills down her back. I grab the base of her T-shirt with both hands, murmur a quick, "Lift up," and she raises her arms so I can take her shirt off. I remain standing behind her, pushing her hair to the side so I can press my cheek to hers and we both stare into the mirror that sits above my dresser.

"You're beautiful," I murmur just before I nuzzle her cheek with my nose, inhaling her fresh, sexy-as-fuck, perfectly Jade scent. "Put your hands on the dresser."

She does as I ask, her gaze meeting mine in the mirror. She's trembling. I can feel her, see it and she presses her lips together, her eyes falling closed when I reach for the back of her bra and slowly unhook it. I push the straps down her arms and the cups fall away from her breasts, revealing her to me. She sheds the bra, tossing it to the floor before she places her hands on the edge of the dresser once more.

"Fucking perfect." I kiss her neck and reach for her breasts, holding them in my palms, tweaking her nipples. She gasps, her butt brushing against my cock and I bite back the groan that wants to escape.

Tonight, right now, is all about her. I want to get her off. I want her to watch as I get her off. And then when it's over I want to turn around and make her come all over again.

And again.

And again.

"Open your eyes, baby," I urge and she does. "Watch what I can do to you."

I go to my knees and curl my fingers around the edge of her cotton shorts, pulling them down her long legs, until they fall to a heap at her ankles. She kicks them off and I sit back on my haunches to admire her pale blue panties that barely cover her ass. I can smell her, musky and sweet, and know for a fact without even touching her that she's soaking wet. She's always wet for me.

"Keep your eyes open," I remind her as I touch her ass, skim my fingers along the lacy hem of her panties. She shudders beneath my touch, her skin so warm and smooth and I lean in, press my mouth to the very spot I was just touching. The agonized moan that comes from the back of her throat makes my dick surge against my fly. "You like that?" I murmur against her skin.

"Shep…" Her voice drifts. She sounds tortured.

I fucking love it.

"You're still watching?" I glance up to catch her nodding, her eyes open and locked on the mirror. "Good. Don't look away. Don't close your eyes. Tell me what you see."

"I see...me."

I pull her panties off, past her hips, her ass, her thighs, over her knees, down her calves, until they're off, and she's completely naked in front of me. Pale and pretty and smooth and wet. "What do you look like? Describe yourself."

She hesitates. I feel it in her body language, the way she stiffens the slightest bit. She doesn't want to play this game. "You know what I look like," she says self-consciously.

"I do. And I love what I see." I press a kiss to the back of her thigh, to the very spot where that little constellation of freckles dusts her skin, and she jolts beneath my lips. "But tell me what *you* see."

"Um, okay." She takes a deep breath. "My hair is a mess."

"It's sexy," I correct, dropping tiny kisses along her other thigh.

"My cheeks are flushed."

"They're always flushed when I'm touching you." I kiss the very underside of her left ass cheek. "I think that means you like it," I murmur against her skin.

"I—I do like it," she admits. "My eyes...they look a

little dazed."

"Hmm." I'm raining kisses on her cheek now. The skin is firm yet soft. I bet no one has ever kissed her here. This territory is all mine—uncharted Jade territory that I'm about to conquer. I feel like scrawling my name across her ass and claiming it as mine.

Property of Shep Prescott. Hands off.

"Do you like it when I kiss you here?" I ask as I run my hands along her outer thighs. I glance up at her to catch her nodding, like she can't even speak. "Spread your legs baby."

"Oh, God." She does as I command, her feet spreading apart, revealing her pretty pink pussy to me and I reach up, lightly drift my index finger along her center to discover she's dripping wet. She whimpers at my touch.

"Tell me something else," I demand. "Tell me what you want."

"Wh-what do you mean?"

"What do you want me to do next?" I touch her again, another teasing press of my fingers to her pussy. She's so soft and wet. I want to put my mouth on her. Suck her. Bite her. Lick her. Fuck her with my tongue. Fuck her with my fingers.

But I need to hear what she wants first.

"Put—put your mouth on me," she says and I smile. She's so easy. I know this is her favorite thing. I can get at least two orgasms a night out of her with my mouth alone.

"Like this?" I hold her hips and lean in, pressing my lips to the very back of her pussy in an almost chaste kiss. "Or like this?" I tilt my head, open my mouth and try my fucking best to consume her in the most obscene way possible.

Her legs shake around me, a whispery, "Like that, like that," falling from her lips just before she moans.

I continue consuming her, licking and sucking her everywhere, pushing two fingers deep inside her. She's babbling nonsense, her hands are gripping the edge of my dresser like she might fall if she let go and I'm kneeling between her legs, getting my girl off all while she watches herself.

Fucking hot.

"Your eyes are still open?" I ask once I pull away from her. I stare up at her, taking in her messy hair and flushed cheeks, bright gaze and swollen lips. Her eyes are open and she's staring at her reflection in the mirror as if she's the most fascinating thing she's ever seen.

Again, fucking hot.

"Yes," she murmurs.

"I want you to watch as I make you come."

"Shep..." She sounds like she's protesting and I cut her off.

"Do it, Jade. Keep your eyes open. Watch yourself.

See how pretty you are when I give you an orgasm." I return my attention to her pussy, attacking her clit with gentle, swirling strokes of my tongue. I push my fingers back inside her body, slowly pulling them out before slipping them inside again, keeping up a steady rhythm that has her body working with me. God, she tastes so fucking good. I can feel her clit swell with every swipe of my tongue and the inner walls of her pussy cling tight to my fingers, like she never wants to let me go.

"Come for me, baby," I urge against her hot flesh, just before I draw her clit between my lips and give it a powerful suck. And then she *is* coming, chanting my name, her pussy quivering, her entire body shuddering. I grip her hips, hold her to me as I continue to devour her, my mouth, my tongue everywhere I can touch her and she's holding my head, her fingers buried in my hair.

I pull away so I can glance up at her. She's still watching herself in the mirror, her lips parted. "Tell me what you see," I whisper.

She looks down at me, her expression full of wonder and pure, feminine satisfaction. "I see a girl who just had the best orgasm *ever*."

I start to chuckle. "There's more where that came from."

"Prove it," she demands as I stand up, rubbing my mouth with the back of my hand. Her eyes track my every movement so I lean in and drop a lingering kiss to her lips, hoping like hell she can taste herself on them.

"Get your ass on the bed," I tell her with a little growl, smacking her butt with the palm of my hand.

She jumps and squeals, then runs over to the bed.

And I have no choice but to follow, tugging off my shirt as I do so.

It's going to be a good night.

Twenty-Five

chapter

Jade

"Don't be nervous." Shep catches my hand and pulls me close to him, dropping a kiss on my forehead. "They're just people. They're not going to bite your head off."

Easy for him to say.

We're in the parking lot of the Shellfish Company, one of the most expensive restaurants in town, of course. Every parking spot is filled but Shep didn't even bother trying to find a space. He left his car with valet parking, which sounds decadent and expensive, especially since I've never done that sort of thing before. Hell, I don't even own a car.

Clearly I'm nervous. I'm babbling in my own head.

He's behaved like the perfect boyfriend the entire

week. We've hardly spent any time apart. If I'm not in class or working and he's not in class, we're together. We talk a lot. Share stories. He's a business major and plans on working for the family company once he graduates. Running the gambling house is like a practice run, he told me, which I found amusing.

When I told him I was a pyschology major it was his turn to be amused. He found that fitting — direct quote. I don't know what to think about that.

With us spending so much time togther, I've stayed at his place every night this week, and that means we've been having lots — and lots — of sex.

Awesome, wonderful, make me forget all of my inhibitions and hang ups, sex. Like, the best sex of my life. It just keeps getting better and better every time we get naked. And he seems just as into me as I am into him. We feel...connected.

It's sort of amazing.

"Are they already here?" I ask as we approach the front entrance of the restaurant. There are a lot of people waiting outside, most of them dressed up, and I'm so glad I wore a dress. A brand new one Kelli and I found when we went to Old Navy yesterday. It's white eyelet, sleeveless, with a full skirt that hits just above the knee and makes me look like sweet girlfriend potential.

At least, that's what Kelli told me when I tried it on for her at the store.

I'm thankful Shep didn't act all perverted when he picked me up, which is his usual way when he first sees me. Not that I don't mind usually, but that's not the reaction I'm looking for. Tonight is all about demure. Not sultry and sexy.

"Probably not. My mother always runs late." He sends me a look as we start to climb the stairs that leads to the front doors. The restaurant is close to the ocean and there's a chill in the air that makes me wish I'd brought a sweater. "She made a reservation though, so we're good."

We enter the restaurant and Shep releases my hand to go speak to the hostess, letting her know we've arrived. I take my chance to admire him yet again. He dressed up tonight. Black pants and a white button-up shirt that sets off his tanned skin, the sleeves rolled up to show off his sexy forearms. Who knew forearms were so sexy?

His hair is actually tamed, like he might've brushed it and I'm tempted to run my fingers through it just to mess it up. I love it when his hair is messy. Which is a lot because every time I get my hands on him they're buried in his hair, tugging and stroking and holding him close...

Yeah. I've got it so bad.

Here's the thing though. I feel awful because I still haven't told him I don't have anywhere to live for the summer. I mean, does he really need to know? Not like it's his problem. But Kelli's furious at me. She doesn't understand why I just can't confess what's going on and ask for his support and help. Because seriously, I need help. I've been looking for a roommate everywhere and have come up empty so far. Enid has committed to giving me forty hours a week at the store, so that's good but I need somewhere to live.

And I have nowhere. Kelli's offer to come home with her for the summer is starting to look like my only option. Though she might pull it if I don't fess up to Shep and let him know what's going on.

He's been acting odd too. I can't put my finger on it and finally chocked it up to him being nervous over this dinner with his parents. He's never introduced a girl to his family before so this is a big deal in their eyes. It's a big deal in my eyes too. So I forgive him for being a little sketchy and staring at me too long sometimes, like he wants to say something but he's not quite sure how to approach it. Every time I ask him what's up, he says *never mind*, or *it's nothing* and I reluctantly let it slide.

Nerves, we all have them. It's been a hell of a week. I'm ready for it to be over.

"My mother just texted me," Shep says as he comes to stand by my side once more. The restaurant's waiting area is packed with people and we're pressed so close to each other I can feel his body heat radiating toward me.

"They just pulled into the parking lot. And the hostess said our table would be ready in a few minutes."

I blow out a harsh breath. "Okay. Good. Great."

"Hey." He takes my hand again, his fingers rubbing against mine in this soothing way that makes me want to purr like a cat. "They're going to love you, I promise."

"Yeah?" I lift my head and meet his gaze, startled when he leans in and drops a sweet, soft kiss to my lips. I really love it when he does that. "What if they don't?"

He tilts his head, his expression incredulous. "How can they not? You're beautiful. Sweet. And you like me. That's all my mom has ever wanted. For some poor girl to actually see something in me," he teases.

"There's plenty to see in you," I tell him sincerely. "You have a lot to offer, you know."

His gaze dims and he shrugs. "Financially, yeah."

I'm taken aback. We never talk about his financial situation. I could care less if he's rich or not, though I did take advantage of that amazing kitchen at his house a few nights ago and made a huge batch of homemade chocolate chip cookies for the boys. I think I now have Gabe and Tristan firmly in my back pocket.

"I don't care about your money," I tell him almost fiercely. "You know this." It's never been about that between us. I tried my best to avoid him from the very start and he chased after me like a man possessed. He wore me down. And not with a bunch of expensive gifts either.

"I do. And I appreciate it." He touches my nose with the tip of his finger. "But that's all anyone has ever really seen when it comes to me. That's all I can offer. That or a quick lay."

I'm about to tell him that's totally not true but then he's turning away from me, an almost pained expression crossing his face. I turn in the direction he's looking to see an elegant, perfectly dressed couple approach us, the both of them smiling though they don't necessarily look happy.

"Shepard." The woman embraces him first, clad in a powder blue skirt suit that I think might be Chanel and a cloud of expensive perfume. Her hair is this color I can only describe as rich butter blonde and it's cut into a perfectly symmetrical bob. She's absolutely flawless. "Aren't you a sight for sore eyes?"

"Mother." He gives her an awkward hug and then turns to the man who looks shockingly just like Shep, only an older version. And he's a little shorter. Shep shakes his father's hand, who offers him a clipped hello in greeting, barely looking him in the eye. The familial love is just overflowing.

Oh, boy. What am I getting myself into?

"This is Jade." Shep is suddenly by my side, his arm curled around mine as he presents me to his parents like I'm some sort of prize. "Jade, these are my parents."

He doesn't offer up their first names so I'm figuring it's not proper for me to use them. "Hello, Mrs. Prescott." I smile, my cheeks hurting from the frozen position they're in. "Mr. Prescott." I'm about to offer my hand but I can tell they're not going to offer theirs in return so I don't.

"Well, aren't you lovely," Mrs. Prescott says, her assessing gaze roaming all over me. I think I just got thoroughly checked out by Shep's mom. "All that red hair...I didn't figure you one with a penchant for redheads, Shepard." She flashes a smile at him.

I want to roll my eyes. Or sock her in the face. But I refrain from doing either. I hate that my hair is always the first thing anyone sees.

He slips his arm around my waist and smiles down at me before turning to face his mom. "There's more to Jade than meets the eye, Mom. She's not just cute freckles and red hair."

Okay. I sort of want to melt at his words. He's the only guy who's ever fully embraced the freckled redhead look I've got going on.

"Mmm, hmm." She studies me with a critical eye, judging me on sight, I'm sure. "Well, it's wonderful to meet you. I'm very interested in getting to know the girl who's finally tamed my boy."

I stiffen at her words. Did she really just say that?

"Oh, I'm not tamed yet," Shep says as he starts to

laugh, as does his father.

His mother just scowls at him. "You're getting too old for the antics, you know. You must settle down sometime, darling."

"I'm not a kid anymore. And there are no antics," he protests and I think of all the many antics he's up to on a daily basis. Hello, illegal gambling house. "I'm freaking twenty-one years old. Not ready to throw in the towel and settle down just yet."

Of course, I know this. But it still sort of hurts, to hear him say it. Ridiculous, considering we've been seeing each other for all of a month, and I'm definitely not expecting wedding bells and engagement rings already. I'm still a teenager for the love of God.

The tension is palpable between them—between all of us—and I smile politely, my brain searching to come up with something neutral to say. "How long are you here for?" I ask, wincing at the lameness of my question.

"We're only here for dinner. We'll drive back down to Los Angeles tonight. Our plane leaves first thing in the morning," Mrs. Prescott explains, her gaze flicking to mine before she resumes her stare down of Shep.

His dad says nothing, just stands next to us and checks his phone. Something I wish I was doing. Anything to not have to deal with whatever's happening between Shep and his mom.

"So Shepard. When did we last see you, hmm?" It

feels like his mom is trying to bait him. Or irritate him. And by the annoyance I see flickering in his gaze, it's working. "You didn't come home for Thanksgiving or Christmas."

"Because you weren't home," he adds.

She waves a hand. "You didn't come home last summer either."

"Again, because you were on vacation."

She rolls her eyes. "You never, *ever* make an effort to see us anymore, Shepard. Are you coming home this summer? You never really did answer that question and I've been hounding you for months."

He sends me a look, one full of nervous apprehension and I wish I knew what he was thinking. He seems worried about...me? But why?

Pressing his lips together, he turns to face his mother once more. "I don't think so, Mother. I'm going to stick around here again for the summer. Play on the soccer league and hopefully hang out with...Jade."

Wait a minute. What?

Shep

I didn't mean to spring it on her like that. Hell, I haven't even asked Jade if she wanted to stay with me for the summer and that's been my plan all week. But like a gutless wonder I kept losing my nerve every time I opened my mouth. I just…I couldn't ask her. Too afraid she might say no.

And fuck, that would hurt more than I care to admit.

Jade's looking at me right now like I've lost my mind and I part my lips, ready to say something, anything to take away that shocked look on her face.

"Prescott, party of four!" screams the hostess, and I'm saved from having to say anything at all.

"Let's go grab our table," Dad says as he strides toward the hostess who's waiting for us, clutching four giant menus in her hand. "I'm starving."

I follow after him and Mom, taking Jade's hand. She's still looking at me, I can feel her gaze on my face but I refuse to look in her direction. I'm trying to come up with the proper way to ask her to stay with me for the summer.

Though I sort of blew that plan all to hell.

"What do you mean exactly, by spending the summer with me?" she finally asks.

My stomach sinks, and my appetite disappears. I didn't want to have this conversation *now*. "We'll talk about it later," I whisper, squeezing her hand.

She pulls her hand out of my grasp and the sudden distance between us feels as large as the Pacific.

Damn it, I should've done this sooner. I'd planned to. I wanted to ask her while we were in bed, just drifting off to sleep, when she's usually draped over me and

I have my arm around her shoulders, drawing circles on her skin with my fingers. It's that time between wakefulness and sleep, when we're both mellow after multiple orgasms.

I could've been all romantic and shit, explaining to her how I couldn't stand the thought of spending the entire summer away from her and I know it's last minute, but hey instead of going home, you should stay with me, Jade. The house is huge and Tristan won't be around, so that would give us plenty of privacy. I could even give you your own room if you want. We could have fun, just me and you. Lots and lots of fun.

But instead, I hit her with it in front of my freaking parents. So stupid.

We're seated at a table with a gorgeous ocean view and I think of my favorite restaurant, the little shack near the beach. The place I took Jade on our first date. The food is way better and cheaper and the atmosphere can't be beat. This place is pretentious as hell. I feel underdressed for not wearing a tie and I can't remember the last time I wore one.

One of the many perks of not living at home anymore, I guess.

I pick up the menu and scan it, as does everyone else at the table. It's an uneasy quiet and I peek over the top of the menu to see everyone's head bent, hiding behind the giant pages of their menu. I'm tempted to laugh.

But I don't.

Instead, I try to figure out what the hell I want to eat and pray for the server to come soon so I can order a fucking drink. It's about the only thing that's going to get me through tonight, I swear.

Within minutes the server is at our table, ready to take our drink order. Mom orders a bottle of wine — surprise — and dad and I both order a beer.

"Do you want something, Jade?" Mother asks, flashing her that barracuda smile. The one that says she'd love nothing more but to tear my new girlfriend — yeah fine I'm claiming it — to shreds.

"I'll just have a glass of water, thank you." Jade smiles up at the server.

"You don't want any wine?" Mother continues.

Jade shakes her head. "I'm not of legal age to drink yet, I'm afraid."

The server makes his escape and my mom turns on Jade like she smells blood in the water. "Exactly how old are you?"

"Nineteen. I'm just finishing my freshman year," Jade admits, then sinks her teeth into her lower lip. She looks...petrified.

Fuck. I just want to wrap her up in my arms and protect her from the barrage of questions Mother is going to throw at her. Poor Jade. Poor me.

Poor all of us.

"Only nineteen?" Mother's lip curls as she swivels her head to aim her gaze right at me. "Awfully young, don't you think, Shepard? This can't be a serious thing. She's a baby."

"We're only two years apart," I say through gritted teeth.

"Two years can be an awfully long time, especially now, at such a crucial point in your lives." Mother returns her gaze to Jade, the smile on her face more like a baring of teeth. "I'm sure you're enjoying yourself with my son. You've probably never been with a boy like him before. Shepard is loads of fun. Very charming. And he has a *ton* of money. But you know this sort of thing won't last."

Jade's jaw drops open. Her lips move as if she's trying to say something but no sound comes out. I think my mother's words just stole her ability to speak.

Me? I'm stunned. I can't even fucking move. Why the hell is she being so awful?

Oh, I know. Because she's my mom. And she's always been awful. I haven't been around her for a long time so I sort of forgot.

"This is really none of your business," I start but Mother cuts me off with a look.

"This is very much my business, considering you are my only son and heir to an absolute fortune. She may look sweet and demure in her cheap little white dress but I've seen girls like her before. She's only with you because of your money." Mother leans across the table, lowering her voice to a harsh whisper. "She's harboring all the signs of a gold digger."

My blood is fucking boiling. So no girl would really want to be with me, it's only because of my money? No wonder I said almost that exact same thing earlier to Jade. I've been hearing it my entire life. "What did you just say?"

Mother rolls her eyes. "A gold digger. I've already told you numerous times, you need to be like your father. When we started dating, I knew how much he was worth, but I also knew how much *I* was worth. It was a match. A *perfect* match." She sends the still silent Jade a withering stare. "This girl is obviously not a good financial match. Very middle class. Possibly even lower middle class."

Her insulting words make me flinch and they're not even directed at me. I'm tempted to tell Mother to shut the fuck up but I hold it in. No need to make a scene at the restaurant. I don't want to embarrass Jade.

"I could care less about any of that shit," I tell her, my voice raising. "And Jade doesn't care either. That you have the nerve to call you and dad a perfect match is fucking laughable. You two despise each other."

"Watch your language," Dad threatens, surprising me that he even has something to say. He usually prefers to loom in the background, only interacting when good shit is going down.

And this is definitely not good shit.

"I'm not going to sit here and let you insult my girlfriend," I continue. "You either apologize to her or we're out of here."

Mother lifts her chin and looks down her nose. That expression used to scare the shit out of me when I was a kid but not anymore. She's all bark and no bite. She always has been. It's why I've gotten away with pretty much everything my entire life.

"Apologize to your mother for using such foul language," Dad says but I ignore him.

"I refuse to apologize for stating the truth." Mother lowers her voice. "This girl isn't the one for you, Shepard. Can't you see that?"

I turn to look at Jade, how her skin is so pale her freckles stand out, her eyes full of a multitude of emotions, none of them good. She's mad, upset, disappointed, nervous...yet all I can see is that she is definitely the girl for me.

"I can't." Reaching out, I take Jade's hand that's lying in a fist on the table and clasp it in mine firmly. She lifts her gaze to mine and I offer her a reassuring smile. "I'm wondering why *you* can't see that she is the girl for me," I say, my eyes never leaving Jade's.

"You can't be serious," Mother starts but I ignore

her.

"Let's go baby," I whisper to Jade and she leaps to her feet so fast I'm surprised she didn't knock her chair backwards.

Mother sputters in protest. Dad is yelling my name. The server is approaching our table, carrying a tray laden with our drinks and Jade and I push past him, though I offer him up an apologetic smile.

No way am I staying through a torturous meal while my mom slings insults at Jade. No fucking way. I'm standing my ground. If I let her get away with this shit now, what will happen the next time I bring Jade around them? Mother will never let up.

And there will be a next time. I can guarantee it. I've been fighting it all week but tonight, right at this very moment, I know without a doubt that I'm falling. Falling in love with her.

So I'm taking care of what's mine.

Jade.

chapter
Twenty-Six

I think I'm in a total state of shock.

I have no idea what happened back there at the restaurant but holy shit, it was weird. I felt like I was in a movie. One of those cheesy made for television movies that they show on Lifetime, with all the overblown drama and exaggerated bad guys — or mom, in this case. The way she looked at me, spoke to me, how she called me a freaking gold digger right there at the table, in front of Shep and his dad.

Unbelievable.

Shep defended me the entire time. He never caved. Not once. He was on my side and oh my God, it felt so good, knowing that he was defending me with an unwavering intensity I don't think I've ever witnessed before.

It was awesome.

Though we haven't spoken since we left the restaurant and that was five minutes ago. I think he's still too mad. Not that I can blame him. I'm mortified over what happened too. His mom is a nightmare. He warned me but he didn't offer up much detail as to how truly awful she was.

And she is definitely awful.

"Jade, I'm so fucking sorry," Shep finally says and I chance a glance at him, the way his long fingers are curled around the steering wheel, his knuckles white. His expression is grim, his mouth drawn thin and his jaw looking like it's going to crack, it's so tight.

"It's not your fault," I start but he cuts me off.

"I should've never brought you there. I thought she'd be cool. I thought she'd accept you and see just how great you are. Instead, she was a total bitch." He stops at a red light and turns to look at me, his eyes full of sorrow. "I'm sorry."

I lean over the center console and reach out, placing my hand on his smooth cheek. "Hey. It's not your fault," I repeat.

He blows out a harsh breath and turns his head so he kisses the palm of my hand. "I hate what she said to you," he murmurs against my skin.

A shiver moves through me. I hate it too, but what's

done is done. "I think she's just trying to defend you. Protect you."

"In the rudest way possible." The light turns green and I drop my hand from his face so he can continue driving distraction free. "Don't make excuses for her. She called you a gold digger, Jade."

"We don't need to relive it," I say with a wince.

He sends me an apologetic look. "Sorry. You're right. What the fuck is wrong with me? What the fuck is wrong with *her?* Jesus." He punches the steering wheel and I place my hand on his thigh, surprised at how rigid the muscle is. He's so tense he feels like he could shatter.

"Calm down. It's over. We survived," I reassure him as I run my hand up and down his thigh. "Let's just go back to your place and relax. Order takeout." Because yeah, I'm still hungry since we never ate dinner.

He frowns. "Damn it, I can't. I have to go to the house and help Tristan and Gabe. The last night it's open, remember?"

How could I forget? Great. Now I'll have to spend tonight alone.

"You could go with me," he continues and I shake my head.

"No." Hell, no. I don't like that place. Last time I went I got drunk and almost snorted a line of coke with the Em and Ems. That was so unlike me. First time I go, I get thrown into a bet and Shep wins me.

That you can't protest.

Yeah, maybe I can.

Sort of.

Okay, fine not really.

"You can stay at my place," he suggests and again, I shake my head. I don't want to be the lonely so-called girlfriend waiting for her man to come home. How pathetic is that?

"Just take me back to my dorm," I say, sounding like a sullen little girl. Feeling like a sullen little girl because this night didn't go as expected at all.

I really thought his parents might like me. That we'd have a fabulous time over dinner getting to know each other with his mother revealing funny stories about Shep when he was a little boy. We'd all laugh and she'd tell her husband that I was the perfect girl for their boy and oh *yeah,* that so did not happen.

What seemed to really piss her off is when Shep dropped that bomb about us spending the summer together, which makes no sense because he still thinks I'm going home over the break. I never told him about Mom selling the house.

It's like a totally weird coincidence.

"What did you mean earlier about the two of us spending the summer together?" I ask.

He's quiet for a moment and I'm about to repeat myself when he says, "Oh. That."

"Yeah. That," I say wryly. "Why did you say it?"

"Well, I'm staying here again for the summer. The thought of going home — especially after what happened tonight — there's just no way. And I know you planned on going back to your mom's but I was going to ask if you wanted to…" His words trail off and I stare at him hard, willing him to finish the question.

"If I wanted to what?" I ask when he doesn't say anything else.

He clears his throat. "I wanted to know if you'd like to uh, stay with me. For the summer. At my house."

"Are you serious?" I squeak. No way can he be serious. We hardly know each other. I mean, okay yeah, we know each other, but it's only been a month. It's like he's asking me to move in with him.

Which is insane. *Insane.* I can't move in with him.

Can I?

Somehow we arrived at my dorm hall. He pulls into a parking spot and cuts the engine, turning to look at me. "I'm dead serious. I've been trying to work up the nerve to ask you all week but it never seemed to be the right time." He shakes his head, looking irritated with himself. "Scratch that. More like I couldn't work up the fucking nerve to ask you because I was afraid you'd tell me no."

Aw. That is like the cutest admission ever. "Why did you think I'd tell you no?"

"Because you *love* to tell me no, Jade. I think that's one of the things I like best about you. You're not afraid to tell me how you really feel. You don't fall for my crap like every other female I've encountered on campus. You've challenged me from the first second we've met and while I love that about you, it can also…scare the hell out of me."

I start to laugh. "Are you saying I scare you?"

He nods, a slow smile curling his perfect lips. "Yeah. More than anything, the way I feel about you scares the fuck out of me."

My laughter dies. "What do you mean?"

He cups my face with one hand, his thumb smoothing across my cheek. "You know I've never done this sort of thing before. That first moment when I touched you… when I kissed you…slipped inside you, I knew."

My heart threatens to pound right out of my chest and gallop away down the street. "You knew what?"

"Exactly what I told my mom—that you're the girl for me. No one else, just you." He leans in and kisses me, his damp mouth lingering on mine, his tongue sneaking in for a quick tease. "I'm falling in love with you, Jade."

Oh God. Did he really just say that? Did he just use the word *love?* Yes, yes he did. "Shep," I whisper against his lips but he cuts me off, deepening the kiss, making me moan as I reach for him. But he breaks away before it can get any more out of control and falls back heavily against his seat.

"I can't fucking believe I have to go work tonight." He runs a hand through his hair, messing it up in that way I prefer. He is so sexy I can hardly stand it. I hate that he has to go to work, too. "I want you in my bed waiting for me. Are you sure I can't convince you to go pack a bag and I'll drop you off at my place?"

"Um…" I want to. I want to say yes to all of the above. There's so much for us to discuss but he has to go and it really, really sucks. Talk about bad timing.

"Just say yes. We can talk when I get home. We can talk tomorrow before you have to go to work. Whatever. Just say yes, Jade." He pauses, his dark gaze meeting mine. "Please."

"Okay," I whisper, unable to stop the smile from spreading on my face. I feel so giddy I swear I'm going to float right out of this car. "Yes."

Shep

I can't remember the last time I was this exhausted.

It's more of a mental thing. If I wasn't busy ignoring the texts from my mom insisting that we talk before they leave town, I was breaking up fights at various tables and kicking out people who claimed they were robbed after losing all their money. Gabe and Tristan were just as busy. The house was chaos, we had to kick out a few belligerent drunks and basically beg everyone to shut the fuck up before they called the cops on us.

The very last thing we wanted to deal with. What Tristan, Gabe and I are doing? Is totally fucking illegal. We could end up in jail. That is some serious shit.

Yet we keep on doing it.

Once we finally got the last person out of there, I raced home, anxious to slip into bed with Jade. I know we need to talk. There's a lot to discuss. I admitted I was falling in love with her for Christ's sake.

But damn, the only thing I want to do is hold my girl in my arms and fall asleep.

I left before Tristan but I know he's right behind me so I hurriedly walk through the house, quietly entering my bedroom and locking the door behind me. The curtain that covers the sliding glass door is still open, letting in soft, silvery light from the moon. There's a perfect lump lying dead center in the middle of my bed and I smile, reaching for the buttons of my shirt when I hear a soft voice say,

"Let me do that."

Jade sits up, letting the sheet fall to her waist, revealing her naked chest to my gaze. My heart stutters in my chest as she leans forward, the sheet slipping off her naked body as she crawls toward the edge of the mattress on her hands and knees.

Oh, fuck. Guess I'm not going to sleep anytime soon.

She rears up on her knees in front of me, her hair a haphazard mess around her head, her body on blatant display. My gaze bounces everywhere, too many good parts for me to look at and she reaches for the front of my shirt, slowly undoing each button.

"I've been waiting for you," she murmurs, her fingers brushing against my bare skin, making me shiver.

"I can see that." My voice is scratchy and I clear my throat.

"How was your last night there?" She tilts her head back, causing all of that glorious red hair to spill down her back and I'm tempted to grab hold of it and give it a tug.

"Awful. Busy. Exhausting." I suck in a sharp breath when she spreads my shirt wide and leans in to drop a kiss on my stomach, just above my navel. I shrug out of it hurriedly, letting the shirt drop to the floor as I watch her kiss me again and again. Fuck, I think she's trying to kill me.

"I can make it better," she whispers against my skin, her mouth traveling downward as her hands curl around the waistband of my pants.

"I bet you can," I mutter, grunting when she slides her hand down the front of my pants, right against my erect cock.

She pulls away with a smile. "I've been thinking long and hard about your offer and I'm going to say yes."

I frown. She's confusing me, kissing my stomach and talking about offers. "What offer?"

Her smile turns coy. "For me to live with you for the summer. I'd love to. Thanks for asking me."

"Oh." Relief floods me. "Good. Thanks for accepting." I'm mimicking her response, making her smile. But I decide to turn it serious. "I didn't want to be without you for months on end, Jade."

"I didn't want to be without you either." She undoes the snap on my pants, then pulls the zipper down, spreading the fly open so she can see how my cock strains against the front of my boxers. With a hum she presses her lush mouth on my erection, delivering feather soft kisses along the length and driving me out of my fucking mind with wanting her.

Yeah. She's definitely trying to kill me. Slay me dead.

"Fuck, Jade," I choke out and she smiles up at me, her hands reaching upward so she can shove my pants and boxers down with one push. My cock leaps toward her and she grips the base, wrapping her mouth around the head and drawing me into her warm, wet mouth...

"No." I push at her bare shoulders. "No, no, no. I can't do this. Not like this."

She releases me from her mouth, backing away slightly with a frown marring her pretty face. "Why not?"

I kick off my shoes and pants and join her on the bed, pulling that curvy, hot as fuck body close to mine. "Because when I come tonight, it's going to be inside you, not down your throat."

"Oh." Her eyes are dilated and I know what I said just turned her on. Good, because it turned me on too. "Well. Have your wicked way with me, Shepard Prescott."

Her invitation is all I need. I'm too anxious for prolonged foreplay tonight. I need to be inside her. Moving within her, feeling her clutch me tight, watching as that glazed look fills her eyes and she throws her head back, her body trembling as she's about to come.

I kiss her wildly, my hands roaming, one reaching out toward the bedside table to find a condom already waiting for me. I grab it, never breaking our kiss and slipping my hand between us, tearing the wrapper open awkwardly and trying to slip the condom on.

"Let me help you," she murmurs against my lips, her slender fingers taking the rubber from my grip and slipping the ring over the head of my dick. She rolls it on, her mouth never leaving mine and I groan at her touch. I'm desperate to get inside her and lose myself. I need this.

I need her.

She removes her hand from my cock and I roll her over so she's pinned beneath me. She opens her eyes and smiles, the look on her face nothing short of breathtaking and I readjust myself, slowly sliding inside her body until I'm filling her up completely.

"Oh." Jade arches her back, sending me deeper and I groan. "God, you feel so good."

I say nothing, just increase my pace, not wasting any time, savoring the drag and pull of my cock slipping in and out of her welcoming body. The way she curls her arms and legs around me, clinging to me, sending me even deeper, if that's possible. The whimpers that sound low in her throat when I hit a particular spot and I try my best to hit it again.

And again.

I can smell her, sweet and sexy, her silky hair is in my face and her breasts are smashed against my chest. She's so wet it's easy to move even faster and I reach between us, touching her clit, circling it and making her cry out. I need to send her over the edge because fuck it, I'm already so close. Being inside her like this, knowing that she's going to stay with me, that we're actually going to try our damnedest to make this work, I'm... overwhelmed. And close.

So fucking close.

That I'm about...

To blow.

Twenty-Seven

chapter

"Did you mean what you said earlier?" My head is on Shep's shoulder, my arm slung over his chest. I'm playing with the scant hair that grows between his pecs, sort of loving it because I've never been with a guy who has hair on his chest before. It's just so…manly.

And sexy. God, everything about Shep is sexy.

"I said a lot of things earlier," he murmurs, his voice this deep, delicious rumble in his chest.

"When you said you were…" I pause and swallow hard. "That you were falling in love with me." If he denies it I will die. Just wither away and turn to dust right in this bed.

He stiffens the slightest bit beneath me. "Yeah," he says huskily, without hesitation. "I meant it."

We say nothing for a moment and my mind is racing. So is my heart. I can't believe it. I seriously cannot believe Shep is falling in love with me but then again...I shouldn't be surprised. I've been falling in love with him too.

I'm crazy about him.

"Does that bother you?" he finally asks.

I lift up so I'm leaning on my elbow. Our gazes meet, his full of trepidation. Silly man. "Of course, it doesn't bother me."

He studies me, turning on his side so he's facing me more fully. "This is the moment where you confess you feel the same way," he whispers.

Smiling, I lean in and press my mouth to his. "Hey guess what? I feel the same way," I murmur against his lips.

He smiles in return. I can feel his lips stretch against mine. "Really?"

"Really. Don't sound so surprised." I kiss him again and then shift away from his big, hot body. Sleeping with him is like sleeping with a furnace, I swear. "Can I confess something else to you?"

"Yeah. Sure."

I roll over so I'm lying on my back, staring up at the ceiling. "I talked to my mom a while ago and she told me that she sold our house. And that she was staying with her new boyfriend while she looked for a new place to buy. Which meant I had nowhere to go for the summer and I was really worried about it."

"Wait a minute. When did this conversation happen?"

"Monday," I admit. I can feel him staring at me but I don't look his way. I feel too stupid. I should've told him. I don't know why I held it back but I did, like an idiot.

"Jade." He's touching me, his hands gentle in my hair as he pushes it away from my face. "Why didn't you tell me sooner?"

"I didn't want to burden you with my problems." I sigh and turn to look at him. "Kelli said I was being stupid."

"You sort of were."

I shove at him and he grunts. "Give me a break. I was unsure about...everything. I didn't know how you really felt about me. It was happening so fast and I was trying to find a roommate all this week and failing miserably. I didn't know what I was going to do."

"And all this time I was trying to work up the nerve to ask you to stay with me. That would've solved your problem in an instant. Crazy." He runs his finger down my nose. "Why didn't you ask if you could stay with me?"

"I already told you. I didn't want to burden you with my problems."

He drops a kiss on the tip of my nose. "Your problems are my problems. We're in this together, baby. Can't you see that?"

I blink up at him, noting the sincerity in his dark gaze. How did I get so lucky that this man is mine? I remember how he drove me crazy when we first met. Now I can't imagine my world without him. "You mean it?"

"Cross my heart, hope to die." He kisses me, warm and sweet, his arm curling around my waist so he can bring me flush against him. "I love you, Jade."

Oh God. Just hearing him say the words makes my heart feel like it could swell to three times its size. "I-I love you too, Shep."

I wrap my arms around his neck as I drown in his kiss, the assured way his lips move against mine, the delicious sweep of his tongue within my mouth. "This is going to be the best summer ever," he whispers against my lips after he breaks the kiss.

Now I'm feeling a little shy. I mean really? What in the world is wrong with me? "Do you want me to help pay rent? Enid is moving me up to fulltime for just the summer."

He pulls away from me slightly. "Are you fucking kidding me? No, you're not paying rent. You won't have to pay a dime, just make me cookies and get me fat. That'll be your payment."

"I can't do that," I say, laughing. "I'll get just as fat."

"At least we'll be fat and happy together." His smile fades and his expression turns serious. "I want you to go back to Enid and tell her you don't have to work fulltime after all."

"But…" I start to protest and he places his index finger against my lips.

"I want to spend as much time with you this summer as possible," he explains, his gaze locked on mine. "I know you need to work and I get that. But I want to be with you, Jade. As much as I can, before the fall semester starts back up and we're busy."

I nod slowly. "Okay," I whisper against his finger. "I'll see what can be arranged."

He smiles and removes his finger from my lips before he kisses me again. "You do that."

Shep

"You look way too fucking happy," Tristan groans as I walk into the kitchen.

Smiling, I grab a mug from the cabinet and pour myself a cup of coffee. "That's because I am."

Gabe is sitting at the island, wearing a pair of tropical print swim trunks and nothing else. "I'm hanging out at your pool today," he declares as a greeting.

I nod. "Sounds good." Too bad Jade has to work this

afternoon. I'd suggest we do the same thing. Not that I want to see these assholes catch a glimpse of Jade in a bikini but...

Damn. I need to get a hold of this possessive wave I feel every time I think of someone looking at my girl.

"What's got your panties in a happy twist?" Tristan asks. "Hey, you never did tell us how dinner with your parents went last night."

"Fucking awful," I say cheerily, dumping a bunch of creamer in my cup. "My mom was a total bitch to Jade."

"Ah, man. I could've predicted that," Tristan says.

"Yeah, no thanks to you and your gossiping ways," I mutter.

Tristan looks pained. "I already told you I'm sorry."

And he did. I knew he was sorry. I just like to give him shit for it.

"It's all good. We held our own and bailed early," I explain as I take a sip from my coffee.

"Where is Jade? Is she here?" Gabe asks.

"Still in bed. *My* bed." Sleeping and cute, all naked and mussed. I'm tempted to run back up to my room and fuck her one more time before she has to go to work but I'll restrain myself.

Barely.

"So she's moving in for the summer," I announce. They both stare at me in quiet shock. "I'm in love with her. And she's in love with me. We're trying to make this work."

"Seriously?" Gabe asks. "She's moving in?"

"Seriously," I confirm. "Just for the summer though." Maybe longer if I can convince her.

"That is pretty fucking serious," Tristan adds.

"I know." I smile. "I can't wait."

"What are you going to do this summer besides play around with Jade?" Gabe asks.

"Probably officially join the soccer league again." I'll need to so I can keep the weight off from all the cookies Jade's going to bake me. "Maybe take Jade on a trip or two for a couple of days. Nothing too far. She's going to work through the summer."

"Unbelievable." Tristan shakes his head. "I never thought I'd see this day, especially not this soon."

"What day?" I ask.

"The day that Shepard Prescott settles down with a girl. A normal, working girl he actually wants to be with." Tristan smiles. "I'm happy for you, man."

"Thanks," I say, settling on the barstool right next to Gabe's. "I'm happy too."

"So no more one and done," Gabe says. "You're over that."

"Totally." I start to laugh. I forgot about the one and done thing. I can't imagine being with Jade only once. I don't think I'll ever get tired of her. "That stupid rule was definitely made to be broken."

Epilogue

Shep

Early August

I stride into the house, polishing off the bottle of water I brought with me to soccer practice when I stop short at the view greeting me in the kitchen.

It's Jade, bent over the oven with the door open as she peers inside, her perfect ass wagging in my direction. She's wearing a brightly printed bikini with a little white coverup skirt over it and she looks like something out of a dream.

A particularly dirty one.

Quietly I sneak up on her, careful not to pounce when the oven door is still open. She closes it and resets the timer, then turns to approach the counter opposite where she stands when she spots me.

And smiles.

"Hey, sweaty man," she greets, a coy smile curling her perfect lips. Her skin is tinged with pink, her hair is pulled up in to a high ponytail and I'd bet big money she just spent some leisure time out by the pool. That bikini barely covers her goods and my hands itch to touch all that bared skin. "How was practice?"

"Exhausting. Hot like the depths of hell." All true. I approach her, drawing her into my arms and holding her close. She pretends to protest, like she hates it when I'm shirtless and sweaty after a particularly hard soccer practice, but I know she's full of it.

She loves me like this. I don't know how many times I've pulled her into my sweaty arms and the next thing I know she's attacking me. Yanking off my shorts and grabbing my cock and trying her best to get me inside her as fast as possible.

My girl is dirty. Insatiable.

And I love it.

"Mmm, well I made cupcakes so that should make your day brighter," she murmurs against my neck just before she kisses it.

I close my eyes and savor the feel of her in my arms. We've established a steady routine over the summer that's worked out perfectly. I love having her living in my house, sharing my bed. She's quite the cook, her skills not just limited to baking. We spend a lot of time by the pool, she works part-time at the candle shop and as every day passes, I realize I'm more and more in love with this girl.

Life couldn't get any fucking better.

"Tell me you made homemade frosting," I murmur against her hair.

She pulls away slightly to smile up at me. "I wouldn't have it any other way."

"A woman after my own heart." I lean in to kiss her but she dodges my lips.

"I thought I already owned your heart," she teases, her fingers dancing across my chest.

My skin tightens at her touch and my cock hardens beneath my shorts. Damn it. It's like she looks at me wrong and I get a hard on. Not that it's a bad thing. We always put my condition to good use.

"You do," I whisper, taking her hand and placing it directly in the center of my chest. "You own every piece of me, baby. Just like I own every piece of you."

Her eyes darken in that way they do when I know she's aroused. I have all her tells figured out. When you spend as much time together as we do, that happens. And I love it. I love her. "I like it when you talk possessive."

"Really? Because when I won you in that bet and I claimed you as my prize, you slapped my face. Hard," I remind her.

She smiles and reaches up to cradle my cheek.

"That's before I knew better."

"Knew better?" I reach for her ass and cup her cheeks, tempted to yank her bikini bottom off and take her right here in the kitchen.

Wouldn't be the first time.

"I had no idea that *I* was the one who was the real winner." She smiles and pushes up on her tiptoes to press a lingering kiss to my lips. "I love you, Shep. Shepard. Sexy Shep. Man of my dreams. Owner of my heart," she murmurs.

"I love you, too," I whisper just before I deepen the kiss.

More than she'll ever know.

Acknowledgements

Writing a book isn't easy, not always. Sometimes it's hard. Sometimes it feels like pulling teeth, each word painfully yanked from my brain.

Luckily enough, FAIR GAME wasn't like that for me at all. I adored writing every word of this book, despite my being incredibly sick during the last few weeks I worked on it. I fell in love with Shepard Prescott the moment he appeared on the page and so did Jade, despite her early protests. I adore Jade too. I love everyone in this book and can't wait for you all to read Gabe's and Tristan's stories.

There are people I need to thank who helped during the writing process of FAIR GAME. First up—huge, massive thank you to Autumn Hull who read. And read. And read this book as I fed it to her in chunks. Thanks for dealing with me, pushing me, and making sure I got this book done on time!

To Katy Evans who fell in love with Shep right from the beginning and encouraged me to keep me going. I don't know how I'd do this writing thing without you.

I have to thank my family for putting up with me while I'm always, always, always working. Your support and patience means the world for me. I love you.

And to the readers, the bloggers, the reviewers, for

reading my books, spreading the word, chatting with me on social media, sending me emails, stopping by to talk to me at a signing...you all means so much to me. I would be nothing without your support so from the bottom of my heart: thank you.

Check out an excerpt from OWNING VIOLET, the first in Monica Murphy's The Fowler Sisters series…

CHAPTER ONE
Violet

Tonight, my life is going to change.

In preparation for it, I spent all day at the spa. Treated myself to a facial, massage, wax, mani, and pedi. My skin is smooth, my face is clear, my fingers and toes are painted a perfect demure pink. My muscles are relaxed and loose, but my brain . . .

My brain is jumpy. My stomach is a mess of nerves. My outward appearance is the exact opposite of my inside because so much is on the line. Everything I've strived toward these last few years is coming to the final pinnacle tonight.

Finally.

I found a dress to wear for this special moment a few days ago at Barneys, one I knew Zachary would approve of. A navy-blue sheath, it hits just above the knee and skims over my curves, subtly sexy because he doesn't like anything overt. Obvious.

Meaning he hates everything my older sister wears, does, says. He doesn't much approve of the way my blunt baby sister acts, either.

But that's fine. He's going to ask me to marry him tonight. Not Lily or Rose.

Me.

There's nothing obvious about me. I'm the epitome of understated. I would make the perfect politician's wife. Standing behind my man, offering my never-ending support all while wearing the pleasant smile I've mastered over the years. There have been a few slipups in the past. I struggled once. Fought for my life, really, and survived.

My father and grandmother like to pretend none of that ever happened. Zachary doesn't even know about it. It's a moment in time — before I met him — the family prefers to sweep under the rug.

It's so ugly, Violet, Father told me once. Wouldn't you rather forget?

So I try. For the family.

Zachary arrives at my apartment right on time because heaven forbid he's ever late. One of the many qualities I admire about him. He's punctual, thoughtful, efficient, handsome, and smart. So incredibly smart. Some call him conniving. Others call him cutthroat. Rumors swirl that there are other women. I'm not stupid. I have my suspicions. They might have even been confirmed once or twice. But when we're engaged, when we're married . . .

That will change. It has to.

Zachary and I have a perfect relationship. The sort of relationship I'd dreamed of since I was a little girl. One that Lily mocks constantly, but what does she know about love?

Sex and addiction and getting into trouble, she knows plenty. But love? I don't think she's had a real relationship in her life.

I have. Boyfriends throughout junior high and high school, then my one very serious boyfriend in college. The one I'd originally thought I might marry. The one I gave my virginity to midway through freshman year. I'd been a real holdout, one of the last remaining virgins among my friends.

He dumped me the beginning of our sophomore year. Right after everything . . . happened. The incident, I like to call it. The thing no one likes to talk about. So I don't talk about it either.

After the breakup, I remained single. Tried my best to rise above everything that happened by focusing on finishing school and then on my career, my legacy at Fleur Cosmetics.

I might have quietly fallen apart for a short period of time that not many know about. We kept it secret. Father didn't want any more public humiliations. We lost Mom so long ago and he always said I was the most like her. Delicate but determined. Smart but not always practical.

I lived up to his expectations for a brief, not-so-shining moment. I needed therapy. I needed medication. More than anything, I needed to be numb. Craved being numb. Feeling emotions only hurt, and I was so tired of hurting.

But eventually I knew I needed to learn how to cope on my own.

Father let me return to work after my brief stint away. And when Zachary Lawrence started working for the company two years ago, getting to know him, I was soon interested. And so was he. I could tell. I didn't care if at first he talked to me only because I was the CEO's daughter. I flirted. I wanted his attention.

And I eventually got it. Got him.

I knew dating someone I worked with wasn't the smartest move, but I couldn't help it. Where else can I meet a man of such good quality? Someone I can trust? I have trust issues. No surprise, considering what I've been through.

While my father calls most of the shots, the company really is a family business. Both Rose and I work there. Even my grandmother still comes in and consults, though she's now eighty-five and mostly retired.

She loves Fleur Cosmetics and Fragrance. My grandma is Fleur Cosmetics and Fragrance. She started the brand. It was her face that appeared in the magazine advertisements and billboards for so many years. Dahlia Fowler is a legend in the cosmetics industry.

And despite my weaknesses and my father's once complete lack of faith in me, I desperately want to follow in her footsteps. With Zachary by my side, of course, considering he works in the brand marketing department and has higher aspirations. The two of us could take Fleur to the next level. I know it. He knows it.

Together, we're a force to be reckoned with. And once we're married . . .

"You're lost in thought."

Zachary's deep voice washes over me and I blink, realize that he's watching me. His brows are furrowed and his mouth is turned down. He looks concerned.

"I'm fine." I smile, hope lighting within me when I see the worry etched all over his handsome features slowly disappear. His blue eyes twinkle as he reaches across the table and takes my hand, grasping my fingers tightly.

"I have something I want to discuss with you," he says in that low, reassuring way of his.

My smile grows and I nod, squeezing his fingers. "Now?"

"Yes." He takes a deep breath and lets go of my hand. Odd. "I've known about this for a while and it's . . . taken everything within me to work up the courage to tell you."

Oh. How sweet. He's nervous about proposing. Zachary's always so confident about everything—I'm surprised. "Go ahead and just say it, Zachary. I'm fairly sure it will all work out in the end."

"I agree. Your father said the same thing."

My heart skips a beat. He spoke with Father. This is serious. This is exactly what I've been waiting for all this time. I can't believe it. My fingers are literally trembling in anticipation of the ring he's about to slip on my finger. I wonder how big it is. I don't like gaudy jewelry. Neither does Zachary. Understated, refined — that's more our style. Perhaps he spoke with Grandma and she gave him her engagement ring, though rightfully that should go to Lily since she's oldest . . .

". . . so he's asked me to test out the new position in London and see if I'd be a good fit. And I said yes."

Wait. What? "P-position? In London? What are you talking about?" I clear my throat, proud that I keep my voice level. I didn't want to make a scene in the middle of one of the most elegant restaurants in all of Manhattan. I could hear my father's voice now.

Violet, that just wouldn't do.

"Your father is sending me to the London office, just on a temporary basis. They've created a new position there since growth in the UK and Europe has been so strong the last couple of years. I'll be trying out the new chief brand and marketing director position both in London and Paris. It's a tremendous opportunity, Violet. One I couldn't turn down. This promotion could change everything." The pointed look Zachary gives me says he's made his choice and there's no chance I can talk him out of it.

"But . . . Wait a minute." I shake my head, a huff of fake laughter falling from my lips. He can't be serious. That's what he wanted to tell me? About a possible promotion? To London? "What about . . ."

"Us?" he finishes for me with that rueful, charming smile. The one that says he knows he's a little bit in trouble but somehow he'll talk himself out of it. As usual. "I won't be gone for long, only a few months. Hey, I bet you could fly over for a weekend. Come to London or even better, Paris. We can explore the cities together."

No offer to take me with him to live there—not that I'd go, especially since it's temporary. But it could turn permanent and he might end up staying. We don't know.

Would I leave to be with Zachary? Only if he promised that we would be married—and he vowed his complete fidelity. I feel safe here. Everything I know, my family, my friends, my career, is here. In New York. Not London or Paris. And what about the ring? The proposal?

It sounds terrible in my own head, but I expected that. A beautiful diamond solitaire ring accompanied by an offer of marriage, along with Zachary's promise of undying love and faithfulness to me. A girl can tolerate only so much and I know it's stupid, but . . . I love him.

I do.

Disappointment threatens to wash over me, but I hold it at bay. I have to.

"I think I know what you were hoping for," he says softly. "But what sort of marriage could we start if we're on two different continents? It wouldn't be fair to either of us. We're still young, darling, especially you. We have plenty of time."

"We've already been together almost two years . . ." My voice drifts and I drop my head, blinking my eyes shut for an agonizingly long moment before I open them again. I refuse to cry. I am twenty-three years old. I refuse to bawl like a little girl.

"And maybe we'll have another year, maybe two years, like this, but I promise, I will marry you." My heart leaps at his words. "I swear. I just—I need this. This promotion is important to me and I'm not the only one your father is considering. I'm a front-runner, but still, there are no guarantees. For you, it's different. This is your family. They'll give you whatever you want," Zachary says, irritation making his voice scratchy. Does he even register the change in tone? "But for me? I have to work at it. Constantly."

I stiffen my spine, offended by his words. They make it sound like I'm some sort of spoiled brat who gets whatever she wants whenever she wants. "I've worked very hard at Fleur since I was in my early teens," I say in protest. "You know this."

He waves a hand, whether dismissing his words or mine, I'm not exactly sure. "You know what I mean. Just . . . let me have this. I'm not a selfish man but I've worked damn hard for this career, Vi." I hate it when he calls me Vi and he knows it. "I'm almost thirty years old. The time for me to do this is now. Before I marry you and we have children and I won't be able to ever leave."

The way he said that makes me think he would feel like he's stuck with the wife and children. In other words, with me and our future children. Why am I letting this bother me? Am I being too sensitive? What he's saying makes sense. He needs to push forward with his career. I understand that. But I need to push forward with my career as well. And my life. My personal life, with marriage and children and . . .

My voice is hesitant as I say, "I could ask my father to step in and offer you a promotion here—"

"No. I refuse to take that sort of handout. I will earn this promotion," he says vehemently. "I want to do this. I would never hold you back, you know."

"That's not fair," I murmur, my gaze locking with his. A mix- ture of anger and sadness fills me, but he doesn't appear sad at all. No, he looks excited. Like this is exactly what he wants. What he needs.

Does this mean I'm not what he wants? What he

needs? "It's the truth," he says simply. "And you know it."

He never told me he was interviewing for the position. And this sort of thing goes on for weeks. Sometimes months. My fa- ther didn't tell me either, and that hurts because he knew what was happening yet never gave me a warning. More than any- thing, though, I hate that Zachary has kept this secret from me.

Makes me wonder if he's kept any other secrets.

Don't fool yourself. He's kept plenty of secrets from you. Why do you put up with him?

I swear my sister's voice is berating me in my head. I can just see Lily's smug expression, telling me she knew it all along. Zachary Lawrence doesn't deserve me. She's said that time and again. So has Rose.

I'm starting to wonder if they're right.

A woman's husky laugh draws my attention and I glance at a table a few feet away, recognition making my stomach sour. God, of course he's here. A million restaurants in all of Manhattan and he'd have to show up in this one. The mysterious, arrogant Ryder McKay, fellow corporate employee of Fleur Cosmetics.

Ryder's with . . . of course, Pilar Vasquez, his former boss, his supposed lover, girlfriend, whatever he might call her. Their relationship is strange, to say the least.

Strange because Pilar doesn't talk about it and Ryder definitely doesn't talk about it either. No one's sure exactly what happens between them, but everyone would love to know.

Not that I want to know. Or really care. His arrogance, the look on his handsome face, the way he strides around the build- ing as if he's the king of all he sees, drives me crazy.

If all goes as planned, that right will eventually go to Zachary someday. He is without a doubt the future CEO of Fleur.

Or me. I could be the CEO. Grandma has said that more than once. If I had half of her confidence, I could conquer the world.

All I know is that Ryder McKay is definitely not on par with Zachary and all of his experience. He's worked at Fleur a bit longer than Zachary, a little over two years. He came to the company via Pilar, who got him a position since she worked with him at her previous employer. Somehow, he's gotten into the good graces of practically every executive who works at Fleur. His charm is dangerous, and I can reluctantly admit he's a valued employee.

Which makes him lethal. And I refuse to fall for him. Zachary hates his guts. Something about Ryder rubs me the wrong way.

Ignoring the disgust curling through my blood, I try my best to keep my attention on Zachary, trying to ignore that the life I'd planned is falling apart in front of my eyes. But Zachary's phone rings, and he takes the call without asking if I mind. Like I don't matter, and I hate that. I hate even more that he turns away so he can murmur into the phone without me hearing.

More secrets. It's probably a woman. That I sit here and tolerate his behavior makes me want to smack him.

Or smack myself.

I'm at a loss. I don't know what to do, how to act, and I can't help my gaze from drifting to where Ryder sits. He's disgustingly gorgeous in a charcoal-gray suit and a crisp white shirt, though he's sans tie and a few buttons are undone at the neck, revealing the sexy column of his throat. His dark brown hair is in slight disarray, as if he's run his fingers through it countless times, and the entire look gives him a rakish air. One that says he doesn't care what people think of him while he sits in a restaurant that caters to some of the richest people in all of Manhattan.

That is the exact sort of attitude Ryder McKay always seems to have and I find it infuriating. Not that I have to deal with him, not much. He was promoted to associate director of package development a few months ago, a position I now can't help but wonder why Zachary didn't apply for, though it would have been more of a lateral move, not necessarily a step up. It would have kept him in New York, though.

Unless Zachary had no desire to stay in New York. . .

I stare harder, wishing I could listen in on Ryder's conversation with Pilar, but I can't hear a thing. His face is shrouded in shadows, the candle flickering in the deep red votive that sits in the middle of the table casting it in golden light. He's very attractive, I can reluctantly admit. Flashing a wicked smile at Pilar, he lets forth a glorious, downright filthy-sounding laugh that sends a spark of heat zipping over my skin.

Only because it sounds so devastatingly wrong and shockingly dirty, not because I have any sort of interest in him. He's too quiet, too mysterious, too . . . dark and full of secrets. That wicked smile is still curving his lush lips as he reaches across the table and takes Pilar's hand, bringing it to his mouth to kiss.

I watch, transfixed, as Pilar laughs, her voice raspy as she seemingly admonishes him. He merely shakes his head in return and drops her hand, his gaze going to mine for the briefest second and then lingering.

I'm caught. Snared in his intense gaze and for a long, charge-filled bundle of seconds, I return his stare. Recognition flares in his eyes and I quickly look away, my cheeks heating, and I'm thankful the lighting is dim so he can't tell. He thinks nothing of me, I'm sure. I'm barely a blip on his radar, and that's just the way I like it. I don't want his attention.

His type of attention . . . scares me.

Glancing across the table, I wave my hand in front

of Zachary's face but he doesn't see me. I hiss out his name, earning a hard glare from him before he turns away.

A sigh wants to escape and I stifle it, chancing a glance in Ryder's direction again to find him still watching me. And he doesn't look away, either. His smile softens and he leans back in his chair. He positively reeks of a man who knows just how to please a woman—a man who has no qualms about flirting with one woman while sitting at a table with another.

I remind myself that I can't stand him. I hate his cocky behavior. His confidence is galling and Zachary can't stand him. I should be disgusted that he's looking at me in such a blatant manner, but . . . I'm morbidly fascinated.

What's it like to think that way? To feel that way? Pilar seems absolutely thrilled to be with him, which only confirms that something is going on between those two. And I wouldn't doubt he'd try and touch her in some inappropriate manner if he hasn't done so already. She probably wouldn't protest, either. She's an eager climber who has no problems stepping on people to get what she wants, both professionally and socially.

They look like they're enjoying their evening, though. Whereas I'm tense and upset at Zachary's seeming rejection they're laughing and carrying on as if they have zero worries. Funny, I can't help but think how lucky Pilar is. To be lost in the pleasure of Ryder's wicked company while I'm lost to my own turbulent emotions at the thought of Zachary leaving me.

Of being alone. Again.

Tearing my gaze away from Ryder McKay, I focus on Zachary, who's off his cell phone and watching me with an expectant expression on his face. "Now, where were we?" he asks, looking genuinely confused. How could he forget that he'd just delivered such life-altering news?

"You were telling me about your possible new promotion." I hold in a breath, count to three, and then let it out in a soft exhale. "I'm happy for you," I finally say, forcing myself to smile. But it doesn't feel genuine. My lips tremble at the corners and I let the smile fall away. "Congratulations, Zachary."

"I knew you'd understand. You always understand. Every- thing." He reaches across the table and grasps my hand again, giving it a gentle squeeze. "If I get the position, I don't see myself staying in London beyond two years. We can make it work, can't we, darling?"

"Of course we can," I whisper. But I'm not sure. Two years with Zachary in another country, meeting numerous women? Most likely bedding numerous women?

For all I know, this could be the beginning of the end.

Made in the USA
Lexington, KY
08 February 2016